"There's such an assurance of narrative voice here, it's easy to call Malfi a modern-day Algernon Blackwood. Mystery and mystique, yes, but the real wonder is how well it's done. I'm gonna be talking about this book for years."
Josh Malerman, *New York Times* bestselling author of *Bird Box*

"This is what it is to be transported: you might think you're on solid ground, but *Come with Me* is a story that will carry you, inescapably, into the uncanny, the horrific."
Andrew Pyper, author of *The Residence*

"Shines as both a nightmare journey of shadows and secrets, and a poignant testimony to love and loss. I read it in a single day because I had no other choice: it's that damn good."
Richard Chizmar, author of *Gwendy's Button Box*

COME
WITH
ME

COME
WITH
ME

RONALD
MALFI

TITAN BOOKS

Come with Me
Print edition ISBN: 9781789097375
E-book edition ISBN: 9781789097382

Published by Titan Books
A division of Titan Publishing Group Ltd.
144 Southwark Street, London SE1 0UP
www.titanbooks.com

First edition July 2021
10 9 8 7 6

A CIP catalogue record for this title is available from

the British Library.

Printed and bound by CPI Group (UK) Ltd. Croydon CR0 4YY

For Wendi Winters
May 25, 1953 – June 28, 2018

PART ONE

HEADLIGHT GHOSTS

CHAPTER ONE

1

Every marriage has its secrets. I understand this, Allison. I get it. Secrets are what allow us to cling to our individual selves while also being one half of a matrimonial whole, and can be as vital as breathing. Fleeting desires, errant daydreams — private things reserved for just one person, the keeper of those secrets, the attendant at the door of the vault. The small secrets are easy to keep hidden — easier, say, than the big secrets, the whoppers, the infidelities and closet addictions that, like some underwater beastie that must ultimately ascend to the surface for a gasp of air, don't remain secrets forever.

I began the process of learning your secret, Allison, something like three months after your death. I call it a "process" because, much like a haunting, it did not reveal itself to me all at once, but rather as a gradual widening and clarity of circumstance. That's just like you, too, Allison — layers of depth upon depth that require effort, require work, to piece together. There had never been anything surface level about you, and the secret that, like reverse origami, I unfolded after your death was no different. It's possible, had I had my wits about me, I would have put the pieces together more quickly. Give me credit, okay? But as it was, I spent those first few months after your death in a sort of hypnagogic trance. You see, part of me had blinked out of existence right along with you — another consequence of the marital union — and what was left in the aftermath only retained the barest essence of a human being.

A cardboard box wrapped in packing tape on our front porch. So commonplace a way to have a piece of your dead wife's hidden life come to light. And I'll admit this right from the start, just so there is no confusing the issue later: I am not proud of where my mind went. Not at first. Something the casual observer may have overlooked… but I was your husband, not someone snatching a glimpse of your life through a window. And just like that, the aperture had opened. And then it widened. And then it widened some more.

I'm of the opinion that when it comes to secrets, there is no end to what we don't know about a person. Even the person who sleeps next to us and shares our lives.

2

It was your darkness that made me fall in love with you, Allison. Darkness of depth, I mean. The way we can peer down a narrow little hole and have our vision robbed by the mesmeric distance of it all. The never-ending-ness of it. You were pretty, yes, but it was the unconventional predatory aura that clung to you — those deep flashes, like flares shot up into the night, that I would sometimes glimpse behind your eyes — that slowly drew me in. Your dark, caustic smile that hinted at some secret knowledge. The cruel way you gnawed at your fingernails, and how, on our first few dates, there were always specks of chartreuse nail polish sparkling along your lower lip. Some grand mystery in the form of a person.

I first glimpsed you alone on a johnboat at the mouth of Deep Creek, where the creek opens up into the bay. You were sitting there with your head down, a dark silhouette, getting drenched in the middle of a springtime downpour. I watched you from beneath the awning of the marina's snack bar, curious about this lone figure bobbing along the choppy waters in the storm. Admittedly, I didn't even know you were female at first — the distance between us, confused by the rain, made you look like an indistinguishable, immovable lump, sorry to say. I started to formulate a story about you, and how you ended up floating out there in the rain on that boat — that maybe you were contemplating suicide after suffering a broken heart... or maybe you were already dead, a casualty of a jealous lover, who had propped your body upright on that boat before casting you out toward the bay.

The scenario only grew increasingly more peculiar when three figures emerged from the water around you, slick as seals in their black wetsuits, and climbed into the boat with you. Only then did you move — a slight tilt of your head, perhaps to posit a question or to extend an order. One of the wetsuited fellows engaged the outboard motor and the johnboat carved a wide arc around the channel of the creek. When it stopped again, farther away from me, I watched as the wetsuits dropped over the side of the boat and vanished again beneath the turbulent, storm-churned surface of the water. You remained curled there in the rain, a dark semicolon rocking on the waves, your head down as if scrutinizing something life-changing in your lap.

The boat ultimately dropped you off at the marina before vanishing into the rainy mist. You had on an army-green slicker, your dark and shiny hair pulled back into a soaking-wet ponytail. Your face was pale, unblemished, almost boyish. You carried a notebook and a camera in a see-through waterproof bag.

I watched you from across the sparse floor of the marina's snack bar as you took up a table far from me, ordered a coffee (black, no sugar), and began scribbling furiously in your notebook. For the next twenty minutes, I alternated between reading a Japanese-language edition of a Haruki Murakami novel and watching you. Finally, when I had summoned enough courage to approach, you didn't even look up at me as you said, "We were searching for a dead body."

This statement — a lie, you would later confess; you were out with divers from the Naval Academy examining oyster beds for an article you were writing for a local newspaper — rendered me speechless. And when you *did* look up at me, I could see that this had been your intention all along. To render me speechless; to knock me off kilter. And that was when I thought for the first time, *Who is this girl?*

So, in that regard, I can hardly blame you for your darkness. I can hardly claim that I was caught unawares by this most recent development. Not completely. I had been forewarned by the first thing you had ever said to me, the first words out of your mouth to a tall, gangly stranger with reading glasses and a chunky, tattered Japanese paperback in his hands. A lie meant as a joke that edged on darkness.

Who is this girl?

After your death, and after five years of what I would consider a pretty goddamn good marriage, I found myself asking that very same question all over again.

3

No one thinks when they first meet a person that there is some cosmic clock counting down the years, months, weeks, days, hours, minutes, seconds until you will stop knowing each other. It doesn't occur to most people when you meet the person with whom you wish to spend the rest of your life that, at some point, one of you will leave. Sure, everyone knows this on a practical level — everyone dies, no one lives forever — but no one looks their spouse in the eye on the night of their wedding and actually hears the ticking of that clock. Its sound is buried far beneath the flash and glamour of what we think our futures hold for us. But it's there; don't be fooled. It ticks for all of us.

You — Allison, my wife — died on an unseasonably warm and rather peaceable December morning, all things considered. At the time of your death, I was most likely wrapping your Christmas present, wistfully ignorant that you were hemorrhaging blood onto a scuffed linoleum floor. I was still in bed when you left the house that morning, awake but with my eyes closed against the bright sheet of daylight pressed against the bedroom windows. I ran a hand along your side of the bed as I stirred. The sheets were cold.

"Hey," you said, bustling into the bedroom. "Did I wake you?"

"No, I need to get up. Where are you going?"

You were wearing a scarlet beret, ringlets of inky black hair corkscrewing down both sides of your face, and a houndstooth topcoat that looked like it might be too warm for such a pleasant and mild December morning.

"Harbor Plaza," you said, hunting around the top of the dresser for something. "I need to pick up a few things. We're going to the Marshalls' tonight for that cookie-exchange thing."

"Ah, that's right."

We would not be going to the Marshalls'.

"If I can find my damn *keys*, that is…"

"Check the mystic pedestal," I suggested.

You tucked a tress of hair behind one ear as you crossed the bedroom and vanished into our walk-in closet. A few years ago and on a whim, you had returned home from a garage sale with a two-foot-tall marble pedestal. I had helped you drag it out of the car and up three flights of stairs — Lord knows how you managed to get it into the car on your own — and, after a time, it had somehow taken up permanent residence in our bedroom closet. It served no purpose other than to attract, inexplicably, random items thought lost from around our townhome with all the force and mystery of a black hole.

You returned from the closet dangling the keys from one hand. "Did you put them there?"

I shook my head.

"Well," you said, "that sufficiently creeps me out. There's no way I left them in there on that thing."

"All hail the mystic pedestal."

You smiled at me, standing there at the foot of the bed in your scarlet beret and topcoat. Something was on your mind — I could sense its urgency in you, desperate to come into the light of day. Something had been on your mind for a while lately. It had risen up like an invisible pillar between us. Over the past month or so you had grown distant toward me, had begun to close in on yourself. My attempts at drawing whatever it was out of you had been met with denial — everything was fine, you were just under a lot of stress at work, this too shall pass. But I knew better. I knew *you* better.

"Come with me," you said.

I rolled over and looked at the clock on your nightstand. It was a quarter after eight. "Too early for me," I confessed, spilling back onto my mound of pillows. Beyond the windows, I could see what looked like a hawk wheeling against a sky the color of bone. "Besides, I wanna try and get some work done."

"Are you sure? We can get breakfast at the Rooster."

Normally, I'd kill for a plate of French toast from the Fat Rooster Café — two slices of artesian bread as thick as Bibles, a dusting of powdered sugar, maple syrup as dense and rich as tree sap. Yet the prospect of negotiating around a throng of last-minute Christmas shoppers overrode any desire I had for French toast.

"Vile temptress," I said, "but I'll have to opt out, love."

"Suit yourself." You came to the bed and kissed the top of my head the way a mother would a sick child. "There's coffee downstairs."

"You're a peach."

"I thought I was a vile temptress?"

"Malleable persona. It's part of your charm."

"Oh, it's true," you said, and left the room.

It was the last time you and I would have a conversation, Allison. The next time I would see you would be in the county morgue, your body laid out on a steel table with a plain white sheet tucked up to your collarbone, an index card placed discreetly over the bullet hole in your skull. And, of course, I can still hear you saying it, over and over, like a curse or maybe a prayer: *Come with me.* Some may say that our destinies are etched in stone from the moment of our births, but I don't believe that. I think that life is what you make of it and the choices are yours. Free will asserts that we all must live with the consequences of our actions... which is why it torments me to close my eyes and hear you say it, even though it's only now just inside my head, *Come with me*, as if the more I think of it the closer I may be to cracking the code to all of space and time and finding a way to slip behind the bulwark of it all, the window dressing and beams and girders that make up the tangible world, and escape with you into that enigmatic, floating sea. Just go. Because my presence with you on that morning, had I gone, may have changed the outcome of what happened.

Some attack of urgency ushered me out of the bed soon after you'd gone. It was like ghost hands leveraging me up and off the mattress, forcing me into the approximation of a sitting position. I climbed out of bed and stood there in a daze until the vestige of that sensation fled from me. Running my hands through my hair,

I went to the closet and shut off the light. You were always leaving that light on, Allison. All the goddamn time.

Rubbing the sleep from my eyes, I went to the windows that looked down on our uncomplicated little spot in the world — the fishhook that was Arlette Street, the parade of townhomes the uniform color of sawdust, the brown hills beyond bristling with the barren, skeletal lightning bolts of trees. I watched you come out of the house and wave to Greg Holmes, out for his morning jog in his headband and gray sweatshirt with the dark armpit stains. You said something that made him laugh before he chugged onward toward the four-way intersection at the end of our development. I watched you get into the Subaru (what you'd always referred to as the Sube), crank over the engine, and pull out of the driveway. Overhead, my friend the hawk was still there, describing pinwheels against the backdrop of silver clouds behind which the morning sun struggled to poke through. I watched the taillights of the Sube flash as you changed gears. Watched you snap your seatbelt into place (you always did this once you were in the street and never while you were still in the driveway, as if wearing your seatbelt made it impossible to drive in reverse). I watched you adjust your beret in the rearview mirror before you drove away. I watched all of these simple contrivances — things I had observed you to do innumerable times before — without so much as an inkling that all the while, that great and terrible cosmic clock was winding down, tick, tick, tick, mercilessly close to coming to a full stop on our time together in this life.

4

That article that the *Herald* did on you? Reporter of the Year? For your Christmas gift, I had it laminated and inserted into a polished wooden plaque so you could hang it on the wall of our shared home office. You were always too modest for such showmanship, but I was proud of you. There was the photo of you on the front page of the Community section, an enlarged version of the one that usually accompanied your byline. You look sly and dark in that photo; that unassuming pink scarf-thing you're wearing around your neck does nothing to cloak your depth. You'd received the honor for your work with teenage girls interested in journalism, offering them space within your column to speak their mind about important issues. These were girls mostly from broken homes, girls who worked part-time while also attending school to help their parents — usually a single mother — pay the bills. For the most part, they did not live in the middle-class neighborhoods the *Herald* serviced, but that didn't stop you from seeking these girls out and lending them a voice. You'd been touched by the gesture when they presented you with the honor at that banquet dinner at the Chesapeake Club, but then confided in me on the drive home (and after quite a few gin and tonics, if we're being honest) that the money spent on the banquet could have been put to better use helping those very girls for whom you'd received accolades for helping. You also said reporters were by their very nature supposed to *report* the stories, not *be* the stories.

"Unless sometimes they are," I'd told you.

After you left the house that morning, I dug out some wrapping paper from the hall closet and swaddled the plaque in chintzy Santa Claus and reindeer foil. I stuck a festive red bow on one corner. *Voilà!*

It was no secret to either one of us where we hid each other's gifts. Hell, it was very nearly a game of temptation, wasn't it? Ours was a modest-sized townhome but that walk-in closet off the master bedroom was enormous. All my clothes and personal belongings neatly filed away on my side of the closet, all your stuff strewn and cluttered and heaped on your side of the closet. Christ, Allison, we were the original Odd Couple, weren't we? Our stuff appeared caught in some perpetual standoff, like cowboys facing each other at opposite ends of a dusty dirt road.

I always kept your gifts in my (faux) alligator-hide footlocker, which I'd humped around with me since my days at the University of Maryland. You always hid mine away inside your hope chest, which you kept shoved beneath a rack of what you called your "office clothes" and looked for all the world like a child's coffin.

I knelt down before my footlocker, lifted the latch, and prised it open amidst a chorus of squealing hinges. As always, the smell of old books and gym socks slapped me in the face. This was the case no matter how many pine-scented air fresheners I dumped in there. Among my old high-school yearbooks, some academic texts, and a few boxed-up novel manuscripts I'd written in longhand on yellow legal pads while still in college (all of them terrible), there were a few wrapped Christmas gifts for you already in there. I moved them aside and made room for the newly wrapped plaque.

I shut the footlocker's lid, grunted as I rose to my feet, and was about to head out of the closet when I noticed something peculiar. At some point, Allison, you had put a lock on the lid of your hope chest. A metal clasp and eyelet with a padlock running through it. It was possible you had done this some time ago, but I was only noticing it now. Something about it struck me not only as odd, but caused a flicker of disquiet to come alive in the pit of my stomach. People put locks on things when they want to keep them safe. People put locks on things when they don't want other people to see what they're hiding inside.

I tugged on the lock. It was sturdy. I couldn't tell how new it was just from looking at it.

Probably got me one hell of a Christmas gift this year, I told myself, though this didn't help settle the disquiet that had risen in me at the sight of that lock.

Ignorant to the fact that, by this time, the trajectory of my life had already been wholly and irrevocably altered, I went downstairs, clicked on the television, then poured myself a large mug of coffee in the kitchen. It had cooled in the pot, so I popped it in the microwave then stepped out onto the back deck for a cigarette while it reheated. Although the day was abnormally warm, the overcast sky looked ready to dump some snow. While I smoked — I did this whenever you were out of the house; you abhorred me smoking — I searched the sky for the hawk I'd spotted twice earlier, but the fellow was nowhere in sight. Somewhere in the distance, probably out by the highway, I could hear police sirens. Closer, a dog barked incessantly into the gray late morning.

When I went back inside, I realized that at least some of the sirens I had been hearing were coming from the TV. I retrieved my coffee from the microwave then stood looking over the counter at the image on the television screen. And, for a moment, I wasn't able to reconcile what I was looking at. In a way, it was like hearing my own voice coming out of a tape recorder — familiar yet momentarily unidentifiable. But then I realized what I was looking at: Harbor Plaza, the outdoor strip mall out by the highway, with its tidy row of shops now partially concealed behind the flashing rack-lights of several police cruisers. Superimposed at the bottom of the screen were the words ACTIVE SHOOTER.

I set my coffee on the counter before I could drop it to the floor. The TV remote was on the counter, so I grabbed it and thumbed the volume louder.

"...where police have shut down the road until they are able to gain control of the situation, where, as we've been reporting, a man opened fire less than twenty minutes ago in the Ease of Whimsy boutique here at Harbor Plaza..."

The image on the screen changed. A different angle of the Harbor

Plaza shopping center, I could see police cars blocking the entrance to the parking lot. There was an ambulance in the background. A snarl of traffic was being redirected by police waving flares. Switching to a third angle, I could see people being speedily escorted by police from the Fat Rooster Café with their hands on their heads. I recognized none of them.

It was always a scavenger hunt to locate my cell phone, but somehow I managed to find it right there beside the coffeemaker. I dialed your number, Allison. It rang six times before it went to voicemail. In the time it took, my body had exuded a staggering amount of sweat and my scalp had gone prickly. I felt like a piece of uranium radiating poison into the atmosphere. I disconnected the call and immediately called you back. Again: six rings, then straight to voicemail.

There's probably too much going on for you to stop and answer your phone, I told myself. *Maybe you even lost it in all the commotion.* It was a mantra I repeated over and over to myself as I got in my Civic and sped down Arlette Street toward the highway. There was a ridiculous amount of traffic, which I attributed to the police blocking off the roads surrounding Harbor Plaza. I sat, unmoving, behind a Chevy Equinox with its blinker flashing and a bumper sticker that said KEEP EARTH CLEAN, IT'S NOT URANUS for what felt like a decade. I was no longer a glowing rod of uranium, but rather had transmogrified into some amphibious thing, clammy with perspiration, fingers joined together by a translucent connectivity of webbing as I clutched the steering wheel.

"Fuck it."

I spun the wheel and tore across the rumble strip at the shoulder of the road, *thump-thump-thump-thump-thump*, loose change in the cup holder rattling, a half-empty bottle of spring water jouncing in the passenger-side foot well. Car horns blared at me. I hit redial on my cell phone and the Bluetooth automatically engaged the car's stereo. The ringing of your cell phone caused the speakers to crackle. Six rings then straight to voicemail. Your perfunctory prompt to leave a message. For the first time in five years of marriage and thousands of times calling your cell phone, I noticed you don't say your name — just a cursory order to leave a message.

None of those people hurrying out of the Fat Rooster with their hands on their heads were answering cell phones. Maybe the police won't let them.

I bypassed the highway exit and instead took the winding back road through a small subdivision. At the end of the road, just as I approached the plaza's intersection, another knot of traffic brought me to a sudden halt.

"Come on, Allison," I said, redialing your number. Ringing and voicemail. Ringing and voicemail. "Answer the damn phone."

It's not like you always answered your phone when I called. I often got your voicemail when I tried to reach you. This was no different.

Up ahead, I could see the lights of the police cars reflected in the shop windows on the far side of the street. Two uniformed officers were rerouting traffic, cars trundling over the grassy shoulders and redirecting themselves. Cars passed by me, heading in the direction from which they'd just come, moving with the cautious, halting crawl of someone who was lost. There was a 7-Eleven gas station to my left, a small collection of people standing out by the pumps observing the situation. I spun my wheel and hopped the curb, scraping the undercarriage, until I was in the gas station's parking area. I jumped out of my car and jogged toward the mob of people, calling, "What's going on? What's going on?"

"Some guy shot up the strip mall," said a woman. She looked stricken, like someone forcefully roused from a nightmare.

"He's dead, he's dead," said a tall man wearing a blue turban. He had a great white moustache that curled to points on either side. He had his cell phone to one ear, a finger screwed into the other.

"Who?" someone else said.

"The shooter, I think," said the man in the turban. "Wait, wait…" He uncorked his finger from his ear and pistoned it above his head. He began speaking into the phone in a language I did not understand.

My cell phone still clutched in one hand, I proceeded to run toward the two police officers directing traffic at the intersection. One of them saw me and shouted something at me but I didn't understand. It felt like bees were swarming around inside my head. Only when the officer came out of the intersection and approached me at a quick clip, one hand held up at me in a stop-running-you-idiot gesture, did I pause halfway across the road.

"Get back!" he yelled.

I uttered something about my wife.

"You're going to get hit," he yelled, motioning toward the confusion of traffic that was trying to reroute in my direction.

I jumped backward onto the curb. From here, I could see the parking lot of the plaza. People were clustered together by the First National Bank. I headed in that direction, vaguely aware that someone — probably that cop in the middle of the street — was once again shouting at me. A truck screeched to a stop as I hurried across the road toward the plaza, the shiny chrome of its bumper mere inches from me. The driver laid on his horn and shouted something while I was simultaneously startled by the sudden whirring of helicopter rotors directly overhead. The thing appeared out of nowhere and cut low as it circled around the plaza, over the street, the nearby trees, the baseball field and firehouse on the opposite side of the road, then back again.

People sat on metal benches outside the bank and stood like herded cattle at the farthest point of the parking lot. Most of them were on cell phones, including a teenage girl who sobbed uncontrollably as she held her iPhone to one ear. I passed through them like a ghost, gripping dark-haired women by their shoulders to turn them around so I could see if one of them was you, Allison. None were. I shoved my way through the mob until I could see a shimmer of broken glass collected on the sidewalk outside the boutique. There were cops and paramedics everywhere. I saw some news trucks and cameras out there, too. Overhead, the helicopter made another pass. I tried to advance up the sidewalk toward the boutique, but another police officer — a woman with striking green eyes and a no-bullshit expression — shoved me back with a hand on my sternum.

"I'm looking for my wife," I said, and held up my cell phone as if it was some verification required for admission. "Her name's Allison Decker."

"Sir, you'll have to stand over there with the others."

"She's wearing a red beret," I said.

The cop's stern expression did not change when she grabbed me around the forearm and led me back toward the crowd. My whole body felt weightless; this police officer could have lifted me over her head with one hand, had she wanted to.

"Listen to me," she said, once we'd reached the outskirts of the parking lot. "See the fire station?"

I'd seen it a million times, of course, but I followed her gaze across the street to where the Harbor Volunteer Fire Department's two-bay brick building stood among a corral of fir trees. Like a dummy, I nodded my head.

"Go there," said the cop.

"But my wife — "

"You need to go there. It's a rally point. Do you understand?"

I didn't — it was as if she were speaking gibberish — but I felt myself nodding my head.

"What's your name, sir?"

"Aaron," I managed. "Aaron Decker. My wife is Allison. She's wearing a red beret." Because how many goddamn red berets were out here bobbing around in some suburban Maryland parking lot?

"Go across the street and wait, Mr. Decker."

Still nodding like an imbecile, I backed away from her until my shoulders struck a van parked alongside the curb. I turned and saw a face in the van's window — a young girl, maybe eight or nine, staring right at me. The fear in her eyes was unmistakable. I glanced around again at the crowd of people, their faces filled with equal parts terror, grief, shock, confusion. One woman was clutching a small boy to her hip, tears streaking down her face. A man in a puffy green jacket kept touching a small cut on his forehead then looking at his bloodied fingertips with incomprehension, a robot programmed to execute some repetitive motion.

When there was a break in the traffic, I hustled across the street toward the fire station. Both bay doors were open. Folding chairs had been set out, many of them occupied by people who had presumably been instructed to do just as I had by the police — come here and... what? Wait?

It occurred to me that you might be here now, Allison. Like me, some no-nonsense police officer may have directed you to come here and wait for the proverbial smoke to clear. That was possible, wasn't it? I dialed your cell phone again as I maneuvered through the crowd inside the fire station looking for you. I saw that other people were doing the same — nearly everyone had a phone to their ear. The difference was, these people were all talking to someone on the other end of the line. Me? Six rings and then voicemail.

A woman with a clipboard came over to me and asked my name.

I gave it to her, then told her I was looking for my wife. I gave her your name. She consulted her clipboard then looked up at me with a solemn expression. My wife was not on her list.

"What does that mean?" I asked.

"It means she isn't here."

"What does *that* mean?"

"We're just gathering information, Mr. Decker. We're trying to make sure people find who they're looking for as quickly as possible."

"My wife. I'm looking for my wife. She won't answer her phone."

"There's a lot going on at the moment," she said, as if by way of explanation.

"Could you tell me what exactly happened?"

"I don't exactly *know*," said the woman. She was middle-aged, overweight, a frizz of dyed red hair like a helmet encapsulating her head. But her eyes were sympathetic. "A man started shooting at people in one of those stores."

"Someone said he's dead."

"I believe so."

"Who else? Was anyone else hurt?"

She touched my arm. My whole body was shaking, and I thought maybe she could feel it. "We're just trying to piece everything together right now, Mr. Decker. In the meantime, you could have a seat. It's best if you sit down. I can bring you some water or maybe a coffee."

"I don't want anything."

"You should sit down."

I found an empty folding chair beside a large metal trashcan. I sat down and stared at the assortment of Styrofoam garbage in the can. In my lap, my cell phone's screen went dark. I didn't dial your number again, not just then, but instead I focused all my attention on it, willing it to come alive, to vibrate and chime with your specific ringtone (birds chirping), for your name to fill the screen, for you to reach out to me and let me know that you were safe somewhere close by, that you had decided to go to the Annapolis mall instead of the plaza, and you were only now hearing about what happened, and shit, so sorry for all the missed calls, but you'd left your cell phone in the car.

An ambulance peeled down the road, sirens blaring. People stopped and watched it go. I bolted out of my chair and wandered toward the street. The fire station was too claustrophobic; I needed fresh air. The mild December afternoon had grown cold beneath the cloud cover, but I didn't care. I shivered, hugging myself, then looked at the sky. Goddamn if the hawk wasn't back, spinning those lazy circles against the low-slung clouds. Only now, from this proximity, I could see it wasn't a hawk at all, but some large carrion bird waiting to feast on something dead or dying on the ground below.

5

By two-thirty, most of the people who had gathered at the fire station had gone. Those who remained looked like zombies, like the last kids picked for dodge ball; there was a contagious scurviness about them that prompted me to keep my distance and refuse eye contact. The crowds across the street had dispersed as well, with the exception of the police and the news crews. The road was still closed.

Still at the fire station, I sat in my chair holding a paper cup of lukewarm coffee. Police officers would periodically come in and converse in hushed voices with the woman holding the clipboard. I recognized one of the officers as the green-eyed, stern-faced woman who had instructed me to come here and wait. The rally point, she'd called it. No one here was rallying. Two minutes earlier, a woman in jeans and a fur-collared jacket had been led away howling. Before that, a guy in a turtleneck had passed out.

I lost count of how many times I called your cell phone. A part of me wanted to just get up, go to the 7-Eleven for my car, and drive home. Chances were good you'd be there waiting for me. I would have bet money on it. Yet something kept me rooted to this uncomfortable metal folding chair.

The green-eyed, stern-faced officer spoke to the woman with the clipboard. The woman with the clipboard regarded her list of names, tracing down the list with a blunt white finger. Then they both looked up and surveyed the remaining population in the firehouse. I was staring straight at them when they both directed their stares at me.

"Aaron Decker," said the officer as she approached. Her face was still stern, but there was something else there now, too. Something I thought might border on compassion.

"Yes," I said, and rose up from the chair.

"I'm sorry to have to tell you this," she said.

And you, of course, Allison, know exactly what she said.

CHAPTER TWO

1

When someone dies of natural causes, the mourning can be a private affair. When they die the way you did, Allison, we're forced to share our grief publicly, at least for a little while. For days after the shooting, I couldn't turn on the news without hearing your name, seeing your face, listening to recounts of what transpired in that little boutique. The *Herald* had provided a photo of you to other media outlets, and that was the one that kept popping up — you in that ridiculous pink scarf.

Around the time you had said *Come with me* that morning, a twenty-three-year-old sociopath named Robert James Vols woke up in his parents' basement. He ingested a bowl or two of Frosted Mini-Wheats (according to the coroner's report), played *Fortnite*, then shot his sleeping parents in the head at point-blank range with a 9mm Smith & Wesson. The pistol, owned by Robert Vols's father, had been legally purchased, and was kept in a lockbox in their bedroom closet. The key to the lockbox was in the top drawer of the nightstand. I guess it was a no-brainer. After the slayings, Vols left the house in his parents' Mercedes. He did so with the pistol tucked into the waistband of his jeans and a hooded fleece pullover concealing it from sight. According to police, he drove straight out to the Harbor Plaza and parked the Mercedes right in front of the Ease of Whimsy boutique, where his ex-girlfriend worked. He entered the boutique with the hood of his pullover up, his hands in his pockets. He stopped and asked another clerk if his ex-girlfriend was working that morning, although he must have known this, because he had parked next to her car, a black Toyota Camry. This clerk — one of the survivors — said Vols's ex-girlfriend was in the backroom. Vols thanked the clerk, and began to meander around the store, feigning interest in the various sundry items the eclectic little boutique had to offer. He peered at his reflection in ornamental mirrors, shook snow globes, poked a finger at bamboo wind chimes, left fingerprints along the stem of a champagne flute. Minutes later, when his ex-girlfriend appeared, Vols walked up to her and shot her in the face. He then turned and proceeded to fire randomly throughout the store. Three more people were killed, including you, Allison. The clerk who survived — a young girl who, I fear, will be forever traumatized by this event — later told me that you were the only person who rushed toward the gunman at the sound of gunfire. She said she saw you shouting at him, waving your hands, and rapidly approaching him. She said it looked like you were trying to confuse and disorient him to buy everyone else some time to get out of the shop. Maybe it worked; several shoppers managed to escape the store during the melee. It also got you killed, though, Allison; the shooter paused for perhaps a second or two, but it wasn't long enough for you to strike him, disarm him, or just get the fuck out of the way. He shot you once in the head, and you went down. He then put the gun in his own mouth and pulled the trigger, abruptly ending the madness.

There was a candlelight vigil held for the victims and their families in downtown Annapolis. I did not attend, but I saw some footage of it on the news: Main Street a somber tributary of people flowing toward Church Circle, a sea of black armbands and slender white candles tipped in a flicker of dancing light like wands capable of magic. There was a celebration of your life held at the Maryland Hall for Creative Arts, where a large poster of your face was set on an easel in the main hall and bordered in a heart-shaped wreath of flowers. I did not attend that service, either.

My sister Trayci came to stay with me for just over a week. She was a rock during the funeral and fussed about the house in that same fastidious, workmanlike way Mom had done when we were kids. Trayci was three years older than me but possessed the spirit and the sheer determination to outlive me by two decades, if she wanted. She'd aged in the time since our last visit, however, which was maybe a year or so ago (too long), and there were now brash streaks of silver in her sandy hair, and the lines that bracketed her mouth had deepened. As she swept crumbs from the kitchen table, manipulated the TV remote, held her glass of Cabernet by the stem, I found myself hypnotized by her hands. Somewhere over the course of this life, Trayci had begun to wear the hands of our mother — thin, precise, cautious fingers, and a soft creeping of the skin on the backs of her hands that somehow made them look both fragile and sturdy at the same time. Our mother long dead and our father, the playboy, living in Europe, Trayci was all the family I had left. She permitted herself one good cry — for me, I suppose, but for you too, Allison; she'd always loved you — and then she swiped at her eyes, cleared her throat, and got down to business. She answered the door when people stopped by to drop off food or pay their respects. I was in the mood to greet no one, and remained, for the most part, on the back deck of our townhome despite the rapidly plummeting temperatures. Twice it snowed while I was out there, and Trayci appeared, dusted the snowflakes from my hair and my eyelashes, then draped a coat around my shoulders. Sometimes she'd bring me hot cocoa.

Reporters came to the house. Trayci kept them at bay, shooing them from our property the way you'd try to scare off a pack of stray dogs by making loud noises. Had she owned a flare gun she would have discharged bright spangles of light at them, I had no doubt. My cell phone became a portal through which news anchors, political aides, NRA representatives and all species of carrion birds could clamber out, rattle their dusty black wings and unspool their hectic, pitiless platitudes into my ear. On the rare occasion when I inadvertently answered one of these calls, the hunger and eagerness in the creature's nearly human voice left me feeling violated. I stopped answering my phone altogether. When the battery eventually ran dead, I let it stay dead. Good riddance.

The sensation of you simultaneously having fled from me and yet seeping into my pores invaded my brain, blurred my sight. There was a presence in the house now. I would catch a whiff of your Tommy Girl perfume in the upstairs hallway. I would glimpse movement in the periphery of my vision, but whenever I looked, there was nothing there. In bed, I'd be sliding toward sleep only to feel your lips brush my forehead, just as they did on the morning you died. The hopeful and hallucinatory mind of the aggrieved, perhaps, although I began to wonder if there wasn't some echo of you that persisted in this house — the dark stain of you, and the life that had been cut short. One evening, after climbing out of the shower, I glanced up at the steamed-over bathroom mirror to find a partial impression on the glass, as if you'd glided in here and pressed your face to the fogged-up mirror. I could make out all the details of you. This shook me, weakened something vital and upright inside me, and I had to brace myself against the wall to keep from collapsing. Had you come in here and done this while I showered? Some leftover piece of you? I went out into our bedroom, walked out onto the landing, my mind frantic and irrational and feeling as if it were speedily unraveling.

Was I expecting to find you out here? Back in the bedroom, there were damp footprints stamped along the carpet, moving in a semicircle around the bed. I cried out, an anguished, grief-stricken mewl, and then realized they were my own footprints. I returned to the bathroom, only to find the image of you already faded from the mirror. I felt like I had missed something important, and that the missing of it brought about some irrevocable tragedy. As if we needed more tragedy. It was then that I wept, my hands planted on either side of the sink, my flushed and hot face staring down into the unblinking eye of the sink drain. I saw a flash of white light down there at the bottom of the drain, an impossible wink of white illumination, there and then gone. And in that moment, I heard — or thought I heard — a disembodied voice, distant yet clear as day, issue straight up from the drain: *"Who's there? Is someone there?"*

I jerked away from the sink, my skin prickling as if some spirit had reached across the void of infinite space and prodded me with an icy finger at the base of my spine. Steeling myself, I peered back down the drain, and saw that it was nothing but an unremarkable black hole once again.

I was losing my mind without you, Allison. Because that's what grief does. It robs us of a part of ourselves, leaving a crater of madness and irrationality in its place.

What if I'd gone with you that day? What difference would that have made? My mind was a never-ending loop of alternate possibilities, of planes of existence where I had gone with you and you had survived, those other versions of us still living happily in the blissful ignorance of my grief. Twice, the stupid Alexa speaker, unprompted, began playing your eighties playlist, Patty Smyth belting out "The Warrior." I let it play, and I cried.

For the first time, I was glad you had no living relatives, Allison. Your father had been killed in an automobile accident when you were just a child, your older sister had drowned when you were both teenagers, and your mother had drunk herself to death years ago, probably due to the misery that had plagued your family. Perhaps this lost family was the reason for the darkness that reflected out of you — that bottomless, lightless cavern that was your soul. You rarely talked about them, although I got the sense that you missed them, or at least longed for the familiarity and warmth of a family beyond just the two of us. It sounds terrible, but in the days following your death I was grateful they were gone, because I didn't think I would have been able to make those phone calls. I wouldn't have been able to have those people in our house, where I'd be forced to interact with them and address their grief and move about like a real live man. I just couldn't have done it.

In my dreams, I was constantly pursuing you through abandoned houses, searching for you among junked cars and through mazes of wire fencing. Dogs wearing the faces of people barked at me. I saw you standing at a bus stop in the rain, then climbing into a boat with men in balaclavas. I saw you in the window of the Fat Rooster Café, eating a plate of French toast, but when I went inside, all the tables were empty, except that your half-eaten breakfast was still there in front of a vacant chair. You sometimes stood at the far end of Arlette Street, in the center of the four-way intersection like a crossing guard, and I would run to you, slow as molasses (as they say), my bare feet pulling hot, tacky strands of asphalt up from the ground, as if I were running through a tar pit. I never reached you in time — you always vanished before I got there. Sometimes, you'd run so fast you'd leave Allison-shaped streaks of light in your wake. Fast and transitory as a comet. And as bad as these nightmares were, it was worse to awaken and realize you were gone in real life.

The cardboard box containing the first clue to your secret life arrived at the house a few days after your funeral. Some UPS guy had placed it on the porch, anonymous as a shoulder-bump in a crowded room. Trayci retrieved the parcel and set it on the kitchen counter, among Tupperware containers full of cookies from our neighbors and a thickening stockpile of mail. I glanced at the box just once and saw that it had been sent from your office at the *Herald*. Presumably, one of your colleagues had cleared out your desk, fitting the culmination of your entire career at the newspaper in a box just slightly larger than a basketball. I contemplated not opening it, and just carrying it directly to the fire pit in the yard where I would set it ablaze. Things would have been drastically different had I done that, of course. But that's not what I did. As days turned into weeks, I just simply ignored it, letting it sit there on the counter. Forgotten.

2

"Why don't you come back with me?" Trayci suggested on the night before she was to return home. "Owen's been traveling but the kids would love to have you."

"I don't think so, Tray. Not just yet."

"Well, I don't like you being alone right now."

"You can't babysit me forever."

"It's still so soon. I wish I could stay longer."

"You've stayed long enough. And I appreciate it. But you've got your own family."

"You *are* my family, Aaron. My little brother."

I summoned an exhausted smile. "Thank you, Trayci."

"Christ, Aaron. What a mess, huh?" For the briefest moment, her face softened. But then she firmed up once more. She hugged me, and when she spoke again, it was with the tone someone might use to talk sense into someone with a mental deficiency. "You listen to me,

Aaron. If you change your mind, there's always a spare bedroom back at my place. You know that. For as long as you need it."

"I do," I told her. "I know that."

"Also, I've made you a list of daily chores."

"Are you kidding?"

"Just some things you should remember to do — like eat, take a shower, breathe. Take it slow when you need to. Those kinds of things. I've stuck it to the fridge."

"You're just like Mom, you know that?" We were on the couch having some beers. I looked at her hands and felt a strange, sad nostalgia for my childhood.

"I just want to make sure you *do* things. And don't just stay bottled up in this house. At least go for a walk around the neighborhood or something. Get some sun on your face. Anything, Aaron. Keep active. Grief hates a moving target."

"Don't worry, Tray. I promise to eat and breathe. All those things. Anyway, I've got my work. I'll just get back to work."

And that's what I did, Allison. For a while, anyway. At the time of your death, I was halfway through translating a Japanese-language Shunsuke Ogawa novel to English. You know I've always been passionate about my work, but I now clung to this Ogawa novel like someone drowning would cling to a life-preserver. On our first date, when I told you I translated Japanese novels for a living, you thought I was pulling your leg. I may have possessed the industrious quality of a career academic, but you were not expecting a white guy from suburban Maryland to have majored in Japanese literature, to have practiced writing Japanese characters with the care and dedication of a surgeon, to delight in the mental acrobatics of finding commonality in two languages where no etymological kinship exists. "It's the alien quality of it all that makes it so beautiful," I had explained to you. Strangely, you'd understood.

I found it also to be a temporary respite from my grief. There is a switch that is flipped when I work, a notable alteration in my brain when I'm operating in Japanese. In the days and weeks after your death, I found that this other-Aaron had somehow remained fully intact and unencumbered in the aftermath of your death while the real-life Aaron — your husband; me — had transitioned into a vaporous phantom who slept for maybe a fitful two hours a night and who wandered the darkened corridors of our townhome like something that should be rattling chains and frightening children. I retreated wholly into other-Aaron during this time. I let him take over. Not just while working, but also in my daily routines. Other-Aaron showered for me, ate for me, went to the grocery store, paid the bills. He donned a windbreaker and slippers so he could traverse the length of our driveway to retrieve the mail. He was thinking and functioning in Japanese, a stranger untouched by the grief that had crippled me, wholly unfamiliar with all of grief's alien aspects and human weaknesses.

Given the situation, I could have asked my editor for an extension on the delivery date of the Ogawa manuscript, but I didn't need one; other-Aaron was fully focused, on target, operating like some mechanical thing engineered to do so. Occasionally, I would peer out of other-Aaron's eyes — formerly *my* eyes — and marvel at the industrious, goal-oriented, emotionless fervor of him. Look at this strange and beautiful thing that had been living inside me all these years. I had no idea he was capable of such majesty.

In the breaks between working on the manuscript and hiding in the shadow of other-Aaron, I began on occasion to peek out into the light of day. Check my email, power my cell phone back on, flip on the television in the living room. I did these things gradually, almost skittishly, tempered by the expectation of you waltzing in the door at any minute, as if this had all been some horrible nightmare. As if to go back to some simulacrum of normality might summon you back into existence. But I was a wreck; indeed, there was something fawnlike about me in these moments, terrified of anything and everything, trembling and vulnerable to the slightest shift in mood. I had avoided the outside world in the weeks after your death, heartsick at the prospect of hearing your name or seeing your face on a screen somewhere. But this is America, where tragedies roll along on a conveyor belt with alacrity. One is boxed up and shipped out just as another arrives, shiny and new, on the showroom floor. Soon, the shooting at Harbor Plaza was replaced with a news story about the search for a missing teenage girl somewhere down south. *Sore ga jinsei da* — such is life.

3

It was other-Aaron who opened the cardboard box that had been sent from your office. I wouldn't have had the courage. Inside were notepads containing your illegible scrawl; a mug that said STOP THE PRESSES: WE'RE OUT OF COFFEE; the nameplate from your desk; random office supplies; some folders containing various people's contact information; a stress ball that looked disconcertingly like a cow's udder; and various other work-related paraphernalia.

The folded sheet of paper was nearly overlooked, Allison. Other-Aaron picked it up, unfolded it, and would have cast it aside had I not been peering out of his — *my* — eyes at that very moment. It was a receipt for a two-night stay at The Valentine Motel in a place called Chester, North Carolina, back in late October. According to the receipt, you paid not with a credit card but with cash.

I stared at it for a long time. At first I considered that it might have belonged to someone else at your office, and that it had gotten erroneously deposited in this cardboard box when whoever it was had cleaned out your desk. But it was your name on the receipt, Allison.

Still, it had to have been a mistake. Obviously I would have noticed if you'd been gone for two nights. I kept staring at the receipt, trying to divine some explanation from it, trying to *translate* these nonsensical glyphs into something my brain could grasp hold of and understand. Two nights in October would have —

But wait. When had I gone to New York to meet with my editor? It had been around Halloween, hadn't it? I'd been in the city for three days. On that occasion *I* had said *Come with me* — those haunting words now, Allison — but you'd been too busy with work and couldn't get away. Or so you'd said.

I went upstairs to the office, rifled through my desk calendar. There it was in my own calligraphic handwriting — I'd been in New York from October 28–30. The same days you were apparently in someplace called Chester, North Carolina, Allison. The same nights you'd stayed at The Valentine Motel.

What the hell were you doing at a motel in North Carolina while I was in New York?

4

I called Tommy Weir from down the block to see if he could bypass the password on your laptop. "It's basically just a big coaster unless you can get in," I told him. I did not let on that I was hunting for something; I simply told him I wanted to have access to your laptop. While Tommy went to work, I clomped downstairs and had a cigarette on the deck. After the smoke, I grabbed a couple of beers from the fridge and carried them up to the office. Tommy had already gotten into the computer.

"I've set up this prompt for you to put in your own password," he said.

I typed something simple that I would remember later, then we both went downstairs to finish our beers on the deck. Tommy had been to your funeral and had paid his condolences then; there was no talk of you now, Allison, and as much as I hate to admit this, it felt good. For that handful of minutes drinking beer with Tommy Weir on the back deck, I felt close to human again. He even told some joke and I laughed. A *for real* laugh.

After Tommy had left, I got on your laptop but found that the search history had been deleted. Also, there wasn't a single file saved on the hard drive. It was as if it had come straight from the factory. I called Tommy up and asked him if he had accidentally jiggered something when he'd gained access to the computer, erasing all the files and browser history.

"No, man, wasn't me. But I noticed that, too," he said. "Probably should have said something. Looks like Allison used a program to wipe the hard drive at some point."

"Wipe it," I repeated. "Like, she erased everything."

"Yeah. It's all gone, whatever was there."

"Okay." I fell silent over the line.

"You all right, Aaron?"

"Yeah." But I wasn't. "Thank you, Tommy."

"Give me a shout if you need anything else."

"I will."

"And it was good to have those beers. Let's do it again soon."

"Will do," I said, and disconnected the line.

5

I felt like someone with a terminal illness as I walked into the offices of the *Herald*. Heads swiveled in my direction. *Who is this creature walking upright between the cubicles, pretending to be a human being?* All those eyes on me, most of them not registering who I was. Some others knew right away. I was greeted by tight embraces and several sympathetic pats on the back from some of your former colleagues. It made me feel like some asshole who'd just missed the game-winning field goal. One woman — I'd met her before at some cookout or something but couldn't remember her name — began to weep behind the tent of her pudgy pink hands as she gazed at me from over the partition of her cubicle. The pity for me in this place was palpable and it made me feel sick. A few people asked how I was holding up. In order to answer, I temporarily summoned other-Aaron, that reliable automaton, to the helpdesk, where he donned my face and provided his perfunctory, socially acceptable responses.

It wasn't a show. You'd worked at the paper for seven years and these people loved you. They felt sorry for me by default, and a little collection of them followed me down the hall to Bill Duvaney's office. On the way I passed your desk, shiny-clean and not a single thing on it. Someone had placed a laminated prayer card from your memorial service on your desk chair. I felt my throat tighten at the sight of it.

Bill Duvaney looked up from his laptop the moment I appeared in his doorway. "Jesus, Aaron," he said, lifting his considerable bulk from his chair and routing over toward me. He wrapped his arms around me, his cologne overpowering, his tie clip knifing into my sternum. "What a surprise. I'm glad you're here. How're you holding up?" he asked once he let me go.

"I guess okay. I don't know."

"This whole thing." He shook his head. Bill had been at the funeral and he'd probably spoken to me that day — so many people had — but I had no memory of it. He was in his fifties, with a dejected, hangdog face, made all the more pitiable by the expression of empathy he now wore. I could see the indentations at the bridge of his nose, left there by his eyeglasses which sat now on the ink blotter on his desk. He had inherited the paper from his wife's family, and I could never quite tell if he grudgingly relished the responsibility of editor-in-chief or felt trapped by this whim of circumstance.

"I hope I'm not bothering you, Bill."

"Not at all, Aaron. Sit down. Please." He waved a meaty paw at one of the empty chairs in front of his desk. "Soda or coffee? There might be donuts in the break room."

"I'm good, thanks."

He closed his office door then went back behind his desk. The cushion on his chair wheezed like a punctured car tire as he dropped his hefty frame onto it. I sat in a chair opposite him and worked my way through a series of ill-fitting expressions, trying to find the right one for such an occasion.

"What can I do for you, Aaron? You name it. Anything you need."

"Back in October, did you send Allison on assignment to North Carolina? Some mountain town called Chester?"

I could tell, based on the tightening of Bill Duvaney's features, that this wasn't the type of question he had been anticipating. "North Carolina?" he said. "Why would I send her to North Carolina?"

"That's what I'd like to know."

"Well, no, I didn't," he said, holding his hands out to profess his innocence. "We're a small community newspaper, why would I send her out of state?"

"I didn't think you would." It felt like something small and hard was attempting to expand in the center of my stomach. "Was she working on anything that might send her down there on her own, even if you weren't aware of it? Some special project she might have been working on?"

"Back in October? She'd been working on a local bake sale, Aaron, and a story on the Halloween display at Sandy Point. She was helping one of our interns digitize our paper files into our computer system."

I felt my head bobbing up and down.

"What brings this up, Aaron? What's going on?"

I considered how to respond. Did I want to air this laundry? I thought about the people out there in the newsroom, in the cubicles and the hallways. I thought about the prayer card on your desk chair, Allison.

"Maybe I'm just being silly," I said.

"You're in mourning," said Bill Duvaney. "It's grief, Aaron. What's it been? Five weeks? No one expects you to click back into reality this quickly."

"I guess you're right."

"Of course I'm right. Your mind, it's all over the place. How old are you?"

"Uh," I stammered. "I'm thirty-two."

"Thirty-two," he repeated, shaking his head as if he was in awe of such a number. "And here you are." Still shaking his head. "At least that son of a bitch had the decency to take his own life."

Bill Duvaney was not the only person to express this sentiment to me. And although I understood why he'd say it and why he felt that way, I was in staunch disagreement. How dare that motherfucker rip you from me then take the easy way out? A part of me yearned for a future paved with months or even years of trial prep and consultations with lawyers and law enforcement to give me an avenue through which I could exorcise my grief and focus my fury. The gunman had not just robbed me of you, Allison, but he had taken away a structured foreseeable future during which I might be capable of finding some resolution to my anger, my sorrow, my nightmares. There would be no resolve for me now. The gunman was as dead as you, Allison.

"Have you been following the news on the guy?" Duvaney went on.

"The guy?"

"The shooter."

"No. Not really."

"He'd been in and out of juvie when he was younger. He'd threatened to kill his parents about a half-dozen times. Police had gotten involved. Back when he was in high school he was taken into custody for threats against some students there. Threatening to shoot up the school, that sort of thing. All the classic signs of a common sociopath, I guess." He reclined in his chair in exasperation. "And what does anybody do? Nothing. That's what. Another one slips through the cracks in the system and everyone wonders how the hell something like this could've happened. We're all so shocked, right? As if it wasn't staring us in the face the whole goddamn time." Something in his voice hitched. He glanced away from me. "And now you see what we're left with?"

"I guess," I muttered.

"We're all left with the aftermath." He looked back at me, pointed at me. "You, Aaron. *You're* left with the aftermath. Christ, you *are* the aftermath." He shook his large, square head. "Those poor people. Your poor wife. Son of a bitch." He cleared his throat and said, "The kid's parents were loaded, you know."

"What kid?"

"Vols," he said. His eyebrows knitted together, as if he was confused by my inability to follow this conversation. "Robert Vols. The shooter. I've got it on good authority that some people are filing civil suits against the parents' estate."

"You can do that?"

"It's what I heard. You should look into it. Why the hell not? I can make some phone calls for you, if you'd like."

"I'm not looking to sue anybody, Bill."

"The family is gone. The parents are dead."

"It's just not something I want to pursue."

"Right," he said. "It won't bring her back. But it might — "

"Might what?"

His face softened. "Listen, Aaron." He turned his laptop around on his desk so that we could both see the screen. "I want to show you something." He pecked out a command on the keyboard then manipulated the mouse. An image blinked on the screen. An image of you, Allison. Not a blown-up image of your byline photo like all the other newspapers and media outlets had used, but of you standing at the center of a heap of smiling children. If memory serves, this was from a story you did on young volunteers. You had wanted to highlight their compassion.

"What is it?" I asked.

"Page two of our memorial issue," Duvaney said. "Everyone on staff is contributing. Even the IT guys. It's coming out at the end of the month."

"That's very nice, Bill." You would have been embarrassed as hell by the fanfare, but I didn't tell him that.

"What I'd like is to get a photograph from you of Allison that we can use for the front page. Everything we've got is… it's stock bullshit, Aaron. They're mostly headshots." Given how things ended with you, he must have realized how distasteful this sounded, so he quickly added: "They're like bad author photos, I mean. I was hoping to get something less staged. Something that really captures her."

"I'll look around the house for something."

"That would be wonderful." He closed the laptop. "I really can't express how I feel, Aaron. We're all just so shaken up."

I nodded.

"Just one other thing," he said, "so you won't be blindsided."

"What's that?"

"You know Allison — she worked her tail off. She was at least three months ahead of schedule on her column."

"Yeah?"

"I plan on running 'Allison's A-List' into late spring, maybe early summer. Unless, of course, you have some objection."

"Why would I object? Allison was very proud of that column."

"I just wanted you to know. I didn't want you to open up a paper a month from now and see her photo, her byline. You know what I mean?"

"I appreciate the notice," I heard myself say from some great distance. I was retreating into the gray again, curling myself into a fetal ball and preparing to disassociate. All of a sudden I wanted nothing more than to be back home.

"I can't express…" Duvaney began, but his words died in the air between us. He lifted his hands off the ink blotter in a gesture of genuine helplessness. "You'll let me know if I can do anything for you, won't you?"

"I will."

"You name it, all right?"

"All right." I stood quickly and felt myself coax a wooden smile to the surface of my face. I suddenly needed to get out of here very badly. "I should go."

Duvaney planted both hands atop his desk to hoist himself out of his chair. He came around the desk and gave me another hug. That tie clip might be the death of me.

"Anything at all," he repeated. "I'm serious, Aaron. We all loved her very, very much."

"Thank you," I said, and fled from his office.

6

A handful of days later, I asked Julie Sumter to meet me for lunch. Probably your closest friend in the area, yet you and Julie could not have been more different. Where you were reserved, contemplative, brooding, a coalescence of dark, enigmatic space dust, Julie was buoyed by a bright, warm center and an unremitting cheerfulness. You liked her because she was genuine. I liked her because she had been good for you.

Julie was already seated at a window table with a mug of tea at 49 West when I arrived. She offered me a sad smile, got up, hugged me tight. I hugged her back, suddenly weakened by the strength of it all. We stood like that long enough to draw attention from some of the other customers. When we parted, Julie's eyes were glassy.

"Thanks for coming out."

"Of course, Aaron."

"Go on," I said. "Sit down. Please."

We both sat, and the waiter was perceptive enough to give us some time to ourselves.

"You're growing a beard," she said. "I like it. Makes you look like a mountain climber."

I wasn't so much growing a beard as I was neglecting certain aspects of my personal hygiene, but I only smiled and nodded in response.

"Is your sister still in town?"

"No, she left a few weeks ago."

"That was good of her to come. Where does she live again?"

"Minnesota. She wanted me to go back with her for a while."

"You didn't want to?"

"It just didn't feel like the right thing to do," I said. "Also, do you know how cold it is in Minnesota right now?"

She laughed. Said, "My parents have a timeshare in Florida. I'm trying to wrangle a week there, get some sun, you know? But it's always booked."

"Allison and I went to the Keys last year for Christmas."

"I remember! Al got me that T-shirt from one of Hemingway's favorite bars."

The sound of your nickname on Julie's lips drove a dagger into my heart. You were Al to your close friends and colleagues. You let them call you this even though you despised nicknames. You said they were juvenile, presumptuous, demeaning. Once, when I playfully called you Allie-Cat after a particularly rousing session of lovemaking, you clammed up and wouldn't speak to me for an hour.

The waiter came over and I ordered a club sandwich, even though I wasn't very hungry. There had been a persistent knot twisting in my gut for some time now.

"I need to ask you something," I said after the waiter had left. "And I just want to say upfront that I'm ashamed to even ask it. My head may not be screwed on as tight as it once was, I suspect, but I need to ask it."

There was a slight drawing together of Julie's eyebrows. She leaned forward and placed one hand atop one of my own. Her palm was warm from holding her mug of tea. I felt as if I'd just confessed that I was dying of some rare disease.

"Was Allison having an affair?" I asked.

Julie sat back in her chair. Her hand lingered on mine for a heartbeat more before it slid away and retreated along the tabletop, her collection of thin silver bracelets jangling. "What are you talking about?" she said, a little breathless.

"I just need to know."

"You're being serious right now? Was Al sleeping around on you?"

I told her about the receipt from The Valentine Motel.

"Well, I wouldn't say that's conclusive evidence of anything, Aaron."

"I was out of town that same week. She went to North Carolina and stayed at a motel for two days while I was in New York. She paid in cash so I wouldn't see the charges on the credit card statement."

"Maybe she was there for a work event. Sometimes she went to those media bazaars."

"It wasn't work-related. I called her every night from New York. She never said, 'Hey, by the way, I'm in North Carolina right now.' I thought she was home. She wanted me to think that."

"Maybe it was a last-minute work thing and she didn't want to worry you about her being on the road while you were away."

"It wasn't work-related, Julie."

"How do you know?"

"Because I spoke with her boss."

"Oh, Aaron." A shadow of pity fell over her face. "You went to her *boss* about this?"

"I didn't get into specifics, I just asked if she had been out of town on assignment for any reason back in October. She wasn't. She never traveled out of state for the paper."

"Allison was not having an affair, Aaron."

"Then how do you explain the motel?"

"I don't know, but I'm sure there are a million plausible explanations. Why is her having an affair the first thing you jumped to? Has she ever cheated on you?"

"Not that I know of."

"Aaron," she said, leaning toward me over the table. "Listen to yourself. This is *Allison* you're talking about. You guys had a great marriage. How did she suddenly become some adulterer in your head?"

"Look," I said. "We'd been having some problems. I don't know what was going on with her, but she'd become distant with me.

Something had been bothering her, been on her mind, particularly those past few months. I tried to talk to her about whatever it was, but she kept insisting it was nothing. Only now, finding this motel receipt, I'm wondering if that wasn't the reason she was pulling away from me."

"Because you think there's some guy out there she was fooling around with? I don't believe that, Aaron. And I don't believe *you* believe it, either. Not really."

A flash of shame caused my face to heat up. Maybe Julie was right. Maybe, in my hopeless confusion, I had allowed my mind to run down avenues I normally would have found illogical. *Could* there be another explanation for that motel receipt? Sure, why not?

Yet —

"Okay, okay," I said, holding up one hand. "Just let me ask you this one other thing, okay?"

"Okay."

"*If* she was having an affair, do you think that would be something she would have told you about?"

"Like, would she have confided in me?"

"That's what I'm asking, yes."

"Aaron, she wasn't having an — "

"That's not what I'm asking right now. I'm asking *if* she had been having an affair, would she have told you about it?"

"Aaron, that's an impossible question to answer. A hypothetical of a hypothetical? Come on."

I glanced out the window. The shop windows across the street blazed with the midday sun. Peninsulas of dirty gray snow extended from storefront doorways and lay in ashy heaps against the curb.

"Listen," Julie said, picking up her cell phone and scrolling through it. "I'm going to give you the name and number of my therapist."

"A shrink?"

"She's good."

"You think I'm crazy now?"

"No, dummy. She does grief counseling. She's someone to talk to. Here. Type this into your phone."

"I don't have my phone."

I could have told her I wasn't wearing pants for the look she gave me. Then she reached down and pulled a pen and a crinkled white envelope out of her purse. She jotted down a name and number on the back of the envelope, then handed it to me. I glanced down at it but did not register what she'd written there. I could have been looking at Sanskrit.

"I'm serious, Aaron. Give her a call."

"All right," I said. I folded the envelope in half and tucked it into the inner pocket of my barn coat.

"And quit worrying about this motel-room thing, will you?"

"I'll try."

"Besides," Julie said, clanging her teaspoon against the rim of her mug. "When a woman has an affair, it's the *man* who pays for the hotel room. It's only the chivalrous thing to do." And then she winked at me to show that, yes, she was joking, but that there was also some truth to the sentiment as well.

I smiled and said, "You're right. You win. I don't know what I was thinking."

"See? Now you're back on planet Earth."

Our food arrived and I made a good show of eating, even though that tight little knot in my stomach kept clenching and unclenching, much like a fist. And behind the facade of it all, other-Aaron, commandeering the motherboard once again, began the processes of translating Julie's words, to break them apart and to separate fact from speculation. Just because the motel bill was paid for in cash and your name was on it, Allison, didn't mean that it was *your* cash that was used. Maybe chivalry *wasn't* dead. Some guy could have easily paid that bill.

7

Everything you had with you on the day of your death — your houndstooth topcoat, your purse, your running shoes, your wristwatch, your bloodstained beret, everything — was packed away in a cardboard box in the annex of our townhome, wedged right there between the water heater and the HVAC unit. Trayci had still been here when the items were returned by the police, and she'd packed them away for me without so much as a word. A part of me had known these things were here, but I hadn't been compelled to go through the stuff until now. Kneeling on the concrete floor and peering into the box, I was overcome by a sudden constriction of my chest at the sight of your neatly folded houndstooth coat; I thought I might suffer a heart attack right then and there. Christ, I welcomed it.

I pulled out your coat, pressed my face to it. The scent of Tommy Girl rushed up and shook me. I shut my eyes and summoned other-Aaron, who materialized from the fog of my grief like Humphrey Bogart. While I collapsed inside myself, other-Aaron dipped his hands inside the pockets of your coat. A ballpoint pen in your left coat pocket. A half-empty tin of Altoids in your right.

Other-Aaron refolded your coat and set it aside. He then dug around in the box, coming upon your beret. There was the rusty bloodstain against the crimson wool, incriminating as a confession. The sight of it would have ended me, Allison, but other-Aaron was as emotionless as a combustion engine, and he only set that aside, right there on top of your coat, and did not linger on it. It was your purse that he picked up next, a cheap Louis Vuitton knockoff. Inside the purse: your wallet, cell phone, compact, two tampons, sunglasses, loose change. One other thing, too — a prescription bottle of pills. Other-Aaron removed it from the purse, but it was me who peered out of my eyes and read the label. Xanax. I popped off the cap and stared down into the plastic cylinder at the collection of oblong white tablets inside.

How long had you been taking anxiety pills, Allison? And for what purpose?

That night, I tried to gain access to your cell phone, but it was as if it had died right along with you. It wouldn't power on and it wouldn't charge. I called Tommy Weir to see if he'd be able to do something with it, but he assured me such a task was beyond his ability. I thanked him, then stood in our kitchen staring at your useless cell phone, wondering if it was possible that some part of you had used ghostly magic to kill the phone. Just as you'd sterilized your laptop, wiping it clean. As if there was something you didn't want me to find.

What does it matter now? Let it go.

But I wasn't sure I could.

8

On the night before I drove to the North Carolina town of Chester to seek out The Valentine Motel, an inexplicable thing happened.

It was the middle of the night and I was in our bed, trying to force my turbulent, depressive mind to just shut down for a few hours and get some sleep. My eyelids had grown heavy but my mind was apprehensive about what dreams might come; it seemed that whenever my eyes shut for a few minutes, a thick, noxious smoke would fill my brain, manic as laughing gas, and cause a series of bells and whistles to engage. And then my eyes would flip open again, my body shaking, my forehead clammy with sweat.

The closet light blinked on.

I didn't move at first. I didn't do anything except stare at the partially opened closet door. In the darkness of our bedroom, that narrow shaft of light was as bright and blinding as the sun. I felt myself waiting to glimpse some diaphanous shape shifting about in that panel of light. Listening for some movement in there.

There was nothing.

"Allison." My voice was hollow.

I climbed out of bed, freezing now in nothing but my boxer shorts. The wind against the townhome sounded like a locomotive shuttling by, creaking the joists and beams and showering the dark windowpanes with bits of debris. When I approached the closet door, I paused. Took a breath. A part of me expected to find you on the other side of that door, Allison. I won't lie. A part of me hoped for it.

The closet was empty. The fixture in the ceiling glowed bright, but there were no ghosts. There was no you. I looked at your clothes, the conga line of your shoes along the carpet, the profusion of hats on the top shelf. Your bathrobe was slung over the beveled mirror like a death shroud; I brushed your robe aside, perhaps hoping to catch a fleeting glimpse of your reflection just behind mine in the mirror glass. But you were not there. I was alone.

I switched off the light and got back into bed, where I wept until my utter exhaustion plummeted me into fitful unconsciousness.

CHAPTER THREE

1

On our third date, we went to dinner at the Docksider, a decent bar and grill on the river where we ate surf and turf and watched sailboats chug up and down the muddy channel. It was dark by the time we left, and we were buoyed and giddy from a few too many rum drinks. I took your hand and turned toward the parking lot, but you pulled me in the opposite direction, and so we cut down toward the river instead. A xylophone of docks yawned out into the water, and there were about a half-dozen sailboats rocking against the pilings. It was late spring and the river smelled strongly of brine. I grew up here and had come to ignore that smell; you were a Pennsylvania girl, whose nose was more attuned to the stink of refineries. "It smells like life comes right up to the shore here, right here, and waits to be born," you said. Then we went back up the boat ramp toward the parking lot.

On our way to my car, we heard a woman crying from somewhere in the dark. Beneath that, the low rumble of a man's voice. As we crossed the parking lot, we saw a couple maybe a few years older than us standing within the sickly orange spotlight of a lamppost and nestled between two vehicles. The woman was in tears, accusing the man of some injustice; the man was trying to hush her while concurrently pleading his case. At one point, the man's voice rose;

the conciliatory tone he'd been using just a moment earlier was now gone, replaced by a surge of anger. He gripped the woman around the forearm. The woman whined and, very clearly, said, "Ouch, you're hurting me."

I squeezed your hand tighter and tried to pull you in the direction of my car. But you pulled me back, your feet suddenly rooted to the pavement. "Hey," you called to the couple. They both turned and looked at you — looked at us — and then the man brought his face close to the woman's. Teeth clenched, he proceeded to berate the woman while she continued to moan that he was hurting her. I saw her try to pry his fingers from her forearm. He, in turn, shoved her back against an SUV. I heard the back of her head strike the SUV's window.

There was a decorative little roundabout in the center of the parking lot — a few pilings strung together by rope, a pair of wooden oars crossed in an X, a plastic egret. You dropped my hand and marched over to the roundabout. You stepped over the rope that had been strung up around it, grabbed one of the wooden oars, and wrenched it free of the display.

"Allison," I said.

You ignored me.

"Hey," you said, advancing toward the couple. I think the woman saw you coming, but the man was blinded by rage. You said nothing more as you came up beside them and swung the oar like goddamn Babe Ruth.

It was a flimsy piece of wood, made brittle from being outdoors, and it cracked in half as you brought it down along the back of the man's neck. Yet you must have managed to strike him just right, because the guy crumpled like a house of cards. His legs folded and he went down — not unconscious, but dazed enough to remain on his hands and knees like someone waiting for a child to climb onto his back and give pony rides.

"Come with me," you said, holding a hand out to the woman.

"Are you fucking *crazy*?" the woman shouted at you. "What did you just *do*?" And then she dropped down to attend to the man, rubbing a hand through his hair and kissing the side of his face.

"Hey," I called to you. "Hey." I touched your arm, but you didn't turn around. You just stared at the couple, perplexed by this turn of events. Suddenly, you were the bad guy. "Let's get out of here," I said.

You dropped the oar and followed me across the lot. I was moving quickly, but there was a dazed lethargy to your gait, as if you were wading through a dream. The look on your face was not one of confusion, however — it was one of anger.

"You fucking crazy bitch!" the woman shouted at you from across the parking lot.

You shoved your hands in your pockets, bladed your shoulders, and marched after me with your head down. As I turned to look after you, I could almost see waves of steam radiating from your body and dispersing into the night. Your sudden fury had left me shaken and unanchored, like something cast adrift in a dark and turbulent sea. I could not reconcile what I'd just witnessed with the woman I believed you to be — the cerebral, pragmatic, compassionate woman with whom I was already beginning to fall in love. It took the remainder of that night for the shock of what you did to evaporate from me. And even then, I never forgot it.

It was this memory that returned to me as I motored the Civic up into the hills of North Carolina. It seemed implausible that you could be both the woman who, in the name of injustice, had cracked a decorative oar over a stranger's head while also being the woman who may have engaged in a romantic relationship behind my back. In the clarity of day, the idea of your infidelity seemed less plausible than during the quaking, riotous, never-ending hours of the night. I had tried to do just as Julie Sumter had advised — to let it go and forget about the goddamn motel receipt. But then I'd close my eyes and wonder what the hell you were doing for two nights in some dive called The Valentine Motel over four hundred miles from our home, and doubt about you and our relationship would begin to cloud my brain all over again.

If I found out about an affair, Allison, what would that do for my grief? Where would that leave me?

Twice I nearly turned back. The second time was as I advanced down a curling strip of asphalt somewhere in the mountains and saw the hand-carved wooden sign on the shoulder of the road welcoming me to the town of Chester. I slowed to a stop in the middle of the road — there was no traffic out here, and I hadn't passed another vehicle in the past half hour — and gazed at the sign.

— *Go back now, none the wiser*, the pragmatic other-Aaron spoke up from behind the gray curtain in my brain.

He was right, of course. Just as Julie Sumter had been right. None of this meant anything anymore, did it?

I didn't turn back. I continued on, carving my way through a forested road marked by the occasional camper or double-wide. It was late afternoon and the sun was an arterial bleed along the western horizon. Ahead, I saw a break in the trees. The road became a narrow bridge over a wide slipstream of gray, frothing water. Men in checked coats and wool caps fished from the bridge; my passage did not appear to disturb them. On the opposite bank, I drove past a small bait-and-tackle shop, a gas station, and a smoldering red-clay chiminea in a gravel parking lot.

The Valentine Motel was about a mile or so from the riverbank, tucked away in the forest. I came upon it rather by luck, since the GPS on my phone had been rendered useless once I'd gone far enough into the mountains. There was nothing special about the place — it was a typical roadside motel, with what looked like a dozen rooms at the far end of a white-stone parking lot. In my mind, I had constructed this place to look like something from a Niagara Falls honeymoon, complete with vibrating heart-shaped beds and a complimentary bottle of cheap champagne waiting on the nightstand. Yet despite the name, this place was more likely where hunters and fishermen caught some shuteye, or maybe slept off too much Schlitz beer.

I pulled into the parking lot. There were a few other vehicles here — mostly pickup trucks — and a large camper was tucked between the motel and a row of dumpsters. Behind the motel, the mountain continued upward, dense with forest. In the waning daylight, I could make out a discreet double-wide trailer back there, animal pelts hanging from the porch eaves.

There was a man in a red flannel jacket attending to the inner workings of a Ford F-150 that was parked just outside the motel entrance. As I crunched across the gravel lot toward the motel door, the man looked up at me. He was maybe in his late forties, with a wave of dark hair curling down to his shirt collar. A cigarette dangled from his mouth.

He raised a grease-streaked hand and said, "Be with you in a minute."

I nodded, then entered the motel lobby. The walls were paneled in wood and there were many framed photographs of men with gruff smiles holding up large fish. A few fishing trophies sat on a shelf behind the front counter, white and furry with dust. On the desk, beside an ancient computer monitor with a plastic hula girl fixed to its top, was a velvet-backed board displaying about two dozen fishing flies, each one as intricate and colorful as an Indian headdress.

The man in the red flannel jacket came in, wiping his hands on a greasy rag. "Don't suppose you know much about engines?" he asked, and offered me a weary smile.

"Sorry."

"It's either the cold or the altitude gets in her every year. Kinda like her owner." He thumped a fist against his chest, still smiling. A tangle of keys chimed against his hip as he maneuvered around the desk. "So what's your poison?" he asked.

"My poison?"

"Muskie? Smallmouth? Walleye?" His eyes — colorless as two pools of rainwater — narrowed as he took me in. "Hell, you're a trout man, through and through. I can tell."

"Oh," I said. "Actually, I haven't come for the fishing."

"Is that right? Well, that's a shame. They're really running now."

As I dug my cell phone from my jacket pocket, I said, "My wife stayed here for two nights back in October. Maybe you remember her?" I showed him a photo of you on my phone.

He peered at it. "Nice-looking lady," he commented.

"Do you remember her staying here?"

"Well, it's just that I don't consider it good business practice to talk about folks who come in and out of here, you know? I mean, you say she's your wife, but you could be some boyfriend out here stalking her, right?" His eyes sparkled and he presented me with a partial smile, to show there were no hard feelings.

I scrolled to a different photo that showed us together, smiling against a sunset on the prow of a friend's sailboat.

"Listen," he said. "You got some question about your wife, how come you don't talk to her about it?"

I slipped my phone back in my jacket pocket and took out the motel receipt. I laid it down on the counter, upside down so that the man could read it.

"My wife died back in December," I told him. "There was a shooting at a strip mall back where we're from, in Maryland. It was... well, it was on the news."

"Ah, Christ," he said. "I'm sorry to hear that."

"I found this receipt after she died. Looks like she spent two nights here back in October. Looks like she paid in cash, too."

He picked up the receipt, examined it. "Cash, yeah," he said. Then he set the receipt back down on the counter. The expression on his face told me that any further explanation on my end was not necessary. This guy knew why I'd driven over four hundred miles to ask him about this. He was wearing a gold wedding band on one thick-knuckled finger.

"My wife's name was Allison Decker," I said, tapping a finger on the receipt to indicate where her name was printed. "Please. Do you remember her coming here or not?"

The man's mouth tightened to a firm, lipless line. The shake of his head was almost imperceptible. "Most of the people come through here, they got beards and beer guts," he said. "I'd remember if someone like your wife came here. I'm sorry."

"Obviously she was here," I said. "This receipt is yours, isn't it? It's from this place."

"Well, yeah, that's true."

"Then she was here. Maybe someone else checked her in?"

"Wouldn't be no one but me. Sheila, my wife, she does the linens and the room cleanings, but I'm the only one checking people in."

"Then I don't understand…"

The man cleared his throat and said, "I mean, look, I can't say a hundred percent, okay? Those rooms open up onto the parking lot, so no one comes in here unless they're checking in or checking out, or maybe if they need change for the vending machines. She could have been with someone who checked in while she went straight to the room or maybe waited in the car. In that case, I never would've seen her."

"And it would have her name on the receipt if someone else paid?"

"I would have put it under whatever name I was given."

"How common is it for someone to pay for a room with cash instead of using a credit card?"

"It happens. Generally, I tack on a ten percent additional charge if you pay cash. You know, to cover any incidentals. Sometimes people ding up the walls or thieve off with the batteries from the TV remote. Stuff like that. If I don't have a credit card number on file, then I'm out the cost of the damage. Doesn't look like I tacked it on to that bill you showed me, though. Whoever it was probably struck me as trustworthy."

"I just don't understand it," I said, more to myself than to him.

"Well, I'm afraid I can't offer much more than that," said the man. "Shame, what you're going through, and what happened to your wife. What a world we live in now, huh? Just terrible."

"Thank you," I said, half in a daze.

"Anything else?" he asked.

I glanced out the plate-glass windows of the motel lobby and out across the parking lot, where, on the other side of the road, the spaces between the trees had grown dark in the oncoming twilight.

"It's getting late and I'm exhausted," I said. "I guess I'll get a room for the night."

"Cash or charge?" said the man, and I couldn't tell if he was trying to be humorous.

2

Was this the room you stayed in, Allison? For those two nights you spent here in Chester — those two inexplicable nights spent here at The Valentine Motel — did you stay in this very room? Room four of twelve, with the vending machines humming right outside the door? The room with the discolored wallpaper depicting green and brown fish leaping in little arcs? The room with the water stain in the shape of Texas on the ceiling? Would I catch the ephemeral scent of your perfume in this place, Allison? Would I feel your cool lips on my forehead as I drifted off toward sleep?

Had someone stayed in this room with you?

3

The town of Chester was no one's destination — except evidently yours, Allison. Rather, it was a byway connecting destinations, a spaceport, a layover between larger towns and cities that appear as swollen black dots on maps. It seemed impossible you'd have come here to gambol with some roughneck from one of these dilapidated, weather-beaten campers; a steely-eyed and bearded bandit trolling for walleye or bass; a good old boy swilling pale beer from plastic pitchers at The Troutman, which turned out to be Chester's only pub.

The Troutman was a rectangular cinderblock building with neon lights filling its smoked black windows. The name of the place hung above the entrance, carved from wood and lit from underneath by a series of floodlights. It was fairly crowded, too, by the look of all the trucks in the lot. I parked close to the road and walked across the lot, which was covered in cedar chips that popped and crunched under my sneakers. The Troutman's front door was held open by a rusty blue oil drum, and I could hear music coming from within, even over the moan of the wind funneling down from the peaks of the mountains. I'd never seen a blackness so black as out here, a sky so dense and luminous with stars.

A blast of warm air greeted me as I walked through the door.

There were a few pool tables near the back, and they seemed to be attracting the most attention. The bar was crowded, too, so I ordered a beer then hunted down a table for myself. There was one in a darkened corner, beneath a collection of taxidermy fish nailed to glossy wooden shields. I sat and drank my beer and watched some men shoot pool.

You would have stuck out like a pink kangaroo in this place, Allison.

Halfway through my beer, a middle-aged woman with an apron slung around her wide hips came over to me. "You need a menu, honey?" she asked, her accent redolent of the mountains.

Even though the last thing I'd eaten had been two Slim Jims with a Dr Pepper, and that had been hours ago while I was still on the road, I wasn't very hungry. Still, I knew I had to eat. "Maybe just a salad?" I said.

"Oh, sugar, let's pretend you didn't say that," the waitress said.

"Okay. Let's pretend I didn't. What do you recommend?"

"What I'm gonna do, darling, is refill your beer and bring you my personal favorite. It ain't even on the menu."

"Sounds pretty special," I said. "Can I ask you a quick question?"

"Sure thing."

I showed her your picture on my cell phone. Because the motel proprietor hadn't been sympathetic when I'd said I was out here inquiring about my wife, I now said, "This is my sister. She was here in town back in October. She stayed for two nights at the motel up the hill. You don't happen to recognize her, do you?"

The waitress placed two meaty hands on the tabletop and leaned so close to my phone that her snub little nose nearly came in contact with the screen. She squinted at the photograph. "Sorry, darling. Don't recognize her."

"Okay, thanks."

"Something happen to her? She gone missing?"

"Yeah."

She covered her mouth with one hand while the other hand fell upon my shoulder. "Oh, Lord. That's just awful."

I felt feverish, claustrophobic. It had been wrong of me to drive all the way down here, hunting for some dark thing.

"Are you a spiritual person?" the waitress asked me.

"Not particularly," I said.

"Well, He's there, no matter if you believe in Him or not. And your sister, I have faith that He will watch over her and take care of her, wherever she is."

"Thank you. That's nice."

Her face darkened. "And even if something has befallen her, rest assured that she is in His warm embrace. When the Good Lord says, 'Come with me,' we don't have no choice. We have to go. And He holds us there and comforts us."

I said nothing to this. Only stared at her.

She squeezed my shoulder before retreating back across the barroom floor.

4

The meal was bologna schnitzel, which was surprisingly delicious. Probably because she felt sorry for me, my waitress brought me a whole pitcher of beer for free. I had no intention of draining it, which was exactly what I did anyway, and I meandered back out into the parking lot sometime around midnight with my head spinning and feeling like my bones were two sizes too big for my body. Because I did not trust myself to keep the Civic from careening into a tree, I summoned other-Aaron, who cranked the ignition, engaged the gears, and drove with dutiful precision all the way back to The Valentine Motel.

The man who had checked me into the motel earlier that evening was standing outside beneath the glowing pink lights of the motel's marquee, smoking a cigarette. I waved to him as I climbed out of my car and fumbled around in my jacket pocket for the key to my motel room.

"Mr. Decker," he called.

"G'night."

"Sir," he said, coming toward me in the darkness.

I paused, one hand still wedged inside my pocket.

"Is my face red?" he said.

"Well, it's pink," I said, nodding up toward the glowing marquee.

"What I mean is, I'm embarrassed to say I misspoke earlier. I had a chat with my wife and it turns out she did check in a woman back in October, name of Allison Decker."

"Is she sure?"

"She described her pretty good. Said she was wearing sunglasses and one of those French hats." He twirled a finger above his head. "A red beret."

5

Next morning, I spoke to the proprietor's wife before heading back home. She was an amphetamine-thin woman with a narrow face and an overbite. She wore her long tawny hair in a braid that came down to the small of her back. It looked like a strong wind might carry her off into the stratosphere.

"I remember her clearly because she didn't look like anyone who normally comes out this way," said the woman. She and I were smoking cigarettes in the motel parking lot while her husband cursed and puttered beneath his truck's hood just a few yards away. "She had on a red beret and sensible shoes. Said she was having car trouble and needed a place to stay until she could have someone take a look at it."

"Was anyone else with her?" I asked. "A man?"

"None that I saw," she said, but then waved at the row of rooms clear across to the far end of the gravel parking lot. "But anyone could have shown up to meet her. I'd be none the wiser, Mr. Decker."

My gaze traced the length of the building. My heart was jackhammering in my throat. "Which room did she stay in?"

"Room Four," she said. "Same room as you last night."

6

It was late by the time I arrived back in Harbor Village. Our street was dark, but there were lights on in all the windows of our townhome. When I entered, I noticed in my haste I'd left the television on, too.

No, not the television, but that fucking Alexa hockey puck, playing your favorite goddamn eighties playlist. George Michael, telling me I gotta have faith.

Sure, I thought. *Fuck you, George.*

I switched off the speaker then went around through the house turning off all the lights. My head ached, my stomach felt like it had been cast in lead, and yet my entire body felt eerily weightless. Upstairs, all the lights were on. I shut them off, too, then climbed beneath a scorching stream of water in the master bathroom. When I closed my eyes under the spray, an image of you popped up in my head, Allison. I chased it away. I couldn't keep doing this. I would drive myself crazy doing this.

After the shower, I climbed into bed and just lay there in the dark, staring at the panels of moonlight that cut in through the bedroom windows. When I shut my eyes this time, it was the neon pink of the motel's marquee that projected against the screens of my eyelids. So I opened them again.

The closet light was on.

I didn't move for a while — I just kept still, the blankets pulled up to my chin, my heart strumming against my ribcage. A part of me thought that if I looked at that lighted doorway long enough, the light might go out. This insanity might stop.

The light did not go out.

I got out of bed and moved toward the closet door. Everything was silent except for the sound of blood funneling through my ears and a faintly flutelike whistle coming from my left nostril.

I eased open the closet door a bit more and peered inside, startled by a figure standing against the far wall and bracketed by our clothes. The figure was me — my reflection in the beveled mirror.

In the ceiling, the light fixture fizzed, blinked, but remained on.

When I looked back down, I found myself staring at your hope chest. And not just at your hope chest, but at the padlock you had attached to it sometime in the recent past. In the aftermath of your death, I had forgotten about the goddamn lock.

People put locks on things when they want to keep them safe. People put locks on things when they don't want other people to see what they're hiding inside.

The latch had been drilled into the lid from the inside, so it wasn't like I could take it apart with a screwdriver. Without a key to the lock, the only way I was getting in there was if I smashed it apart. It hurt my heart to consider this, but if I'm being honest: I considered this. The wood was strong, the chest well-made, so it would take more than a sturdy hammer to do the trick. An axe? We had one in the shed, didn't we?

I turned to head out of the closet, already picturing myself chopping your hope chest into kindling, when something caught my eye and made me freeze.

Atop the marble pedestal was a small brass key. I stared at it in disbelief, because surely, *surely*…

"All hail the mystic pedestal," I said, and picked up the key.

It fit into the padlock with ease. When I turned it, the lock popped open.

— *Do you really want to do this?* other-Aaron spoke up from the recesses of my admittedly jittery mind. *Once you open this you'll never be able to unopen it.*

I opened it.

CHAPTER FOUR

1

The first thing I saw when I opened your hope chest was a tidy row of wrapped Christmas presents resting on a mat of folded sweaters. A pang of grief resonated through the center of my body, fierce enough to leave me momentarily breathless. I removed the presents and the sweaters from the chest one at a time, setting them in a heap beside me on the floor of the closet, and paused only when I saw the first of the items you'd been concealing beneath them.

A gun.

My knowledge of guns was limited to what I'd read in books or seen on television. It was a revolver, black-bodied with a walnut handgrip. The steel barrel gleamed. I crouched there peering down at the thing, a prickling sensation creeping up the nape of my neck. I wouldn't have been more surprised had I opened the lid to find a rattlesnake inside. That this thing was in our house — that it was here and I hadn't known about it — was so impossible that I had to question whether I was awake or dreaming. You had always been against handguns in the home. Even after a series of break-ins in Harbor Village last year, you had refused to entertain the notion of keeping a handgun in the house for protection.

I picked it up, turned it over in my hands. Like a venomous snake, it felt dangerous just holding it. I found the cylinder release and engaged it. The chambers in the cylinder were empty, but that didn't dissolve my unease. Instead, I knelt there holding the thing, wondering why it was here and why you hadn't told me about it. Wondering if things might have been different if you'd had it with you that day at the strip mall...

I set the gun atop the mound of sweaters, reached back into the chest, and removed a rectangular cardboard box of .38-caliber ammunition that you'd tucked between two folded afghans. A wave of noxious heat coursed through my entire body. I set the box of ammo on the floor, then wiped my sweaty palms along my thighs.

Above my head, the closet light blinked several times. An indecipherable Morse code. The scent of your Tommy Girl perfume caused me to turn and gaze out into our bedroom, as if in anticipation of your impossible return. I waited. I begged for it. Kneeling there on the closet floor in supplication. Once the muscles in my thighs began to ache, I turned away. My face was warm, my hands were shaking, and there was a javelin of ice advancing its way through the marrow of my bones.

I removed one of the afghans to reveal a clear plastic bag, the kind that bed sheets and quilts come in. But there were no bed sheets or quilts inside this one. From inside the bag, the smudgy countenance of a child's doll stared out at me.

I unzipped the bag and slid the doll out. It was the kind with the fabric body and the rubber head and limbs. Only this particular doll was missing its arms, as though they'd been torn from its torso. The thing was old, it smelled like death, and its cloth body had turned the grayish-greenish-brown of an aging bruise. One of the doll's eyes were missing; when I tipped it backward, its remaining eye winked shut. I replaced the doll back in the bag, the stink of it still on my hands.

One final thing was hidden at the bottom of your hope chest,

Allison, buried beneath an old bed sheet. I removed the remaining contents from the chest, stripped the bed sheet away with a magician's flourish, and found myself staring down at a thick accordion folder with a series of industrial rubber bands stretched around it to keep it closed. The discovery of the gun had been a shock, but something about this thick file unsettled me on a more basic level, stirring into alertness that distant, reptilian part of my brain. The part adept at recognizing danger.

I extracted the file from the chest, marveling at the thickness and heft of it, and set it in my lap. It occurred to me that it could contain anything — work papers, tax records, love letters from old boyfriends, college transcripts, original copies of your freelance newspaper articles, or proof of my stupid suspicion of your infidelity. Pretty much anything at all.

But what the file contained, of course, was a history of the dead.

2

Inside the accordion folder were six individual packets, each one held together by a large binder clip. Each packet had a cover page — a single white sheet of printer paper on which you'd printed a name, date, and a location:

MARGOT IDELSON (2006) – Norfolk, Virginia

SHELBY DAVENPORT (2008) – Bishop, North Carolina

LAUREN CHASTAIN (2011) – Vineland, New Jersey

MEGAN POLLOCK (2013) – Whitehall, Delaware

GABRIELLE COLSON-HOWE (2016) – Port Tobacco, Maryland

HOLLY RENFROW (2018) – Furnace, West Virginia

Just seeing those names caused a serpent of dread to tighten into a coil at the center of my body. The names meant nothing to me, and I had no context for what any of this was… but some innate part of me stirred uneasily at the sight of those names.

Inside each packet were newspaper articles and stories printed off the internet concerning the murders of these people — people who turned out to be teenage girls. Some of them contained black-and-white photos of the victims, smiling school-photo faces with ringlets of pale hair, clavicles adorned with slender necklaces, some of them with braces on their teeth. You'd printed maps from MapQuest, charting the miles to these various small towns up and down the east coast in red marker, towns whose names were unfamiliar to me and as remote as distant satellites. Most disconcerting were the pages and pages of handwritten notes you'd taken that corresponded with each specific packet — pages torn from spiral-bound notebooks, their margins frilly from the tear, or long sheets of yellow legal paper. Within your notes were names and phone numbers, people identified as law enforcement personnel from various locations, family members of the deceased, many others. I realized that some of these notes were from what appeared to be interviews you had conducted with some of these people. Most of these notes had dates written in the upper right-hand corners of the pages. Some were from the past few years, which was troubling enough — it meant you had been doing this behind the backdrop of our marriage without me ever realizing it, whatever this *was* — but even more disturbing were the ones from *before* our marriage. What was all of this and how long had you been collecting this information? The length of time you had spent in this dark world staggered me, Allison. And not just in your head, either, but in actuality. You had been traveling to these places, speaking to these people in person. You'd been doing this for years, it appeared. And, of course, all of that intel conspired to arrive at the heart of the question here — namely, what exactly had you been doing?

And through it all, a finger of guilt edged up through the middle of my soul. My mind had jumped immediately to infidelity when I had come across that motel receipt, but Julie Sumter had been right — there *were* other possibilities. I'd own the guilt because it meant you'd been faithful all along, yet my confusion over this new discovery was quickly overshadowing it. Because it was true that you'd been hiding *something* from me.

I spent time with these files, spent time combing cautiously through the computer printouts and all your handwritten notes. It occurred to me that these printouts may have been the reason you'd wiped your laptop's hard drive, although I couldn't fathom why. Whatever this was, you had graduated toward a frenzy — among the more recent files, your handwriting became even more illegible and hectic than normal. In particular, I found a loose sheet of yellow legal paper tucked between the two most recently dated folders. I slid it out and stared at it, unable to reconcile exactly what I was seeing, or how it related to the other information you had collected in the folders. Like someone writing in the throes of a fugue state or while possessed by a spirit, the same phrase had been furiously scribbled over and over again, as if screaming from the page:

Gas Head will make you dead

It wasn't just the cryptic nature of the phrase or the fury with which it had been so clearly written that resonated with me, but the certainty that I had heard it somewhere before. Nonetheless, it was meaningless to me, as informative as a line cribbed from an unfamiliar poem.

I turned the page over and saw the phrase repeated on the other side, along with a drawing that could best be described as a bar graph without any demarcations: six rectangular columns of varying size standing in a row, like someone had rearranged the tone bars of a xylophone.

Again, the light above my head fizzled and dimmed. I stared at it, then looked away, the afterimage of the bulb radiating like a wound in the center of my vision.

3

"I don't understand what the hell she was doing," I said to Bill Duvaney one afternoon, as we sat having lunch at a restaurant in downtown Annapolis. He had been adamant about taking me out to eat for nearly two weeks now, a show of goodwill on his part, and to make sure I was getting on without you, I suppose. It was kind of him, and there was no ulterior motive that I could discern, but I'd been avoiding him because I didn't think I had it in me to don a mask and socialize with anyone yet. Particularly not someone with whom my only connection had been you, Allison. But in the end, I finally acquiesced. And as it turned out, *I* was the one with the ulterior motive. If there was a person who might be able to shed some light on your morbid obsession, it might be your boss, a newspaperman to whom something like this, no matter how dark it might seem to me, might make an ounce of sense.

"Well, it's certainly unexpected, but I don't know if it's all that unusual," Bill said. Before him on the table was the accordion file containing all your research. He had glanced at some of the newspaper articles and at your handwritten notes with all the gravitas of a heart surgeon, but the look on his face now wasn't quite so solemn.

"Come on, Bill. You don't think it's unusual that my wife was going to all these places, talking to all these people, these cops and whoever else? Asking questions about unsolved murders? And the whole time, she never said anything about it to me. She was sneaking around behind my back and keeping this a secret like some... I don't know..."

"Like some reporter," Bill finished.

"Yeah, but nothing you were paying her to do. It had nothing to do with her work."

"Maybe it was a pet project. There's a whole breed of people out there who fancy themselves detectives. They find cold cases, try to solve them from their living rooms while surfing the internet on their laptops."

"She wasn't just surfing the internet. She was going to these places. I checked the dates of her hotel stays. Some of them correspond to dates when I was out of town. She was waiting for me to leave so that she could get back out there and dig around in this stuff. Others are from before we met. And not just that, but this first murder?" I dug the packets out of the file, found the one I was looking for. "This girl Margot Idelson? She was killed in Norfolk, Virginia, in 2006. Allison would have been seventeen at the time, Bill. *Seventeen*. What was she doing researching some girl's death back then?"

"Who's to say she took all these notes contemporaneously? Maybe she only started looking at all these murders in the past year or so."

I shook my head. "I don't think so. The handwritten dates on some of the notes certainly don't point to that." The dates on the notes aside, there was something about the way they were written that conveyed an immediacy to the event you were researching, although I didn't possess the mental acumen to figure out exactly why I felt that way. Something in my gut, perhaps.

"Well, Aaron, whatever it is, the answer died with Allison," Bill said. "What does it matter now?"

Lowering my voice, I said, "She bought a gun, Bill. A revolver. She had it hidden away in a trunk in our closet with the rest of this stuff."

Bill's eyebrows climbed toward his receding hairline. "A *gun*? Allison?"

"Back when we were having all those break-ins in the neighborhood, I suggested the possibility of getting a gun for protection, and she wouldn't even consider it. Started citing statistics about gun owners accidentally shooting their spouses. Yet she goes out and buys one and hides it from me. I don't get it."

"Maybe it wasn't protection for the home," Bill suggested. "Maybe it was protection for her, while she was on the road."

"Jesus," I muttered. "It's like I didn't even know her, Bill."

"I think you're making a big deal out of this stuff because your emotions are all over the place. Allison's death, it was sudden, Aaron. It was cruel. Your focus on this stuff is just a way to keep your connection to her." He picked up his ice water and frowned at what appeared to be the remnants of someone's pink lipstick on the rim of the glass. "Hell, maybe she was writing a book," he suggested, setting the dirty glass down. "She learned about all these random unsolved cases, these poor girls, so maybe she wanted to give them a voice. Maybe she didn't want them to be forgotten. It's just like what she did with her column, only on a more grandiose scale. If you ask me, that sounds just like something Allison would do."

It was true. I found myself thinking of our third date, and how you'd cracked that guy over the head with an ornamental oar because he was roughing up his girlfriend. It *was* just like you, Allison. Bill was right. You had a streak inside you that burned brightly whenever you witnessed some injustice, especially if it was perpetrated against a young girl at the hands of some perceived asshole. So... was that it, then? Had you been writing a book about these forgotten girls? Had it been your intention to give them a voice and grant them immortality on the pages of a manuscript? Or had it been something more than that?

"If that's what she was doing, writing a book," I said, "then why wouldn't she tell me about it? I would have supported her writing a book."

"You would have supported her running all over, doing this type of research in all these remote places, crashing in motel rooms by herself, talking to God knows who? With a gun in her purse, no less?"

"Of course. I'm not some macho asshole, Bill." Yet even as I said this, I wasn't sure it was one hundred percent truth. Would I have been okay with it? "Anyway, it couldn't be a book. If it was, what was she waiting for? These murders span over a decade. She could have published the son of a bitch by now."

Our waiter came by, set a Manhattan in front of Bill, a diet soda in front of me. Bill scowled at my sobriety. When the waiter left, I rummaged through the files until I found the single sheet of yellow legal paper, the one with *Gas Head will make you dead* printed ad nauseam across both sides of the page.

"And then there's this," I said, handing the paper to Bill. "Does that phrase mean anything to you? Have you ever heard it before?"

He scrutinized one side of the page, then the other. "'Gas Head will make you dead.' Means nothing to me. This was with the rest of this stuff?"

"Wedged between the two most recent files."

"Maybe it's a song lyric? Did you try googling it?"

"I have. Zero results. It's not a song lyric. It's nothing that exists anywhere on the internet."

"It could just be some mental flotsam that had been swirling around in her head. Looks like daydream doodling. Reporters are always making little sketches in the margins of their notes. I see it every day. See?" He pointed to the thing that looked like an unlabeled bar graph. "Just doodles." He handed the paper back to me. "Why's this bugging you so much?"

"Because I've *heard* this before, this 'Gas Head' phrase. I can't remember where, but it's familiar to me. It means something. I just don't know what."

"Well, what can you do? You can't ask her about it. You can't ask her about *any* of this, Aaron. She's gone."

I took a deep breath. My gaze clung to the files of dead girls spread out across the table, the crinkled sheet of yellow paper with that eerie phrase all over it.

"We were having some problems in the past few months, just before she died," I said in a low voice. "Allison had become cold, distant. She wasn't sleeping. Something was bothering her and it resonated through our marriage, but she wouldn't talk to me about it. If it had something to do with this stuff" — I waved a hand over the files — "then I want to know. If something here was what was pulling her away from me in the end, Bill, then I want to know what it was."

"That's a lofty expectation," Bill said. His eyes looked sad.

I felt anxious and unsettled. I told Bill I was going outside for a smoke, then excused myself from the table. My campaign from the rear of the restaurant to the sidewalk felt like a mountaineering expedition. The afternoon was chilly, the skies terminally gray and clustered with storm clouds. I smoked while watching the traffic. A group of tourists meandered up the block at the far end of the street; I kept expecting you to appear among them, your eyes bright, your smile radiant, your dark hair curling and framing your face. By the time I'd smoked my cigarette down to the filter, a pattern of raindrops had collected on the windshields of the cars parked along the curb.

Back at our table, Bill Duvaney had the files opened again. It was not your notes he was studying, nor the newspaper articles you'd printed off the internet. All six faces of the murdered girls stared up from their respective files, a lineup so tragic that I paused beside Bill's chair and just stared down at them from over his shoulder.

Bill looked up at me. "What do you see?" he asked me.

"Tragedy," I said.

"Look more closely."

I looked at the pictures but didn't understand what it was he wanted me to see.

"A pattern," Bill said. "A *type*."

"A type of what?"

"A type of victim."

I looked at him.

"Sit," he said.

I pulled my chair around to his side of the table and sat down.

"All of them young, blonde, pretty," Bill said. "Could be these murders are actually connected."

"Connected," I said, and looked at him. "You're talking about a serial killer?"

"I'm no police detective," he said. "If the articles were more specific regarding how each girl was killed — and they're not — then maybe the connection would be even clearer. But look at them. Look at their faces."

"Jesus Christ," I muttered, my gaze volleying from photograph to photograph. It was true — the similarity between each victim was uncanny. How had I missed this before? "Jesus Christ, Bill. What do I do with this?"

"Who's the most recent murder victim?"

I pointed to one of the photographs. "Holly Renfrow, killed last fall," I said. "Seventeen years old, from a town called Furnace, West Virginia. The newspaper articles Allison collected about her death are vague as to the specific cause, just like you said, only that police suspected foul play. In Allison's notes, though, she listed Renfrow's cause of death as a drowning."

Bill was watching me, grinning.

"What?" I said.

"You've really studied this stuff," he said. "Perhaps it's transference. Allison's obsession becoming yours."

"I don't know about that."

"Every obsession needs a home," he said. "Anyway, if I were you, I'd take this stuff to the police out there in Furnace, show them what you've got. Let them piece it all together."

I considered this. My gaze hung on the photo of Holly Renfrow. There was a better picture of her included in the file, a color photo you had gotten from someone — a relative of Holly's? — at some point. But something about this black-and-white one caused my throat to tighten.

"What's wrong?" Bill said from some great distance.

"You think that's what Allison would want me to do? Take this stuff to the police, I mean."

"Why not?"

"Because as far as I can tell, *she* didn't."

"What do you mean? In all six cases Allison's got notes in there from conversations with police."

"Yeah, but about each *individual* murder," I said… or was it other-Aaron speaking through me now, translating the documents laid out before us? "There's no evidence here that she took this serial-killer hypothesis to the cops. She clearly kept these files for herself. Hidden. Hidden even from me." I looked at Bill. "What if there was a reason for that?"

"Well," Bill said, "you can't ask her, so you've only got your gut to go on, I suppose. Do what you think is right, Aaron."

I didn't say anything to that. What I was thinking of was the closet light, blinking on and off, on and off, as I sat on the floor poring over the contents of your hidden files. Inside the nerve center of my consciousness, other-Aaron opened his eyes and did the math. I was temporarily comforted by the familiar sound of his sleek machinery rolling away inside my head once again. And just like that, it became suddenly, transcendently clear: a memory of something you'd showed me, something silly and futile, something that might prove a way for a haunted man to commune with a ghost and find the answer he seeks. Other-Aaron retreated, bowing like a sensei as he vanished into the shadows of my brain.

4

There was a thing you showed me early on in our courtship that I'd never forgotten, Allison. A game, really. What would you call it? A silly thing that you showed me only once, but that had resonated in the back of my mind since your death. A symbol of you and of everything you'd left behind in your wake.

You had driven us that night, out to some raucous dinner with colleagues of yours, and we kept making faces at each other from across the room to make each other laugh. It was at Bill and

Maureen Duvaney's house, a handsome brick Tudor perched above the Chesapeake Bay. The more inebriated everyone got, the louder their voices and the looser their tongues became. I had watched these people in awe, trying to reconcile your relationship with them, how your introversion and cavernous depths functioned alongside their boisterous natures.

At one point in the evening, a woman appeared on the porch dressed in multicolored silk robes and wearing a pleated floral-patterned turban on her head. Jewelry jangled from all her limbs, and when she walked, it was like the clinking of castanets. She was Madam Golganor, seer of futures, rider in the chariot of the cosmos. A robust and red-faced woman, she downed several drinks, told a number of sexually explicit jokes, then ultimately settled down at the Duvaneys' dining room table with a crystal ball that very clearly had a MADE IN CHINA label stuck to its wooden base. For a shot of bourbon, she'd impart wisdom; for a shot of rye, she'd divulge the secrets of the universe; for a Tom Collins and a slice of cake, she'd tell you what your future held.

Your coworkers all took turns with the increasingly intoxicated Madam Golganor. Riches were in store for some; true love on the foreseeable horizon for others. I'll admit, she was a riot, and her injection of dirty limericks between each telling only added to the absurdity of it all.

When it was your turn, you refused. Politely, demurely — but a refusal. Instead of forcing you, they turned to me. "Go on, Aaron," Bill Duvaney said, clapping me on the back. His face was flushed and I could smell the alcohol seeping from his pores.

I sat across from Madam Golganor at the dining-room table. She waggled bejeweled fingers over the glass orb. My future was predictably hazy at first, but then Madam Golganor's eyes widened, her red, clownish lips formed a circle, everyone erupted in an

"Ooooooh," and then one of Madam Golganor's stubby little fingers popped up. The room went silent.

"I see... I see," she said, closing her eyes now. Her hands swam across the globe of glass. "I see... *a woman*."

"Ooooooh," went the crowd.

"A woman... in a red beret," said Madam Golganor. "She is there but she is hazy. She is trying to speak. She is trying to tell you something. I fear I may require an additional libation in order for your destiny to be fulfilled."

Someone set a glass of amber liquor in front of her; Madam Golganor's eyes flipped open and she downed the shot like someone about to be marched out in front of a firing squad.

"Ahh," she said, her eyelids settling closed again. "There. There. Yes, she is hazy, this woman, but I can hear her. I can hear her warning for you, Aaron Decker — because that is what it is, I fear. A warning."

"Ooooooh," went the crowd.

"What is it?" I asked, playing along. I saw you smiling darkly at me from across the room, a glass of red wine in your hand.

"This woman in the red beret says, 'Don't. Open. The. Door.'"

"Ooooooh," went the crowd.

"What door?" I asked.

But something funny had happened to Madam Golganor's face then. A stiffening of her features. When her eyes opened, they were strangely sober. Fearful, almost. She looked at her crystal ball then up at me and then back at her crystal ball again. Then she sparkled back to life, clapped her hands, and shouted, "There once was a man from Nantucket!"

Finally, you told the others you weren't feeling well and got us both the hell out of there. Instead of driving back to either of our apartments (this was before we had moved in together, remember), you took me to a firehouse carnival where, in our nice dinner-party attire, we'd bought wristbands and rode on all the rides twice. You won me a stuffed panda by tossing rings onto bottle spouts. Then you drove us out to Manresa, which was an old Jesuit retreat renovated into an assisted living facility on the Severn River. You steered your car down a narrow gouge in the trees until we emptied onto a flat scrim of land overlooking the river. On the other side of the river, the lights of Annapolis burned like sodium flares. I assumed you would park facing the water, but you didn't. You cranked the steering wheel and spun the car around until the river and those hazy pinpoints of light were at our backs and we were facing down that narrow chasm in the woods through which you'd just driven us.

You shut down the engine and turned off the headlights.

I rolled in your direction. Kissed your face, your neck. "This was a fantastic idea," I mumbled around a mouthful of your lower lip.

"In the back, mister," you said, already climbing over the console and squeezing between the two front seats. I wasted no time following your lead, already shimmying out of my pants as I passed from the front of the car to the back, crashing on top of you in a heated little twist. You were in a gown that zippered in the back. I tried to get it undone; "Fuck it," you'd breathed into my ear, and hiked the hem up past your hips.

Afterwards, we curled together on that tiny back seat like a couple of lazy kittens. I dozed a bit, lulled into peaceful slumber by the sound of your breathing, and awoke only when you extracted yourself from my embrace and climbed back into the driver's seat. I tugged on my pants and followed suit, spent and weak and satisfied, spilling myself into the passenger seat as though I had been liquefied.

You swiped a hand through the fogged windshield. A black arc appeared on the glass. "You know," you said. "I own a red beret."

"Yeah, but you're not a ghost."

"Who says ghosts are confined to one particular place in time? What if ghosts are able to transcend? What if once you become a ghost, you have always *been* a ghost, and you can go anywhere, uninhibited by space and time?"

"Like you coming back from the dead to talk to me at a dinner party where you also happen to be, quite alive," I said.

"Ghosts are time travelers," you said.

"Maybe they are."

"Bloody Mary," you said, changing the subject. "Do you know it?"

"The drink?"

"The game, dummy. Didn't you ever play it when you were a kid?"

"That thing where you look in the mirror and say her name three times?"

"Yes, only when I was a kid, we said it five times."

It wasn't exactly like Bloody Mary. You had another name for it, I think — Headlight Ghosts? Yes, that was it. You explained the rules, even though there really weren't any rules. You even said so yourself: "There really aren't any rules. You go with your gut."

The game was to sit in silence and stare at the darkness ahead of us through the windshield. Convince yourself there was a ghost out there. Imagine the ghost standing just beyond your line of sight, melded with the shadows and the trees, a dark figure out there in the night. Visualize the specter in your head and force your eyes to see it. Force them. Then, *very slowly*, you counted out loud from ten down to one. If you were with someone in the car, you counted in synch with them. Like a chant. A prayer. And you let the tension build as you counted. The anticipation of what could be out there in the dark.

"And then on one — " you said, flipping on the vehicle's headlights.

The tree line flooded with light. The wooded passageway through which we had driven seemed to open like an aperture.

"Did you see one?" you asked me.

"A ghost?"

"You didn't, did you?"

"No."

You weren't disappointed. "Let's try it again."

We must have sat there clicking those headlights on and off for close to an hour that night, Allison. Finally, in the end, I screamed and pointed and stomped my feet and said, "Oh my God it's a ghost look at it oh my God it's coming for us!"

You laughed and slapped my arm. But you remained staring at the mist that swirled within the glow of the car's headlights.

"What?" I said. "What did you see?"

"Two figures," you said, your voice low. "Holding hands. Just for a moment — there and then gone."

I followed your gaze. For a moment, I even convinced myself that there were figures hovering out there in the darkness, shifting beyond the reach of the headlights, forms created from shadow and fog and imagination. Two distinct figures, just as you'd said. But there was nothing there, of course — just the swirl of mist, the sphere of light, and a world of darkness beyond.

You took my chin in your hand and turned me to face you. And then you kissed me. Then you started the ignition again.

"You don't really believe in ghosts, do you?" I asked as you drove us back through the woods.

"It has nothing to do with ghosts," you told me. "It's a game all about the power of perception. If you can visualize the ghost strong enough in your mind, it'll be there for a split second when you first turn on the headlights." But then you turned and stared at me, your eyes wide in mock horror. "But don't be fooled, Aaron Decker — I'm haunted as fuck."

"You're freaking crazy, too, lady," I said. "And keep your eyes on the road so we don't smash into a tree."

"Oh, brother, I'm gone," you said.

5

Thinking of that night, I drove out to Manresa and out to that plateau of land that overlooked the Severn River, this time in your Subaru. It had been years since we'd come out here, and it was closing on midnight, so it took me some time to locate the rutted dirt passageway that cut through the woods. In fact, I feared it might have become overgrown and vanished altogether over the years. But no — the Sube's headlights caught it, a narrow black tunnel boring through the trees. I spun the wheel and drove into the woods, tree limbs scraping along the sides of the car. As I drove, a lump formed in my throat, one that gradually swelled to the size of a grape then a strawberry then a plum. There was the pang of heartache in my chest to accompany it, too. By the time I came out the other side, onto the flat grassy ledge that stood high above the river, my face was hot, and the palms of my hands had grown cold.

I did just what you did on that night — I turned in a circle until the car faced the way I'd come, that black tunnel in the trees. Then I turned off the headlights. Darkness fell around me like a black cloak. In the rearview mirror, I could see the shimmery diamonds of light across the river.

Despite the blinking closet light, *was* this something you would have wanted me to pursue? Or was I about to become a grave-robber digging through the memory of your work? I had come to an impasse that was cluttering up my mind. My heart, too. I closed my eyes. Felt my whole body shaking. I'd asked if you believed in ghosts and you had said, *It has nothing to do with ghosts. It's a game all about the power of perception.* Which, I realized now, wasn't exactly an answer to my question.

I opened my eyes and began to count down from ten. My voice cracked on six. A single tear, hot as magma, seared down my left cheek on three. The word "one" issued from me in a breathy whisper.

If you can visualize the ghost strong enough in your mind, it'll be there for a split second when you first turn on the headlights…

I turned on the headlights.

What was out there in the darkness was a vaporous cloud of mist that swirled and roiled and appeared to struggle to take on solid form. I watched it undulate within the glare of the headlights. A second tear spilled down my face. My breath was fogging up the windows.

You were not out there. There was no ghost. Even that spectral mist, I realized, was just exhaust spouting from the tailpipe and swirling in the breeze around the car.

A sob ruptured from my throat. My breath had laid a sheen of fog across the windshield, and just as I reached out and cranked on the defogger, I saw a handprint right there on the inside of the windshield, just slightly to the right of the steering column. A handprint. *Your* handprint, Allison. A print that had been there for months, surely. Because to think otherwise would mean —

The fog began to fade, causing your print to dissolve into the clearing glass. I quickly turned off the defogger; the fan died with a wheeze. Your handprint remained until it slowly receded back into the glass, blending there, fading in the shifting temperature and moisture inside the car.

A handprint on the glass. Much like a hand extended, as if in welcome. As if to beckon, to speak. Not just to send me forth on my own —

(come with me)

— but to join you on your journey.

PART TWO

THE FLOATING WORLD

CHAPTER FIVE

1

Furnace, West Virginia, looked as if the apocalypse had come and gone. It was only about a two-hour drive from our place in Harbor Village, but in actuality, it was on the dark side of the moon. I made the drive in your Subaru, Allison, while ingesting a steady diet of your eighties rock, which were the only CDs you had in the car. Your fascination with this music always astounded me. Christ, you were born in 1989. I'd always found it uninspiring and silly, but something about those sappy tunes kept me alert and on point and — saccharine as it may sound — as if you were right there in the car with me.

I drove across a stone bridge that arced over the roiling, slate-colored waters of the Potomac River. I could see the town of Furnace from this vantage along the opposite bank, visible as a collection of tiny train-village houses and storefronts and at least one church spire. Hills rose up in the background, brown and cold-looking, connected in places by the oxidized blue girders of ancient train trestles. Chimneys exhaled white smoke into the overcast sky, where it seemed to get snared like cotton in the leafless canopy of trees.

The town itself was really just a central cobblestone road, unimaginatively named Main Street, that campaigned between the hills in a serpentine asphalt ribbon down to the river. Storefronts flanked either side of this road — quaint little mom-and-pop saltboxes with large front windows, colorful awnings, and placards of cheery country greetings on the doors. Beyond Main Street, a network of crudely paved roads scrolled up into the hills, where whitewashed houses could be glimpsed between the burgeoning curtain of springtime greenery. According to my internet research, Furnace's population was around 250 people, which made it even smaller than neighboring Harpers Ferry. It was serviced twice a day by the *Capitol Limited*, one of only two Amtrak trains that connected Washington, D.C. with Chicago. In the mid-1800s the town was known for its musket factories, the remnants of which were visible from the western Maryland side of the expansive stone bridge, each one looking like a small brick prison.

The official municipal police force was the Furnace Police Department, and it consisted of three sworn full-time officers, two sworn part-time officers and a single civilian employee. According to your notes, you had come out here last summer, after the body of seventeen-year-old Holly Renfrow was discovered by some local fishermen who spotted something pale and human-like snared in the root system of a tree that had fallen into the Potomac River. You had met with the chief of police, Hercel Lovering, but given your minimal notes regarding the encounter, I surmised that Lovering had probably been tight-lipped and hadn't told you much. Chief Lovering was a tall man with hard-edged features, close-cropped sandy-colored hair, and eyes of such a piercing blue they might as well have been chipped from some priceless gem. He looked like a Marine, or maybe one of those astronauts from the 1960s. He was waiting for me at a booth inside The Foundry, which, at one point in the town's history, had been an actual foundry, but was now a rustic diner with wagon wheels for chandeliers.

Chief Lovering stood as I approached the table. "Mr. Decker," he said, and shook my hand. His grip was strong enough to roll my knucklebones. "I'm so sorry to hear about your wife."

I'd left a voicemail on Lovering's desk phone the day before — the number had been scrawled on a Post-it note in your handwriting, Allison, and stuck to a photocopied newspaper article of Holly Renfrow's death — where I found myself rambling after the automated prompt, which, at some point, had unceremoniously yet blessedly cut me off. When he called me back ten minutes later, my face had still been hot with embarrassment.

"I won't lie," I said. "It's been rough."

"It's such a goddamn shame," he said, still squeezing my hand. "This country's gone to shit." He released his grip and waved a big bear paw at the table. "Take a load off."

We sat together at the table. Lovering was in uniform, with patches on the arms that showed two rifles crossing each other bisected by a straightaway of train tracks. I could smell his pine-scented aftershave from across the table. I imagined you meeting with this grizzly bear of a man — perhaps right here in this very diner — and could hardly reconcile the image of two distinctly opposite individuals seated across from one another.

"The meatloaf here is fantastic, if you're in the mood to grab something," Lovering said.

"I stopped at a Burger King on the drive in. Maybe just a cup of coffee."

"Even better." Lovering held up two fingers over his head. I turned around and saw a rail-thin fellow whose body was packaged in a starchy white apron nodding vigorously, eager to please. It occurred to me that in a place like this, the position of police chief was probably right up there next to godliness.

"I appreciate you meeting with me," I said. "I hope I'm not pulling you away from anything."

He glanced at his wristwatch — a bulky device, something a scuba diver might wear — and said, "I got a half hour or so. Though I probably could've answered whatever questions you've got over the phone. Saved you the drive."

"I don't mind the drive."

"So what can I do for you?"

"Well, this is going to sound a little odd, but I've only recently learned that my wife came out here last fall, and that she was looking into Holly Renfrow's death. Do you recall meeting with her?"

"I met with a lot of people last fall, after Holly was murdered. As you can imagine, we were a little busy."

"Did she say why she'd come out here? My wife?"

"Why she came out here?" He raised an eyebrow. "Said she was a reporter."

"Allison was a reporter, yeah — for a neighborhood paper out in Maryland. She wrote a column called 'Allison's A-List,' which basically highlighted accomplishments of local teens in our area. She wrote about bake sales and grand openings. Stuff like that."

For the first time since my arrival, Lovering's eyes fully engaged mine. "Then what the hell was she doing out here following up on a murder?"

"I think she believed Holly's murder was connected to the murders of some other teenage girls she'd been researching," I said, placing the accordion folder on the table. "I found all her research in a trunk in our closet after she died. There are six girls in total, going back about thirteen years. They're spread out up and down the east coast and separated by a few years."

"What are you saying?" Lovering asked.

"I'm saying Holly Renfrow's murder might be the work of a serial killer."

The rail-thin waiter in the stiff white apron arrived, a mug of steaming coffee in each hand. He set them on the table. "There you go, Chief," the waiter said. His voice was reedy, like a woodwind instrument.

"Hey, Tyler. How's your momma?"

"Oh, she's feeling better. Much better. Still achy though." Almost apologetically, Tyler swung his gaze in my direction. "She's had both knees replaced," he informed me, wincing as he said it, as if he shared his mother's pain.

"Give her my regards," Lovering said, not looking at him. In fact, he was still staring at me. I couldn't read his expression.

"Oh, absolutely. Can I get either of you anything else? A menu?"

"We're good," Lovering said. He began to systematically tear open sugar packets and, one by one, dump them into his coffee.

The waiter executed an uncomfortable little bow and then departed.

I met Lovering's rail-spike gaze. "I take it my wife didn't bring this up with you when she was out here."

"No, son, she did not."

"Maybe it sounds crazy to you, but Allison had always been something of a… a victim's advocate, I guess you'd say." I was thinking of our third date again, Allison, and how you'd clobbered that asshole with the novelty oar in the parking lot of the Docksider.

Lovering folded his arms over his chest and leaned back in his seat. I hadn't expected him to be so standoffish at the news. Maybe he thought I was crazy.

I cleared my throat and said, "Look, this folder is filled with information on all six murders, including Holly's. And it's not just stuff printed off the internet. Allison had been traveling to these places and talking to people about these murders. She did the same thing out here; you weren't the only person she spoke to here in

Furnace after Holly was killed. My wife, she was *invested* in this. She was making connections that I don't think anyone else was making. And I didn't even know she was doing it until after she died and I found this stuff."

"What connections?" Lovering asked.

"Well, the girls, they all look the same." I described them while simultaneously reaching for the file so I could show him the photographs, but his big hand fell atop the folder, suggesting that he rather I not open it here. I withdrew my hand, feeling somewhat admonished. I said, "Holly's was the most recent murder Allison had been looking at. That's why I came here to speak to you about this. I'm no police detective, but I can go through the files with you, help decipher my wife's handwriting. Whatever you need."

Lovering's nostrils flared as he exhaled across the table. "Just how many people did your wife talk to out here?"

"Well, uh... let me see..." I reached for the accordion folder once more, waiting to see if he'd stop me again. He didn't. I took out the mini-file on Holly Renfrow's murder, flipped through the pages of photocopied news stories, internet printouts, and handwritten notes, saying the names as I came across them in your nearly illegible handwriting. "Rita Renfrow, who I assume is a relative of the... uh, of Holly."

"She's the mother," said Lovering, flatly.

"Right. Okay. Her. Then my wife, it looks like she made several phone calls to the medical examiner's office, but I can't say if anyone had ever called her back or spoken to her. There's not much information on that. Then there are the two fishermen who found Holly's body in the river – uh, who are – "

"Geoff Rupp and Richie Dolan," Lovering provided.

I glanced up at him. "Right. Right." Peering back down at your notes, I said, "Then there's a list of names here, labeled as friends of

Holly's, but it's unclear whether or not Allison actually spoke with any of them. Also, there's a woman named Denise Lenchantin. According to my wife's notes, she was an eyewitness who might have had contact with Holly Renfrow's killer the same night Holly was murdered?" I looked up at Lovering, who was gazing out the window. I could see the tiny red scab beside his left earlobe where he'd cut himself shaving, delicate as an eyelash.

"That must be the waitress," he said.

"She had contact with Holly's killer?"

"No, she didn't. There's no connection there," Lovering said. "This Lenchantin woman, she's over in Hampshire County. She came forward once news of Holly's murder hit the media. Claimed someone tried to abduct her the same night Holly was killed. Something about a flat tire and a guy pulling up around eleven o'clock or so. But the distance is too far and the time is a bit too close to work out. Hampshire's three counties over, and this Lenchantin woman, she lived just beyond Romney, if I recall, so we're talking maybe like an hour and a half from here. The timeline is too tight."

"Right, okay." I looked back down at your notes. "And then there's another guy on here, name of Dean Partridge. Is that right? Partridge? My wife's handwriting is terrible. Not sure who — "

"Oh, for shit's sake," Lovering said, pushing himself back from the table. He raked a set of blunt fingers along the ridges of his brow.

"What?" I said. "You know him?"

"He's one of my goddamn officers."

"Oh." Trying to backpedal, I said, "Or maybe I've got it wrong. Like I said, my wife's handwriting is for shit, really…"

Lovering swatted at the air between us. "Forget it," he said. "Dean's my wife's nephew. It's not like I'm gonna give him the boot, for Christ's sake, much as I'd like to." He slurped his coffee then set the cup down on its saucer with a clink. Grimaced. "What do you say we grab a couple to-go cups for these coffees and take a drive, huh? This ain't really the place to jaw about this."

2

"Holly Renfrow was with some friends at the Exxon station over the bridge the night she disappeared," Lovering said as we drove back down Main Street in his police car. "You probably passed the place on your way into town. Her friends said she split around ten that night after she got into an argument with one of them."

"What's a bunch of teenagers doing hanging out at a gas station at night?"

"There's some of those old arcade games in the back," Lovering said. "They were drinking, too. Fella owns the place, he don't pay much attention as long as they're feeding quarters into the machines."

"This looks like a pretty small town. Did you know the Renfrows? Holly?"

"I did," he said, then corrected: "I do. Went to school with Rita, the mother. This whole thing, it hit us pretty hard. We've all had a time of it." He cleared his throat and said, "Anyway, there's not much to do around here if you're a teenager unless you've got your driver's license, which Holly had, although her mother was using the car that night. Holly got a ride out there with one of her girlfriends but split on foot after the argument."

"What was the argument about?"

"Some shit about a boy. What else? Her friend had been seeing some guy she liked. You can imagine."

We were headed now in the direction I had come when I'd entered town, approaching the stone bridge. Directly ahead, the landscape opened up and hinted at a great height below which the Potomac River churned and frothed and carried unnamable things far downriver. The police car thumped onto the bridge and coasted along until we were at the midway point — the zenith of the arch — and overlooking the wide reach of the river.

"How long was she missing before her body was found?"

"Two days," said Lovering. "The ME determined she'd been in the river for about that long."

"How exactly was she killed? The newspaper articles weren't very detailed."

"She drowned."

"How does murder factor into a drowning?"

Lovering slowed the cruiser to a stop. The sky above the river was a cold gunmetal color, the water below like chiseled slate. Lovering looked at me, those gemlike eyes gleaming. "She had her hands bound behind her back before she was thrown in the river to drown. When those two fishermen found her, her hands were still bound at the wrists behind her back with electrical wire."

"Oh. Jesus Christ, I didn't know that."

"I'm sure your wife learned about it, talking to all those people like she did. It ain't in her notes?" I couldn't tell if he was being facetious or not.

"No, it wasn't in her notes." My voice was small.

Lovering geared the cruiser into Park then got out of the car. I set the stack of papers on the passenger seat and then followed him out.

It was like standing at the top of a skyscraper, the wind was so fierce up here. Lovering had parked in a narrow breakdown lane. There was a sidewalk here, which we both stepped up on to, and a concrete railing that looked down on the rapids below. I peered over the edge and saw a number of large black rocks cresting above the whitecaps, sleek as obsidian. It was maybe seventy feet to the water from this spot on the bridge.

"Locals call this the suicide bridge, even though we haven't had a jumper since the eighties," Lovering said. Then he pointed due west along the rocky bank. "Body was discovered about a mile up that way, along the west bank of the river. Snarled up in the branches of a big deadfall that was partially submerged." He ground some sidewalk grit under one boot. "Her cell phone was found right about here. Screen was smashed. It either happened by accident when she came into contact with her killer, or it was busted on purpose by the guy. People know they can be traced by phones, so the guy probably wanted it gone."

"Right," I said. I couldn't say much more, for fear I might cause myself to be sick.

Lovering gestured to the open sky above our heads next. "Notice there're no lights out here? No lampposts on the bridge? It's dark as hell on this thing once the sun goes down. This is probably where he approached her."

I glanced down the length of the bridge, from one side to the other. The whole span was maybe a quarter-mile at most. But the height was dizzying; vertigo wrapped its chilly arms around my throat.

Lovering gazed over the railing and down at the turbulent waters below. It was brief, but I caught it nonetheless — a distant look that clouded his otherwise sharp blue eyes. "My guess is he got her in his car and took her someplace first. Maybe he intended to rape her, but the ME could find no evidence of sexual assault. Small favors, right?"

I couldn't muster a word.

"He pushed her into the river somewhere farther along the bank somewhere, is my guess. Guy was probably thinking she'd drown and the body might coast all the way out to the Chesapeake and get lost for a while. Probably would have, too, had that tree not been there to catch her."

"How do you know he took her someplace else? How do you know he didn't just push her over the side of the bridge right here?"

Lovering jerked his square head toward the concrete railing. "Those big rocks down there? My guess is she would've gotten caught up on one of them, maybe would've landed on one if she'd gone over here. That she was found a mile west of here suggests he'd dumped her beyond the rocks where the river flows deeper. Was probably hoping she'd never be found."

I considered it all. After a moment to catch my breath, I said, "How come you're telling me all this when you wouldn't tell my wife?"

"Because this was still an open investigation when your wife came out here."

Surprised, I said, "Wait, what — you've solved the case? You caught the guy?"

"In a manner of speaking." Hercel Lovering looked at me, gave me a humorless smile. The tip of his sharp nose was red and there was now a prominent vein, shaped like a wishbone, at the center of his forehead.

"I don't get it. What's that mean?" I said.

"Das Hillyard," he said. "Local sex offender. Was convicted for diddling a couple of underage boys when he was working over in Preston, spent time on Misery Mountain."

"What's Misery Mountain?"

"Hazelton Penitentiary. Anyway, he's on the security footage from the Exxon station that night. Maybe twenty minutes before Holly leaves on foot, he shows up, buys some lottery tickets and a can of chewing tobacco. He's there on videotape eyeballing Holly and her friends. So naturally, I grilled him over and over on the Renfrow murder and he started doing the tap dance. He broke down in tears a few times. Those kiddie-diddlers, they can really turn on the waterworks when they want to. It's second nature to 'em, like how a squid will shoot out black ink."

"He confessed?"

"Nope. He just had the good sense to drop dead."

"What do you mean?"

"Back in January, we get a call from Hillyard's mother. It's her house; Hillyard was staying with her. She's upset, says her son's dead. Me and Dean — loose-lips Dean, remember? — we go up to Hillyard's place out on Farmington Road and find him stiff as a board in his La-Z-Boy recliner. Looked like he'd been dead for days, rigor mortis locking up his knees. Old mother's blind, so Lord knows how long he'd been dead in that house before she started to smell him. His feet were about six inches off the floor. He had a syringe poking out of his arm."

"Holy shit," I said.

Lovering rubbed the back of his neck with one hand. "Heroin overdose. Looked like a rabid dog, all that dried foamy shit around his face. He'd pissed himself, too, and the whole place stank to high heaven."

"But he didn't confess," I reiterated.

"We didn't need a confession," Lovering said. "We found Holly Renfrow's sweatshirt inside his house."

I opened my mouth, but all that escaped it was a hiss of air.

"Not as neat and clean as I would have liked, but there it is, Mr. Decker. Case closed."

"So what do we do now?" I asked.

"Do now with what?"

"The other murders," I said. "You need to contact the other police departments and let them know that this Hillyard guy might have been responsible for killing those other girls."

"Das Hillyard wasn't no serial killer, Mr. Decker."

"But if you'd just look at my wife's research — "

"You got any proof other than these girls look somewhat alike?"

"No, I don't, but it's a start. Like I said, I'm not a detective. You guys can investigate. That's what you do."

"Let me ask you, Mr. Decker," Lovering said, planting his hands on his hips. "What timeframe are you looking at for these other murders?"

"The earliest was in 2006."

"Well there you go," Lovering said. "Hillyard went to prison in 2005 for what he done to those boys over in Preston. He served thirteen years and was released at the end of last summer, a few months before he got the itch and killed Holly. Whatever connection you think you see here — whatever your wife thought she saw — it just ain't there."

"Well shit," I said. Something akin to a laugh juddered up my throat, but there was no humor in it. I turned away from Hercel Lovering, planting both hands on the cold concrete railing of the bridge. On the horizon, a chevron of birds carved a passage across the gunmetal sky.

"You want to know what I think, Mr. Decker?"

"Yes, of course."

"I think you're looking for something that isn't there, son. You're missing your wife and trying to hold on to something."

"Maybe you're right," I said, not facing him. The wind was drawing water from my eyes and I didn't want this guy looking at me like that.

Lovering said nothing for a while. We listened to the wind rattle the trees along the shore. After a time, he said, "It's been solved, Mr. Decker. If your wife was trying to get to the bottom of these murders, she can at least rest easy on this one."

"Thank you," I said, but kept my gaze averted. Seventy feet below, the rushing of the water sounded like television static. Suddenly, it was all I could hear.

3

There is a word in Japanese, *ukiyo*, which has no English equivalent. In Japanese, it means "the floating world," and in essence it refers to living in the here-and-now with complete and utter detachment from the rest of the surrounding universe. This was how our cruelly brief marriage had been for me: a dome beneath which we were fully immersed in each other and the rest of the world be damned. Everything we did — every dream and idea and epiphany we ever had — we shared with each other. This was my understanding, anyway. I had thought you'd felt the same way. I would have bet on it. But as we'd made love and shared meals and curled up on the couch together to watch movies and spent fall afternoons tossing a Frisbee at Quiet Waters Park — all those things beneath and within and surrounded by our dome — a part of you, Allison, was elsewhere. How else can I say it? A part of you was navigating unfamiliar interstates, probably with a revolver in the glove compartment of the Sube, a small spiral-bound notebook tucked inside your coat pocket or wedged inside your purse. A part of you crept into the hills of West Virginia or traversed the muddy riverbanks of southern Maryland, hunting for the stink of death in the air. A part of you had collected and studied photographs of victims who had met untimely, brutal deaths, young women for whose murders no perpetrators had ever been apprehended. There you were, having lukewarm coffee at some dreary hour of the morning with a police deputy of some rural backwater, discussing how long it would take to strangulate someone with your bare hands and whether or not submergence in a river would wash semen off a corpse. While I cooked dinner and bought concert tickets online and mowed the postage stamp of our backyard, you were surreptitiously examining maps of West Virginia, Delaware, New Jersey, Maryland, Virginia, North Carolina, so many remote places, marking circles where victims had gone missing and etching crosses where, presumably, their bodies had ultimately been found. A chronicler of death — who would have thought? Certainly not me. Certainly not the man to whom you'd been married for five years. That when we held hands in the park or in a movie theater, some clandestine part of your mind was occupied with thoughts of pale, water-bloated corpses or frail bodies left to decompose in the woods. That when we kissed, a part of your mind was consumed with the amount of pressure it took to crush a windpipe. That maybe your occasional bouts of insomnia had not been a result of too much coffee or stress from work but the repercussion of a mind frantic with the details of some young girl's final moments on this planet — of silt and grit beneath purpled fingernails, dead leaves snared in moss-slickened hair, eyes recessed into sunken jack-o'-lantern sockets. You kept all this stuff in our house; you kept all this stuff in your mind. I could decipher the progression of your thoughts — laid out for me in your frenetic, slapdash handwriting on sheets of yellow legal paper and charted by the dates of countless newspaper articles, some more than ten years old — as you pursued some dark and unfathomable obsession further and further into the shadows.

It was this notion that consumed me as I drove home from West Virginia and my meeting with Hercel Lovering. It caused a throbbing bolt of anger to temporarily replace my grief. I welcomed it, because since your death, I'd felt as if I'd died, too, and it was becoming a permanent state for me. Yet anger makes us feel alive. So I let it fuel me for as long as it would, which turned out not to be very long at all.

Because when I stepped into our townhome that night, I broke down all over again.

As if I needed corroboration, I fired up my laptop in the kitchen and googled "Holly Renfrow" and "Das Hillyard" and the town of Furnace, West Virginia. I found the news stories from January detailing Hillyard's death, and his conviction in absentia of the murder of Holly Renfrow. The articles confirmed what Lovering had told me — that Hillyard had spent over a decade in prison for molesting two young boys. There was a color photo of Hillyard alongside one of the articles, a conspiracy of soulless black eyes, sunken, pockmarked cheeks, and an air of profound apathy that possessed not even the slightest modicum of humanity.

This prompted me to question the status of the other murders. Had they been solved at some point, too? I started from the earliest case — Margot Idelson, killed in 2006 — and worked my way forward. From what I could tell, none of these other cases had been solved. In fact, there existed very little information on the older cases, and nothing current. The exception to this was the 2016 murder of a teenage girl named Gabrielle Colson-Howe, from Port Tobacco, Maryland. There were some current stories written about her, keeping her in the public consciousness, and even mention of her on some message boards. Perhaps this was because her death was still relatively recent; it was the second most recent murder in your files, behind Holly Renfrow's death last fall. Yet on closer inspection, I realized — or, more accurately, other-Aaron realized — that the articles and the posts on message boards all shared a single commonality: the same author.

Roberta Negri's name appeared as the byline to the newspaper articles written about Gabrielle Colson-Howe's death back in 2016. She had also authored the more recent articles, posted on various blogs and social justice websites instead of online newspapers. These newer articles had nothing more to add regarding Colson-Howe's murder, but merely served, as far as I could tell, to keep the dead girl from being forgotten. "Still No Justice for Murdered Teen," said one headline. A grainy photo of Colson-Howe — the same one as in your files — accompanied the article. Another was headlined, "Colson-Howe Murder Remains Unsolved — Police Have No Leads," and showed a photo of a grief-stricken woman holding a stuffed bear to her chest; the caption identified her as the murdered girl's mother. I had come across the reporter's name, Roberta Negri, in your files, too.

The accordion folder was on the kitchen table beside my laptop. I opened it and slid out the file on Gabrielle Colson-Howe's murder. I opened it, roved through the pages, and saw that I was correct: Roberta Negri was also the author of the newspaper articles you had printed from the internet and tucked away in here. On one of the printouts, you'd scribbled a phone number beside Negri's name. It wasn't the phone number that gave me pause; it was the sketch of six rectangular bars beside the phone number that caused an icy disquietude to surge through my body. It was the same design, albeit more hastily rendered, that you'd drawn on the sheet of legal paper, among the repeated Gas Head phrase.

A breathy, soundless exhalation in my left ear caused a chill to ripple down my spine. I whirled around in my chair, my heart ratcheting up into my throat. The sensation that someone had been standing directly behind me, whispering in my ear, echoed throughout my consciousness with unwavering certainty...

But the kitchen was empty. Beyond, the living room was dark, the windows that faced the backyard shuttered against the night. I heard the distant ticking of a clock echoing from somewhere in the house.

I closed the laptop then slid the file back into the accordion folder. After some hesitation, I took out Holly Renfrow's file. I opened it to the last page of your notes and, with a pen that I had scrounged from a junk drawer, wrote Das Hillyard's name right there on the bottom. Underlined it. Circled it. Closed the file.

"Case closed, Allison," I said to the empty kitchen.

I'd never been much of a drinker, but I knocked back two shots of bourbon before heading upstairs to bed. The alcohol seared down my throat. At the top of the stairs, I reached for the hallway light switch, but the light would not go on. I stood there in the darkness, feeling as insubstantial as dandelion fluff, and I might have just curled up right there at the top of the landing had I not turned my head and peered down to the opposite end of the hallway.

A figure stood in the open doorway of our office.

My breath snared in my throat. I couldn't move. A chill rippled through my body.

"Allison?" I said, my voice cracking.

The figure did not move.

Snapping from my paralysis, I advanced down the hallway toward the open office door. As I drew nearer, the figure — black as pitch — receded into the darkness of the room.

"Allison!"

I struck the doorframe and fumbled for the light switch. Braced myself. The lights came on, stinging my eyes. It revealed nothing but an unoccupied office, my neatly kept desk against one wall, your cluttered one against the other.

I stood there in the doorway for an unknowable length of time, as if my stillness and dedication might lure you back into existence. Finally, I rerouted to our bedroom and slithered beneath the sheets. Sleep hit me like a wall, but my lingering angst caused me to wake up several times in the middle of the night, certain that some enigmatic monster with a skull swollen with hot air and splitting down the seams had been hovering over my sleeping body in the moments before I opened my eyes. Other times, I'd wake up to see the shape of Robert Vols, your murderer, crouched in one darkened corner of our bedroom. His hood up over his head and a pistol tucked into the waistband of his pants, he'd nod casually in my direction then saunter out into the hallway where he'd vanish within a panel of moonlight.

CHAPTER SIX

1

In 2016, in the early part of August, the body of a teenage girl who had been missing for the better part of two weeks eventually turned up along the shore of the Potomac River in southern Maryland, directly beneath the expanse of the Harry W. Nice Memorial Bridge. Her body had swelled and purpled, and some of her clothes had been sloughed away in the river's current. When she was found, her blonde hair was already green with algae. Her fingertips and some of her toes were missing, having been scavenged by crabs, and she was ultimately identified by her dental records as the missing girl: Gabrielle Colson-Howe, sixteen years old, from nearby Port Tobacco. The tiny Maryland village of Port Tobacco was home to just a mere half-dozen families, so the disappearance and subsequent death of the girl hit everyone who lived there very hard.

The body was most likely carried by the river's current for several miles, the pale and naked arms ghosting through underwater fronds, a sneaker coming loose and gradually climbing toward the surface where it bobbed and rocked, unnoticed by anyone, like a tiny seagoing vessel. The glint of a gold ankle bracelet may have attracted the attention of curious fish. The girl's body thumped against the occasional underwater rock formation, maneuvered through tangles of submerged tree limbs, wove between the taut lines of crab pots like an actor weaving between cables backstage in a theater.

Two wanton boys lurking about the embankment shooting at gulls with a BB gun discovered Colson-Howe's body beneath the bridge, where garbage tended to collect and where the discarded camps of homeless people — moldy nylon tents and damp sleeping bags — stood like tiny evacuated villages. The boys had vanished beneath the bridge to smoke cigarettes that they had purloined from a nearby construction barge, grateful to have a respite from the blazing summer sun, and that was when they saw it. The pale nakedness of it seemed to radiate with a dull internal light beneath the dark shadow of the bridge. They did not know what it was at first. Surely, they did not suspect it was the corpse of a teenage girl. They approached it, their sneakers squelching in the muck and their cigarettes dangling from their lips as they advanced toward the pale white shape. The nearer they drew, the more the thing began to take on the likeness of a human being. Facedown, motionless. Maybe a homeless person who'd gotten drunk and drowned in the river? It had happened before. But the twinkle of that ankle bracelet seemed *wrong*. Not a homeless person.

Both boys stopped advancing when they realized it was a dead girl. Her shirt, wet and streaked with mud, torn in places to expose marbled flesh, was partially twisted about her throat, and the river had stripped her black tights down so that they trailed like a comet's streak from the one sneaker that remained on her foot. The other foot — the one with the ankle bracelet — was bare. The toes had been nibbled down to the knucklebones.

The boys — ages eleven and twelve, friends since they were in training pants — stood there beneath the bridge while vehicles thundered overhead and the stink of diesel exhaust clouded around them like a funk. They studied the girl while they finished their cigarettes. The corpse's bare buttocks were bruise-gray and networked with blue-black veins. Large bottlenose flies crawled over the exposed flesh, and a cloud of them clotted in the air above the corpse's head like a halo. One of the boys — the more brazen of the two — grabbed a stick and poked at the mottled, graying flesh along the body's left flank, where the ribs stood out, clearly defined. The flesh yielded like dough. The boy pushed the tip of the stick more firmly against the body until it left behind a dime-sized puncture wound that did not so much bleed as drool out a thread of gray river water.

The boys smoked another cigarette each while contemplating whether to plant a BB in one of the exposed buttocks of the corpse. In the end they decided against it, and when they'd finished their smokes, they headed home to tell their parents what they had found.

2

I learned this story about how the two boys discovered Gabrielle Colson-Howe's body beneath the bridge from Roberta Negri, the author of the newspaper articles in your file. Negri had interviewed both boys extensively back in 2016, immediately after the police had spoken with them. There was no evidence in your notes suggesting you had spoken to the boys yourself, but you had certainly met with Roberta Negri — "Call me Bobbi" — and discussed the particulars of it.

When I called Negri's number to request that she meet with me, I thought I'd have to refresh her memory of you — it had been almost three years since you'd been out to Port Tobacco, from what I could discern from your handwritten notes, Allison — but she cut me off midway through my explanation.

"Allison Decker. Jesus Christ, *yes*. Mr. Decker — Aaron? — I recognized your wife on the news back in December. I wrote a piece on it. Of course I remember her. I was heartbroken to hear about it. I remembered meeting with her."

"I was hoping you might have some time to meet with me, too."

She agreed to meet me at a crab house in Newburg, which overlooked the river not too far from where Colson-Howe's body was discovered by those two boys three years earlier. When I pulled into the parking lot and got out of my car, I saw a woman wearing a red ball cap and an army-green windbreaker that rippled in the strong wind. She was leaning against a bright blue Yaris and smoking a cigarette, a backpack slung over one shoulder. As I approached, she seemed to age before my eyes — her posture was suggestive of someone in their late twenties, insolent and carefree, but she was closer to fifty. Her face, pale and spangled with small red freckles and not unattractive, was deeply lined and worn-looking.

"Hey." She held out a hand, and I shook it. "Aaron Decker? Call me Bobbi. I was so sorry to hear about what happened to your wife."

"Thank you. And I appreciate you meeting with me."

"No problem." She sucked on her cigarette. "Just let me finish this, will you? I allow myself three a day and don't like to cut 'em short."

"I'll join you," I said, digging my own pack of smokes from my jacket. In the wind, I chased the tip of my cigarette with my lighter until Bobbi brought her hands up and cupped the flame for me. "Thank you."

We smoked, and I watched the fog recede from the shoulder of the road and retreat back into the trees.

"You a reporter, too?" she asked.

"Me? No."

"So you're out here doing what?"

"Trying to find out what the hell my wife had been doing."

Bobbi looked at me.

"I only recently learned that she came out here three years ago, after that girl died. Apparently, Allison had been looking into a bunch of murders, and I thought maybe they might be related. But now I'm not so sure what to think."

Bobbi pulled on her smoke, then exhaled a cloud that was quickly dispatched by the wind. "That's not the truth," she said.

"What's not?"

"Your wife didn't just come out here after Gabby's death."

"No? What do you mean?"

"It's the reason I remembered your wife when I saw her picture on the news after the shooting at that strip mall." She looked at me, her eyes like steel. "It's because she lied to me when we first met, and I never forget the face of someone who's lied to me."

I stared at her for the length of several heartbeats, digesting what she'd just told me. Wondering if I was misunderstanding something...

"Fuck it," she said, pitching her half-smoked cigarette on the ground. "Go inside? I'm freezing my tits off out here."

3

We were seated at a long wooden table beneath a plate-glass window with the image of a blue crab frosted onto the glass. I told Bobbi to order whatever she liked; lunch was my treat.

"So what do you mean she lied to you?" I asked once we'd placed our orders with the waiter.

Bobbi said, "It wasn't Gabby's death that prompted your wife to come out here, Aaron. Your wife came out here before Gabby's body was ever found."

I shook my head. "What do you mean?"

"Gabrielle had been missing for maybe a week or so by that point and the police initially thought she had run off somewhere. A runaway. Everyone assumed it, even her parents. She was a problem kid from a broken home, hung around with the wrong crowd. She'd run away before. There was a town hall thing held in Port Tobacco, where she was from, and another larger meeting out here in Newburg. Local PD got a bunch of folks together, that sort of thing. Your wife attended both events. I talked to her — I always make it a point to talk to a new face in the crowd — and when she said she'd come in from Annapolis, I thought it was very strange. Why would a reporter come all the way down from Annapolis to look into a local runaway? She told me she was a freelance reporter for some major newspapers, magazines, but I later looked her up online and saw that she worked for some community paper. Nothing else."

"That can't be right," I said. "You're sure this was before the body had been found?"

"Of course I'm sure. We were still dealing with the local PD when your wife first came down here. Once the body was found, jurisdiction went to the MDTA — Maryland Transportation Authority Police — because of the location of the body beneath the Nice Bridge. That's their realm."

"What was she doing out here?"

"Nothing a reporter wouldn't normally do. Hung around, asked questions, took notes. I invited her to lunch because I was curious why she'd come here to cover a story on a local runaway. Said she was writing a larger piece on teenage runaways. I guess it made sense. To be honest, I didn't think too much of it at the time. But then a week later, Gabby's body was found under the bridge. That changed everything. There was a press conference with the MDTA out here in Newburg. There's your wife again, another face in the crowd. She'd come back. And I thought, Jesus, that's strange."

"What was so strange about it?" I asked. "She'd already been out here once when the girl went missing, why not return for the press conference?"

"Because it didn't fit with her reason for being out here in the first place. This wasn't a runaway. It had turned into a murder investigation. A bit out of scope for what your wife said she'd been out here writing about the first time I met her. And what really struck me was that she didn't seem too surprised that Gabrielle had turned up dead."

"Wait a minute. You're saying she knew this girl was going to turn up dead from the beginning." It was more of a statement than a question. I was rolling it around in my head and letting other-Aaron analyze it for authenticity. I couldn't fathom how such a thing would be possible.

"I'm just saying it was *weird*," said Bobbi. "I wanted to know the score, so I took her out to lunch again. She played it off like it was some terrible coincidence — that this runaway story she'd been interested in had now turned into a murder investigation. A believable enough story, sure. Yet my Spidey sense started tingling at that point, you know? Journalistic intuition."

"What'd you guys talk about over lunch?"

"The murder. Your wife had a list of people she wanted to interview — Gabby's friends and family, the police. She asked me about the boys who found the body."

"Oh yeah?"

This was when she told me the story of the two boys who discovered Gabrielle's body beneath the Nice Bridge, not leaving out any of the gory details.

"Your wife took notes and asked some questions. I remember thinking, man, this chick knows an awful lot about murders for someone supposedly doing an exposé on teen runaways. I mean, she had that list of potential interviewees already prepared. It's one of the reasons I checked out her background after she'd left."

"How was she killed? The newspaper articles don't say."

"Yeah, well, the police, they had to wait for a coroner's report. They don't like to speculate to the media and an autopsy takes time. How squeamish are you?" She began to dig through her backpack.

"I don't know."

"I've got a contact in the coroner's office," she said. "One of the reasons the local cops hate me."

What she laid down on the table between us were several eight-by-ten glossies, full color. I was staring down at them before I could stop myself — before my brain could even register what I was looking at in that top photo. I turned it around so it was right-side up, and felt my breath catch in my throat.

"Jesus Christ," I uttered.

"You said you weren't squeamish."

"I didn't actually say that," I corrected.

I was unable to pull my eyes from the photograph of Gabrielle Colson-Howe's mangled body. And that's exactly how it looked — *mangled.* As if a great pair of hands had grasped her and twisted her, knocking all her limbs out of joint, and leaving behind discolored bruises along her exposed flesh.

They were crime-scene photos. There she was, half-sunk into brown marsh water beneath the stanchions of the bridge, a pale, crooked arm, a shoeless foot stripped of its digits, the gleam of a gold ankle bracelet. I turned to the next photo and saw a dime-sized hole in the corpse's abdomen. I asked what it was and Bobbi reminded me about how one of the boys had admitted to poking the body with a stick. Another photo, and there was the girl's face, turned unnaturally on her neck so that the right side of her face lay submerged in brown water. Her left eye blazed out — or, rather, an eye socket filled with a bulb of whitish jelly — and I could see the mud that had hardened in the creases around her nose and mouth and at the corner of that single horrific eye socket.

"She was strangled and dumped in the river," Bobbi said, shuffling through the photos herself now. She came to one that showed the girl's shirt twisted around her neck. "See the shirt hiked up like that? Most likely it happened in the river, the current tugging it up out of place like that, because she wasn't strangled with it. The son of a bitch who did this, he used his hands. There were indentations made by the killer's fingers along her neck. I've got some clearer photos from the coroner's office that show the bruising on the neck, if you want to see 'em."

"No, thanks."

Our waiter arrived with our food. He was a middle-aged guy with a few days' stubble on his chin and a look of bleary disinterest in his eyes. He glanced at the photos spread across the table then met my gaze as if I were the responsible party for what had befallen the girl in the photographs. His disinterest turned to disgust as he set our food down on the table — a crab cake for Bobbi, a club sandwich for me, and two steaming mugs of coffee. At the sight of the food, my stomach executed a somersault.

"Sorry," I said to the waiter, and turned the stack of photos upside down.

Bobbi did not seem to notice; she slid her plate in front of her and unspooled her utensils from their napkin sleeve, eager to dig in.

"What about any suspects," I said after the waiter had gone. "It's been three years. No leads?"

"Like I said, the police are pretty tight-lipped when it comes to open cases. I know they questioned some Aqualand folks at the time, brought 'em in. Grist for the mill. Someone from there seemed the most likely suspect, according to police."

"What's Aqualand?"

"A little community of double-wides near the foot of the bridge. There's a lot of drug problems out there, a lot of domestic violence. Same with the Port Tobacco RV rec area. There's some Section Eight housing nearby, too. What *I'm* saying is there are countless potential leads every which way you turn your head in just a ten-mile radius. My guess? I think she was attacked and killed right there in Port Tobacco and then dumped in the river somewhere up that way. Keep it simple, right?"

"Then how'd she wind up under the bridge?"

"There's a fairly large spring in Port Tobacco, connected to the Potomac by a series of creeks. Her body could have been dumped in the spring and traveled along one of the channels out to the river, where it ultimately washed up beneath the bridge. There are also some pretty large drainage tunnels that go underground. The footing on the Maryland side of the Nice Bridge has a habit of collecting whatever floats by, whether through the drainage system or the river itself. The bridge gets jumpers from time to time, too, and the bodies wash up along the shore. They're generally a mess, like they've been hit by a truck or something, the bodies. I've seen my share of floaters. You know, some years ago, the carcass of a fully grown hammerhead shark washed up there. Can you imagine? DNR came and collected it with a winch hooked to the back of a pickup truck. I've got pictures."

"What about you?" I asked. "Did you ever have a suspect in mind?"

"A suspect? You mean like a specific individual? No. But cases like these, it's usually someone the victim knows. A crime of passion. A crazy boyfriend. Something like that."

"Did she have a boyfriend?"

"Lord. Only about a half-dozen," Bobbi said, rooting around in her bag again. "Not to sound shitty, but Gabby wasn't exactly a Girl Scout, if you know what I'm saying."

She produced another photo from her bag and handed it to me. I was relieved to see that this one was what appeared to be a school photo of Gabrielle Colson-Howe, not another crime-scene photo. It was the same photograph used in the missing poster you had in your notes and alongside some of the newspaper articles, only those had been black-and-white reproductions and of poor quality that did not truly highlight the intricate details of the girl's face. This photo, however, was crisp and full color. The girl had delicate, pixie-like features, a cascade of blonde hair, a coyness behind her bright green eyes. Much like you, there was a depth to this girl, a secret chamber that I recognized hidden far within her.

"She's pretty, isn't she?" said Bobbi.

"She is."

"Anyway, Gabrielle and her friends bought pot from some guy at the RV park on occasion," Bobbi went on. "I've done stories on the drug culture out here, particularly among high-school kids. I mean, I'm not condemning them — hell, I've got a guy, too, right? — but it doesn't make for a clean case, far as the police and their leads go. The night Gabby went missing, her friends were partying on the beach. Not down where her body was found, but farther up the creek. The spring in Port Tobacco closes after dark, but kids go there to do whatever kids do. They'd stolen a bunch of beer and cigarettes from a convenience store. There were one or two guys there that night who'd been, you know, involved with her. According to her mother, Gabby had been sexually active since she was twelve."

"*Twelve*? Jesus Christ. That seems impossible."

Bobbi laughed, patted the top of my hand. "You're cute."

With palpable reluctance, our waiter returned to refill our coffees. I thanked him, but he didn't respond. His eyes suggested he was still disgusted by me, and he was quick to depart without uttering a word. I took a long pull of my coffee, and said, "So I guess these boyfriends were all interviewed by police?"

"Of course. But, see, I don't think it was some kid from town she was hooking up with. I think it was most likely someone else she was involved with that no one knew about. Not even her friends. A secret lover or somebody like that."

"She wouldn't have told her friends about some guy she was seeing?"

"Not if it was weird," she said around a mouthful of crab cake.

"What's weird?"

"Like, if it was some older dude. Some guy she might not want her friends to know about for whatever reason. Or maybe the guy was married. I mean, who really knows? It's just a hunch. But something like this… like I said, it's a crime of passion, man. You gotta really wanna fucking kill somebody to choke 'em out like that. I mean, do you have any concept of what it takes to strangle someone to death? You really gotta work at it. It's much more intimate than shooting someone or even stabbing them. And it takes *time*. No one ever thinks of it like that, but it's true. It's probably the most intimate thing in the world. Even more than rape."

"Was she…?" I let my voice trail off.

"Raped? No, she wasn't. The current of the river stripped half her clothes off but the coroner found no evidence of sexual assault. My source at the coroner's office said the only clear indication of physical trauma was around her neck. Remember what I said about the distinct bruising around her neck where you could make out the individual impressions of fingers? That was it. Did I mention I got the photos from the morgue, too, if you wanna see 'em."

"That's all right," I said.

Bobbi flipped over the crime-scene photos so that they were face-up again and spread them across the table with one hand. "Here. See? See this?"

It was a close-up of a section of the girl's neck, where the shirt had been pulled aside. There were speckles of mud on her pale flesh and a solitary band of seaweed tangled in her hair. Purple bruises in the distinct shapes of fingers were clearly visible against the colorless skin of the girl's neck.

"To hold someone down like that and strangle the life out of them," Bobbi said. "Man, that takes something."

"Don't they usually scrape underneath the fingernails for bits of skin? DNA or whatever? You see it in the movies."

"Of course," Bobbi said. "There was nothing. Nada."

Shaking my head, I leaned back in my seat. The coffee was good but it wasn't sitting well. "You keep referring to her as 'Gabby.' Did you know her personally?"

"No, I didn't. Not back in 2016, anyway. But since then, she's never really left my mind. I guess I got to know her post-mortem." She frowned, a glob of tartar sauce tucked into one corner of her mouth. "Boy, that sounds morbid."

"I noticed you'd written some more recent articles about her," I said.

"Just trying to keep her top-of-mind. Look, the cops may never bring anyone to justice in this case, but that doesn't mean this poor kid should be forgotten."

"That's exactly what my wife would have said. And it's why I came here to talk to you." I opened the accordion, took out the individual files, and fanned them out like playing cards across the table, placing them atop the photos of the girl. "Like I said, Gabby's wasn't the only murder my wife had been investigating."

Bobbi peered down at the files. A forkful of crab cake halted midway to her mouth.

"There's six in total, including Gabby's. To date, and as far as I know, only one of them has been solved — the murder of a seventeen-year-old girl from West Virginia named Holly Renfrow. I was already out there and spoke to the chief of police. Renfrow was killed when some local degenerate tied her hands behind her back and threw her in a river to drown. The guy overdosed on heroin back in January. The murder took place last fall."

"I knew I liked your wife," Bobbi said.

"At first, I thought Allison might have made a connection between all these murders, and that the guy who'd killed Holly Renfrow had killed all the others. But that's not the case. That guy had been in prison for over a decade, so he couldn't have killed any of these other girls. So then I started wondering if Allison's motivation might be the same as what you're doing with Gabby — to keep the memories of these girls alive, or maybe even to give them a voice and tell their story. To keep them from being forgotten. Only that can't be it, either."

"Why not?"

"Because she'd kept this stuff hidden for years. What voice has she given to Margot Idelson, killed back in 2006? Or Shelby Davenport, murdered in 2008? Those murders happened over a decade ago. If she'd wanted to keep these girls in the public consciousness, just as you've done for Gabby, she wouldn't have kept their stories locked up in a trunk in our bedroom closet."

"And you came here to see me because you thought I'd have an answer for you? For why your wife had been investigating these murders?"

"I came here because I don't know what the hell I'm looking at here. And this stuff was important enough to my wife that she'd devoted herself to it, so I want to make sure whatever she was looking for doesn't get *overlooked*."

Bobbi slowly moved her head up and down. Her gaze, clinging to me, was intense.

I produced the sheet of legal paper from between two of the files. I pointed at the six columns you had meticulously drawn on the page, then pointed to one of the Gas Head phrases that surrounded the drawing.

"Does this phrase mean anything to you? 'Gas Head will make you dead.'"

"Never heard it before in my life."

"What about this weird diagram thing? These six rectangles?"

Bobbi shook her head.

I opened the Colson-Howe file, flipped to the printout of the newspaper article where the same drawing had been sketched beside Bobbi's byline. Said, "See? It's here, too. Right by your name."

"I see that," she said, "but it still doesn't mean anything to me. I'm sorry." She paused. "Except…"

"What?"

"Six rectangles," she said. "Six murders? Maybe there's a correlation there."

"Like what?"

"I really can't say, Aaron. It's just a guess. I don't know."

"Could you look at this stuff for me? Go through it, see if it means anything more to you than it does to me? Maybe make sense of something I've overlooked?"

She reached down and flipped through a few pages of the Colson-Howe file. "I don't know what I could possibly make of all this stuff."

"Please," I said. "I don't know what I'm doing. I translate books for a living, I'm not a reporter. My *wife* was the reporter. Just like you."

She met my eyes. Since your death, Allison, I have grown to hate the look of pity on someone's face when they realize what has happened to you and, by proxy, what has happened to me. The look

Bobbi Negri gave me in that moment was no different, yet this time I did not shy away from it, did not become embarrassed or angered or ruined by it. This time — and to speak frankly, Allison — I willed myself to look as pitiful as possible.

Bobbi set her fork down. She studied her wristwatch.

"I live less than a mile from here," she said, collecting her crime-scene photos and tucking them inside her backpack. "You grab the check and meet me outside. You can follow me back to my house."

"Thank you," I said.

She gathered her backpack, popped a final bit of crab cake in her mouth, then slipped out of the restaurant. A moment later, the waiter arrived as I was wedging your files back into the accordion folder. He set the bill down on the table, and I could feel his gaze on me, intense as a laser beam.

"Sorry about those photos," I said, digging out my wallet.

"Show some respect next time," he said. "I knew that girl."

"I'm sorry," I said, and left him a considerable tip.

4

B obbi Negri lived in a bungalow-style stone house buried among a sprawl of shaggy firs. The river was not visible from her property but the briny scent of it hung in the air like a garland. A collection of wooden birdhouses populated her lawn, and there was a Jackson Pollock smattering of bird shit on the flagstone walkway that led toward the ivy-trellised front door.

The interior of the house was dark and musty, a conglomeration of food smells clinging to the walls. Although I could see no cats, litter boxes were stationed in all four corners of the cramped foyer, strategic as the placement of roadside bombs.

A dowdy, middle-aged woman appeared at the opposite end of the hallway. She had a hefty hardcover book tucked under one arm. "You're home early today, Bobbi."

"The unpredictable life of a small-town reporter." Bobbi repositioned her backpack and pulled off her windbreaker, which she draped over the handle of an umbrella poking from a ceramic umbrella stand. "How was she today?"

"In and out. She's refusing to turn on the lights again."

Bobbi sighed. "Thanks, Dory. You can head on home."

The woman repositioned the hefty tome under her other arm, grabbed a purse that looked equally heavy, and zippered up her fleece pullover. She eyed me somewhat suspiciously as she moved past me in the hall.

"See you tomorrow, Bobbi," she said, then squeezed out the door and clomped down the stairs.

"Dory's my ma's caretaker," Bobbi said as I followed her down the hall.

"Is your mom okay?"

"Alzheimer's. It comes and goes."

"That's too bad. I'm sorry to hear it."

"It's getting to the point where I'm going to have to put her in a home."

The kitchen was at the rear of the house, an outdated little alcove with an assemblage of pots and pans hanging from a ceiling rack. The kitchen table was burdened with reams of paper and an old manual typewriter. Wilted daisies drooped from a ceramic vase. Behind the table stood a rank of aluminum filing cabinets, and there were pages torn from newspapers pinned to the walls, a few of them in spotty frames.

"Sweet old typewriter," I said, running the pads of my fingers over the keys. There was a clean sheet of paper in the roller. "You actually use this for work?"

Bobbi dumped her backpack on a chair. "It's for my mom," she said. "I dictate to her, make her type. It helps keep her mind active and alert. Plus, the typing keeps her hands strong and staves off arthritis."

"That's smart," I said.

"Well, it's becoming futile, but we don't give up, do we?" She offered me a weary smile.

"No. I guess we don't."

I helped her relocate the reams of paper onto the kitchen counter. She left the typewriter and the vase where it was, setting down a laptop (which she had taken from her backpack) down beside them. Her crime-scene photos reappeared, set now in a tidy stack between the typewriter and laptop.

"I'm going to grab some stuff from my office," she said, already heading down a darkened hallway. "Do me a favor and put on a pot of coffee."

The coffeemaker was on the counter, but I had to hunt for the coffee. I finally located it in a rotating cabinet tucked between the dishwasher and the refrigerator. The filter from the previous batch of coffee was still in the machine. I tossed it in the trash, washed out the filter basket and the carafe, then proceeded to make a fresh pot.

On my way back to the rotating cabinet to put the coffee back, I was startled by a figure in the next room — a small parlor, the shades drawn — staring out at me. Before my mind could settle what I was seeing, the figure said, "Jeffrey."

It was an elderly woman in a wingback chair. A shawl was draped across her lap. With the shades drawn and no lights on in the room, it was too dark to make out the woman's approximate age, but her voice made her sound nearly prehistoric.

"Jeffrey," she said again.

"Ma'am."

I took a step into the room. The woman did not move; only her eyes — furtive, moist little buttons in the darkness — confirmed for me that the figure seated in the wingback chair was in fact alive, and the one who had spoken.

"Did you clean your shoes off, Jeffrey?"

"I'm not Jeffrey, ma'am."

"You need to clean your shoes before coming into the house, Jeffrey. We've talked about this."

My eyes having grown accustomed to the gloom, I could see she wasn't as old as I'd originally thought — maybe in her early seventies at most. She was swimming in a too-big sweatshirt with the Baltimore Ravens logo on the front. Her hair was a wiry mass tugged into a ruthless bun behind her head, and streaked with bands of silver.

"Do you hear me, Jeffrey?" said the woman, a note of agitation in her voice now.

"Yes, ma'am. I cleaned my shoes before I came in."

"Good boy." Her head turned slightly, as if to look at something just beyond where I was standing. "What about your friend, Jeffrey?"

The question prompted me to turn and stare into the dark corner of the room. There were picture frames on the wall and a radiator against the baseboard. No one was there.

The woman in the chair leaned forward and studied the dark corner at the opposite end of the room. "Who is that?" she said.

The longer I stared into that darkened corner, the easier it was to convince myself that there was someone standing there staring back at me.

"Allison?" I muttered, and stepped further into the room. The darkness appeared to coalesce into the suggestion of something solid and real. Something *there*.

"Who *is* that?" repeated the old woman at my back.

Extending a hand, I grazed my fingers through the darkness at the far end of the room. I felt nothing except a cold draft of air. The chill of it resonated throughout my entire body.

In a papery whisper: "Don't be afraid, Jeffrey."

"Allison…"

"Don't. Be. Afraid."

A hand fell on my shoulder, nearly sending me through the roof. Bobbi stood there, embarrassed to have startled me. She turned to the woman in the chair. "This isn't Jeffrey, Mom. This is my friend Aaron."

"Jeffrey's a good boy," said the woman, adjusting the shawl draped over her legs. "He's cleaned his shoes just like he's supposed to." She looked at me and I could see a muddy disconnection in her eyes. A smile creased her face. Then she looked past me and at the far corner of the room again.

"This isn't Jeffrey, Ma," Bobbi said, more sternly now.

The woman turned back toward us. Those moist little eyes blinked. Clarity filtered across her face. "Oh," she said. She leaned over and clicked on a lamp beside her chair, the light pooling in a sedate yellow glow across her lap. She smiled at Bobbi. "Hello, dear. Should I get up?" She gripped the armrests of the chair, as if to stand.

"Sit, Ma," Bobbi said. "Aaron and I have got some work to do. We'll be right here in the kitchen. Do you need anything?"

The old woman settled back down in her chair. "No, Bobbi, I'm just resting my eyes for a bit." She looked at me. "Nice to meet you, young man. Aaron, is it?"

"Yes, ma'am. Pleasure's mine." I had to push the words out of me; I was still chilled by what had just transpired… or what I *thought* had transpired.

Bobbi pulled me back into the kitchen, where the coffeemaker burped and trickled on the countertop.

"Jeffrey was my brother. He was killed in a car accident like ten years ago."

"I'm sorry."

"Most times she's okay, but when her mind gets all fuzzy, she starts talking to Jeffrey."

I cast a glance over my shoulder, back into the parlor and at the darkened corner of the room. Half expecting to see you standing there, Allison.

It was madness, I confess.

5

We sat together at the kitchen table while Bobbi combed through your files. Occasionally she would study a line or two from your notes and then type something on her laptop; other times, she would ask me to decipher your handwriting. Together, we demolished the entire pot of coffee while the daylight drained from the kitchen windows. At one point, Bobbi excused herself from the table. She slipped into an adjoining room — what looked like a cramped little laundry room off the kitchen — where she proceeded to make a number of phone calls on her cell phone. When she returned to the kitchen with her cell phone clutched in one hand, she told me to put on a second pot of coffee.

"Who were you on the phone with?" I asked her.

Instead of answering me, Bobbi said, "What was the name of the girl who was murdered last fall? The one in West Virginia, whose killer overdosed on heroin?"

"Holly Renfrow."

"You said you went out there, spoke to the police chief?"

"Yeah." I scooped fresh coffee grounds into a new filter.

"How did you say she was killed?"

"She drowned."

"But *how*?"

"Her hands were tied behind her back and she was thrown in the river."

"Tied with what? Do you know?"

I remembered what Chief Lovering had told me. "Electrical wire, I think."

"And you said you initially thought these murders might be connected?"

"It was just a hunch. The victims all look the same — the same profile, you know? But the guy who killed Holly Renfrow couldn't have killed these other girls, because he was in prison."

"Come here," Bobbi said, setting her cell phone on the table so she could shuffle through the crime-scene photos. I came up beside her just as she separated one photo from the stack and slid it in front of me.

This photo was a close-up of Gabby Colson-Howe's left hand. I tried not to look at the missing digits, taken away by fish or crabs or whatever else, and instead examined what Bobbi Negri was pointing at: a ring of dark red lacerations around the wrist, stark and undeniable against the otherwise pallid flesh.

"Those are ligature marks," Bobbi said. "I was just on the phone to my source at the coroner's office. According to him, Gabby's wrists had been tied together with something before she was strangled to death. You asked about scrapings under the fingernails? That's why there was none — her hands had been bound behind her back while she was being strangled."

"Just like Holly's," I heard myself say.

"I asked my guy what he thought Gabby had been tied with. You know what he guessed? Some sort of thin wire. Very unusual."

"Jesus Christ," I muttered.

"You were right from the start, Aaron," Bobbi said. "Your wife had been hunting a serial killer."

6

I stayed for a dinner of Hamburger Helper and cans of Budweiser. As I set the picnic table out back, Bobbi's mother, Lois, ambled out of the living room and sat at the kitchen table before the old typewriter. I heard her clack a few keys as I carried a handful of napkins and plates to the table in the backyard. When the food was ready, Lois joined us, her Alzheimer's in temporary remission throughout the meal. The crispness of the air and the scent of the nearby river were invigorating.

"What is it you two have been so stealthily working on all afternoon?" Lois asked once we'd all finished our meals. We were watching the boomerang shapes of small bats zigzag across the deepening sky.

"It's getting too cold for you out here, Ma," Bobbi said, handing me a fresh beer from the cooler at her feet.

Lois dismissed her with a flap of her hand. "Nonsense. Is it top secret?"

"Just some project my wife had been working on."

"And where is this wife of yours now?"

"Ma," said Bobbi.

I offered a gentle nod in Bobbi's direction — *It's okay.* I told her you'd passed away in December, and left it at that.

Lois tented her hands at her breast, as if in prayer. "Oh no. Was it sudden?"

"Yes."

"She still haunts you." It was not a question.

"Yes."

"It was that way with Jeffrey. My son. He was killed in an automobile accident."

"I'm sorry."

"It's good for them to haunt you in the beginning. It's how we grieve. It's how we get through it without them."

"I suppose so," I said.

"But after a time, we must let them go. They need to rest and we need to move on. Do you see?"

"It's too soon for that," I confessed. "I'm not ready to let her go."

Lois leaned closer to me from across the table. Her hands were still clasped at her chest in prayer. "Do you want to know a secret?"

I nodded. Bobbi said nothing.

Lois said, "*We haunt ourselves.* In the end, if we don't come to peace with it, if we can't resolve it, we haunt ourselves."

I looked at her face — her rheumy, glittery eyes, and the stark black lines around her mouth. As I watched her, I saw something dark and introspective overtake her features. The glitter fled from her eyes. It was like a mist creeping over a city.

"You're not Jeffrey," Lois said. Her mouth formed a scowl. "You're *not.*" There was undeniable hatred in her voice, as if I was not only not her son, but some imposter here to fool her into thinking I was.

"Okay, Ma," Bobbi said, casually rising from the picnic table. "Let's call it a night. It's getting late."

While Bobbi took her mother upstairs, I cleared the plates and empty beer cans from the picnic table, soaked the glassware in the sink, then sat down at the kitchen table to digest all that Bobbi had figured out following her phone call to her source in the coroner's office.

At one point, my gaze shifted to the single sheet of paper in the roller of the typewriter. Prior to joining us for dinner, Lois had hammered out a single phrase in the center of the page. I read it now —

once, twice, three times — and couldn't help the chill that shuddered down my spine as I did so:

YOU WILL DIE

That was it. That was the whole of it. An elderly woman in the throes of Alzheimer's, this phrase could have meant anything — or nothing — at all. Yet in that moment I was suddenly, profoundly certain it was a missive left behind for me to find. A dire warning the old woman had, in her confused mental state, snatched out of the ether and transcribed for my benefit. It made me uneasy, those three words.

— *You're just scaring yourself*, other-Aaron advised. *You're like some superstitious fool divining portents in tea leaves.*

It was nearly nine o'clock when Bobbi reappeared, arms folded over her chest as she leaned in the kitchen doorway. I was still at the kitchen table, all six of your files open to the static black-and-white photos of the dead girls. I had forced myself to dismiss the note Lois had left behind in the typewriter.

I glanced up at Bobbi. "Remember when I said the victims all looked the same?"

Bobbi nodded but didn't say anything.

"I bet that's how my wife knew to come out here when Gabby first went missing. Allison didn't have to wait for a body to show up. Gabby fit the profile."

"Keep in mind that while the evidence linking Gabby's and Holly Renfrow's deaths is pretty solid, at least in my estimation," Bobbi said, "we don't know for certain about how the other girls were killed. You said it yourself — newspapers leave out all the juicy details. Sometimes they do that because their readership doesn't want to know, and they cater to that. Other times — *most* times — it's because the cops are keeping their cards close to the vest. They rarely talk about the particulars of cases like these to the media unless they think it might help their investigation."

"Can we make some more calls? Get some info from some of these other coroners?"

"I don't know how successful we'd be with something like that, Aaron. My connections outside this town are fairly limited. You might have better luck going back to the police at this point."

"I'm a little gun-shy about going back to the police." I considered all we had learned. "What does this mean about Das Hillyard? That he didn't kill Holly?"

"It would seem so."

"Police chief said Holly's sweatshirt was found in his house."

"There could be a million reasons why that sweatshirt was found in his house. He could have found it on a park bench. Doesn't mean he was a murderer. Maybe he was just a thief."

"And a convicted pedophile," I added.

"Well, even that doesn't fit, does it? What interest does a pedophile have in teenage girls?"

"If they're truly connected, why was Gabby strangled and Holly thrown in a river to drown?"

Bobbi shook her head. "I don't think like a murderer, Aaron. I don't know."

"So what do we do now?"

Bobbi went to the fridge and returned to the table with two fresh cans of beer. She handed one to me. "There's an article in the Renfrow file that talks about a woman who was approached by some creepy guy in the middle of the night when she blew a tire," she said.

"Yeah. Denise Lenchantin. Chief Lovering said what happened to her wasn't connected to what happened to Holly."

Bobbi shrugged, suggesting she didn't put much stock in any

particular theory at this point. "I'd be curious what she had to say to your wife. If we're dealing with an honest-to-God serial killer here, Aaron, it clearly can't be Hillyard. Which means someone else is out there. It might very well be the guy who stopped that Lenchantin woman on the road that night."

"You think I should talk to her," I said. It wasn't a question; I already knew the answer.

"It's what I would do," Bobbi said. Then she added, "It's what Allison would do."

CHAPTER SEVEN

1

Denise Lenchantin finished her shift at the Coal River Diner just after eight in the evening. She was still clearing tables when I arrived and introduced myself. We had spoken earlier on the phone, and she had agreed to the meeting, but my arrival now seemed to catch her off guard. She was a slim, attractive woman in her early twenties, dressed in an unflattering Pepto-Bismol-colored waitress uniform with an aquamarine ribbon in her dirty blonde hair. Hefting a tray cluttered with greasy dishes and half-eaten wedges of pecan pie, she summoned a weary smile then suggested I wait for her across the street at a pub called The Mineshaft. I slipped back outside, the air having dropped a good fifteen degrees since the sun had gone down, and I hurried across the curl of blacktop that separated the neon-lit diner from the pub. Fronted by a massive gravel parking lot populated with four-wheelers and pickup trucks, The Mineshaft looked like the kind of bar where the bouncers carried batons.

I stepped inside, a guy in a charcoal peacoat, a cornflower-blue Van Heusen button-down, and a leather satchel over one shoulder that, in this environment, might be mocked for resembling a woman's large purse. I waited for the jukebox to screech to a halt and for heads to swivel in my direction. But no one paid me any attention as I wove through the dim barroom and selected a stool at the far end of the bar.

I looked around, noting that there were no pool tables in here, no karaoke machines, no tight little bandstand for live music on the weekends. This was a place for serious drinkers — people who did not come for a good time or to simply burn a paycheck, but career alcoholics who opted for the only form of acceptable suicide, which was to drink themselves to a premature death. Most of the men in here sat by themselves, hunched over the bar or at tables just beyond the cones of light issuing from the milky cataract bulbs recessed into the ceiling. Men in hunting attire whose heavy beards gave them all an air of anonymity. For the first time, I understood the futility of trying to hunt down a killer in these hills. The Mineshaft looked moderately populated with America's most wanted.

I ordered a Budweiser from a middle-aged tattooed woman working the bar, then dug through my satchel and took out the packet on Holly Renfrow. When the bartender brought over my beer and saw that I was reading an article about a murdered teenager, I stammered out some pathetic excuse while simultaneously stuffing the papers back in my satchel.

"Takes all kinds," the bartender said, cutting me off. "You want something to eat?"

"I'm waiting for someone."

Without a word, the bartender departed for what was probably more enthralling conversation with the gray-haired lumberjack a few stools away.

2

Forty-five minutes, a second beer and a plate of chicken wings later, and I was convinced that Denise Lenchantin had decided to bail on our meeting. Just as I was about to wave over the bartender and request my bill, Lenchantin came in. She'd gone home and changed her clothes, I saw, which accounted for her delay. Coming through the pub's door on a burst of frigid air, she wore an electric-blue halter top beneath a black leather motorcycle jacket, and charcoal-colored jeans that clung to her like body paint. She looked lost for a moment, then smiled as she noticed me seated at the bar. She approached, a fat handbag studded with silver buttons and fringed trim clutched under one arm. She'd ditched the hair ribbon, too, her golden hair spilling down past her shoulders now.

"You mind if we grab a table instead?" she said as she came up to the bar.

"Sure."

I followed her to an empty table. She hung her purse over the back of her chair before she sat down. I sat opposite her, with a clear shot of the bar and the front door beyond. The men in this place were not subtle in their appraisal of Denise Lenchantin; not only had heads turned upon her arrival, but at least one fellow at the bar had swiveled completely around on his stool so that he could stare at the back of her head. I glanced at him disapprovingly, but he seemed unperturbed by my reproach.

"I almost didn't recognize you," I said, feeling it necessary to say something; her transformation from dowdy waitress to someone who could have been modeling in a magazine seemed to demand some sort of acknowledgement.

"Sorry you had to wait so long, but I wasn't coming in here dressed like a bag of cotton candy." She poked a cigarette in her mouth.

"You can smoke in here?"

"Unless these are strictly for show," she said, picking up the black plastic ashtray that sat in the middle of the table.

The tattooed bartender arrived with a pitcher of beer and two pint glasses. She set them on the table.

"Any fresh ink?" Denise asked the woman.

The bartender hoisted one leg of her nylon pants to reveal what looked like Gumby giving it to Pokey in the rear, just above her ankle.

Denise laughed. "Excellent! Oh, shit! I love it."

The woman swiveled her gaze in my direction, as if anticipating a more in-depth critique.

"And they call the *horse* Pokey," I commented.

The expression I received in return could have been a grin, a grimace, or evidence of sciatic pain. She dropped her pant leg and went off to reclaim her station behind the bar.

Denise Lenchantin filled both pint glasses then slid one over to me.

"Thanks," I said. "Although I don't think I'll be able to help put much of a dent in this pitcher. I'm a bit of a lightweight, and I've already had a couple."

One of her hands sprung out and clutched me about the wrist, before I could even lift my glass off the tabletop. "Hey," she said, all serious as a heart attack now, leaning closer toward me from across the table. "I've been thinking about your wife ever since your phone call. That's fucking dismal, man."

I felt my face go through the motions of appreciation, but said nothing.

"You don't gotta be polite about it," she said, still squeezing my wrist. Her fingernails, shining with metallic silver polish, looked like bolt heads. "What was it, an accident? Some kind of accident?"

"Well, not exactly." I told her about the shooting at the plaza. It was something I hadn't planned on doing, but once I started, I found that I couldn't stop. Also, for much of the day, I'd felt you right here with me, Allison, crazy as that sounds. Talking about you now seemed almost natural. As if there were three of us seated around this table instead of just two.

"Jesus fuck, man, I remember hearing about that on the news," she said, shaking her head in astonishment. "I just didn't make the connection to your wife, is all. I mean, it sounds shitty, but this stuff happens so much now that you just kinda lose track of all the shootings. Am I right?"

"Sadly, yes," I admitted.

She released my wrist and sat back in her chair. She brought her beer to her lips and downed half of it in a series of thirsty gulps. When she set the glass back down on the table, there was a crescent of red lipstick on the rim.

"That guy keeps staring at you," I said. "Dude at the bar."

She looked over her shoulder, saw the guy, waved to him. Almost in a daze, the guy raised a hand and waved back. His bearded face never cracked a smile.

"You know him?" I asked.

"Not a clue," she said, turning back around and topping off her beer from the pitcher. "I used to work here, though, you know. He's probably a regular. Hell, they're *all* regulars. You'd think the money would be better working in a bar than in a restaurant, but look around. These guys aren't exactly big tippers, you know what I'm saying? But you get used to the stares. It don't bother me." She shrugged. "At least I didn't have to dress like cotton candy when I worked here."

"I'd like to talk about what happened to you last fall," I said.

"You're talking about that creepy dude in the car? The story I told your wife?"

"Yes. The guy you reported to the police after Holly Renfrow was murdered."

"Right, yeah." Her face tightened. "Fucking animals, right? This guy just walks into a shopping center with a gun and ruins your fucking *life*? I'm sorry, I'm just thinking of your wife again. Makes me crazy. Hey — you wanna do some shots?"

"Uh, no, I'm okay. The beer's fine."

"Just one round," she insisted, and before I could protest further, she was out of her chair and stomping in her clunky heels over to the bar. The guy on the barstool who had been ogling her since her arrival repositioned himself on his stool so that he could look directly at her ass now.

This was hopeless, Allison.

Despite an absence of music, Denise Lenchantin danced her way back to our table, an amber-colored shot glass in each hand. She placed a serving of the suspicious liquid in front of me.

"What's this?"

"Brake fluid."

"What?"

"I'm fucking with you. Just tequila," she said. She raised her own glass. "Listen, listen — to your wife, okay? Andrea."

"Allison."

"Fuck! Allison! I'm sorry. I'm terrible."

"It's okay."

"It's not. What a shit I am."

"It's fine."

"To Allison!"

I raised my shot glass and clinked it against hers. Booze sloshed down my wrist and soaked the cuff of my shirt. The smell of it made my eyes water. "To Allison."

We both downed the shots. Like a flaming arrow, the tequila fired straight down my gullet where it detonated in my stomach like a nuclear bomb.

To my astonishment, Denise bent over and kissed the top of my head. I caught a whiff of her perfume, dizzying and floral, before she dropped back down in her seat on the other side of the table.

"This guy that approached you back in the fall," I tried again.

"Yeah, right," she said, nodding vigorously now. "Total fucking creep."

"Can you tell me what happened?" I asked.

It had been around midnight and she had been getting off her shift at the diner. She got in her car and was heading home along a wooded roadway that curled around the hillside. It was a beautiful vista during the day (she told me) but could be downright creepy at night. She hadn't gone more than a mile when her car, an old Ford station wagon from the eighties which she'd inherited from her parents, began to thump-thump-thump. She pulled over, walked around the car, and saw that the rear passenger-side tire was flat. At that point, she had considered calling her father or even her boyfriend to come and get her, but she decided it was too late to disturb either one of them. She had a spare and a jack in the trunk, and she'd changed tires before.

She had only just opened the trunk when she heard a vehicle approaching. She looked over her shoulder and watched as a pair of headlights carved a passage toward her through the darkness. Its engine was loud, an eight-cylinder job (she knew a bit about cars from her father, a mechanic by trade), and it clawed its way down the road through the otherwise silent night. The vehicle slowed until it came to a stop beside her car.

"I thought he was a cop at first," she said, "because he had one of those floodlight thingies on the side of his door. Shined the light right in my eyes."

"Was it a police car?"

"If it was, it was one of those undercover cars like a detective would drive. Like in the movies? I mean, it didn't have the lights on the roof and wasn't painted like a cop car. It was just a plain sedan, I think four doors. Brown or gray — I couldn't really tell in the dark. But he wasn't a cop."

"How do you know?"

"Because I asked him," she said. "He didn't say yes right away, but then he said he was. But by then, I could tell he was full of shit. He called himself a 'policeman.' Cops don't call themselves policemen unless they're talking to goddamn five-year-olds, am I right?"

"I guess you're right," I said.

"Also, it was the way he said it that creeped me out. Like, he stretched out the word, you know? *Po-leeeece-man.* Like that."

"Yeah," I said. "That's creepy."

She took a long swallow of her beer.

"Go on," I said. "Keep going."

3

The vehicle idled in the road parallel to her own, trailing a cloud of exhaust in its wake. The floodlight attached to the driver's door was impossibly bright. It blinded her.

"You look like a ghost," the driver said, his voice barely audible over the rumble of the car's engine. It was a man, his voice deep. "Gave me a scare. Standing out here like this on the side of the road."

He kept the floodlight trained on her face, which made it impossible for her to see any details beyond the light — not of the vehicle nor of the driver himself. When she sidestepped out of the glare, the driver repositioned the light so that it blinded her again.

"Flat tire," she said, holding up a hand to shield the light from her eyes.

The man said nothing; she listened to his car idling there in the middle of the road. It was the only sound she could hear.

"You a cop?" she asked.

"I'm always here to help," he said.

She recognized that this was a non-answer, and that the lizard part of her brain was already recoiling from this stranger.

"I can help," he said, and she detected a hint of urgency in his voice this time.

She didn't want his help. "That's okay. I've got a spare and a jack in the trunk. If it's — "

"Spin around," said the man.

She thought she'd misheard him. Or maybe in her increasing apprehension she'd misinterpreted some advice he was offering about changing a tire. "Excuse me?"

"Like a ballerina," he said. "Spin. Around."

Her hand still in front of her face, she took a step back until her thigh thumped against the quarter panel of her car. The driver repositioned the floodlight again so that it filled her vision.

"I don't think so," she told him.

The driver said nothing. She couldn't see him behind the light, but she could hear him shifting about inside the car. All at once, a million different and terrible things began to shuttle through her mind. There was a tire iron right here in the trunk — would she be able to use it as a weapon? If it came to that? She picked it up, its iron-cool weight feeling insubstantial in her grasp.

"How 'bout killing that light, man? I'm going blind over here."

"This is no place for you," the man said, ignoring her request. There was an odd singsong quality to his voice. "Come with me."

"What?" she practically wheezed; her throat felt like it was constricting, making it difficult to talk, to breathe.

"Leave the car," said the man. "Come with me."

"I don't think so."

"It's safer that way. I'm a policeman." *Po-leeeece-man.*

"No. I don't think so."

"You shouldn't change a flat out here in the middle of the night. You're liable to get struck."

"Yeah, well, I don't think so." It seemed all she was capable of saying. She forced herself to sound casual, unafraid. Like not showing fear to a snarling dog. "Thanks, but no thanks."

When she thought she heard the latch open on the car door, she moved quickly around to the passenger side of her own vehicle, stepping onto the grassy shoulder of the road and feeling a bit safer with her car between them. Fear rose up in her, strident as a klaxon, and the tire iron suddenly felt like it weighed a thousand pounds as she carried it with her. Yet instead of panicking, she put her cell phone to her ear and pretended she had just received a call.

"Yeah, hi, Dad," she said into her phone, loud enough for the stranger to hear. "Yep, I'm just down the road. Keep driving until you see me. A nice man has stopped to help me, too."

At this point, she had moved far enough out of the glare of the floodlight so that her vision had returned. From this vantage — near the front of her own vehicle now and still moving, staring at the headlights of the stranger's car — she saw that the driver had climbed out of his car and was standing in the road between the two vehicles. She had heard the door unlatch but hadn't actually seen the man get out of his car. His sudden appearance there in the road terrified her.

"I'm just past the bend, Dad," she said into her phone, still pretending to speak with her father. "Okay, great. Can you see the car lights? Great." She paused, her body prickling with apprehension. Her grip tightened on the deadly weight of the tire iron, which she kept down at her side. "Hold on, I'll find out," she said into the phone. And to the stranger — the dark shape standing in the middle of the road, slowly being swallowed up by the cloud of exhaust unspooling from his car's tailpipe — she called, "Hey, mister, my dad wants to know your name."

The man said nothing. She stared at him — at the shape of him — while her heart thrummed in her chest. Despite the chill of a late autumn night, a great heat roiled out from her waitress uniform and caused sweat to pop from the pores along her cheeks. Sweat stung her eyes and she quickly mopped it away.

"What's your name, mister?" she asked again. "My dad's just up the road and he wants to know."

4

Denise Lenchantin paused here to refill her beer. She refilled mine, too.

"Christ, kid, you know how to build suspense," I said. "What the hell happened next?"

"Nothing. He just got in his car and drove away."

"You scared him off."

"Well, I was freaked the fuck out myself. I really *did* call my dad after that, woke him right up, and he was there in like no time, right? He changed the tire and followed me home. I told him about the guy and what he'd said to me, and just the overall creepy vibe he gave off. But we didn't do anything about it. Not then. It wasn't until later, when I heard about that girl in Furnace, Holly what's-her-name, and how the police were asking anyone with any information to come forward, blah blah blah, I thought, shit, what if that creepy son of a bitch was the same guy killed that girl in Furnace? Holly, right? I mean, it happened on the same fucking *night*, right? So, I reported it."

"You were smart," I told her. "That thing you did with the fake phone call, it probably saved your life."

"Don't say that. You're giving me chills, man."

"Well, it's true. Quick thinking."

"Listen," she said, and leaned forward across the table toward me again. "You work in places like this, you learn how to stay on your toes, know what I mean?"

"What happened when you went to the police in Furnace?"

"I gave them a statement. They asked if I could identify the guy, but I told them it was too dark and I didn't see his face. I didn't see anything about him. I couldn't even give them a good description of the car. Except, well, it really *stank*."

"What do you mean?"

"The exhaust. It was fogging up the road and it smelled like the freaking car was on fire. I mean, I know when a car's burning oil, but this thing, it was like ready to explode."

I nodded, unsure what to make of this.

"But anyway, back in January, they found the guy who killed that girl. Did you know that? Turns out he was some local pedophile or something. Anyway, he killed himself." She put a finger-gun to her temple, pulled the trigger. "Blew his brains out."

"His name was Das Hillyard. And he didn't shoot himself. He overdosed on heroin."

"Yeah? Wow. I guess... well, dead is dead, right?"

I thought of our closet light coming on seemingly by itself, and the stark impression of your handprint materializing on the windshield of the Subaru. The figure that materialized in the doorway of our home office. But in the end, I said, "Yes. Dead is dead."

"They said it wasn't the same guy. The guy in the car who I saw that night and the guy who killed that girl. Furnace police said that Hillyard guy didn't own a car like the one I described. He had a truck or something. Which means your wife was wrong. Allison. Allison." She jabbed a finger to her temple, as if to imprint your name on her brain.

"Wrong about what, exactly?" I asked.

"Well, your wife thought it was the same person. But this was before the cops knew it was that Hillyard guy. They didn't have any suspects when your wife came out here. Nobody knew nothing."

"You're right. I think my wife believed that the guy who stopped to talk to you on the road that night was the same guy who killed Holly Renfrow. And I agree with her. But it wasn't Das Hillyard."

If this took her by surprise, she didn't show it.

"How many times did my wife come out here?" I asked.

"Well, we met just once. But we spoke a little bit on the phone before that. I told her what happened to me and she wanted to meet."

"Did she say why?"

"I guess she wanted more details."

"Did she say why she thought the man who stopped you was also the man who killed the girl in Furnace? What made the connection for her?"

"Oh," she said, "it wasn't just the girl from Furnace. Your wife thought this guy had killed a bunch of different girls."

"She told you this?"

"Oh yeah. Talk about freaking me the fuck out, right? You're telling me this guy who pulled up next to me on that road was a fucking *serial killer*? No thanks." She held up one hand like a crossing guard halting traffic.

"What else did she tell you?"

"I don't know. I can't remember." She smiled wanly at me. "I'm sorry, man." But then her eyes widened. She looked like she'd just remembered she left the oven on at home. "Wait. There was that thing with the yearbook."

"What yearbook?"

I could see the memory rushing back to her, the wheels and gears spinning behind her eyes. "Shit. Shit, yeah. Now I remember."

"What, Denise?" I said.

"Your wife had some girl's yearbook. She wanted to know if I'd be able to pick the guy out of a photo. If I'd recognize him, you know? Like those lineups on cop shows?"

"Hold on. I'm… I'm confused. My *wife* wanted you to identify the guy who came up to you on the side of the road in someone's yearbook? Like, a school yearbook?"

"That's right. But I told her I didn't get a good look at the guy. I didn't even look at the photos."

"I don't understand," I said. "Whose yearbook was it?"

"Uh," she said, squinting at me as if I'd suddenly transformed into a blazing inferno. "I don't know. She just said that the guy went to school with one of the girls he killed. She got a copy of the yearbook and wanted me to look. I guess maybe it was that Holly girl's yearbook?"

"You're fucking kidding me."

"Hey, man. Creepazoids gotta go to school somewhere, too, right? Shit, I went to school with about a million of 'em." She laughed, all teeth.

"This would mean that my wife had a suspect," I said.

"Well, yeah. That's what I'm saying."

"That can't be."

"I'm just telling you what happened." She turned in her chair and began rooting around in her purse.

"Denise, are you sure it was Holly's yearbook?"

"I don't really know."

"Because a guy who went to school with Holly would've been too young to kill some of the other girls. Unless…" *Unless he wasn't a student*, was what I thought but did not say. "Do you remember the name of the school?" I asked her instead.

"No name. I have no idea. What's the name of the high school over in Furnace?" She produced a tube of lipstick and applied it to her lips, painting them a startling red.

144

"I don't know the name of the high school in Furnace. Did you actually see the yearbook?"

"Yeah, but I don't remember what name was on it. Like, the school name, I mean."

"Do you remember what the yearbook looked like?"

"Yeah. It had a green deer on the cover."

"A green deer," I said.

"That's right. You know it?"

I felt like banging my head against the table. "No," I said. "No, I don't know it. Denise, did she say anything else? Anything about who this guy is or why she thought she had a suspect?"

"No, man. Sorry." She finished off her beer then emptied the rest of the pitcher into her glass. "She just didn't."

5

I had a belly full of beer but felt stone sober as Denise Lenchantin and I walked out of The Mineshaft.

"This is me," Denise said, pausing beside a beat-up station wagon in The Mineshaft's gravel parking lot. "Where're you?"

I nodded across the street, where the Sube was still parked at the diner.

"Which car?"

"The Subaru." I pointed it out to her.

"Okay. Just making sure."

"Making sure about what?"

She hoisted one shoulder in a halfhearted shrug. "When you called me earlier, asked to meet, I was thinking maybe *you* were the guy. You know? And then my mind started to go wild, man. Like maybe your wife had a hunch that you were killing all these girls and so she started investigating, but now she's dead, and here you come right on her heels, maybe for the same reason your wife came — to see if I could identify you. You and your car with the police light on the door."

"I'm not the guy," I assured her.

She held up one finger, as if to make a point. Her face was close to mine and I could smell the alcohol and cigarettes on her breath. "Maybe you don't even know it," she said. "Maybe you've got a split personality, like in the movies. I'm being playful, can you tell?"

"That's some imagination."

"At least you're leaving a paper trail, picking up the bar tab and all," she said, folding her arms across her chest as she leaned back against the station wagon. "Cops would be on you in no time if I disappeared. My guess is Janet would be more than happy to rat you out, too. She didn't like you much."

"She the bartender with the classy tattoo?"

Denise laughed.

I looked across the street, where the Coal River Diner glowed like a nuclear reactor. "That's where you were working the night that guy ran into you?"

"Yep. Fancy joint, huh?"

"They got security cameras out here in these parking lots?"

"Here? Fuck, no."

"Anyone ever tell you they saw someone messing with your car that night? Messing around with the tire?"

"Jesus, you think that's what he done? That guy?"

"I don't know." I looked her over. "You sober enough to drive home? I can get you an Uber."

She brayed laughter. "No fucking Ubers out here, man," she said. In one fluid motion, she reached out and hooked a finger in the belt loop of my slacks.

"Uh, hey." I took her arm in one hand and jiggled it to release her grip, but it just made the situation more suggestive. She tugged me toward her. "I don't think that's such a good idea, Denise."

She smiled and stared at me. Yanked again on my belt loop. The tip of her nose nearly collided with mine.

"Listen," I said, tugging with a bit more force on her arm. "Denise, I'm sorry."

"It's okay. I'm not drunk."

"It just isn't…" I stammered. "This isn't the thing to do. I can't. Allison…"

"Allison," she repeated. Her hand fell away. "Yeah. Well. Whatever."

For the first time, I realized she possessed some of the same qualities as the killer's other victims — blonde, slim, pretty, with petite features that were almost too youthful. If she were a few years younger, she could have fit neatly among all those black-and-white newspaper photos shuffling speedily through my brain. A whole history of dead girls.

"Be careful," I told her, "and have a good night."

"Watch your six," she said, and blew me a kiss.

I hurried across the street to where the Sube sat beneath the sickly glow of neon lights radiating off the diner's rooftop sign. I climbed into the car, tossing my satchel onto the passenger seat, and started the engine. "Manic Monday" came on the CD player. I lowered the volume and sat there, the car in Park, while I watched Denise Lenchantin smoke a cigarette in the parking lot of The Mineshaft all by herself.

She looked like someone's victim.

6

It was well after midnight by the time I got back to Furnace. As I coasted down Main Street, the combination of exhaustion and alcohol edged me closer and closer toward sleep. My mind continued to wander and my head kept nodding. I recalled having passed a motel on the opposite side of the river earlier that day, and as I drew closer to the river, I could hear it calling my name.

When I hit the stone bridge, I slowed the car to a crawl. Chief Lovering had been correct about one thing — with no lampposts on this bridge, it was as if I were about to drive clear off into space. The heavy cloud cover, which had been there all day like a bad omen, blotted out the moon. The only light was the feeble issuance from the Sube's headlamps, meek and futile in such tremendous, expansive darkness.

I stopped the car halfway along the bridge and shut down the engine. The driver's window was halfway open, and I could smell chimney smoke carried along on the cold night air. I was parked in roughly the same spot Lovering had parked his cruiser the day he'd driven me out here to point out the place beyond the bend in the river where Holly Renfrow's body had been found.

"Who came and took you, Holly?" I said to the darkness. "What monster came across your path on this bridge?"

As I gazed into the dark, I sensed a faceless predator, silent and lethal as poison gas, creeping toward me across the stone bridge. In my head, I was listening to Denise Lenchantin's story again. Of the man who had hidden behind a sphere of dazzling white light, saying, *Leave the car. Come with me.*

Come with me.

I turned off the headlights, and sat there in the dark. My breath was coming in shallow gasps now. Still, I found my voice, and counted aloud from ten down to one. Slowly, poignantly, as if each number was a heartbeat.

"Ten… nine… eight… seven…"

The darkness at the far end of the bridge looked as dense as a wall.

"... six... five... four..."

Your voice took on a presence in my head: *It has nothing to do with ghosts. It's a game all about the power of perception.*

"... three... two..." and my heart was galloping now, "one."

I flipped on the headlights, and there she was, Holly's ghost advancing toward me along the bridge, snared in the glow of the headlights, an insignificant figure who defied description, except for the youth and the beauty of her, gnashing bubblegum, trailing a hand along the concrete railing, her face illuminated by the bluish light issuing from her cell phone, her platinum hair swept to one side, resting in a coil on one shoulder...

I stared at her, my heart tightening in my chest. She took a few more steps in my direction then stopped. Looked up at me, as if sensing my presence, the two of us bridging some unfathomable gap between space and time and death. Her gaze hung on me, and even from this distance, I discerned a flicker of apprehension in her eyes. A fear of things to come. A sense that —

Nothing. Nothing was there. I blinked my eyes and saw only the wall of absolute darkness swallowing up the far side of the bridge. In that moment, I knew two things at once — that my overtaxed mind had tricked itself into seeing a ghost, and that maybe, at the end of the day, that's exactly what ghosts really *were*. A composite of all we need them to be. Our aching desire that makes them real. And if that's true, where were you, Allison?

Where were you?

Air shuddered from my lungs. Despite the cold night, my neck prickled with perspiration and the palms of my hands felt made of glue.

Feeling as though something bleak and dangerous had seeped in through the pores of my flesh, I cranked over the ignition and sped away.

CHAPTER EIGHT

1

I spent the night in the motel in Maryland, about fifteen or so miles from the border of Furnace, West Virginia. I was you, Allison, tracking a killer and bunking down in seedy roadside motels. Telling no one. Just like you.

I feared a series of brutal dreams were lying in wait for me just beyond the edge of sleep. As it was, a memory filtered through the veil of semi-consciousness as I lay there in bed, a memory of a phrase and of a faceless, distant thing known as Gas Head. In those moments, I remembered… but my weariness, coupled with an overindulgence of alcohol, saw to it that I was unceremoniously dispatched into the country of Unconsciousness without so much as a whimper.

2

One humid summer evening, after we'd finished several bottles of wine and climbed drunkenly up the stairs toward our bedroom, groping and kissing each other's necks, you said, "I want us to try something."

In the bedroom, you stripped off my clothes with precision while I went at yours with a distempered, inebriated sort of hunger —

tugging, pulling, twisting. When we were both naked, you kissed my lips, licked the tip of my nose, and pulled something from the top drawer of your nightstand.

"What are those?" I asked. It looked like a shoelace tied in two loops.

"Flex cuffs. Police use them when they don't have enough handcuffs."

"Yeah? What are you doing with them?"

"I found them in a box of junk at the office. Leftovers from Police Week."

"Thief."

"That's me," you said, smiling in the half-light coming through the bedroom window. "Now turn around."

"Me?"

"I don't see anyone else here."

"Lord," I said, grinning, shaking my head.

"You don't trust me?" Then you reached down and grabbed me. Hard. "Someone does."

"Yes," I had to agree. "Someone sure does."

I turned around and you bound my wrists behind my back.

"Too tight?"

"No, ma'am."

"See if you can pull out of them."

I tried, but the flex cuffs provided too much resistance.

"Snug as a bug," I said. Despite my initial reticence, I was rock-hard; all the blood had rushed from my head to my groin.

"Good," you said, and shoved me down on the bed.

I rolled over and you climbed atop me. You waited for no invitation, impaling yourself on me like an assault. Your fingernails left crescent-shaped indentations in the sparsely haired flesh of my upper chest.

"Come on," you urged, breathlessly. "Don't you want to touch me? Don't you want to reach up and grab me?"

"Yes."

"Do it."

"I can't."

"Try."

"I'm trying." And I was — tugging against the restraints, my hands an uncomfortable ball of flesh and bone pressing into the small of my back as you rocked on top of me.

Then, just as sudden as this all began, you climbed off me. Your body glistened in the moonlight coming in through the window, and something about you looked spectral.

"You look like a ghost," I said through heavy breaths.

"Shhh," you said. "Don't."

"Don't what?"

"Come here. Roll over. There's something else."

"Help me," I said, my legs flailing over the edge of the bed. With my hands bound behind my back, I couldn't shift my weight to my legs.

You pulled one of my ankles to the floor. I stood there panting like a dog. I felt like I could level a small forest with my erection.

"Turn around," you said, producing a pair of scissors from the nightstand drawer. "I'll cut those off you." You snipped them off; they dropped to the carpet. But when I tried to turn around, you braced me with your hands on my biceps. "Put your hands back."

"Back where?"

"Back here."

I slipped my hands to the sweaty pocket of flesh at the base of my spine. You worked something over them and onto my wrists. Tugged them tight. Too tight.

"Ouch!"

"Don't be a baby," you said, and kissed my ear.

"These hurt."

"They're plastic. The others were nylon."

"I like the nylon better."

"Duly noted."

I made for the bed, but you tugged my wrists, halting my progress.

"No," you said. "On the floor."

"Help me."

You helped me down on my knees. I sat, then swung my legs around. You came around to face me, crouched down, sat astride my hips. You were a goddamn sieve.

We went at it in that fashion for several minutes. As I was nearing the end, you shoved me backward, throwing your weight against me. I went down, not flat on my back but against the mound of my hands. The floor less forgiving than the mattress, my bound hands pressed like a stone into my spine. You kept grinding against me, and your weight only added to the pain.

"Allison — "

"Move them."

"Okay. This hurts."

"Then break free."

"Come on. Stop. Stop."

You didn't stop. You railed against me, droplets of tangy perspiration pattering across my face and stinging my eyes. My hands ached from the weight of us and my back ached from the dull pressure of my hands which were now balled into fists and quickly growing numb.

"Allison," I grunted, bucking my hips to knock you off me.

You moaned, kissed me full on the mouth. Clamped your thighs around my waist. "Come with me," you said.

My orgasm felt like it started at the base of my brain and blew through the trunk of my body with the force of a bullet fired from a gun. My whole body tensed, spasmed. Atop me, you whipped your head back, your fingernails slicing deeper into my flesh. Your body shook and you moaned. The delicate stalk of your neck looked shiny and blue, like polished steel, in the moonlight. Something like a laugh burst from you. Then we both went limp. Like a cat, you rolled off me then curled in a fetal position against me on the floor, exhaling sex-breath in my face.

Between gasps for air, I said, "Get... these fucking things... off me," and rolled over onto my side. You clipped them with the scissors and I immediately sat up and rubbed at my wrists. "That was a bit much," I commented.

"You seemed to enjoy yourself all right."

"Yeah, well, men are fools."

"No argument here," you said.

I went to the bathroom to examine the damage to my wrists. The nylon bands had irritated my flesh so that it had turned a raw-looking pink; the plastic bands had actually left deep impressions in my skin, made with such force that I could see the brand name — Loop Riot, LLC — engraved backwards along one wrist.

You came in, studied my wrists. Ran a finger along the abrasions, an archeologist fingering a groove carved in sandstone. "Oh shit, baby, I didn't realize."

"Yeah..."

You kissed the insides of my wrists, the outsides of my wrists. Sawed that finger back and forth against the raw places on my flesh then kissed my lips. "I'm sorry."

"Next time, they're on you."

You laughed. Said, "Most likely *not*."

"I'm gonna have a shower. Pop in?"

"I'll go keep the bed company," you said, and slipped out of the bathroom.

I took a quick shower then joined you in bed. You were already asleep, but I kissed the side of your face anyway and rolled over onto my pillow. I was halfway to dreamland when you uttered, quite clearly, a phrase that struck me as wholly, completely bizarre —

"Gas Head will make you dead."

I rolled over and said, "What?"

You did not respond.

"Allison? Are you awake?"

You'd talked in your sleep before, but nothing so clear and projected as that. *Gas Head will make you dead.*

So bizarre, I laughed. Then I settled back down and closed my eyes, intent on asking you about it in the morning.

But by morning, I had forgotten all about it.

CHAPTER NINE

1

Pink, sinewy, glistening: dead things hung in rows from the roof of the Renfrow porch. I was halfway up a walkway of wobbly slate pavers when a man in a fleece jacket and a knit cap came around the side of a pale yellow A-frame, mopping grease or maybe blood from his hands.

"Hello," I said, pausing in my stride. I gave this guy my best smile.

"This here's private property. No soliciting. There's signs posted up the drive."

"I'm not soliciting. I'm looking for Rita Renfrow."

"Yeah? Who're you?"

"My name's Aaron Decker. My wife, Allison, was a reporter. She met with Rita soon after… well, last fall. She was here about Holly."

"Right, I remember," said the man. His beard, black as a bear's pelt, covered half his face. His eyes sparkled. "She here with you?" He peered past me, down the driveway and toward the road.

"My wife passed away in December."

"What do you mean?"

"I mean my wife is dead."

At this, he offered a perfunctory nod, then said, "All right, come on." Without waiting for me to move, he turned and lumbered back around the side of the house.

I followed him, using the branches of nearby spruce trees as handholds, since the front and side of the property sloped at a precarious angle toward the road below. Behind the house was a building smaller than a garage but larger than a tool shed. There was an ATV inside, its frame painted camouflage green. A mangy-looking dog of some indeterminable breed sat in a patch of sun, its leash tied to a stake in the ground. At my approach, the dog sprung to its feet and began barking at me. A small novelty skull hung from its collar.

"What were those things hanging from the porch?" I asked.

"Beaver," said the man. He climbed a set of wooden steps and tugged open a sliding glass door. "Rita!" he called into the house. "Come on out here a minute, will you?" Then he leaned against the doorframe where he continued toweling dark gunk from his hands. To the dog, he said, "Shut the fuck up, you bastard."

The dog shut the fuck up and dropped back down to sun itself in the pane of light. Yet its eyes remained on me, distrustful.

"Are you Rita's husband?" I asked the guy.

"Boyfriend." He looked up and pointed farther up the hillside, where the foliage was denser and, beyond, I could see distant houses. "I'm Chip. My place is up the hill. But Rita, she's got this nice work shed. So, well…" Almost ashamed, he cocked a thumb at the shed.

"That your ATV?"

"Sure is. You ride?"

"Can't say I do," I said, and grimaced at the thought of careening around this sloping hillside on that suicide machine.

"Probably smart," Chip said. "I busted six bones on that thing."

"All at once?"

"Huh?"

"Never mind."

A woman appeared in the doorway. She looked scarcely older than me, and despite the chill in the air, she wore only jeans, a ribbed wife-beater and an open flannel shirt. Bright pink moccasins adorned her feet.

"That reporter lady who was here asking about Holly last fall," Chip said to her. "This is her husband."

"I'm Aaron Decker," I said, and approached the woman with my hand extended.

She shook it. Said, "Where's your wife?"

"His wife's dead," Chip said, as he tucked the filthy towel into the rear pocket of his jeans.

Rita Renfrow's eyes volleyed from me to Chip then back to me again. "What's he mean?" she asked me.

Because I didn't have it in me to explain the details of your death, Allison, I simply said you'd passed away in December from an accident and left it at that.

"Well, that's just terrible," Rita said, and the expression on her face softened the slightest bit. She was haggard but pretty, with tawny hair pulled back in a girlish ponytail. Had she lived an easier life she might have even been beautiful. "Hurts my heart to hear it, Mr. Decker. I liked your wife. She was very compassionate. She was very kind to me."

"You can call me Aaron."

It was Chip who nodded at this as he tromped down the steps and, with his head down, cut a straight path toward the work shed and the ATV. The little dog barked once at his approach and then fell silent when Chip uttered a barrage of curses at it.

"I apologize for showing up out of the blue like this," I said. "I hope it's not an inconvenience. Can we talk for a few minutes?"

"House is a mess," she said, stepping outside. "But sure, we can sit out here."

There was a picnic table beside a shallow rock garden, and Rita headed toward it now, digging a pack of cigarettes from the breast pocket of her flannel shirt. Her jeans, I noted, were tight-fitting, the rear pockets studded with rhinestones. They looked like cheap imitations of some expensive brand.

I joined her at the picnic table. She offered me a smoke and I took it.

"I spoke with Hercel Lovering," I told her. "Chief of police?"

"I know who he is. Went to school with his brother. Believe it or not, those Lovering boys used to be heartthrobs around here." She waggled her eyebrows, but her eyes were dead.

"He says your daughter's killer died of a heroin overdose back in January," I said.

"Das Hillyard." It seemed to pain her to speak his name. I understood her pain. "It's good he's gone, I guess. He was a monster, you know. Did some nasty things to some boys in Preston a while back. Spent some time in prison for it. I guess maybe they should've kept him there." She flicked ash from her cigarette. "They found her sweatshirt in his house, you know."

"Yes, I've heard that."

"Herce says Das Hillyard most likely approached her, maybe offered her a ride that night. Came up on her like that." Her gaze sharpened and she stared me dead in the eyes. "I don't necessarily know if that part's true. I don't like to think that's the way it happened. Holly was too smart to go off with someone… well, with someone like Hillyard."

"Your daughter knew about Hillyard's… uh, what he'd done?"

"You mean to those boys over in Preston? Wasn't no secret around here. It's just…"

"What?" I said.

"If he killed himself by shooting junk up his arm, well, I guess that's just fine and dandy — world's a better place with one less murderer and child molester in it, you ask me — but I'll tell you, Mr. Decker, I would have liked to hear him say it."

"A confession?"

"An apology."

I nodded, though I personally didn't believe someone who possessed the black wherewithal to strangle a teenage girl to death was much inclined to apologize for anything.

"I would've liked to hear him say what he'd done to her and that he was sorry," she went on, her whole body trembling now. There was a vacuous, absent look in her eyes, as if she were on valium, or like someone had siphoned some vital fluid from her veins. "He should have at least given me that."

I understood that burning hate, Allison. That missed opportunity. Your killer, Robert Vols, had taken his own life moments after taking yours. He'd left me unanchored and incapable of finding my footing in this world without you. He'd left me powerless to make sense of his senselessness, because he had taken his final, mad, fleeting thoughts with him to hell. Here was a mother who was tormented by that same bitter loss without the inviolability of resolution.

"But oh well," she said, swiping at the moisture leaking from her eyes with the heels of both hands. Something like a dull smile flashed across her face, quick as lightning. I convinced myself I'd just caught a glimpse of the woman she'd once been, before her daughter had been stolen from her. "At least I know the monster is dead. That's the only thing that gives me any peace."

I opened my mouth then closed it again. Fortunately, other-Aaron stepped in and said, "Did my wife explain to you why she was out here investigating your daughter's murder?"

"She was nice, your wife." That faraway look in her eyes...

I nodded, waited for her to continue, but she didn't. I asked the question again: "Did she explain why she came out here? Why she talked with you about Holly?"

"What do you mean? She was a reporter. I talked to a lot of reporters after she... after it happened. But your wife, she was different. She was compassionate. She listened to me. She wanted to see Holly's room so I took her up there, showed her around. I gave her one of Holly's school pictures."

"I know," I told her. "She kept it. I have it with me now."

Rita nodded.

"What about one of Holly's yearbooks? Did you let Allison borrow one?"

Rita didn't respond. Her eyes were distant again, lost in the fog of memory.

"Rita, did my wife happen to mention to you the possibility that whoever killed Holly may have killed other girls?"

The fog fled from her eyes. She stared at me, the cigarette trembling in one upraised hand. "What do you mean? That Das Hillyard killed other girls?"

"I don't believe it was Hillyard who killed your daughter."

She shook her head, frowning. A vertical crease appeared between her faint eyebrows. "What's *that* mean?"

It was Hercel Lovering's voice in my head now, warning me to leave well enough alone. But if you were right, Allison — if you were right and Lovering was wrong — then I couldn't just walk away from it, could I? Not after all you'd done. And not after what had happened to those girls.

"I think my wife came out here because she thought your daughter had been... had been hurt by a man who had done this to other girls in the past. She had been researching other murders, girls who died in similar circumstances."

"You're telling me Das Hillyard didn't do it? He didn't do... that... to my Holly? Someone... you're telling me... *someone else*..."

"It seems that way to me," I said.

She hung her head as a sob ratcheted up her throat. The sound startled me, shook me. I kept my eyes on the lengthening ash of her cigarette until a shadow fell across the picnic table. Looking over my shoulder, I saw Chip standing there, his eyes two dull oil spots above the nest of his beard. He looked agitated and uncertain.

"What's going on?" he said.

"I'm sorry," I said. I went to get up from the table, but Rita clapped a hand over one of mine, halting me in mid-rise.

"You sit back down," she said, her lower lip quivering. Her cheeks were streaked with tears, but her eyes were hard and sober now. "You don't just say something like this then get up and leave, mister."

"What's going on, Rita?" Chip said. Behind him, the dog began barking again.

"He don't think Das Hillyard killed my Holly," she said.

"My wife came out here because she identified a similarity in the way Holly was killed to another girl three years earlier, and maybe a handful of others, too," I said. "She'd been... she'd been tracking these murders, studying them. If you knew my wife, you'd know she wouldn't make a mistake, that she was diligent and dedicated and had been looking into these things for years..."

My voice broke. I saw my own grief reflected in Rita's face, and felt everything come loose inside me in an instant. I struggled to keep it together, but my hands began trembling on the tabletop. To my surprise, Rita reached out and squeezed one.

"Go on," she urged me.

I took a breath then said, "Hillyard couldn't have killed the other girls because he'd been in jail since 2005 for what he did to those boys in Preston. And I don't think he just killed Holly, because there were similarities between how Holly was killed and at least one other girl, back in 2016, when Hillyard would have been in prison. So, either my wife was completely wrong about this — which means that *I'm* completely wrong about this — or Hillyard didn't kill any of them, including your daughter."

"Her sweatshirt," Rita began.

"Maybe there's another explanation for how Hillyard got it," I said. "I don't know. I really don't. I don't know what to say. I'm sorry. I'm sorry."

I shouldn't have come here. This was wrong. I felt like I was slicing open fresh wounds that had scarcely begun to heal. What you had accomplished with tact and decorum and great tenderness, Allison, I had bulldozed and razed to the ground.

Rita's hand slipped off mine. To Chip, she said, "Go inside and get us a couple of beers, will you?"

Chip nodded then slunk away into the house. The dog stopped barking as soon as Chip disappeared through the sliding glass door.

"You've got me thinking of a man now," Rita said. She examined the filter of her cigarette with something like melancholy before pitching it into the dirt and digging a fresh one from the pack. "A man down at the bottom of the hill one night."

"What man?"

"Couple nights before... before it happened, Holly goes out to drag the trash down to the curb at the bottom of the hill. It's dark. When she comes back inside, she's all nervous and shaking and, like, pretty freaked out. She says there was a man across the street, watching her. She said she didn't see him until he called her name. Scared the tar out of her."

I glanced over my shoulder and peered down the slope of the hillside, but from this vantage I couldn't see the road. Only trees. "Who was he?"

"She didn't know."

"She didn't recognize him?"

"She didn't see him clearly; it was too dark. He was just there, watching her from across the street. Almost like he was trying to hide from her. That's how she said it."

"Why hide if you're going to call out her name?"

"I don't know."

"Did you tell this to the police?"

"Not that night, but after… after what happened, yeah, I told Hercel myself. I had forgotten about it at first, but I eventually remembered. I told him in case it was all connected, you know?"

"What'd he say?"

"Herce wanted a description, but I couldn't give any. He came out and checked around the woods on the other side of the street — about where the guy would have been standing — but he found nothing. Then later, after they found Holly's sweatshirt in that bastard's house, Herce said it was Hillyard, that he'd probably been watching…" Her voice hitched. "That he'd probably been watching her for days." Rita's gaze leveled on me. "But if it wasn't Hillyard — if that's what you're telling me — then who was it standing out there, calling to my girl?"

"I don't know."

"Because whoever it was, he had to know her, right? To call her by her name like that?"

"I guess so."

She lowered her voice, as if confiding a secret. "I went out there that night. Holly was so frightened. I went across the street to look around. I didn't see nobody. There's woods there, and I went partway into 'em, but then I started spooking myself. I kept thinking someone was in them woods with me, moving around me and watching me. I kept thinking someone would come out from the trees and grab me. Or just stand there, maybe call *my* name. I don't know. Anyway,

I hurried on back into the house and bolted the door. And that was that."

Chip returned with two Buds, the caps already off. He set them down on the picnic table without uttering a word, then meandered back toward the work shed. When the dog started yapping, he told it to shut the fuck up or he'd string it up a tree.

For the next few minutes, Rita and I drank our beers in relative silence. She was working her way through her pack of cigarettes, too, and offered me one again. I accepted, grateful, and confessed to her that I had been smoking for quite some time behind your back, Allison. Maybe you knew and never said anything, but I thought I did a pretty good job keeping it from you.

"I guess I don't have to hide it anymore," I said, inhaling.

"The secrets we keep," she said, grinning sadly at me now. "Am I right?"

I couldn't help it — I coughed up a laugh. Rita's grin transformed into an actual smile. She reminded me of her daughter in that instant. Or of her daughter's photograph, anyway.

— *You'll be dreaming of those crime-scene photos for a long time*, other-Aaron, ever the pragmatist, spoke up in my head. *Those images of Gabrielle's body face-down in the mud beneath that bridge? Her fingers and toes missing, that solitary eye socket as blank as a keyhole. The marks on her wrist. Let's not forget about those photos.*

Other-Aaron was right, of course: There would be no forgetting those images.

"Once she was gone, it was like a part of me broke off and floated away," Rita said. She was staring off into the trees. Small brown birds leapt from tree branch to tree branch, peeping in the cool spring air. "Sometimes I still feel her presence. That's why I don't go into her room very much; it's too painful. It's like sometimes she's still here. Do you ever feel that way about your wife?"

"All the time," I said.

"And then, other times, I feel like that broken piece of me is still hanging around, too — a part of me out there, not bound by our reality, wandering in and out of time, lost, doomed like a ghost to go through the motions. It's like there are two of me, walking along on different paths now, on different timelines. My hope is that this other version of me can slip back to a time where Holly is still alive. Is that crazy?"

"No."

"In a way, that makes me a ghost, too."

Me too, I thought.

"So, what happens now?" Rita asked after she'd finished her beer. I stared at her as the wind pulled fine threads of smoke from the tips of our cigarettes.

"Rita, did you lend my wife one of your daughter's yearbooks?"

"I don't remember doing that."

"Is it possible?"

"Anything's possible. My mind was a mess back then." She smiled weakly. "Still is."

"Would you mind if I took a look at the yearbooks your daughter had?"

"I guess. How come?"

"Allison had a theory that the killer might have been in one of Holly's yearbooks."

"In her *yearbook*? Like, someone she'd gone to school with? A classmate?"

Or a teacher, I thought, but did not say.

"That seems impossible to me," Rita continued.

"Do any of her yearbooks have a green deer on the cover?"

Distantly, Rita shook her head. "I don't know, Mr. Decker. I don't know. But I can take you up to her room and you could look for yourself."

"Is that okay with you?"

Her mouth went firm. She said, "You a cop?"

"No."

"A reporter?"

"No. I translate Japanese novels into English."

"Yeah? That's a thing?"

"That's a thing."

"So then what are you looking into all this for?" She said it as if we were working through a crossword puzzle together.

"I want to finish what my wife started," I told her.

2

We stepped into the house, but did not go farther than the foyer at first. There was a resistance here — not from Rita, but from the house itself, as if to instill in me the sense that I was an interloper, a trespasser. Someone who did not belong here. There was a wall cluttered with family photos, old wedding pictures with sepia tints, many photographs of a teenage girl whose face exuded an indescribable iridescence. The place smelled unclean, but it wasn't as messy as Rita Renfrow had led me to believe. Rather, it was the smell of neglect in the wake of tragedy — a musty, forgotten odor that made me think of old warehouses and abandoned buildings.

I followed her up a creaky stairwell to the second floor, cattail-pattern wallpaper on the walls, a teal carpet with stains peppered indiscriminately across its threadbare surface. From the corner of my eye, I saw a tabby bullet along the upstairs hallway, zoetrope-like behind the staves of the banister as we climbed the stairs.

"I keep dreaming that there's someone in the house," Rita said as she labored up the stairs. The ascent seemed to take a lot out of her, both spiritually and physically. "A man. I get up and come down the hall here. I look in Holly's bedroom. Sometimes he's standing in there, a dark shape against the windows. Other times I catch him, like, fleeing down the stairs and going outside. He's like a ghost but, like, you could touch him and feel him if you just reach out. I never touch him, though. I'm never quick enough. Once, I followed him out into the front yard and I was halfway down the hill before I realized I was sleepwalking or something and that there was no one there. And now I'm wondering if it's the guy, you know? The one across the street who called her name? If it wasn't Das Hillyard, then who was it?"

— *It was Gas Head*, said other-Aaron. I remembered my half-dream from the night before in the motel, a half-dream that was also a memory. You had muttered that strange phrase in your sleep: *Gas Head will make you dead.* That's where it had come from, but I still didn't know what it meant.

Holly's was the last bedroom at the top of the stairs. A pair of windows looked down the slope of the wooded hillside and to the road below. The windows were open, the sheer curtains billowing like ballgowns. It was, for all I could determine, the bedroom of a typical teenage girl. Posters filled the walls, and there was a small desk and vanity with a gaming console on it. A large TV sat on a bureau and faced the bed, which was packaged in a bedspread with what looked like embroidered marijuana leaves on it. The carpet was brown shag, and it was littered with clothes, grubby with dried gunk, pockets of it filled with small colored beads, shards of broken pencils, a single glittering earring. The closet door stood open, and I could make out a wall of junk in there as well, everything held together by sheer force of will.

"When your kid dies, you find that you're not afraid of nothing no more," Rita said. She did not enter the room.

I stepped inside Holly's bedroom, looked around. A traitor, a grave-robber. The reek of old cigarettes caused a momentary pang of grief to rise through the center of my body. How many times had I snuck off to smoke so you wouldn't smell it, Allison? That one pitiful vice now, in the wake of your death, felt like a betrayal tantamount to infidelity. And yet I was still doing it.

"The cops searched her computer and all her social media, back when they were still looking for the guy," Rita said from the doorway. "They looked through her phone, too, which they'd found back, well... I mean, she'd left her phone behind and they were able to search it, even though it was broken. They found it on the bridge. I really don't know how all that technology works." Her voice snagged. "I was surprised to learn she'd been applying to colleges. Imagine that? Hadn't said anything to me. Not that I got the money to send her anywhere."

"Was she a good student?"

"Not good enough for a scholarship."

"Neither was I," I said, which was a lie.

Still in the doorway, Rita said, "See those? On the mirror?"

"These?" I pointed at the collection of photographs that were glued to the frame of the vanity.

"Look at her," Rita said, her voice sounding farther away than it actually was. "She was just a baby, really. That's all. Seventeen ain't no age to die."

Holly Renfrow was mostly with friends in the photos — a gaggle of bright, shiny girls and boys, peace signs and sexy poses, kisses for the camera, Halloween costumes, funky hairdos and overdone eyeshadow, the mangy mutt from the yard, a teenage boy kissing the side of another girl's face, someone's rust-eaten blue Firebird, roasting marshmallows before a campfire, cigarettes in their mouths.

"I try so hard not to think about what happened to her," Rita said. "Those last moments of her life. But there it is, whenever I shut my eyes. These images just sort of jump into my head and I can't get rid of them. Cops say she wasn't… you know… raped or nothing. So I guess there's that." She turned away from me and stared off down the hallway. "That other girl," she said. "How'd she die?"

I didn't want to say it, but I felt I had an obligation, now that I was here dissecting this woman's misery. "She'd been strangled."

"Is that how you made the connection between her and Holly?"

"What do you mean?"

"That they were both strangled."

I looked up at Rita's reflection in the vanity mirror. "Chief Lovering said Holly had drowned."

"Technically, yeah, I guess so," Rita said. "Holly was still alive when she went into the river. Maybe not conscious, but alive. She'd breathed water into her lungs. That's what the medical examiner's report said. But it also said that whoever had done that to her, there was evidence that she'd been… I mean, that someone had been… been choking her before she fell in the river… that her throat showed, uh, signs of… uh, signs that she…"

I straightened my back and turned around. Stared at her. She was lost again, her eyes unfocused and bleary, wandering the halls of her memory.

"Rita," I said.

She blinked and her vision refocused on me. "Guess it was a mistake reading that damn thing," she said. "Gives me nightmares." She shivered, then said, "Do you mind shutting the windows? I open them to air the place out every once in a while — she was always smoking up here, and not just cigarettes — but it's starting to get cold."

I went to the windows and peered out. I could see their mailbox down there beside the road, a wooden mallard with rotating propellers for wings. I could see my car parked down there, too, and the patch of dirt across the street where the mysterious figure might have stood and called to Holly a few nights before she was killed. Had he been able to see into her bedroom window from down there? Had he spied on her for nights prior to murdering her?

I shut one window, then the other. Those ghostly curtains went still.

"Thank you," Rita said from the doorway.

"Rita, do you remember seeing a dark-colored sedan in the street or parked nearby? Something like an unmarked police car, with one of those spotlights on the door?"

"I don't remember. I don't know if I would have noticed."

"Did Holly say if she saw a vehicle that night?"

Rita shook her head. She was gnawing on a thumbnail, a medicated look in her eyes.

"Okay," I said. "I'm sorry."

"Her yearbooks are on the bottom shelf," Rita said. She motioned toward a rank of bookshelves that stood beside the vanity. Paperback novels and hardback Harry Potter cluttered the top shelves while the bottom held the slender volumes of yearbooks, textbooks, magazines, and random frills of loose-leaf paper.

I crouched down to examine the spines of the books on the bottom shelf. Somewhere in the house, the chirping of a cell phone drew Rita from the doorway; she said nothing as she slipped back down the stairs and disappeared.

Holly had just started her senior year when she was murdered, and had amassed three yearbooks from Jefferson High School. I slid all three volumes from the shelf and saw right away that none of them sported a green deer on the cover. Jefferson High School's mascot was a cougar, its roaring muzzle rimmed in gold. There would be no confusing it. I opened one of the yearbooks and saw the countless signatures from Holly's friends and classmates, the bubble-hearted sentiments and goofy drawings, the *see you next year*s.

I closed the book and slid them all back onto the shelf when, at my back, the dog barked — two sharp reports that sounded like a starter's pistol. I turned around to see the dog from the yard now standing in the center of the room, barking not at me but at the open closet door. Something moved inside the closet — the transference of a figure from one side to the other.

The closet light blinked on. There was no one standing in the closet, but in the new light, I could see Holly's clothes swaying as if disturbed by some presence.

I stood up and approached the closet. The little dog took a tentative step backward, not because of my approach, but as if it sensed something it did not like emanating from that open closet door. I felt a twinge of apprehension, too. I swept aside the clothes that had been swaying when the light had come on, bracing myself for whatever tragic and impossible thing that might be crouching behind them —

(I keep dreaming that there's someone in the house)

— but of course there was nothing there. Just the wall.

I looked around at the rest of the clothes, the board games and puzzle boxes stacked on the top shelf, the jumble of sneakers and a pair of ice skates on the floor, the stuffed animals with droopy heads wedged into one corner. There was an open cardboard box on the floor of the closet, a pale pink sweatshirt folded inside it. It hooked my attention because of the bright red label on one of the box's flaps that read PROPERTY OF FURNACE WV POLICE DEPARTMENT. I knelt down and lifted the sweatshirt out of the box. SAINT FRANCIS YOUTH LEAGUE was printed in blocky red letters across the front of the sweatshirt.

At my back, the dog whined then ran out of the bedroom.

Overhead, the closet light flickered.

I brought the sweatshirt to my face, inhaled its scent. Like the rest of the room, it smelled vaguely of cigarettes.

Rita spoke up from the doorway, startling me. "Saint Francis Youth League. It's a local youth group. They do cookouts and camping trips in the summer, help the elderly in the winter. That sort of thing."

"This was the sweatshirt Hillyard had in his house?"

Her face went grim. She nodded, her eyes growing distant again.

I folded the sweatshirt and placed it back into the box.

"Did you find what you were looking for?" She looked at the bookshelf while she hugged herself.

"I don't think so," I said. "I'm sorry to have wasted your time."

Rita nodded. She covered her mouth with one hand as if she might be sick.

Before leaving, I asked if she still had a copy of the medical examiner's report.

"I burned it," she said. "Right out there in the fire pit. Made me sick to keep it in the house. It was a mistake, Mr. Decker, reading that horrible thing. A huge mistake."

3

We stepped back outside. Rita shivered as a gust of wind wove through the hillside, rattling the leaves in the trees.

"It's cold out here," she said. "Doesn't really warm up around here until late summer. And even then, we've only got a few good weeks of real heat." She smiled at me, a smile that was soft and not without grace. It hurt my heart to witness it. "Anyway, take care," she said, and headed back into the house.

I turned my face skyward. It was as if the mention of how chilly it was had caused an icy bolt to tremor through my body. Overhead, the sun poked a spear of white light through the otherwise oppressive clouds. Shivering, I headed back across the yard toward the slope of the hillside that led down to the street. Inside the work shed, Chip clanged around and muttered to himself. He appeared in the doorway as a broad-shouldered silhouette, rubbing the nape of his neck with one big hand.

The sensation that I'd overlooked something vital rose up in me then — a breathy, other-Aaron whisper that burned in my right ear and stirred the hairs on my neck to attention. I was still thinking about the car that had stopped alongside Denise Lenchantin on the night Holly was murdered. Days earlier, a man had been out here calling out to Holly. Had the same car been parked somewhere along this road? Had someone else seen a similar vehicle in the vicinity the night Holly was killed?

Chip noticed me, nodded in my direction. I raised a hand in return, then wound my way back down the hillside to where my car was parked in the road.

4

Trina Garton had been Holly's best friend, and she had been with her at the Exxon arcade the night of Holly's murder, along with a local kid named Ian. Trina and Holly had had an argument over a boy, which was the reason Holly had left on foot that night. Trina worked at the Burger Barn, a fast-food joint where all the employees wore paper hats and red suspenders. I got all this information from your notes, Allison. It seemed you had spoken with the girl on your visit out here last fall.

Trina was seventeen, pretty, waifish. Her hair was long and chestnut-colored, limp beneath her paper hat. She was still visibly shaken over what had happened to her best friend as we sat talking in one of the booths inside the Burger Barn.

"Did she ever mention someone hanging around her house, maybe in the days before she was killed?" I asked the girl.

Trina had been gazing out the window, where a pair of crows pecked at some bloody gruel on the pavement. She looked at me now. "How'd you know about that?"

"Her mother told me. Holly mentioned something about it to you, too?"

"Holly didn't keep no secrets from me. She said a man had been watching her. A man who knew her name. She saw him outside her house one night, but she started to think he was always hanging around, even if she couldn't see him."

"Why would she think that?"

"Because she could smell him."

"Smell him? What's that mean?"

"When she saw him across the street, she said she could smell him, a smell like a fire. Like something burning. And then she'd smell it again somewhere else, and wonder if he was lurking around. Only…" Her voice trailed off.

"Only what?"

"Only she started thinking maybe it wasn't a man at all."

"What does that mean?"

Trina turned away from me, directing her gaze on the crows in the parking lot again. "I don't know," she said, her voice barely a whisper.

"What about a car? Like an unmarked police car with a light on the door? You know the kind I'm talking about?"

She shrugged, wouldn't look me in the eye.

"Did you ever notice a car like that driving around?"

"I don't know."

"Were you driving that night?"

"The night Holly was killed? Yeah."

"I know you guys got into an argument and that's why Holly left."

Trina seemed to become smaller before my eyes, and I realized this had not been the thing to say to this girl. It sounded too accusatory.

"Are there any schools around here that have a deer as a mascot?" I asked, changing the subject.

"What?" She looked at me.

"A deer," I said. "You know — as a mascot?"

She raised her narrow shoulders in a shrug before returning her gaze out the window.

"Trina, what happened was not your fault."

She nodded fervently, bouncy little jerks of her head. She did not meet my eyes, but kept her gaze trained on the crows snacking on roadkill in the parking lot.

"Anyway, I'm sorry to bring all this up," I said, sliding out of the booth. "I'm sorry about what happened to your friend."

I went outside, patting down my pockets for my cigarettes. There was one left in the pack. I shook it out, lit it, then thought of you. I pitched it to the ground and crushed it under my shoe. Mentally exhausted, I leaned against the Sube while I listened to a train whistle in the distance. When I looked across the parking lot, I saw Trina crossing the tarmac toward me. She was hugging herself with her thin arms, much like Rita Renfrow had done while standing in the doorway of her daughter's bedroom. Her dark hair billowed out behind her.

"That car," she said, coming up to me but still not meeting my gaze. "I think I saw it that night."

"Yeah?"

"After Holly left, me and Ian went looking for a place to… you know… to park?"

"Ian's the guy who was with you two that night, right? He's your boyfriend?"

"Yeah. I mean, we're kinda dating. We went to the overlook that night. It's this place where we sometimes go? There's a lot of trees and you can't really see it from the road, so kids sometimes go there? So we went, but there was a car there, and I remember thinking it was a cop. Because of what you said."

"The spotlight on the car door?"

"Yeah."

"Do you remember anything else about the car?"

"It was brown, a brown car. That's all I remember."

"Was someone in the car?"

"I don't know."

"Did you happen to see the license plate?" I knew it was a long shot.

"No. We pulled in then drove back out. Ian had some, you know, some pot? We didn't want to get stopped by any cops."

"Did you tell this to the police?"

"About the pot?"

"About the car."

"They never asked about it. Should I have?"

"It's okay."

She nodded. She was staring at her sneakers. Across the parking lot, the crows shrieked and, startled by something, took to the air.

"How do I get to this overlook place?" I asked.

5

There was a narrow strip of asphalt that cut through the woods, and it reminded me of the night you and I drove out to Manresa and searched for headlight ghosts. It concluded in a paved parking area at the cusp of a high ridge. Trash was strewn about the underbrush — empty beer bottles and discarded packets of cigarettes, mostly. Through the trees, I could see the openness of the sky, and knew that this ridge overlooked the river. I got out of the car and stood there for a moment, not moving, as if to harness something pertinent and illuminating from the atmosphere. I heard birds chirping and the wind murmuring through the trees. I heard, too, Rita Renfrow's voice, speaking up in the center of my brain: *When your kid dies, you find that you're not afraid of nothing no more.*

If this was where Trina Garton saw the brown sedan that night, was this also the spot where Holly had been taken to by her murderer? It was certainly secluded enough from the main road.

Rita Renfrow's voice trickled in again: *Holly was still alive when she went into the river. Maybe not conscious, but alive. She'd breathed water into her lungs. That's what the medical examiner's report said.*

I crept through the trees, veering away from a used condom that looked like a large drip of snot dangling from a tree branch. The ground was not flat, but rather sloped at a sharp angle pitched down toward the edge of the ridge. As I drew closer to the edge, I used nearby tree branches as handholds. Bits of gravel and sand slid out from beneath my shoes and bustled in compact little avalanches down the slope.

Then, suddenly, the ground fell away beneath my feet. Tree limbs were stripped from my hands, slicing my palms, as I fell backward onto my ass and slid through the underbrush toward the edge of the cliff. It rushed up out of nowhere, the weedy ledge suddenly right there, illusory and precarious. At the last minute, my senses re-engaged and I managed to dig the heels of my shoes into the crumbly brown earth while scrabbling at the ground with my hands, halting my progress. Rocks and debris cascaded over the edge of the cliff; I watched them tumble down into infinity, my heart hammering against my chest, my breath coming in shaky gasps.

One of my legs swung out over the edge of the cliff. I felt gravity's ravenous tug on me and grappled for anything, scraping at the earth with my fingers. I snagged a sizable root that arched from the loose soil and pulled myself up.

I was more cautious now, seeing how easily the loose ground had surrendered beneath me. Far below, the Potomac roiled and frothed. Men fished from the opposite shore, tiny colored splotches from such a distance. Against the horizon, I could make out the stone bridge spanning the river.

I drew myself into a seated position and tried to catch my breath.

— *If Holly's killer had approached her on the bridge then brought her to this spot to murder her, maybe the arrival of Trina and Ian had spooked him before he could finish the job.* It was other-Aaron, reasoning his way through it all. *Perhaps he had bound her hands and attempted to strangle her, only to see Trina's headlights coming through the trees. Seeing an opportunity, perhaps Holly had gotten away. Perhaps she'd run in a blind panic and had gone over the cliff herself.*

It would explain why Holly hadn't been strangled like Gabby had.

I peered over the edge and looked down, careful to keep a sturdy grip on a nearby tree limb to prevent me from falling over the side. What I saw was a partially submerged deadfall directly below, its black and shiny branches rising up out of the tide and clawing at the air. Perhaps the very same deadfall that had snared Holly's body as the river's current tried to wash her out into the bay.

CHAPTER TEN

1

I pulled the Sube into the parking lot of the Exxon station where Holly had last been seen alive. The place was larger than a typical gas station, and I could make out the neon ARCADE sign in one smoky black window. There were a few men in hunting attire loading up their trucks with coolers and fishing gear in the parking lot. I got out of the car and went inside.

The store was empty. "Come Go With Me" by the Del-Vikings played on tinny speakers, but otherwise the place was dead quiet, except for a steamy hiss emanating from a coffee station against one wall. I headed down an aisle toward the rear of the store, where, in an adjoining room, about a half-dozen arcade consoles stood against the wall like suspects in a lineup. There were a couple of Formica tables in here, too, and a trashcan painted to look like R2-D2. The air back here smelled of overheated electronic equipment. I looked up and saw a video camera tucked into one corner, where the wood-paneled wall met the acoustical ceiling tiles. I didn't enter the room, merely observed it from the doorway, and tried to imagine Holly Renfrow, a girl I did not know, in this place while her own cosmic clock counted down the seconds until her death. I leaned against the doorframe. There was no door on the frame, and the frame itself was covered in graffiti — mostly names or initials or crude little slogans written in different colored marker or carved into the wood itself. How many generations had marched through here and left their initials on this doorframe?

One set of initials caught my attention over all the others, and not simply because it was directly in my line of sight. Printed with a stark black Sharpie were the initials ALD. Allison Leigh Decker.

This wasn't you, of course. They could have been anyone's initials. And while you had come out here, spent some time here, most likely even visited this place during your investigation, I found it highly implausible that you would pause in your research to print those three letters among all the others right here on this doorframe, exactly where I happened to be standing. The idea was ludicrous.

Nonetheless, I took a pen from my coat pocket and printed ALD — Aaron Lee Decker — directly beside yours. When I finished, I found that my hand was shaking and my heart was galloping in my chest. A clammy, amphibious sweat sprung from my pores.

A shift, then — not so much in the atmosphere, but in my immediate line of sight, where a narrow channel had appeared and was yawning straight ahead of me, the colors of that world duller than the surrounding world. I could still see the arcade, the tinted windows, the R2-D2 trashcan, but it was like peering through the crack of a partially open door, the interior slightly distorted and off-color. I adjusted my weight from one foot to the other to alter my perception, and with it the channel slewed from view. I shifted back and it returned — a passage carved through the center of this world, or so it appeared, my flesh tingling, the Del-Vikings growing fainter and fainter on the speakers until the music was nothing more than a distant pulse of static...

"The hell you doing?"

I nearly jumped out of my socks at the sound of the man's voice. I whirled around to find a towering, lanky fellow sporting an eye-patch gazing down at me with his solitary peeper. The son of a bitch looked at least seven feet tall. He wore a nametag that said GARY.

"I'm sorry," I said, shoving the pen back in my pocket as quickly as possible. "I didn't mean to…" I motioned at the doorframe. "I thought this was, like, a thing."

Gary said nothing, only cast a red-hot laser beam at me from his one remaining eye. The patch he wore over the missing eye looked like it was made from an old catcher's mitt, which gave it an eerie, flesh-like quality.

"I'll just grab a pack of smokes," I said. It was the first thing that came to mind.

"Behind the counter." He pivoted and moved toward the counter at the front of the store. His gait was uncannily like the swinging-armed stride of Bigfoot in those old blurry filmstrips.

Before following him, I glanced back in the direction of the arcade, desperate to glimpse that odd rip in the fabric of the universe I thought I'd seen a moment ago. But there was nothing there. Or if there was, I was no longer permitted to view it.

"That security camera in the back room," I said, coming up to the counter. "Is that the only one in the store?"

Without looking up from scanning my smokes, Gary pointed over my head toward the front door. I turned and saw two additional security cameras bolted to the metal doorframe, one facing the counter and one pointing out into the parking lot.

"I'm working with a reporter who's investigating the murder of that teenage girl who was killed out here last fall," I said. "I understand there was some surveillance footage from the night she was here? The night she died?"

He made a sound that might have been an acknowledgement or might have been him clearing phlegm from his esophagus.

"Do you think I'd be able to view the footage?"

He slid my smokes across the counter then quoted me the amount owed. I dug out my wallet and paid the guy in cash.

"You police?" he asked.

"No, sir."

"What you interested for?"

"Like I said, I'm working with a reporter who was looking into it."

"Murder's been solved," he said as he counted out my change. "Nothing to investigate."

"Yeah, so I've heard. I'd still like to look at that footage, though, if you'll let me."

He handed me back my change in silence.

"You don't recall seeing a brown sedan with a spotlight on the driver's door that night, do you?" I asked him. "Maybe looked like an unmarked police car?"

"Hundred dollars," he said.

"What?"

"Hundred dollars. To look at the tape."

"Seriously?"

He hoisted one pointy shoulder in a lazy shrug then wended down the length of the counter toward a closed door marked PRIVATE.

"Okay, wait," I called after him. "Fine. A hundred bucks. You got an ATM?"

His impossibly long arm rose up over a tall display of scratch-offs. He pointed toward the ATM, which was wedged between a rack of straw sombreros and the coffee station. I went to it, fed it my ATM card, then groaned at the ridiculous five-dollar service fee.

When I returned to the counter, the fellow had one finger working around beneath his eye-patch while his other hand was extended to receive the money. I laid the five twenties in his palm. To my surprise, he produced a queer little change purse from his hip pocket, folded the bills into it, then tucked it away again.

"A'ight," he grunted, and beckoned me to follow him with a flap of his long arm.

We went into the room marked PRIVATE. It was a cramped, narrow little chamber, with shelves of electronic equipment, including a flat-screen television monitor on one cinderblock wall. There were some cleaning supplies back here and a couple of folding chairs propped up in one corner. A poster of Miley Cyrus as Hannah Montana stared out at me from the wall above the chairs, unsettling in its out-of-placeness. The whole room smelled like a toilet had overflowed in here.

Gary went to the shelf and rummaged around some of the items. "Burned a disc for the police and made a copy for myself, in case some magazine wants to pay big bucks for it," he said, producing a rewritable DVD in a white paper sleeve. "You ain't the only one come looking to watch it, either."

"Who else came to watch it?"

"Pretty gal. Newspaper reporter."

"When was this?"

"Couple days after they found the girl's body down at the river."

"Allison," I said.

"Don't recall a name."

"How much did you charge her?"

"Nothing." He sneered at me, his one eye blazing like a lighthouse beaming through night fog. His teeth were irregular little coffee beans. "Like I said, a pretty gal."

He removed the disc from its paper sleeve, bent over, and fed it into the DVD player. The TV came on automatically, a bright blue screen that was quickly replaced by a quadrant of images, each of the four boxes on the screen a different location in or around the store. I recognized the arcade, the main part of the store, the parking lot, and what appeared to be an alleyway behind the store where overgrown trees hugged a large dumpster.

"You get a lot of thefts back there?" I pointed in particular to the image of the dumpster.

"Came across a bobcat one night taking out the trash."

"There was a bobcat taking out the trash?" I offered a meager grin to show I was joking, but he ignored it.

"Made a noise like a garbage disposal before running off into the trees," he said. "Had teeth like bolts. Since then, I check the camera before I go out back at night."

I examined the other three screens. It was nighttime on the video, and the parking lot footage was a patchwork of shadow and light. When the occasional car drove by on the road out front, all I could see were headlights and the barest suggestion of a vehicle. If a brown sedan were to drive by, I probably wouldn't be able to identify it. The footage of the interior of the store showed only Gary standing behind the counter, stacking cartons of cigarettes on an overhead shelf.

It was the footage of the arcade that drew my attention. Two teenage girls sat at one of the tables while a tall boy in basketball shorts played one of the arcade games. The footage had a slightly fish-eyed distortion to it, but I could tell that the girl with blonde hair seated at the table was Holly Renfrow. She possessed the delicate profile that I'd seen in her photographs, undeniable on this security footage. When she turned her head, I saw that her hair had been shaved down to the scalp on the right side. The friend seated opposite her was Trina Garton. They were both smoking cigarettes.

"Do you know any of these kids?" I asked.

"Well, she's the dead one," he said, tapping Holly's image on the screen. "They're all from town. Don't know their names."

"Do you live in Furnace?"

"I got a place up on the hill," he said, which didn't actually tell me anything. He handed me a slender black remote control. "Watch it as many times as you want. I'm going back out."

"Is Das Hillyard on this footage?"

"Sure is," Gary said as he sauntered out of the room.

"What does he look like?" I'd seen the lone photo of him online, along with the news article of his death and subsequent conviction in absentia back in January, but I wasn't sure I'd be able to recognize him on the video.

"Like a goddamn pervert," he said, and closed the door, leaving me alone.

The only light in the room came from the TV, so I tripped over a mop that was leaning against a wall on my way to retrieve one of the folding chairs. I set the chair up in front of the TV and watched.

There was the date stamped in one corner of the screen, a scrolling time-code beside it. By 9:43 pm, it was clear that Holly and Trina were engaged in an argument that was growing more heated by the second. The teenage boy in the basketball shorts — Ian, I assumed — occasionally glanced over his shoulder at them, but for the most part remained entranced by the videogame. A minute later, a man in a fishing vest entered the store. He was tall and slender but with a swollen bulge of belly protruding beneath his tight-fitting thermal shirt. He went down one aisle, absently observed some items there, then turned in the direction of the arcade. There was no audio to go along with the footage, but I could tell just by looking that Holly's and Trina's voices were probably growing in volume as their argument became more heated. Ian turned away from the videogame console at one point and interjected something but neither girl seemed to pay him any attention. It was most likely the girls' argument that had attracted Das Hillyard's attention.

After several seconds, Hillyard turned away from the arcade room and sauntered up to the counter. His features swam into digital focus — pocked, sallow cheeks, narrow little eyes recessed behind squinty folds, hair greased back into a scraggly ponytail. On the video, his age was indeterminable. I was reminded of the photo that had accompanied the news article from January; I got the same loathsome sense just watching him amble around the store on the video. He purchased a container of chewing tobacco and some scratch-offs from Gary then wound his way back toward the front of the store. He paused and cast a final glance back at the arcade room — on the other screen, the girls were standing and arguing now, Holly jabbing an accusing finger at Trina — before exiting into the night. The parking lot footage followed him to a dilapidated, two-tone Ford F-150. He got in and the headlights momentarily washed out the screen. In the store, Gary slipped out from behind the counter, crossed the floor, and stood in the doorway of the arcade where he could be seen talking to the teenagers. Hillyard's pickup backed out of the parking lot and trundled onto the road as Gary returned to the front counter and Holly pitched her cigarette butt onto the floor of the arcade. Trina turned away from Holly, sidling up beside Ian, who flapped his arms, the expression on his face one of futility. Holly turned and headed for the door, but stopped as Ian began talking to her. He seemed upset, civil, placating. This was just a guess, of course, judging by his expression glimpsed through a fish-eye lens. Holly, I could see, was crying. It was a simple teenage spat, nothing more... but knowing the outcome, it struck me as unimaginably tragic. No wonder Trina Garton couldn't look me in the eye as I asked her questions about that night. She would carry the guilt of that night with her for a long time.

Ian followed Holly out into the store, perhaps trying to convince her not to leave. Holly was having none of it. When he reached out to grab her forearm, she slugged him and marched right out into the parking lot. Rubbing his arm, Ian watched her go, then retreated like a wounded puppy back into the arcade, where Trina sat on the tabletop lighting another cigarette. Ian was the boy they'd been fighting over, I suddenly realized. The way Holly had struck him when he'd reached for her arm, coupled with the look in her eyes: It was no wonder Trina's guilt was overflowing.

I leaned closer to the TV screen and watched Holly Renfrow campaign across the parking lot until the darkness swallowed her up. Hillyard had already driven off and there were no lights beyond the parking lot. It was as if Holly had vanished like a ghost into the night. And in a way, she had.

I had been so occupied with what had transpired in the arcade while simultaneously studying Das Hillyard on the store camera that I did not pick up on what was happening in the back alley until my third viewing of the video footage. Moments after Holly had fled the convenience store, a pair of headlamps blinked on in the darkness of the back alley. There was a vehicle parked behind the dumpster and a meshwork of autumn tree limbs, something that had been there all along but hadn't been visible until the headlights came on. I could not discern the make and model of the vehicle in the dark and given the grainy footage of the surveillance video. The headlights shrank incrementally as the vehicle reversed beyond the trees. For a moment, they were blocked completely by the dumpster... but then they reappeared and swerved out of view of the camera completely, heading toward what I estimated to be the main road. A thick cloud of exhaust rolled in front of the camera. A handful of seconds later, those same headlights appeared on the road that ran in front of the gas station parking lot. The vehicle moved more slowly than any of the others that had passed along that stretch of road throughout the night — methodical and plodding, like a predator stalking prey. I could not make out any details of the car as it coasted by, except that it expelled a cloud of dark smoke in its wake. But I didn't need to. I was convinced that it was a brown sedan with a spotlight on the door.

2

One-eyed Gary was changing the filter in one of the coffee makers when I came out of the back room.

"Can I keep this?" I asked, holding up the DVD.

"I'll burn you a copy," Gary said. "For twenty bucks."

"Are you serious?"

"Twenty," he said.

I paid him another twenty bucks, and Gary vanished into the backroom to burn me a copy of the disc. He was grinning smugly when he reappeared, and handed me the DVD in a paper sleeve, which I tucked into the pocket of my peacoat. Before heading back out into the daylight, however, I paused, a thought having just occurred to me. It was your face that swam across the screen of my consciousness, Allison.

"That pretty reporter who showed up here a few days after they found Holly's body in the river," I said. "You got video footage from that day, too?"

One-eyed Gary chewed on the inside of his cheek. Something akin to suspicion danced in his eyes, but it quickly fled as he watched me open my wallet again. "I can probably dig it up for you, sure," he said.

"How much?"

He extended his hand, quoted me a price, and I paid it.

3

There you were, on a grainy bit of surveillance footage, your dark raven hair obscured by a red beret. You spoke with Gary behind the counter, flashed your smile. He was right — you did not need to pay this man any money. It was your charm, your aura, your persuasion that got you in the door. He led you into the room marked PRIVATE and you stayed in there, watching the surveillance footage that I had also just watched. Did you see the same thing in it that I saw, Allison? Those headlights coming alive in the dark like eyes? Or were you already targeting someone specific, someone who was featured in a dead girl's yearbook with a green deer on the cover? If only I could read your mind via the transmission of this video footage, suck your thoughts like a psychic vampire, maybe another piece of the curtain would be swept aside, another section of the puzzle dropped into place. How could I tell? How would I know?

When you exited the room, you went straight to the arcade. The camera in there picked you up, your features distorted by the fish-eye lens. You did not enter the room but merely surveyed it from the doorway. Taking in information just by proximity. You turned to leave, but then paused. You examined the graffiti on the doorframe — the initials wrapped in hearts, the phrases scrawled with marker or engraved by a blade. You headed down an aisle, tugged a marker from a metal arm poking out of the shelf. You opened the package, returned to the doorway, and printed something — your initials — on the frame. Then, realizing that the cameras were watching you, you looked up and stared directly into one. Your face — a face I hadn't seen in months — stared up at me. *You* stared up at me. Here I was, looking into your eyes while you stared back into mine. In that moment, we were together again, gazing into each other's souls.

4

Back in my motel room, I fired up my laptop and fell backward into the past. For each of the six girls, I searched for the names of their high schools and for images of their mascots. Margot

Idelson, the killer's first victim, had attended John Tyler High School in Norfolk, Virginia, up until she was found dead ten miles from her home, her body face-down in a shallow creek, in the fall of 2006. John Tyler's mascot was not a green deer but a bulldog with a spiked collar.

Next, I traveled to 2008, to Bishop, North Carolina, where the body of sixteen-year-old Shelby Davenport was found in a quarry. The Bishop High School mascot was a Viking, but after I conferred with your notes and the articles detailing Davenport's death, I learned that she had been homeschooled and had not attended Bishop High.

I repeated this process for Lauren Chastain of Vineland, New Jersey; for Megan Pollock of Whitehall, Delaware; and for Gabrielle Colson-Howe of Port Tobacco, Maryland. I conducted an image search for each high school's yearbooks with the terms "green" and "deer" included in the search bar. There were no green deer in sight.

— *Maybe there was no yearbook at all,* other-Aaron piped up. *Maybe Denise Lenchantin just had too much to drink that night and was confused. Or maybe she was just trying to impress you. She wanted to seem helpful so she made something up. Besides, how the hell would Allison have concluded that the killer had gone to school with one of his victims? There's nothing in her notes to suggest that.*

That was true, but —

— *But nothing. Lenchantin made it up. You're searching for a ghost.*

I didn't believe that. It didn't seem… *right.*

— *There's something else that isn't right,* said other-Aaron. *Did you notice, or did it slip right by you?*

What?

— *Back at the convenience store? On the videotape?*

Had I missed something?

— *Yes,* said other-Aaron. *Yes, you did.*

"Tell me," I said out loud, and looked up from my laptop, as if expecting other-Aaron to be right there in the room with me, perhaps perched on the edge of the bed. Of course, there was no one perched on the edge of the bed. I was alone in the room. And as if to underscore my loosening grasp on reality, I was suddenly hearing Denise Lenchantin's voice in my head from the night before: *Maybe you've got a split personality, like in the movies. I'm being playful, can you tell?*

Someone knocked on my motel room door, startling me. I closed my laptop, swung off the side of the bed, and peered through the peephole in the door. It was Chip, Rita Renfrow's boyfriend. He was standing out there wearing an army-green nylon jacket and he had his big beefy hands wedged into the pockets of his jeans.

I opened the door and said, "Chip. What are you doing here?"

"I think we need to talk," he said, the words shuttling out of his mouth on a nervous burst of air.

"How'd you know I was here?"

"It's the only motel close to town. I saw your car." He jerked a thumb over his shoulder to where the Sube was parked.

"Right," I said, opening the door wider. "Come in."

He hurried inside but did not seem to relax even after I closed the door.

"Chip, what's the matter? What's wrong?"

"Look," he said. "I need to tell you something. I been thinking about it since you came by the house earlier. I just thought I'd come talk."

"Okay."

"So, yeah," he said, shifting from one foot to the other. He reminded me of a kid about to confess some misdeed to the school principal. "Holly's sweatshirt. The police didn't find it in Das Hillyard's house."

I stared at him, thought I'd misheard him. "What do you mean?"

"Those cops were in and out of Rita's house since this whole thing happened. I was there on one of the days they came by. The cops. They searched Holly's room a couple times after… you know, after they found her. But after Hillyard was found dead, they came and carried some stuff out of Holly's room. They took that sweatshirt with them."

"The pink one," I said, to make sure. "Saint Francis Youth League."

"Right, yeah. That one."

"You're sure about this, Chip?"

"I saw them carry it out of the house."

"Who did, exactly?"

"Hercel."

"Chief Lovering," I said. "He took the sweatshirt from Holly's room? You saw this?"

"Right. I don't think he realized that I saw him, and I didn't think nothing of it until later, when they said they found it in Hillyard's house. I knew that wasn't true, but I figured the guy was a piece of shit, and that he probably *did* kill Holly, so I wasn't gonna say nothing. Cops, they gotta do what they gotta do. Also, it gave Rita some closure, you know? She wanted them to catch the guy who did it so I figured no harm, no foul."

I was nodding along with his story, trying to appear cool and collected, but inside, my body was boiling over with a heat that felt like molten lava. If I opened my mouth, a jet of steam might burst out.

"When you came around the house saying that Hillyard might not have done it and that the real guy might still be out there somewhere, well, I don't know, man. I guess I thought I should tell you what I saw."

"You're positive about this, Chip?"

"Swear to God, man."

And that was when I realized what other-Aaron had just been hinting at regarding the video footage: Holly Renfrow had not been wearing that pink sweatshirt in the surveillance video. She had been dressed all in black on the night she had been murdered.

"Jesus Christ," I said, and ran a shaky hand through my hair.

"Look, Mr. Decker, I don't wanna get nobody in trouble. I just thought you should know."

"I'm glad you told me," I said.

"And I didn't say nothing to Rita. I don't think she'd take it too well. You get me?"

"I get you."

"I'm saying don't say anything to her."

"Right," I said. "I understand."

"And another thing," he said, and cleared his throat. "You came and told Rita that Holly's killer's still out there. You stirred that all up after she thought Hillyard had done it and that the case had been closed. Well, lemme just say you better find the guy who really did it and make this thing right for her again. Because now she's in hell all over again."

My throat felt tight. It was all I could do to eke out the word, "Okay."

Chip wrung his hands together then went to the door. "You never saw me," he said. "I was never here."

"You're a ghost," I told him.

He slipped out of the motel room and into the waning daylight.

5

The Furnace Police Department was housed in a historic brick building that looked like it had once been an armory during the Civil War. There were wrought-iron bars on the windows and the brickwork appeared to have sustained a barrage of small-caliber rounds at some point in its long history. It sat downhill from a quaint stone church, the land between the two buildings studded with ancient tombstones and flowering dogwood trees.

I pulled up outside the police station to find Chief Lovering standing on the cemetery grounds, hands on his hips, scrutinizing a section of the stationhouse roof that appeared to be sinking. He turned in my direction as I pulled into a spot beside a police cruiser and got out of the car.

"Is that Aaron Decker? Mr. Decker, you're becoming a permanent fixture around here," Lovering said as I approached.

"I think you made a very big mistake," I responded, moving toward him down an aisle of tombstones.

Hercel Lovering did not seem perturbed in the least by my statement. His hands still planted on his hips, he kept his gaze leveled on me, his face expressionless. He said nothing.

"I know you took Holly's sweatshirt from her bedroom," I said. "It was never in Hillyard's house."

"Is that right," he said. It was not a question.

"Rita's boyfriend saw you take it from the house."

"Charles Zacks doesn't know his ass from a hole in the ground."

"I also reviewed the security footage from the Exxon station from the night Holly was killed. She wasn't wearing the sweatshirt. She's dressed all in black. My guess is she probably stopped wearing pink right around the same time she stopped playing with dolls."

Hercel Lovering took an easy step in my direction. For now, his hands were content to remain on his wide hips. "Mr. Decker, I've been very patient with you, feeling bad as I do about what happened to your wife. But I've only got so much patience to go around, you understand?"

"Holly's killer is still out there. That man who stopped Denise

Lenchantin in Hampshire County the same night Holly was killed? I think that was the guy. I think my *wife* believed that was the guy."

Lovering frowned. "You're talking about that waitress again?"

"You told me Lenchantin was approached around eleven o'clock that night, making it impossible for Holly's killer to drive the ninety miles from Furnace to Romney in such a short time. But Lenchantin's shift ended at midnight that night, not eleven, giving Holly's killer an extra hour to make it out there."

"Mr. Decker —"

"My wife also believed that the killer knew one of his victims, that he'd either gone to high school with her or was maybe even on the faculty."

"You're back on this serial killer kick," Lovering said.

"Chief, I'm willing to sit down with you again and tell you everything I know. We can go over all my wife's work, all the deductions and links she made, all the connections. I'm not a cop; this isn't what I do. But I could show *you*."

"Das Hillyard killed Holly Renfrow, Mr. Decker. I don't care what you think you know or what that moron Chip thinks he saw. I don't care what sort of wild deductions you think you can make from reviewing some security footage. This case is *closed*. There is no serial killer. I told you before, Mr. Decker — you're looking for something that ain't there."

"The girl from Maryland, killed in 2016," I said. "Her hands were bound behind her back with wire, just like Holly's."

Lovering's stoic expression did not falter. He took a step toward me. "You like playing police detective? You're looking for something to solve, Mr. Decker?"

"I'm not playing anything. These are the facts."

"After we spoke, I read about what happened to your wife. The guy who did that to her killed himself, too. You got no answers because that madman took all the answers with him when he blew his brains out. So, now you're trying to find answers elsewhere. Well, Mr. Decker, it just don't work that way."

"Please," I said. "I'm not judging what you did. I don't care about that. What I care about is finding the real killer. He's still out there, and when he kills again—when he kills some other teenage girl in another county or state or wherever—this time you'll be partly responsible. Because I'm telling you he's out there, that he's been doing this for a long time, and I don't think anyone has ever been aware of him except for my wife. So *please*, Chief. Please hear me out and take this seriously."

Lovering's mouth stretched into a wide, carnivorous grin. His steely eyes narrowed. I couldn't tell if he was trying to look smug or if the sun was in his eyes. "I think," he said, "that you've been in my town long enough, Mr. Decker. I think it's time you go on home."

"You're making a mistake."

"Goodbye, Mr. Decker." Hercel Lovering turned on his heels and strolled toward the stationhouse doors.

"Please," I called after him. "Please sit down with me. Let me show you what I've got. Let me explain."

Without another word, he disappeared inside the stationhouse, leaving me standing by myself in the graveyard. Surrounded by the dead.

CHAPTER ELEVEN

1

You once said to me that you and I existed outside this plane, where space and time were wound into a ball and not in a straight line. We would always be together because we had *always* been together. We were acting out all our moments simultaneously right now. Ghosts, you had told me, were time travelers not bound by the here and now.

2

It was fully night by the time I turned onto Arlette Street and coasted along its serpentine bend toward our townhome. Ours was the only house without its porch lights on. Even the light from the streetlamps seemed to recoil from our home, as if, in my brief absence — or perhaps in yours, Allison — it had turned into something diseased and unhealthy and wholly uninhabitable.

I had debated with myself during the entire drive back from Furnace whether or not I should place a call to the district attorney's office and let them know what corruption Hercel Lovering had orchestrated. Yet each time I convinced myself to do just that, it was Rita Renfrow's face that floated before my mind's eye. Chip had been right — because of me, Rita no longer had the closure she thought she had. Was I the hero or the villain in this scenario?

As I stepped through the front door of our townhome, I was greeted by the sound of "Voices Carry" playing on the Alexa speaker in the living room. What this did was reduce me to tears right there in the foyer. I dropped to my knees and sobbed like an injured child. I cannot say how long I stayed that way, but several songs had played by the time I got up, went into the living room and unplugged the fucking thing. Without a second thought, I dumped it in the kitchen trash.

Upstairs, I entered our bedroom, dropped my satchel containing your files onto the ottoman at the foot of our bed, then stripped off every stitch of my clothing with my eyes half-shut in the dark. When I climbed into bed, it was like someone clawing their way along some scorched desert landscape. My mind plummeted into sleep the moment my head hit the pillow.

It was not dreamless. Things happened. I can't remember most of what I dreamt, although I am certain — and this certainty is born from experience — that many of those dreams were about you, Allison. But they were also corrupted by flashes of grotesqueries — of pale, rotting corpses staggering through the darkness as if spirited into half-life, spilling black river water onto our bedroom carpet as they drew nearer toward me in my slumber. I kept seeing the faces of young women, billiard pockets where their eyes should have been, teeth bashed from their skulls. An impossibly tall, impossibly thin man stood over me in bed, the profile of his face a composite of sharp geometric angles. As he stared down at me, his head proceeded to swell as —

(gas)

— steam hissed from popped seams along his cranium. His eyes blazed silver as he reached down and cupped my testicles with a set of ice-cold, elongated talons, and levered his head close to mine, where he whispered in a voice like thunder, *diddle-diddle-diddle*, until he squeezed —

I awoke in darkness, blanketed in sweat. Though not *complete* darkness: at some point, as I thrashed within the straitjacket confines of my nightmares, our closet light had come on. Blink — like an epiphany. The doorway glowed with a soft yellow light, laying down a strip of illumination along the carpet from one end of our bedroom to the other.

I sat up in bed, my back against the headboard. I couldn't take my eyes from the lighted closet. You might walk out and into the bedroom at any second, Allison. My heart was galloping.

The closet light blazed. I got out of bed and stood there, naked, my body chilled by the sheet of sweat that coated it. My throat had tightened, but I managed to call out your name nonetheless. Held my breath. Waited for you to waltz out and greet me. Ached for it. *Oh please, oh please.* In that moment, inside myself, I agreed to take you in any form, in any ghostly condition, that you might wish to appear to me. It didn't matter. My grief was so palpable in that moment that my entire body began to tremble and I thought it possible that I might just break apart and crumble to the carpet in broken shards of crockery, a powdery heap that had once been a person, which only you, in your spectral majesty, might reshape into something even more exquisite and true.

But you never came out of that closet. Of course not. Instead, I went inside, wincing at the over-bright ceiling fixture sizzling and popping like an Alka-Seltzer commercial. The intensity of the light was so great I thought it might burst, but it didn't. It remained on, the heat coming off it in impossible waves.

The only thing in the closet was a trembling, pale-skinned cretin wearing my haggard, grief-stricken face, staring back at me from the glass of the beveled mirror. Nude, thin-ribbed, gaunt, haunted.

Trembling and afraid, like something peeled from its shell and battered about.

"Allison," I said, my voice a croak. "If you're here…"

If you're here, what? What?

The light in the ceiling made a *zzzzzz* sound. But nothing more.

I turned off the light and slipped out of the closet in pitch darkness, my pupils still resonating with the image of the light fixture as I felt my way back toward our bed. My whole body shook. As I reached the mattress and ran one hand along the sweat-dampened sheet, I looked up and saw another light on out in the hallway, shimmering along one wall.

I headed out of the room. The light was coming from the room at the end of the hall — our shared office that we no longer shared. Creeping down the hall, one hand running along the railing that overlooked the foyer below, I advanced toward the office, my breath wheezing from my constricted throat. I thought of the image I saw — or imagined I saw — standing in this very doorway nights earlier. The certainty that you were in that room right now was so profound in that moment that I felt a grim and terrible smile crack the lower half of my face. My arms itched to embrace you. A taste in my mouth was *your* taste, as if in anticipation of a kiss. As if —

The room was empty. You were not here. My desk was on one side of the room, neat and tidy, unused for some time now. Your desk, overflowing with papers and books and DVD cases and an honest-to-God rolodex, had gone unused even longer, although it looked more lived-in and homey than mine. The light that burned was from your desk lamp, a ceramic Cheshire cat whose lampshade was a sombrero. Some gaudy thing you had picked up at a yard sale one summer. The bulb beneath the sombrero burned as intense as the fixture had in the closet — so stridently that I could hear the insect-buzz of the current transmitting through it.

I stood there, waiting for you to materialize out of nothing right before my eyes. But when that didn't happen — when the grim smile faded from my face and the taste of you drained from my mouth — I was left with nothing but a hollow jack-o'-lantern sensation, as if someone had taken a sharp utensil and scooped out all my vital bits.

I was halfway across the room, meaning to switch off the Cheshire-cat lamp, when I froze. My gaze had swung haphazardly across the jumble of madness strewn about the surface of your desk, only to lock onto a coffee mug bristling with pens and pencils. A mug you'd had for years, dating back to your childhood, Allison. A white mug with a green elk's head on it. Not a deer, but an elk. ELK HEAD HIGH SCHOOL, it read beneath the image. *Your* high school, Allison.

I turned and faced the bookshelf that spanned the wall between our two desks. Japanese novels, my own translated works, textbooks on publishing and journalism, yet at the bottom, a hodgepodge of personal papers and books. Was it possible…?

There it was, Allison. Hiding in plain sight, as they say. Right there on the bottom shelf. Dropping to my knees, I slid your yearbook off the shelf and onto the floor. It struck the carpet with a muted thud. It was right here all along, Allison — your old high-school yearbook with the image of a green elk on the cover.

On your desk, the Cheshire-cat lamp blazed like a supernova before the bulb blew out, dousing me in darkness.

PART THREE

THE
OTHER
YOU

CHAPTER TWELVE

1

The yearbook with the green elk on the cover was for the 2003–2004 school year. You would have been a freshman back then. Sitting cross-legged on the carpeted floor of our shared office, a fresh bulb in the Cheshire-cat lamp the only illumination, I turned the pages, the black-and-white faces of students framed in their rectangular boxes churning over to reveal a fresh crop of new faces, all of them strangers to me, all of them adults now. I turned pages until I found you, Allison — or someone who purported to be you. Allison Leigh Thompson. Despite your inner mystery, you had always been outwardly vivacious, cunning, sly as a fox and yet playful as an otter. You'd been both daring and sultry, and your beauty had always been a step above girl-next-door; more cosmopolitan, fashionable.

The teenage girl in the yearbook photograph who bore your name looked nothing like the woman you would become. This girl wore a blonde, shaggy mop of hair, choppily cut, uneven, short like a boy's. The expression on your face was difficult to decipher, like an image reproduced over and over again until all the fine details have been granulated to incoherence. The only recognizable quality was also your darkest one — your eyes. Even at fifteen years old, they professed a dark maturity that hinted at impossible depth.

I had never seen childhood photos of you before. By the time we had gotten together, you told me none existed. After your mother had died, you had sold your familial home and had escaped the town of Woodvine, Pennsylvania, with little more than the clothes on your back. The fact that you'd had your high-school yearbook with you and never shared it with me struck me now as some indistinct betrayal. I couldn't understand why you hadn't showed it to me before. Moreover, if you'd been so concerned about keeping it a secret, what was it doing here in the office and not hidden in your trunk? Had you tucked it away on the shelf after showing it to Denise Lenchantin, only to forget it was here and to hide it away again? Yet in the moment, these were not the most pressing questions. The question at the forefront of my brain right now was why you *had* shown it to Denise Lenchantin. You told her that the killer had gone to school with one of his victims, but there were no dead girls among your records who had attended Elk Head High School, no dead girls who had lived in your hometown of Woodvine, Pennsylvania, or any of the surrounding towns.

I sat there, nude and cross-legged on the floor, studying each page with the care and deliberation of a crime-scene investigator, scrutinizing the faces of your long-ago classmates, wondering which one — if any — was the murderer for whom you'd been so desperately searching. This opened up a passageway in my mind, one in which other-Aaron functioned as a sort of de facto guide, my personal Virgil, and together we wound through the spiral of your past, and I could smell the scorched brimstone of your obsession as both other-Aaron and I pursued some non-specific figure into the black. Who was the killer? How had you figured out this person's identity after all these years? Or had you known since you were a teenager? Had you come across the monster back then in its primordial form, its full terribleness still incubating yet not unnoticed by you, only to spend the remainder of your adult life hunting the monster down?

— *That is not it*, said other-Aaron. *That does not fit. That does not* translate.

That was true — because all evidence led me to believe that you had spent over a decade trying to uncover the identity of the killer, not trying to hunt down a specific person you already believed to be the culprit. Not until the end, anyway. Not until the Holly Renfrow murder, when you had asked Denise Lenchantin to look at a photo in this yearbook. Whose picture had you wanted Lenchantin to look at? What had finally tipped you off, Allison? What was the clue I could not see?

— *So what are we left to deduce from this?* posited other-Aaron. I could smell the oil burning as his machinery kicked into overdrive. *That Allison had been tracking an unknown killer who, in the end, just so happened to be from her hometown? A sheer coincidence that the killer had attended high school with her?*

True. The coincidence being that if you *hadn't* begun your obsession already knowing or thinking you knew the identity of the killer, then what were the odds he would turn out to be someone with whom you had gone to high school? A miraculous coincidence, indeed. This would be the part in translating a novel where I would pause and shudder at the sheer crudeness of such a convenient literary device.

But this was real life. Unlike fiction, real life labored under no obligation. Stranger things have happened, so they say.

Except I wasn't buying it. I had missed a piece of the puzzle, maybe the most important piece, and the realization of this turned my uneasiness into something more closely related to panic. Moreover, I had become increasingly aware of the Great Cosmic Clock, now a profoundly proper noun in my mind, ticking and ticking as if to count down the seconds leading to my own demise. As if my own life suddenly depended on solving the mystery you had left behind, unfinished.

— It could just be that Allison was wrong about the killer's identity in the end, other-Aaron suggested. *If all the clues led her to the wrong deduction, and she had made a leap in logic near the end — if she hadn't gone to school with the killer after all — then that would eliminate the coincidence and put us back into reality.*

It would also thrust me back to square one. A false lead and I was deaf, dumb, and blind once again. Believing this also suggested that you had gone off the rails at some point, and that your obsession had ultimately clouded your judgment. After all this time fruitlessly searching for a killer, you had concocted one. Summoned him into existence and gave him the face of a high-school acquaintance. Or even a friend.

It was this notion that caused me to realize there was something unusual about your yearbook. There were no signatures in it, Allison. No missives from your friends, no goofy drawings, no *have a great summer*s or *see you next year*s on the panels of blank pages toward the end of the book. Pages left intentionally blank for that reason. No one had signed your yearbook, Allison, and this, for whatever reason, troubled me.

2

I awoke on the floor of our office, thinking the house was on fire. It was only daylight, potent and disorienting as it blazed through the windows on this side of the house. Your yearbook was a bird that had crashed down from the sky, upside down and with its wing-like covers splayed on the sawdust-colored carpet. I gathered it up, got dressed, and then carried the yearbook downstairs.

In the kitchen, I fixed up a pot of coffee then dug the Alexa speaker out from the trash. I plugged it in, watched as the color bar whirled, then stared at it in silence. It had always amused us how the thing would periodically turn on unprompted. That had taken on a different meaning since your death, of course, and I had tried hard to relegate it in its place and to refuse to assign any supernatural significance to it since then. But no longer. I waited for it to come on now, almost in anticipation of hearing your voice, static-laden and tinny, come through the speaker. I waited, with no sense of amusement, but with a staunch, bracing hope.

Nothing. Nothing.

"Allison," I said to the empty kitchen.

The device lit up and Culture Club's "Do You Really Want to Hurt Me?" spilled out of the speaker.

"What the hell, Allison," I groused, shaking my head. "Come on."

Boy George crooned, and I poured myself a cup of coffee. I drank it out on the deck with the door open, listening to the music. I still had the pack of smokes I'd purchased back at the Exxon in Furnace; as if in defiance of you, I dug out the pack and had a cigarette on the deck while I finished my coffee. Boy George transitioned to Neil Sedaka singing "Oh! Carol," and I pitched the filter of my cigarette into the yard, lit another, and contemplated smoking the entire pack. If it was possible to smoke yourself to death in one sitting, I would have tried it then. I looked down into the yard and saw you down there, sunning yourself on a beach towel or pruning the peculiar breed of flowers that sprouted every spring along the fence line, those budding strawberry-looking things with the thorns. I saw you drinking a beer, heard you laughing at a joke, felt your fingertips graze the back of my neck as you slipped by me.

Inside, the music stopped. The silence that followed was so jarring and uncomfortable that I hugged myself, then slipped back into the house, a man guilty of some travesty. Maybe I was.

Your yearbook, which I had placed on the granite island in the center of the kitchen, lay open just as I had left it. Only difference was I had left it open on your photograph, Allison — the unidentifiable fifteen-year-old version of you. Now, probably due to my leaving the door open while I smoked, a breeze had turned the pages. On one page were a bunch of advertisements. On the other was a full-page memorial for a female student who had apparently died during the school year. My own senior-year high-school yearbook had a similar page, dedicated to Michael Beamish, a lacrosse player who had died in a car accident his junior year. A dedication or tribute or whatever. The one in your yearbook was of a beautiful teenage girl, stunning ringlets of blonde hair cascading down her shoulders, her smile iridescent, her eyes possessive of that same dark majesty that I had recognized in *your* eyes when we'd first met. The dead girl's name was Carol Thompson, and you'll forgive me, Allison, for not making the connection immediately upon reading the name. You had mentioned your sister so infrequently that I should not be held accountable for my temporary oversight. Truth is, I did not realize who she was until I was halfway up the stairs, my body yearning for a hot shower.

When it struck me, I froze midway up the stairs, then spun around and hurried back down. Your dead sister's face was still smiling up at me from the glossy yearbook page. I could see the similarities in your features — delicate, almost fragile, and emboldened by an innate brazenness that made you (and her) look almost dangerous. It was the way nature sometimes makes beautiful things poisonous.

The only thing I knew about your older sister Carol was that she had drowned when she was a teenager.

Something prompted the Alexa to come alive, this time with Manfred Mann's "Don't Kill It Carol."

I looked back down at your sister's photo. I felt snared in some sort of dream state, my body moving with a preternatural slowness.

Your sister Carol drowned in a river. I never had a reason to question this, Allison. Why would I?

The music still playing, I grabbed the yearbook, raced up the stairs to my office, and began the process of digging up the bones of your long-buried sister.

3

We had been living together for less than a month in a tiny Eastport apartment when you returned home from attending a two-day media bazaar in New Jersey with blisters on the palms of your hands and a noticeable change in your demeanor. Something had shaken you. As usual, you put on a front, masked yourself, mummified your true emotions beneath layers of gauzy wrappings. It was what you did when you didn't want me seeing your vulnerabilities, or when you wanted to pretend that you didn't have any. When I asked about the bazaar, your responses had been curt, noncommittal. It had been great; you'd had a wonderful time. Then you would smile and change the subject. This bothered me. I wondered if something had happened during those two days in Jersey. Even though our relationship had still been fairly new, I'm ashamed to admit that my mind first went to infidelity. Had something happened between you and some guy while in Jersey? I wanted to come right out and ask you — perhaps that would have been the mature thing to do — but I was a coward in that regard. Maybe I didn't want to seem needy or insecure. Maybe I didn't want to anger you by suggesting I didn't trust you. Or maybe I didn't want to know about it, if in fact that was what had happened. Instead, I gently poked you — *What's wrong? You're not yourself. Did something happen? You can talk to me.* All those old chestnuts. People are funny creatures, aren't they?

You, Allison, had been deft. Like some ninja or acrobat, you had always managed to negotiate your way around my queries, leaving me dizzy and tongue-tied. It was one of the things I admired about you but also one of the things that frustrated me.

"What happened to your hand?" I asked.

You were lying on the couch watching TV, your left hand extended so that it dangled over the edge of the couch. I could see your palm glistening in the TV light, and when I bent down to examine it I could see a rind of fresh blisters along the pad of flesh beneath your fingers. The shininess was from some salve you had applied.

You pulled your hand away from me and sat up. Your hair hung over half your face so that only a single eye stared out at me. I thought I saw a flash of… *something*… behind that eye. Quick as a lightning strike on the surface of an ocean.

"It's from writing all day," you said, pulling your legs up under you.

"You're right-handed."

"Typing," you said. "Both hands." You mimed typing in the air between us.

I took your right hand, turned it over, saw a collection of even worse blisters along the soft pads of your palm. They glistened with salve.

"Jesus, Allison."

"It's nothing. I've got tender palms."

I laughed, but didn't find it funny. You were holding something back and it worried me. "How'd you get these from typing? Looks more like you've been swinging a baseball bat for about ten hours straight."

"They had some old manual typewriters at the bazaar. They were so kitsch I couldn't keep away." You held up both your hands, palms out, as if in surrender. "Occupational hazard."

"Allison, did something happen on the trip?"

"I *told* you — no. I'm just tired and maybe a little disillusioned."

"About us?"

"No, loser. About my work."

"What's to be disillusioned about? I thought you loved writing for the paper."

"I do. I just worry that I'm not making much of a difference. You know?"

"Then what else would you like to do?"

"I don't know."

"Allison…"

"If I think of something, I'll let you know." You wrapped your arms around my neck, drew me closer, kissed me on the mouth. "Let's go upstairs."

"Just don't touch me with those gross hands of yours."

"Touchy touch touch," you said, and pressed your salve-coated palms against the sides of my face.

If you were trying to sidetrack me, Allison, it worked.

However, I wasn't totally blinded by you. That night, after sex, you cried out in your sleep. You sometimes did this, although most of the time I never could comprehend the jumbled nonsense that you said. This night, however, it was clear that you were calling out for your sister. You said her name several times. Finally, when I jostled you awake, you sobbed then sat upright against the headboard. Your body was shiny with sweat and I imagined I could hear your heart pumping.

"Bad dream," you said, swiping a tangle of damp, matted hair out of your face.

"About what?"

"Can't remember."

"You kept calling out, 'Carol, Carol.' Your sister."

You looked at me in the half-light; our bedroom in that tiny apartment was never fully dark, with the orange-hued sodium lamps in the parking lot outside perpetually radiating against the windows.

I waited for your response but you didn't say anything; instead, you tossed the sheet aside and got out of bed. I watched you walk naked out of the room and into the hall. The bathroom light clicked on, followed by the faucet.

I got up, tugged on my boxer shorts, and followed you into the bathroom. I stood in the doorway while you washed your face at the sink. When you looked up, you caught my gaze in the mirror.

"It's not the first time you've called out her name in your sleep," I said.

"It's nothing."

"Doesn't seem like nothing."

You dried your face on a towel but didn't respond.

"You never talk about her."

"I don't want to."

"I understand that," I said, "but maybe that's why you keep dreaming about her. She's coming to your mind whether you want to talk about her or not."

You went to the medicine cabinet, took out a tube of ointment, and squeezed some onto the palm of one hand. Your blisters looked like angry red bullet holes in the harsh bathroom light. Then you sat on the closed toilet lid and massaged the salve against your skin.

"I know you don't like to talk about her, or about your family at all, but maybe keeping that stuff packed away is causing you stress. If you're not comfortable talking to me about it, maybe you could talk to a therapist or something."

"Oh, please."

"Don't brush it off. It weighs on you, Allison. I just want you to find some peace. Maybe I'm wrong, but it seems to me like you carry this thing around with you all the time like some black cloud. Sometimes I don't even think you're aware of it. You've been doing it so long it's become part of your personality."

You looked up at me, angular shadows falling across the right side of your face. "You don't know me, Aaron. I love you and we've got something great between us, but you really don't know me."

"Then *let* me know you."

"That's impossible."

"Why?"

"Because I don't even know *myself*. I'm a tornado — spinning, spinning, spinning." You gave up a humorless laugh. "I've worked very hard to bury the bad stuff in my past. My sister's death — yeah, it *is* a cloud. You're right. But it's not your cloud."

"You're wrong about that," I said. "We're together, aren't we?"

Your eyes simmered. You were a million times right, Allison: you were a tornado. I saw dead leaves and tree branches and all sorts of debris swirling behind your eyes. Spinning, spinning, spinning.

"One thing I know," you said, "is that the longer you spend in darkness, the easier it is for that darkness to become reality. It *takes form*, it gains *life*. I've spent a lot of time in darkness, Aaron, so much so that I've churned it up and stirred it to the surface and made it this real, tangible thing. It lives alongside me. It moves when I move. It's in the bedroom right now, waiting for me to come back."

"This is… what? Metaphorical?"

"Is it?" And you sounded hopeful, as if I could give you an answer that might fix whatever darkness roiled and churned inside you. "When you spend so much of your life sifting through dark and terrible things, you give those things the power to become real. The ghosts don't leave you alone."

I came into the bathroom, knelt down in front of you on the fuzzy pink bathmat.

"Jesus," you said. "Please don't tell me you're about to propose while I'm sitting naked on the toilet lid."

We shared a laugh. Your eyes remained stone sober.

"Carol drowned when she was seventeen. It ruined my mother. She became mired in grief until she drank herself to death. The whole thing ruined me, too. She was my older sister. I looked up to her, admired her. Loved her. And then, one day, she was gone. Just gone. And after my mother died, I was alone."

"I'm sorry."

"Yeah," you said, though not unkindly. You even smiled at me. "It's what we say, isn't it?"

"I love you, Allison."

"You're okay," you said.

"Is that something you'd want to do?" I asked.

"What?"

"Get married."

"Jesus, Aaron. Your romance is shit."

I reached over and flushed the toilet, which caused you to laugh. We never talked about your sister after that.

4

You lied, Allison. Your older sister, Carol Thompson, had not drowned. In 2004, her body had been discovered in a shallow, rocky offshoot of the Elk Head River on the outskirts of Woodvine, Pennsylvania, most of her clothing stripped from her body and her skin the color of wax paper. The cause of her death was strangulation. Few other details were available in the online news articles, but what I was able to determine was that in the fifteen years since your sister's death, no suspect had ever been apprehended. If there had ever been any suspects at all, the news articles did not say.

There had been an outcry in 2004, as one would imagine. A seventeen-year-old girl brutally murdered and then dispatched of in such a heartless, grotesque fashion caused something of an uproar in Woodvine and in neighboring communities. Things like that simply didn't happen in small towns like Woodvine, where good, hardworking people were always friendly and no one ever locked their doors. There'd been a rally, a march, a candlelight vigil. A wreath of flowers was placed on the stone footbridge that arched over a narrow section of the Elk Head River, not far from where your sister's body had been discovered. It was like what happened to you all over again, Allison. That one family should sustain so much tragedy seemed not only an injustice but an impossibility.

And then, just like with your death, Allison, people began to forget. The news articles became scarce until they ceased altogether. Local papers stopped reporting on the status of the investigation, which had been stalemated from the very beginning. That a murdered teenage girl could vanish from the public consciousness so tidily and unceremoniously was a travesty in itself.

With Carol being your serial killer's first victim, I was afforded an answer to your motivation. You weren't just hunting a murderer, you were hunting your *sister's* murderer. Yet this revelation only compounded the questions in my mind. Why hadn't you told me about any of this? Why the lie about her drowning? Was it just that horrific for you that you made up a lie and stuck to it, just so you wouldn't have to relive any of it in the retelling?

I was your husband, Allison. Your family would have been my family, whether they were still here or not.

5

Phone calls to the Woodvine Police Department were of little help. The 2004 murder of Carol Thompson remained unsolved, and the police were unwilling to provide me any information that wasn't already public knowledge since the case was technically still open. I told them I was family by marriage to the deceased, hoping this might loosen them up a bit. They told me to submit a photocopy of my driver's license and our marriage certificate as proof, which I did, but all they supplied in return were heavily redacted copies of old police reports. These reports failed to provide me any details that weren't already online, with one exception: I discovered that the name of the detective who had been investigating Carol's murder had not been redacted from one page of the report — a detective with the decidedly cop-like name of Peter Sloane. I called the Woodvine PD and requested to speak to Sloane, but was told that he had retired years ago. When I asked how I might get in touch with him, I was informed (rather curtly) that their policy prohibited them from giving out that sort of information.

I took to the internet and searched for Sloane's whereabouts. I checked the usual social media sites, but the name was too common. There were too many rabbit holes. When I felt defeated, other-Aaron reminded me that anyone — *anyone* — could be found online in some capacity nowadays. I narrowed the search to include "Woodvine," "police," and "detective" among my search terms. What I found was a newspaper article from a few years back detailing the grand opening of a pub called Pistol Pete's in the town of Swarthmore, Pennsylvania. According to the article, the owner, Peter Sloane, was a retired police detective from Woodvine, Pennsylvania. The accompanying photo showed Sloane and his wife (according to the caption) standing in front of a Bavarian inn, the pub's name in copperplate font on the tinted front window.

I telephoned the pub and asked the woman who answered if I could speak with Sloane.

"Can I ask who's calling?"

I told the woman my name and that I was a relative of a woman who was killed in Woodvine, Pennsylvania, back in 2004. "Mr. Sloane was the detective on the case," I said. "I'm doing some research and would like to speak with him."

"Is he expecting this call?"

"He's not, no. I'm calling out of the blue. But I was going to be in the area and I was hoping he might find the time to sit down with me for a bit. I've got some questions about the case."

"He's retired from all that," the woman said.

"Are you the manager?" I asked.

She laughed — a sharp whip-crack that conveyed little humor. "I'm the wife."

I made a sound over the phone that suggested she'd caught me off guard: a little wheeze that scrambled up the stovepipe of my throat.

"Listen," she said, all business; she sounded like a retired police detective herself. "He'll be in tomorrow around noon. Stop in for lunch. I'll let him know you're coming."

"Great. Thank you so much."

"Just don't get him riled."

Before I could ask what she meant by that, the line went dead.

CHAPTER THIRTEEN

1

Pistol Pete's was situated in a shopping center that looked like it should have been on a brochure for skiing in the Swiss alps. It was tucked between a mattress store and a European bistro, the type of place someone might drive by without realizing what it was. Pistol Pete's could have been a pawn shop for all anyone knew.

I entered the place at exactly noon, having made the 115-mile drive in under two hours. It was a typical neighborhood tavern, with a central bar and booths around the perimeter of the dark, wood-paneled interior. There was a stage beneath a wall of TVs where a guy with a ponytail was checking the tones on a Fender amp, an acoustic guitar strapped to his chest. The place was doing a fair amount of business, with much of the bar and several booths occupied by men and women in business attire.

I went to the bar where a guy in his twenties was drying pint glasses with a dishtowel. "What can I get you?" the guy asked. He had a metal barbell through his septum.

"I'll have a Yuengling," I said, nodding at the tap handle. Across the bar, a guy in a rumpled tweed jacket with his necktie askew sat stirring a bowl of what looked like clam chowder, a dour expression on his face. He was examining something on his cell phone, the glow of the screen making him look like Bela Lugosi in that ancient *Dracula* film.

The bartender filled a pint glass and set it down in front of me on a coaster.

"Is Peter Sloane around?" I asked.

"Wow," said the bartender. "Haven't even taken a sip and already you're looking to complain to the owner." He looked me up and down. "You a friend of his?"

"I've never met him, but I called to schedule a meeting. My name's Aaron Decker. He's probably expecting me."

Truth was, I didn't know what Peter Sloane was expecting. If anything.

The bartender waved over a waitress, a wide-hipped gal with a shock of spunky purple hair, and said something close to her face. The waitress shifted her gaze toward me, nodded. She had a cat's paw print tattooed along the left side of her neck. I smiled at her, prompting her to quickly look away. I watched as she disappeared through a doorway at the back of the bar. The whole thing looked like a mob hit was about to take place. The bartender came back over and said, "Mr. Sloane will be out in a few minutes. Why don't you have a seat over there?" He motioned with a thrust of his chin toward the nearest empty booth, hidden in a dark section of the bar against one wall.

"Thanks."

Some sporting event was on the TVs; something happened on-screen and the men and women around the bar cheered. The old fellow in the rumpled tweed sports coat glanced up, his face under-lit by his phone as if by a pool of radioactive liquid; he looked like someone jerked awake on a subway. I sat at the booth and watched the guy with the ponytail jigger with his amp, strum a few chords, jigger with his amp again. When he looked up and — rather dismally, I thought — surveyed his audience, I saw on his face the bleary-eyed countenance of someone perpetually stoned and inherently distrustful of others.

I was halfway through my beer when a man in an embroidered western button-down shirt and glasses perched on the bridge of his blade-thin nose came over to the booth. He was bald except for a tight wreath of graying hair at his temples. He looked more like an accountant than a former police detective. "Aaron Decker?" he said.

"Mr. Sloane." I stood, shook his hand. "Thanks so much for your time."

"Go ahead, sit down." He sat opposite me in the booth. He was maybe in his sixties, in good shape, and with a relaxed air about him. He removed his glasses and set them on the table. "Full disclosure," he said, his hands spread wide to suggest he had nothing to hide. "My wife thinks this is a bad idea."

"You mean meeting with me? How come?"

"High blood pressure. She thinks I handle stress poorly." He tipped me a wink.

"You were a police detective for twenty years," I said, recalling the bio in the newspaper article.

He held up two fingers in a V. "Twenty-*two* years," he corrected. "And I tell her, it's not work-related, the high blood pressure. It's genetic. My old man had high blood pressure. *His* old man had high blood pressure. Anyway, it doesn't matter, she doesn't listen to me. I'm retired but I still answer to the boss, if you know what I mean."

"Sounds reasonable."

"You hungry?" He raised a hand and waved at the waitress with the sprout of purple hair. She sidled over and Sloane ordered a pitcher of beer and a plate of cheeseburger sliders. When she left, he folded his hands on the table and said, "So you're who now?"

"My wife was Allison Thompson. Her sister Carol was murdered in Woodvine, Pennsylvania, in 2004. She was strangled to death and found in a river. According to what I've read, you were the lead detective on the case."

"Carol Thompson, yeah," he said, and for a brief moment his easygoing expression fled from his face, replaced by something dark and haunting. "Haven't forgotten that one. I've seen some stuff, but that was, hands down, the single worst thing that happened while I was in Woodvine. She was seventeen at the time, I think. Just brutal, what happened to her. You said your wife is her sister?"

"She was, yeah. My wife died back in December."

"Is that right? Hell, I'm sorry to hear that. What happened to her, if you don't mind me asking?"

I glanced down at my hands, which were tapping nervously on the tabletop. "She was killed in a shooting at a shopping mall just before Christmas. Back in Maryland, where we live. Lived. Live." I was suddenly nervous.

"Annapolis," Sloane said, his face expressionless. "Gunman was some shitbag in his twenties. Parents had money."

"That's right," I said, astonished that he was familiar with the incident. "Most people don't remember it."

"It was just a few months ago," Sloane said.

"This country has a short memory," I said.

"It happens too often," Sloane added. "People get numb. I don't think it's callousness or even a short memory, although maybe you're right."

"Then what do you think it is?"

"Fear," he said. "Used to be something like this happened, it was an anomaly. It didn't fit in with the fabric of the world, and so people could afford to be horrified not only by the violence and terror of it, but by the sheer *absurdity*, the *impossibility* of it. That kid in Texas takes potshots from the university observation deck, kills over a dozen people, and the country is petrified not just by horror but by disbelief. That was in the sixties. Back then, something like that, people could watch it and still not relate to it. Something like that would never happen to them, right? But now, it's like every week there's something on the news. People are no longer exempt. It's no longer an absurdity. So what do they do? They try to erase it from the public consciousness as quickly as possible. None of us are just spectators anymore. We've all got a stake in the game."

"That just sounds so bleak."

"Bleak, yeah. And dangerous. You keep turning away from stuff like this, it allows it to grow and fester in the dark." His lips tightened, and he said, "I'm sorry about your wife, Aaron. It's a terrible thing."

I nodded and found, in that moment, I could not say anything more about it.

"I got a memory of her being just a kid, your wife," Sloane said, his voice a bit more cheery now. "She was a smart kid. Bold, you know? In a way a lot of kids aren't. I'm glad to hear she got out of that town. Places like that are like a prison sentence for someone as smart and bold as your wife. You ever been?"

"To Woodvine? No, I haven't. My wife never talked about it all that much. I guess there was a lot of heartache for her there."

"It's a quiet, isolated little town. Very evangelical, with a church on every corner. A place where everyone knows everyone else. A *safe* place, though not without its" — he seemed to hunt for the word — "its idiosyncrasies, shall we say? Most people, they spend their entire lives living in a place like that. They're born there, they eke out an existence there, they die there. Few people ever get out. And when they do, they very rarely ever come back. It's like breaking free from a trap you didn't know you were caught in."

"You got out," I said.

Peter Sloane grinned, and thumbed at the cleft in his chin. "Well, I'm the exception to the rule, and not just because I got out but also because I wasn't born there. I got *in*, you might say. Wife and I are from Philly. I had a heart attack in my early forties — early forties, how about that, right? — and Dottie, my wife, she thought the pace would be slower in the sticks. Mostly, it was." He set both his hands down on the tabletop. "But you didn't come here to get my bio, did you?"

"I did not," I said, and offered him a tired smile. "Like I said, Allison never talked about where she grew up. She mentioned her sister only a handful of times. She told me Carol had drowned when she was a teenager. I've only recently learned the truth about what happened to Carol since Allison died."

Sloane nodded, as if this was the most basic thing in the known world.

"I called the Woodvine PD but they weren't very helpful," I added.

"Well, technically," he said, "it's still an open investigation. They can't tell you much."

"I'm hoping you can," I said, cutting to the chase.

He spread his hands open on the table and made a face that suggested something akin to regret. "Nothing more I can really tell you, Aaron, other than what you probably already know from looking into it on your own. It was in all the papers for a while. The town took it real hard, and of course everyone was frightened for a time. We never caught the guy."

"Was there ever a suspect?" I asked.

I watched as Peter Sloane's mouth tightened the slightest bit. Something in his eyes turned hard, but it was a fleeting observation, quick as a minnow darting through shallow surf — there and then gone.

The waitress arrived with our pitcher of beer. She poured two glasses then told us our cheeseburgers would be out shortly. Peter Sloane waited for her to depart before talking again.

"You ever have the good fortune to meet your wife's mother?" Sloane asked, and I could easily discern the sarcasm in his voice.

"No, sir."

"Lynn Thompson was what you might charitably call 'colorful.'

She was an alcoholic, and when she wasn't drunk, she sleepwalked through an eight-hour shift as a receptionist at the local refinery to earn a paycheck. The girls' father had been a long-haul trucker who was killed in a highway incident when the girls were little, so there'd never really been a father in that house. Rumor had it Keith Thompson had practiced the same recreational activities as his wife, and that he'd had a blood alcohol level three times the legal limit when he drove his semi through a guardrail and down a ravine somewhere in Colorado. Maybe you already know this."

"I knew her father had been killed in an automobile accident when she was young. That was it."

"Anyway, I'm sure being widowed with two young kids isn't generally a recipe for success, but Lynn Thompson took a nosedive and never looked back. Her manager at the refinery kept her on for a while because he felt sorry for her, but he could only do that for so long. The same day she got fired just happened to be the same day the railing on a two-story set of metal stairs came loose, and down went Lynn. Dislocated her hip, broke her leg, whatever else. Coincidence? You tell me. But as you might guess, it's the mental anguish that really rattled her. She threatened a lawsuit but settled for what was probably a modest payout from AstroOil, the parent company.

"The girls fended for themselves for the most part. A few neighbors and some of the local churches occasionally stepped in to help where they could, but depending on what state of inebriation Lynn was in at the time, she responded to these charities with either a cold thanklessness or outright contempt for anyone who dared insert themselves into their lives.

"As you can imagine, she wasn't too discerning when it came to her love life, either. I'll spare Lynn Thompson the indecency of any detail here, Aaron, but you seem like a fellow who's capable of using his imagination."

"I never knew it was like that. Allison had said that her mother was an alcoholic, that she basically drank herself to death, but she said it was because of her sister's death. She never talked about any of this stuff."

"Worst part was when Carol began to emulate her mother. Most natural thing in the world, but here we got a smart, attractive, outgoing teenage girl who's got no other role model and can't help but begin to mimic her mother's behavior. It's all she ever knew, right? She got into drinking, some casual drug use, was fooling around with boys when she was at an age that was just young enough to be cringeworthy."

This statement made me think of Gabrielle Colson-Howe, and how Bobbi Negri had mentioned that Gabrielle had been sexually active since she was twelve years old. Hearing your sister described in such a similar fashion disheartened me, Allison. There existed such a clearly visible blueprint for misery — particularly for teenage girls — yet everyone always seemed to ignore it.

"Carol had been grabbed for drinking with friends in the school-yard on a number of occasions," Sloane went on. "You try to impress upon them that they're headed in the wrong direction, that the path they're choosing to take will only lead to problems in the long run. And sometimes you even start to get through to one or two of them. But then they go home and find Mom or Dad passed out on the sofa, empty bottles scattered around like bowling pins, maybe a joint smoldering in an ashtray, and then what hope do they really have?"

A woman in a paisley blouse and sensible shoes marshaled over to our booth. I recognized her stern, birdlike features from the photo in the newspaper article about Sloane and his wife.

"Mr. Aaron Decker," she said, proffering a hand. There was a smile on her face but it did not appear to be wholly welcoming. "Dorothy Sloane. We spoke on the phone."

"This is Dottie, my wife," Sloane said.

I shook her hand and thanked her for passing along my message to her husband. I started to say how much I appreciated their time and what a wonderful little place they had here, but she cut me off without ceremony.

"This whole thing happens under one condition," she said. "My husband does not need to play police detective, Mr. Decker. He's retired from that business. Now, he runs a fairly successful bar where our crab cakes will rival any you've ever had."

"Well," I said, "I'm from Maryland, so that's a pretty bold statement."

"We got a plate of sliders coming," Sloane groused at his wife.

"Forget it," said Dottie. "I'm bringing Mr. Decker the crab cake." Then she leveled a finger at my face. An impressive diamond gleamed from her knuckle. "For the record, I think this is a bad idea. He's got a bum ticker."

"Christ, Dot," Sloane said.

"Promise me you won't get him all worked up," Dottie said, ignoring her husband and not taking her eyes from me.

"I promise," I said, and crossed my heart.

"Yeah, well," she said, narrowing her eyes.

"I'm trustworthy," I assured her.

"Yeah, *well*," she said again, but with a bit more emphasis, then tipped her glance at her husband. That index finger swiveled over to him. "Twenty minutes," she said. "No more."

"Okay, boss," Sloane said, and saluted her.

"You know your limitations, Peter. Don't be obtuse."

"I get it, I get it," he said, flapping a hand at her. "You're eating into my time."

Her face softened then. Her smile reappeared, more genuine this time. She touched the back of her husband's head, then marched over to the stage to consort with the stoned musician who was still trying to tune his guitar.

"She thinks running a business is less stressful than being a cop," Sloane said. "Anyway, do I look like I'm ready to roll over dead?"

"She's just worried about you."

"I don't golf, I don't bowl. Give me a break, right?"

I laughed. But then it occurred to me that when I reached Peter Sloane's age, there would be no you there to worry about me. No gentle hand grazing the back of my head. I would be alone.

"Enter James de Campo," Sloane said. He had lowered his voice, but that did not mask the disdain in it. "You asked if there was ever a suspect? Good old Jimmy. This guy was the latest in Lynn Thompson's sordid parade of men. A real piece of work, and just the type of guy you could imagine someone like Lynn Thompson ending up with. It's like goddamn science, the way bad elements gravitate toward each other."

"So he was a drunk, too," I said.

"He was the raging storm cloud in an already overcast sky, if you'll forgive the poetic license," Sloane said. "Lynn Thompson didn't just pop up around town half in the bag anymore; now she was sporting some, ah, ocular discoloration, if you catch my meaning." He motioned around one eye with his index finger. "Neighbors complained about the fighting and we were always dispatching officers out to their place on Cane Road. They lived in a shitty little A-frame a ways off the main road, tucked behind some trees and a distance from some of the other neighbors, so you can imagine how loud they must've been.

"Of course, Lynn never pressed charges. They never do. I had a good sit-down with her at one point, too, told her she was setting a poor example for the girls, letting this kind of thing go on under her roof. It didn't do any good."

"What about Carol and Allison?" I asked. "They obviously had witnessed the abuse."

"They didn't just witness it," Sloane said, picking up his beer. He brought it halfway to his lips but did not close the distance. "They were *subjected* to it. They were *victimized*. James de Campo terrorized that household."

"I can't believe this," I said. "This sounds like someone else's life. Why would she not say anything about this to me? Why keep it a secret?"

Sloane sipped his beer then set it back down on the table. "I don't have an answer for that. Maybe it's better to pretend things like that never happened in the first place in order to move beyond them. Maybe she had to lie to herself to do it, and that meant lying to you."

"I wish I'd known."

"Wouldn't have changed anything."

He was right — it *wouldn't* have changed anything. Except that it would have been a large and vulnerable part of you that I could have shared, and maybe helped you cope with, helped you carry that weight.

— *You're wrong*, argued other-Aaron. *That was not Allison. She was the last person who needed some Prince Charming to swoop in and tell her everything would be all right. She would have been disappointed in you had you tried. And what would you have done, anyway? Knowing this would have just made you feel helpless and futile. She was always stronger than you.*

"He broke your wife's leg, you know," said Peter Sloane.

It was my turn to pause with my beer halfway to my lips. "What?"

"The story was she fell down the stairs. I never bought it. She went down those stairs, all right, but I'd bet dollars to donuts James de Campo was standing at the *top* of those stairs when it happened."

"She had metal pins in her leg," I said, rubbing my own left leg beneath the table as if to feel your phantom scar, as I had so often done when we'd lain in bed together. "She said she'd fallen out of a tree when she was a kid and broke it."

"Yeah, well," Sloane said, and drank some more of his beer. "I talked with Allison, tried to get her to tell me what really happened. She was, I don't know, maybe thirteen or fourteen at the time. And even at that age she was the smartest one living in that house. I thought she'd tell me, because even though I could tell she was afraid of de Campo, I knew she also hated him, and hate can be one hell of a motivator. But in the end she stuck to the story — she'd been carrying a load of laundry and took a header down the stairs.

"Again, I went to Lynn, told her you gotta press charges. This shit will keep happening and that drunk fool might even wind up killing someone if she didn't use her head and tell him to hit the bricks. But again, it was like talking to a doorknob. Something about Lynn Thompson, when you told her something she didn't want to hear, you could actually see doors and windows shutting up inside her. Like the way you'd close up a ship in preparation for a storm? Batten the hatches. That was Lynn Thompson — always battening the hatches."

"What about de Campo? Did you confront him about it?"

"I did. I told him I knew he'd hurt that kid and that he needed to leave Lynn Thompson and her girls alone. But he just laughed it off and told me to get off his girlfriend's property. Heck, I think he proposed to Lynn just to spite me, because it all happened around the same time."

"Proposed? They were married?"

"I don't think it ever came to that. Carol's death put a stop to it, you might say."

"I assume you're telling me all this because you believe James de

Campo was more than just a suspect," I said. "You think he murdered Carol Thompson."

Peter Sloane's eyes sparkled above the rim of his beer glass.

2

The crab cake arrived and, in Dottie Sloane's defense and despite my rapidly diminishing appetite, it was fantastic. I said as much after she came by the table to gauge my assessment. Pleased but not surprised, she bowed her head, satisfied, like a defense attorney who'd just proven her client innocent.

After she had left, Peter Sloane said, "They'd had a fight that night."

"Lynn and Jimmy?"

"Jimmy and Carol," Sloane said. "It seemed that once he and Lynn became engaged to be married, the damn fool had become instilled with some sense of proprietorship over Lynn's girls. And not in the protective sense, mind you. Often in public he'd smile and hug them and call them 'my girls.' He didn't say it with any sense of pride or anything, more like a butcher posing with his best hog just before the slaughter. Back before they were engaged, his aggression was meted out whenever the girls happened to be around, but for the most part, I don't think he bothered too much with them. After he and Lynn had gotten engaged and he was living in the house full-time, he began to take, I'd guess you'd say, more of an interest in them. And not in a healthy way."

"Jesus," I said, holding up a hand. "If this is headed in the direction I think it is…"

The look on Peter Sloane's face suggested I wasn't too far off the mark. "How about I just cut to the chase," he said. "The night Carol was murdered, she got in a fight with Jimmy. He'd been drinking all day and was primed for it. Along with his beer muscles, he'd developed an unexpected sense of modesty, and laid into Carol for, well, let's say for her penchant for entertaining various boyfriends."

"This fucking guy," I muttered, shaking my head.

"Yeah, exactly," Sloane commented. "The fight got physical. Jimmy struck her across the face, shoved her against the wall. Lynn stepped in, tried to douse the fire, but he got handsy with her, too."

"He admitted to hitting them?"

"No," Sloane said. "It was Allison who came forward and told me what she saw. Once Carol's body was found, something changed with her. She was no longer keeping her mother's secret."

"Good for her."

"That's right," Sloane agreed. "Her sister's death changed her, all right."

More than you know, I thought.

"Carol ran from the house that night and never came back," Sloane said. "We didn't get a call at the station from Lynn until two days later, when Carol hadn't come home and none of her friends knew where she had gone. Some officers went out to the house, took statements. They all knew the problems that were going on in that house, so no one thought anything of it. Carol had run off before. But then later that night, one of our guys radioed in to dispatch. He's got a body in the Elk Head. I went down there, and yeah, I didn't need a coroner to tell me it was Carol Thompson." He paused here and seemed to study my eyes. "How much do you want to hear, Aaron?"

"All of it," I said.

He nodded, satisfied. "The girl was naked from the waist down. Her wrists were secured behind her back by a length of electrical wire."

"Wire," I muttered, the word nearly sticking to the roof of my mouth.

"There was heavy bruising around her throat and a wound in her scalp; blood had dried in her hair and in streaks down her face. Later, the coroner confirmed the cause of death was strangulation. Her killer had choked her to death and then dumped her in the river."

"Her pants had been removed? Was she raped?"

"No, no indication that she was raped. No sign of any molestation whatsoever."

"Then why had her pants been removed?"

"Well, now you're asking questions I don't have answers to. Maybe it was a crime of passion and the killer couldn't get it up in the heat of the moment. I don't mean to be crude, but, well," and he shrugged one shoulder. "Maybe it was meant to confuse the authorities. I can't say. All I can confirm is that she wasn't raped."

"Maybe she was struggling too much." I found that I wanted to believe this, Allison — that your sister had, in the final moments of her life, fought enough to dissuade her murderer from that particular brand of heinousness.

"Doubtful," Peter Sloane said, dashing apart that last bit of hope I'd held onto. "Coroner determined that Carol Thompson had been incapacitated — that the contusion on her head was from some blunt object that suggested her killer had knocked her out, or at least attempted to — and then her hands were bound behind her back, most likely after she'd gone docile. The hands behind the back, it could be a fetish thing, or in a more practical scenario, it would have prevented her from fighting back while he strangled her. You can't gouge at someone's flesh if your hands are tied behind your back while you're being strangled. There was no skin or DNA under Carol's fingernails."

"Jesus," I muttered. I was thinking of what Bobbi Negri had relayed to me regarding the state of Gabby's body when she'd been found — how there'd been no evidence beneath her fingernails, either.

How she'd been naked from the waist down but not raped. The same pattern, so many years apart...

"There were bruises alongside her flank," Sloane continued, running a hand down the length of his own ribs for illustration, "and also on her thighs and shins. Coroner surmised this was from the weight of her attacker, bearing down on her while he strangled her. It takes some effort to kill someone like that, you know. It's not something that's over in a handful of seconds."

"That's what I've heard," I said, my own throat suddenly feeling very tight.

"There was a broken bone in one of her hands, too, which suggested that she'd been lying on her back with her hands tied while she was being strangled. The weight of her body, along with the weight of her killer who was probably on top of her, straddling her, would've broken the bone."

"Any chance she remained unconscious the whole time?"

The look Peter Sloane gave me suggested that anything was possible, although he didn't personally believe it to be in this particular case.

The prospect of such a death caused the back of my own throat to seize up even further. I imagined a woman, any woman, on the ground with her hands tied and pressed into the small of her back, while some faceless monster straddled her, squeezing the life from her with such force that it caused a bone in her hand to snap. I could almost hear the sound of it giving way: a shameful clacking sound, like snapping a chopstick in two.

"So, now we've got a murder investigation on our hands," Sloane said. "Crime-scene guys came in from Pittsburgh, did a workup of the scene, but ultimately came away with nothing. Meanwhile, I targeted de Campo."

"What'd he say?"

"Nothing at first. Told me to pound sand. That was when Allison came forward and told me about the fight he and Carol had the night Carol ran out of the house. Allison told me that Jimmy had left the house soon after Carol had that night. In a rage."

"No shit."

"So, I readdressed Jimmy. Brought him down to the station. He admitted they'd had a fight, but he tried to play it off like he was the victim — that Carol had come swinging at him, unprovoked, and that Lynn had joined in. Pity this poor hardworking man, right?"

"Fuck him," I said.

"He said he was furious after the fight and left the house to go get a drink at a local pub. But he was already so piss-drunk by the time he showed up that they turned him away. He caused a bit of a ruckus there, too, when he was told to hit the bricks."

"So that was true," I said. "He really went to a bar."

"Yeah, he did. He also wound up driving to a liquor store and picked up a six-pack of Iron City. It was after that when he was unable to account for his hours. No alibi, in other words. According to him, he'd spent the rest of that night in his truck getting shitfaced in the parking lot behind the local movie theater. He said he fell asleep out there, drunk off his gourd, and didn't get home until the next morning, sometime after Lynn had already begun making phone calls to Carol's friends."

"Did you believe him?"

Peter Sloane rubbed again at the small, dark cleft in his chin. He stared down at his beer, where the foamy head had dissipated. "I don't know. I certainly couldn't charge him with anything. I tried to entice him to come in and take a polygraph, but he shut me out. I went back to Lynn, asked her to tell me about the abuse, the times he'd hit her and the girls. I thought I might leverage her grief against any twisted loyalty she had toward de Campo. I was hoping to get enough for an arrest warrant. But she was useless, was in shock. She refused to believe that Jimmy could have anything to do with Carol's death, and she refused to acknowledge any of the physical abuse. I tried the same thing with Allison, but she was so messed up over her sister, I felt like I was making things worse for her, so I gave her some space. Maybe in hindsight that was a mistake."

"Why?"

"Because I ran out of time. By the end of the month, James de Campo had packed up his shit and moved out of town, never to be seen again."

For some reason, I thought about you in that moment, Allison, and the circumstances surrounding your own death — about how the officer had come over to me in the fire station to tell me that you were dead. I didn't cry. I didn't scream and shout and throw things. What I did was float along the sidewalk with the officer to a police car, where they showed me your purse and the ID within it. It was you; I'd told them this with perfect clarity and an unanchored sense of serenity that, in hindsight, felt like a dream, an anesthetization. Later, when I was brought to the morgue to identify your body, I did so with the perfunctory motions of an android summoned into reality from some dystopian science-fiction novel. I did all this while some part of my brain continued to insist that it was all wrong, all a mistake, and that you would be coming home that night, no matter what the reality of the situation was. The crying and the throwing of things didn't happen until much later, once the initial shock had worn off.

A group of men cheered at something on the TV from across the bar, rousing me from my memories. I looked up and saw a group of patrons high-fiving each other.

"Whatever happened to him?" I asked, still watching the people across the bar. I felt aloof, disembodied, and needed to watch other people in real situations just to anchor myself to the real world.

"Last I heard, he took up with some woman from Atlantic City. If there could be anything halfway good that comes from something so tragic as that girl's death, it was that the son of a bitch disappeared from their lives after that. He left them alone. Far as I know, anyway."

The people across the bar settled back into their table. Conversation was jaunty and alcohol-fueled.

Peter Sloane leaned closer toward me over the tabletop. His voice lowered, he said, "What's this about, Aaron? There's something more going on here with you that you're not telling me."

I looked at him. My mind whirred like industrial machinery. "After Allison died, I learned that she'd spent the past fifteen years or so trying to hunt down her sister's killer. And not just that. Somewhere along the way, she began to look into unsolved murders of other teenage girls. Girls who looked somewhat the same as Carol and had been killed in similar fashion. Allison died believing that whoever killed Carol had also been killing other young women up and down the east coast for the past fifteen years. Someone who's still out there."

Sloane sat back in his seat. "You're talking about a serial murderer," he said.

I unloaded on him, told him about the similarities in the murders you had uncovered during your own investigations, Allison. I led him from your sister's murder in 2004 to the death of Margot Idelson in 2006, the young woman from Norfolk, Virginia, whose body was discovered half submerged in a shallow river and in a fashion that was nearly identical to the way Carol had been found. I told him about Gabrielle Colson-Howe, and how there had been ligature marks around her wrists. Same as Holly Renfrow last fall, her hands bound in wire. Same as your sister.

"A reporter friend of mine tried to confirm that some of the other girls had been found with ligature marks on their wrists, too," I said, "but the police weren't telling her anything over the phone. But I'll bet you a thousand bucks all of these girls died from strangulation with their hands tied behind their backs."

"Jesus Christ, Aaron."

"The most recent victim, Holly Renfrow, her cause of death was listed as drowning because she'd fallen into the river with her hands bound. She could have been unconscious. But according to her mother, who'd read the coroner's report, there was bruising around her daughter's neck. At first, I wasn't sure why her death was different from the others, but after going out to the spot where I believe she was killed and where she'd fallen into the river, I think I pieced it together."

"Okay," said Sloane, which I took as a prompt for me to continue.

"It was left unfinished," I said. "He'd been following Holly Renfrow, watching her for days. He'd been outside Holly's house a few nights before she was killed. Her mother told me that Holly had seen him there, across the street. He called to her by name. And although I can't be sure, I think he was parked behind the gas station the night she was killed — the last place Holly was seen alive. He was waiting for her to leave, waiting for an opportunity to get her alone. Just like with Carol. Just like with all the others."

Sloane gave a slow nod of his head. I couldn't read his expression.

"He abducted her, and drove her to a place he believed to be secluded. I was there. It's like a scenic overlook, high up on a wooded ridge overlooking the Potomac River. He managed to bind her wrists up and probably started to strangle her but at some point she happened to get away from him before he could actually kill her. I think another car showed up that night — some kids looking to park, who also happened to be Holly's friends — and it spooked him. Holly saw her chance, got away from him, running down the slope toward the edge of the ridge. But the hillside is really steep out there and it had been dark. I think she accidentally fell over the cliff and went into the river. With her hands still tied behind her back. Christ, I nearly went over the edge myself when I was out there."

"Aaron, how the hell do you know all this?"

"Like I said, I went out there, spoke to some folks — the girl's mother, the local police, a potential witness. Just like my wife had been doing." I refrained from adding *behind my back*, even though that was exactly how I felt. That was the truth of it.

"Was Allison in law enforcement?"

"No, she was a reporter," I said, "but she was also tenacious as hell. And obsessed. Here, let me show you this."

I opened my satchel, removed the fat accordion folder, and slid out the mini-files of each murder. Paperclipped to the top file — the one concerning the death of Holly Renfrow — was the school photo Holly's mother had given to you, Allison. Platinum hair, the collar of a suede jacket popped, petite features that looked so fragile. I'd stuck it to the top of the packet because it seemed wrong to bury her likeness beneath all that dense, morbid paperwork. The photo caught Peter Sloane's eye; he picked up the packet, stripped the photo from it, stared at it.

"That's Holly," I said. "Physically, the similarities between all the girls are — "

"I see it," he muttered, staring at the photo. "I remember what Carol looked like. Allison, too." He set the packet down on the table and looked at me hard. "I'm at a loss here, Aaron," he said. "I'm a bit blindsided, I guess. I wasn't expecting this."

"Whoever he is, he's smart and he's careful," I said. "No more than one victim a year, and he always skips a year, sometimes two. If Carol Thompson was his first victim, then the rest all look very similar to her because I think he's recreating that first experience with her, over and over again. I've read stuff like this online about serial killers; they do that. That's how Allison knew to key in on certain girls. The girl who was killed in southern Maryland? Gabrielle? Allison went down there when she'd first gone missing, before a body was ever found. She was scouring the internet, searching for similarities. Gabrielle Colson-Howe had the same look as Carol, as Holly Renfrow, as Margot Idelson from 2006. All the others. If they looked like Carol and they disappeared or were murdered, Allison keyed in on them."

Peter Sloane just stared at me.

"Do you think this is something James de Campo is capable of?"

"Son," he said, "I can't fathom this is something *anyone* is capable of." He sifted through the documents I had placed on the table. "This is a large hunting ground for a serial killer," he said, shuffling through the papers and noting the various locations where the bodies had been found over the years.

"How much do you know about serial killers?" I asked him.

He glanced up at me. "I saw those Hannibal Lecter movies," he said, then returned his attention to the printouts and newspaper articles spread across the table. The maps with the crosses on them. Everything you had collected. "Have you shown this stuff to the police?"

"I tried to explain it to the police chief in West Virginia, the guy who investigated Holly's death, but he shut me down. He said this wasn't proof of anything and he had his own ideas about who killed Holly. Someone who could not possibly have killed these other girls. A guy who conveniently died of a heroin overdose."

"I don't know, Aaron," Sloane said, sifting through the paperwork. "That thing about the wires used to tie their hands, that's pretty specific. I mean, Jesus Christ. Yeah, okay. But that's just two girls, right? Two of the six? We'd need more than two to establish a pattern."

"I can't get any more info than that."

"Well, maybe this is something, maybe it isn't. I can't really say. This might be FBI territory. Whatever it is, it's well beyond my pay grade."

"There was a woman in West Virginia who was approached by someone who tried to get her to come with him in his car," I said, not willing to be dissuaded. "This was the same night Holly Renfrow was killed three counties away. This woman was a little older than his other victims, but she looked the part. Maybe he saw an opportunity with her. Maybe he was frustrated when Holly got away and fell into the river before he could... well, before he could do to her what he'd set out to do..."

"She get a look at the guy?" Sloane interjected.

"Well, no, not exactly. It was too dark. She didn't see his face."

"How do you know it's the same guy?"

"Because the witness described his car. A dark-colored sedan with a floodlight on the door, like an unmarked police car. In fact, the guy told her he was a police officer. 'Policeman,' was what he said. The night Holly was killed, some kids she was friends with saw a similar car parked at the overlook where I think Holly's killer took her, where she fell into the river."

I couldn't decipher the look that was now on Peter Sloane's face.

"Also," I said, "it was what Allison believed. For the most part, I'm just following her lead here." I slid the yearbook with the green elk's head on the cover from my satchel and set it on the table between us. "Allison also had a suspect. Someone she believed was in this yearbook and had gone to high school with her and Carol."

Sloane shook his head. "No," he said flatly. "Come on, Aaron. How do you know that?"

I told him how you had wanted Denise Lenchantin to identify someone's photo from the yearbook.

"But I have no idea who it is," I said. "And now, given your story about James de Campo, I'm not sure what to think. He obviously didn't attend high school with them."

Sloane stared at the yearbook and didn't say anything. I wondered if I had just soured our discourse with what must have sounded like wild suppositions. He was probably thinking I was nuts.

"I feel like the little silver ball in a pinball machine," I confessed to him.

Without a word, Sloane opened the yearbook and began turning the pages. When he arrived at a specific page, he paused with it half-turned and scrutinized it. Then he turned the book around so that I could view the page right-side up.

It was a black-and-white photograph of a group of school custodians. Sloane pointed to the man standing at the front of the group, a bleary-eyed shit-kicker in his late forties with a scrim of beard stubble, hoops in his ears and his long hair greased back from his face. He was not smiling in the photo as much as he was smirking, like he knew some terrible secret of which no one else was aware. It bothered me just looking at him, as if something about him was radioactive.

"That," said Peter Sloane, "is James de Campo."

3

"Now keep in mind," Sloane was saying, as I continued to stare down at the yearbook photograph, "this isn't proof of anything. That your wife was seeking confirmation from some witness doesn't mean de Campo killed anyone. You understand that, right?"

I looked up at him. "What do you mean?"

"I mean your wife was bringing her personal experiences into what may be a completely unrelated event. Or series of events. If she believed that James de Campo killed her sister back in 2004, then every time a similar murder happened somewhere, she was looking for clues, for evidence, for anything that confirmed her pre-existing belief. And now that's what you've been following — your wife's beliefs, not hard evidence."

"The waitress and the yearbook photo — " I began.

"Your wife wanting to show this waitress woman de Campo's photo in this yearbook isn't proof of his involvement in any of these murders; it only speaks to the fact that your wife wanted corroboration of her *own* belief. Do you see the difference?"

Yes, I did see. Peter Sloane was right — this was not unwavering proof that James de Campo was guilty of anything, except being in the forefront of your mind, Allison. Yet even knowing that, I could not shake the sudden jolt of *certainty* that zapped like electricity between the synapses of my brain. I could almost raise one hand and see sparks of current arcing between my fingers like some super villain.

"'Gas Head will make you dead,'" Sloane said.

I looked up at him. "What?"

He was holding the crinkled sheet of legal paper with that phrase written over and over again on it. He tossed it down on top of the yearbook.

"Do you know what that means?" I asked him.

"Yeah. It's an old ghost story. Every town's got one, right? If you were a naughty little kid in Woodvine, Pennsylvania, Gas Head would get you."

"That's it? Some stupid urban legend?"

"Far as I know," Sloane said.

"What about this drawing? These six rectangles?"

"Beats me," Sloane said.

I sat back against the cushioned seat. "A ghost story," I muttered, half thinking aloud. "What's it have to do with these murders?"

"You wallow in dark stuff, Aaron, and monsters tend to float to the surface. Maybe that old legend came back to her the more she dug around in this stuff."

"I guess," I said, staring down at that phrase. How stark and angry those words looked...

Peter Sloane redirected his gaze from me and out across the barroom floor. I felt a fresh set of eyes pressing upon me, boring into the panel of flesh between my shoulder blades. When I looked across the bar, I saw Dottie Sloane seated there, gazing at us from overtop a pair of bifocals and tapping a clipboard against one knee. She didn't look very pleased that I was still here talking with her husband. When she saw she had my attention, she tapped her wristwatch. It seemed my twenty minutes were done.

"Don't let that stink-eye intimidate you," Sloane muttered conspiratorially. "She won't turn you to stone."

"No, but her eyes are burning a hole in the side of my face," I confessed.

"Listen," Sloane said, rising up from the table. "Take your time, finish your beer. Hang around for a bit and watch the game. In the meantime, if it's okay with you, I'd like to photocopy some of these news articles. I've got a Xerox machine in the back, won't take me five minutes. I'll see what I can do about loosening some lips regarding some of the older murders with these other police departments."

"That would be excellent."

He gathered up the articles from the table and then ambled away. I watched him tuck the news articles in the rear pocket of his pants as he went over to his wife and proceeded to rub her shoulders. She said something to him while keeping her gaze trained on me. He responded with joviality, smiling and still rubbing her shoulders as he said something in response. Whatever it was, she wasn't buying a word of it.

I gathered up the remainder of your papers and stuffed them

back in the accordion file, then dumped the whole thing back into my satchel. On the riser at the front of the bar, the guitarist was strumming the chords to a familiar song, although I couldn't name it. When I closed my eyes, the yearbook photo of James de Campo resonated in my brain like the afterimage of a flashbulb explosion. It was still right there in front of me on the table, and I found I was helplessly drawn to it. Those features, dark and brooding. His refusal to take a polygraph. Had you known with certainty that it was de Campo fifteen years ago or just suspected it, Allison? Had you spent the past fifteen years trying to prove your suspicion or had something only recently brought James de Campo back into your consciousness? If so, what had it been? What was I missing?

Peter Sloane's voice, like the flutter of a paper streamer in my head: *Keep in mind this isn't proof of anything.*

In my excitement, I never stopped to wonder why, given the depth of your research and all your copious notes, James de Campo's name never once appeared anywhere in your file.

4

There was nothing but a clump of white foam at the bottom of the beer pitcher by the time Peter Sloane returned to the table.

"It's kismet. Turns out he's less than an hour away," he said, sliding a manila folder across the table like some secret dossier.

I looked at the folder then up at him. "What's this?"

"It's called a TLO report. I had a friend in the department do a rush job and send it to me. It's got de Campo's last known address."

"No shit," I said, opening the file. The newspaper articles he'd borrowed were on top. Beneath them was a printout that looked imposingly official.

"Also, I had him run a quick criminal history," Sloane said. "Pretty much what you'd expect — assaults, drunk and disorderly, one case of assault on an officer."

"Has he spent any time in prison?"

"Not prison, no, but some county jail time up and down the coast. But that doesn't mean he's a pussycat. Guys like de Campo have an uncanny ability to avoid getting hemmed up. Sometimes I think God favors drunks and bastards. Anyway, burn that stuff when you're done with it. I never gave you anything. Understand?"

"Yes."

He put his hands on his hips. "So, what are you going to do when you find him?"

"I don't know yet. I'm making this up as I go."

"What would your wife have done?"

"I'm not sure. I'm learning she was maybe not the person I thought she was."

"I'm not so sure that's true," Sloane said.

"Maybe you're right."

"Listen," he said, digging a cell phone from the breast pocket of his western-style shirt. "Let's exchange numbers. I'll let you know if I have any luck calling those other departments. Meanwhile, you keep me posted on how things turn out with Jimmy."

"You think it's him, don't you? Despite what you said about not having any proof of anything."

"You *don't* have proof. There's nothing there. I'll reserve judgment. I'm cautious that way." The smile that came to his face was weary, melancholic. "After all this time, I'd just like to see Carol Thompson get some justice."

I stared down at the documents Sloane had given me. "He's not just going to admit anything to me, even if he *did* do it," I said. "Would it be proof enough if we were able to show that he traveled to the places where these other girls were murdered? If he was, say, in Furnace, West Virginia, at the time Holly Renfrow was killed, then that would be something, right? And in Newburg in 2016 when Gabby was murdered? All of those places over the years."

"If you could prove it," Sloane said, "then maybe that would be something. But it'll be hard to do."

"And if he's driving the same type of car that Lenchantin saw and that the kids at the overlook saw that same night," I added. "That would at least be something, right?"

He shrugged. "Maybe."

"Just maybe?"

"An old sedan with a spotlight on the door? Hell, I still drive one. It's not as uncommon as you'd think. It's not like you have a license plate number."

"He's not going to want to talk to me, is he?"

"Just watch yourself, Decker," he said, clapping a hand on my shoulder. Then he left, ambling toward the shadows at the back of the bar.

I looked back down at the paperwork Sloane had given me. Three arrests for assault and battery, one against a police officer. There was a burglary charge that was nearly a decade old. Some jail time on the books, just as Sloane had said, although I couldn't tell from the printout just how long he'd spent behind bars. An arrest and nol pros for drunk and disorderly. And, of course, that old standby, the DUI.

James de Campo had bounced around a lot, too. The burglary arrest was in Delaware. Two of the assault charges were in Pennsylvania and the third took place in New Jersey. Without comparing the timeline of arrests to your notes, I didn't know just how close he was to the places where the girls had been killed in those approximate areas, nor if the timeline of his arrest would preclude him from being the killer, but just reading the guy's rap sheet caused a widening bubble of exhilaration to buoy up through my body.

There was a photograph of de Campo included in the packet, too — either a mug shot or a driver's license photo, I couldn't be sure which. Absent was the grimy smirk from the yearbook photo, having replaced it with a dour, sullen downturn of his mouth. His hair was still long and shellacked back in a greasy curtain. De Campo's eyes looked like two black buttons someone had pressed into the pale, weather-worn fabric of his face.

I flipped to the rear of the packet. Peter Sloane had highlighted James de Campo's last known address in bright yellow marker. According to this, he was currently living in Pennsauken Township, New Jersey.

I shoved the manila folder into my satchel, along with all your papers, anxious to get on the road. The waitress returned and told me the meal and drinks were on the house. I tried to argue but she wouldn't listen. I thanked her, left a chunk of cash for her tip on the table, gathered my stuff, and was about to head out of the tavern when something above the bar caught my attention. One of the TVs had switched from the sporting event that was still on all the other sets to a black-and-white, slightly pixilated image — the grainy, wavering footage of a security camera. As I walked closer to the television, I saw that the image on the screen was of the interior of the Exxon station in Furnace, West Virginia, the place where Holly Renfrow had last been seen alive. The impossibility of what I was looking at rendered me instantly motionless: I froze right there in the middle of the restaurant, my body suddenly cold, my extremities quaking. I could not remove my eyes from the screen. A figure came in through the convenience store's door, a woman in a tilted beret and houndstooth topcoat. You, Allison. You paused just in the entrance of the store, glancing around, just as you had on the video footage I had watched back in that cramped, stuffy storage room in West Virginia. Yet here you were. I watched as you looked directly at the camera, your face a pale white mime-face beneath the dark cant of your beret. Yet unlike on the actual video footage, this camera zoomed in, closer, closer, until your face filled the screen. Your countenance was comprised of tiny digital squares, glowing with ghostly illumination, each individual square as potent and majestic as an entire solar system.

You stared out at me and I stared back. Opened your mouth, spoke, but there was no sound. You brought up one hand, palm splayed. Had I been closer, I would have reached out and placed my hand against yours.

"Sir," said the waitress with the purple crest of hair, as she tapped me on my shoulder. "You dropped something."

I looked down and saw that your yearbook had slipped out from beneath my arm; it lay with its covers splayed on the sticky linoleum floor like something that had been shot out of the sky. I looked back at the TV and saw that the sporting event was back on the screen.

"You okay?" the waitress asked.

"I am, yeah. Sorry. Thank you."

I bent down and gathered up your yearbook. When I stood, I saw that Dottie Sloane was studying me from the opposite end of the bar. There was a witchlike quality about her that caused me to instinctually take a step backward. But then her features softened and something like pity flashed across her face. This did not make me feel any more put-together.

I raised a hand at her, then headed for the door, my joints feelings loose, stripped, and on the verge of disassembling.

CHAPTER FOURTEEN

1

The Delaware River is just under 400 miles long and boasts a shoreline that runs through five states — New York, New Jersey, Maryland, Delaware, and Pennsylvania. In the summer of 2011, a sixteen-year-old girl named Lauren Chastain vanished from her home in Vineland, New Jersey. After a week-long search, a couple of hikers discovered her body washed up along the muddy reeds of the Union Lake reservoir, which was fed by the Maurice River, one of the tributaries of the Delaware. Much like Gabrielle Colson-Howe, Lauren Chastain's body was severely decomposed, and she was ultimately identified through her dental records. According to the information you had collected, Allison, the cause of Chastain's death was a crushed windpipe due to strangulation. None of the news articles mentioned anything about Lauren Chastain's wrists having been bound, but of course I had my own thoughts on that subject, as I know you did, too. I hoped Peter Sloane might yield more definitive intel from his police department contacts.

According to the paperwork Sloane had provided, James de Campo had been living in Pennsauken in 2011, at the time of Lauren Chastain's murder. My GPS claimed it was about forty miles from his residence in Pennsauken to Vineland, New Jersey, where Chastain had lived and had gone missing. It was another fifteen minutes from

Vineland to Millville, New Jersey, which was where the river emptied into the Union Lake reservoir, where Chastain's body had been found. There was a map of the Maurice River and the Union Lake reservoir among your notes about Lauren Chastain's murder, the New Jersey Division of Fish and Wildlife emblem in the lower right-hand corner of the map. I could only surmise that the red cross you'd printed on the map where the tributary enters the reservoir was where Chastain's body was found. The whole round trip could have taken de Campo approximately two hours.

It fit perfectly.

Where things grew hazy was trying to factor James de Campo into the other murders. What had brought him to Norfolk, Virginia, to murder Margot Idelson in 2006? What had sent him all the way to Bishop, North Carolina, to then kill Shelby Davenport two years later? Was he deliberately spreading out his hunting ground (as Peter Sloane referred to it) in an effort to thwart police and to remain undetected? How was he finding these girls? Based on their photographs, they all looked somewhat similar — sleight of frame, blonde hair, delicate features — which, I surmised, gave de Campo a victim type. But how was he able to locate girls who all looked fairly similar over such a vast area? Had he been stalking them over the Internet? Whatever the answers to these questions were, I was becoming increasingly certain that the man who had killed your sister and all those other girls was now less than an hour from me.

As I approached the Delaware River on my way to Pennsauken, a hot ball of lead began to cultivate itself in the center of my queasy stomach. It seemed my excitement had begun to sour into apprehension the nearer I came to James de Campo's residence. Driving across the Walt Whitman Bridge into Jersey, the faces of all those dead girls turned on a great wheel inside my head. By the time I reached the Jersey side, I felt as if I was going to throw up. First exit I came to, I veered off the highway, pulled into a gas station parking lot, and managed to open my car door just in time to dispatch a trembling, bitter ribbon of acid onto the pavement. When I was done, I went into the gas station and bought a travel-size container of mouthwash and a bottle of water. Over the next fifteen minutes, as the sky purpled with the threat of a storm, I sat in the car and listened to your shitty eighties music. I was trembling. And when my cell phone trilled, I nearly jumped out of my skin.

It was my sister Trayci. I stared at her name and number on the screen until the call went to voicemail.

2

Lafayette Street was a rundown residential strip of roadway situated beside an industrial park, and was flanked on both sides by one-story houses that looked like boxcars cut loose from a train. The houses stood against a backdrop of transmission towers equipped with flashing beacons at their tops. Telephone lines drooped like garlands only about eight feet above the sidewalk.

The storm had arrived, pounding out of the sky with a vengeance, by the time I pulled the Sube up to the curb in front of James de Campo's address. It was a brick-fronted ranch house with an overgrown front yard and a prominent NO SOLICITING sign posted behind the panel of glass in the front door. A bathtub Madonna rose up like a phoenix from the weeds, weather-washed to a spectral white, except for her outstretched hands, which looked grimy with moss. Two vehicles sat in the driveway — a white Hyundai Sonata and a red Toyota short-bed pickup. No brown sedan.

On the drive over, I had concocted a story that I hoped would prevent James de Campo from slamming the door in my face at the sheer mention of the circumstances surrounding your sister's murder. Perhaps he'd be compelled to hear me out if I told him his name featured prominently in your notes — notes for a book you were planning to write about the unsolved murder of your sister. If I led him to believe that a book was going to be published, he might agree to talk to me, if only to get out his side of the story. At least, that was my hope. It was the best I could come up with.

I waited for the thunderstorm to lessen to a drizzle before I got out of the car and walked up the wobbly concrete pavers toward the porch. I noticed that there were bars on the front windows. There was no doorbell so I knocked. I could hear a television blaring from inside. Overhead, thunder rolled across the sky; I managed to blade my body so that I was protected under the narrow awning of the porch from the drizzle spitting down from the clouds.

The door opened partway and a woman peered out at me. She was in her sixties, bleached blonde, with a year-round tan. She wore a loose-fitting terrycloth robe that gaped at the front, exposing the upper portion of a leopard-print bra and a silver crucifix nestled between her freckled cleavage. She eyed me with unmasked suspicion. "No soliciting," she said, tapping a curled fingernail against the glass pane in the door.

"I'm looking for James de Campo."

"You with the IRS?"

"No, ma'am. My name is Aaron Decker. I married a woman named Allison Thompson. She'd been writing a book about the death of her sister back in 2004, in Woodvine, Pennsylvania, and I was hoping to speak to Mr. de Campo about — "

"Holy shit, you got some balls," the woman said, cutting me off. "You don't fool me. Get out of here or I'll call the cops."

"Ma'am — "

"That girl is the devil," the woman said, her face tightening.

"What?"

"We don't want nothing to do with her. I'll call the cops myself."

"I think you're thinking of someone else…"

"Oh, *sure*. You think I'm a moron, buddy? Get lost."

"I don't understand."

"What do you *want*? What are you doing here?" Holding her robe closed with one hand, she peered past me at the Sube parked in the street. "Where is she? Where is she?"

"Allison's dead," I said. "She died back in December."

This statement did not appear to alleviate the woman's suspicion; if anything, her eyes narrowed further.

"Please," I said. "I don't know what you're talking about. What happened? Did something happen between Mr. de Campo and my wife?"

Some species of laughter erupted from the woman's throat. It sounded birdlike and raw. "Did something *happen*? Who do you think I am?"

"Ma'am, I have no idea what you're talking about. I swear."

"What'd you say your name was?"

"Aaron Decker."

"Your wife tried to kill my husband, Mr. Decker."

I opened my mouth to say something more, but nothing came out. I thought I'd misheard her.

A metallic clacking sound issued from somewhere behind her in the gloominess of the house. A shape ambled into view, a swarthy, plodding silhouette with broad shoulders and big arms. A man's voice accompanied it, rough as a foot callous: "Who is it?"

"The devil's husband," she said in a strange singsong voice, shoving the door open while stepping aside. This wasn't an invitation for me to enter, but to allow the figure inside the house to get a better look at me. "Some guy who married Allison Thompson. *Her*."

The man shambled into the doorway. He used a walker, which accounted for the metallic clanking I'd heard, and he moved with evident difficulty although he otherwise seemed to be in good shape. It was James de Campo, all right, though he looked like he'd aged a hundred years since the yearbook photo had been taken. He still wore his hair slicked back and curling behind his ears, but it had gone the color of smoke. His face was thinner and crosshatched by the scars of childhood acne, something that wasn't readily visible in the yearbook photo or in the mugshot Peter Sloane had included with his paperwork. A steel-colored goatee wreathed his mouth, neatly trimmed. I might not have recognized him at all if it hadn't been for his eyes — the same sly, calculating eyes from the yearbook photo. Predatory eyes. It was proof that age does not dilute the people we are.

"James de Campo," I said.

"I hear you right, son? Allison Thompson's dead?"

"Yes, sir."

"Tell me how."

"She was killed in a mall shooting back in December."

"Was she the shooter?" de Campo asked. There was no trace of sarcasm in his voice. I noticed a droop to the left side of his mouth, as if he'd suffered a stroke and never fully recovered.

"Of course not. What the hell is going on?"

"Come in out of the rain," he said.

"Jimmy," said the woman, clearly displeased, but he ignored her.

I entered the house, careful to stand dripping on the tiny floor mat in the cramped little foyer, while the woman in the robe and leopard-print bra maneuvered around me to close the door. There was a living room with a ratty-looking sofa and recliner against one wall and a large bell-shaped birdcage containing two ashy-gray cockatiels in one corner. The TV was on but muted, some televangelist with a ventriloquist dummy's plastic face and a three-piece suit, and there was a smell in the air of staleness and desperation.

"This isn't a good idea, Jimmy," the woman said, peering past the NO SOLICITING sign and out into the street. It was as though she did not believe me, and expected to find you standing out there on their lawn.

"I'm full of good ideas," Jimmy responded. He clanked over toward the recliner and, with some difficulty, managed to drop his considerable bulk into the chair. He was wearing a green New York Jets sweatshirt and loose-fitting sweatpants with holes in the knees. His slippers looked orthopedic — delicate fabric equipped with straps and clunky soles. "Sit," he grunted at me, motioning toward the sofa.

"I'm putting clothes on," announced de Campo's wife, and she hurried off down the hallway.

I sat on the sofa, a smell like unwashed laundry and body odor wafting up from the cushions. De Campo snatched the TV remote from a side table and clicked off the set. Hanging on the wall above the TV was what looked like a paint-by-numbers portrait of Jesus Christ, as if done by a careless child with little artistic ability. Christ's eyes were a startling, wolfish yellow, and appeared to dribble in streams down His sunken cheeks.

"The hell are you doing here?" James de Campo asked. "And don't feed me no shit about writing some book."

I glanced down at my hands, which were clutched together between my knees in a nervous tussle. "Carol Thompson," I said. "Allison's sister. I'm sure you remember what happened to her back in 2004."

"What's it to you?"

Because I didn't have an answer for that, I said, "Your wife. What did she mean when she said Allison had tried to kill you?"

"Pretty much that," he said, quite matter of fact. "First time, she showed up right there on our porch. Raving like a lunatic. Like a madwoman."

"*First* time?" I said.

He ignored me. "I didn't even recognize her. Had all her hair chopped off and dyed black. Been a few years since I'd seen her, as it was."

"When was this?"

"Hell, it was years ago. I remember she was eighteen at the time, because she could've been charged as an adult for what she done to me."

"What'd she do?"

"Came at me with a knife." He rolled up the right sleeve of his sweatshirt to reveal a puckered whitish-pink helix of scar tissue, about three inches in length, running along the inside of his forearm. "Never thought I'd see that girl again in a million years. She'd been a kid last I'd seen her, and like I said, she didn't look the same no more."

"How'd she find you?"

"Good question. Never got around to asking. Was too busy trying not to get stabbed. Also, she wasn't in the… well, she wasn't in the best frame of mind. Brenda wanted me to send her away but she was making a scene on the porch and she wouldn't leave. I told her to come in and we'd talk. Not that I had anything to say to her, but I didn't want her out there rousing the neighbors and getting the police involved. Anyway, she didn't want to talk. She wanted to lecture me on what a piece of shit I was. She also wanted to poke me in the gut like a rib-eye. Picked up a steak knife that was on the kitchen counter and came at me like Jack the fucking Ripper."

He mimed a jabbing motion at my belly, causing me to jerk backward on the sofa. The cockatiels squawked and fluttered about in their cage.

"I wrestled the knife from her, but not before she split me open" —

he traced a finger along the scar on his forearm — "and then I threw her out in the street. She stood out there screaming at the house, chucking rocks at the windows. Busted two of 'em. Brenda called the cops. By the time they showed up, Allison had left, but the police, they eventually picked her up at a gas station or someplace nearby. Asked me if I wanted to press charges."

"Did you?"

"I don't much like dealing with police," he said.

"Why'd she attack you?"

"Because she's fuckin' crazy."

"Mr. de Campo, I spoke with Peter Sloane earlier today. He was the detective who'd been investigating Carol Thompson's murder back in 2004. He was — "

"I remember who he is," he said flatly.

"Sloane said you picked up and left Woodvine soon after Carol was killed."

"Rumors were going around. I lost my job. Had to move on."

"This would be your job as a custodian at the high school?"

He grunted a noise that approximated an affirmative response.

"But you and Lynn Thompson were engaged."

"Carol's death changed things. I didn't want to be there no more."

"Why did Allison come here? She must've wanted to hurt you for a reason."

James de Campo leaned forward in his chair. It looked like it pained him to do so, and I thought I could hear the creaking of his body. He massaged his right knee with one large hand as he spoke. "Why don't you ask me what you came here to ask me, buddy, and quit with the bullshitting."

I swallowed what felt like a mouthful of sand, and said, "Did you kill Carol Thompson?"

Something like a bitter grimace flashed across his face as he reclined back in the chair. "You're as nuts as your dead wife. No. I never touched the girl."

"That's not what I heard."

"Yeah? Well, fuck you."

"Furnace, West Virginia," I said. "Holly Renfrow. Newburg, Maryland. Gabrielle Colson-Howe. Vineland, New Jersey. Lauren Chastain. Bishop, North Carolina. Shelby Davenport. Whitehall, Delaware. Megan Pollock."

"Son, you *are* nuts. What the hell are you talking about?" he said, and even as I continued to prattle off names and locations, I couldn't help watch him rubbing one hand down the length of his right leg, an aggrieved, pained expression beneath the genuine confusion and mounting agitation on his face. My certainty dwindled to a brief pinpoint of light. I glanced at his walker and at his orthopedic slippers and tried to imagine him dragging Holly Renfrow into the woods beyond the overlook, negotiating along that perilous slope of hillside that concluded in a drop down to the Potomac River. A slope on which I'd lost *my* footing and nearly sent myself over the side. It seemed it'd be a physical impossibility for him.

The cockatiels clanged around in their cage, disconcerted. I could smell them.

"Allison came here raving like a madwoman," I said. "Your words. Why?"

De Campo reached into the collar of his sweatshirt and produced a bronze medallion on a slender gold chain from around his neck. He leaned forward so I could get a good look at the triangle embossed on the medallion. I made out the words *Unity, Service, Recovery.* "That's five years, seven months sobriety," he said, not with pride but with a sense of regret that seemed to come up from a wellspring deep inside him. "I wasn't the cheeriest motherfucker back when I knew those two girls."

"You broke my wife's leg."

"You know," he said, tucking the medallion back into his sweatshirt, "part of the Twelve Steps is asking forgiveness of those you've hurt, but what they don't tell you is you probably won't remember half the shit you done. So there's that."

"So you're saying what? That Allison came here to confront you because you were a piece of shit to her and her sister when she was growing up? That it wasn't because she thought you killed Carol?"

"Hell, she knew I didn't kill her sister. She came here because she was fucked up in the head. Sister's death messed her up pretty good and she didn't know what to do about it. Maybe she blamed me because it was easy to blame me — I got one of them faces, I guess — but she knew I had nothing to do with it. You should've seen her when she showed up here on my porch. She looked like some homeless kid been eating outta trashcans. She was angry. That night Carol died, me and Carol, we'd been going at it, all right? Arguing. I don't know. I was drunk and she was running around the neighborhood like a cat in heat. Maybe I laid hands on her; I can't remember, but I'll own it. That's why she left the house. She wouldn't have been killed if we hadn't been fighting — that's about the whole of it, least as far as Allison was concerned, right? So, yeah, sure, I'll take the blame. Allison had no problem blaming me for it. Took a swipe, got some blood, there you go. I thought maybe that was the end of it, and maybe that's why I decided not to press charges. Honestly, I don't know. I was still drinking pretty heavy back then."

"But it wasn't the end of it, was it? You said that was the first time. What else is there? What else happened?"

"Happened," screeched one of the cockatiels, startling me.

James de Campo grimaced again, either from the pain in his throbbing right knee or from the memory of what he was about to tell me.

3

One evening back in 2013, before James de Campo had yet to embrace the comforting glow of sobriety, he had finished his custodial shift at the AMC theater in Pennsauken Plaza and had stopped on his way home at a local bar called the Cougar's Den. True to its namesake, the place was populated primarily by middle-aged women in tight-fitting jeans, their cleavage on full display, their hair teased into an imitation Elvis pompadour. Jimmy had come here to ogle these women while knocking back vodka tonics with the authority of a squadron commander. After about an hour, he was seeing double and chatting somewhat morosely with a woman who sported a visible Van Halen tattoo upon the canvas of sparsely freckled flesh above her left breast. At some point, the woman vanished for the ladies' room, running a set of acrylic fingernails along the nape of his neck as she departed, but then she never returned. That was the rub of it. For Jimmy de Campo, it sometimes seemed like the ladies' room at the Cougar's Den was a black hole into which random bimbos and middle-aged, sex-hungry divorcees were occasionally and inexplicably dispatched.

When he looked up from his fifth or sixth vodka tonic, he met the stately gaze of a young woman seated at a lone table across the barroom. Her features, delicate, were illuminated solely by the glow of a flickering candle in a glass jar seated at the center of the table. She was fairly attractive, what with her long, inky ringlets of hair and her ghost-white complexion, but it was the fact that she was the youngest woman — the youngest *patron* — in this place by at least three decades that commanded Jimmy's attention.

"Who's the broad?" he asked the bartender, a guy named Steve who occasionally had to call the cops when shit got too rowdy in the place.

Steve appraised the woman. "Beats me. Never seen her before."

"What's she drinking?"

"Merlot."

"Is it expensive?"

"Six bucks a glass."

A bit pricier than his rail drinks, but he said, "What the hell, send her one over on me."

"A regular Don Juan," Steve said, and poured a glass.

When the drink was sent over to the woman's table, Jimmy, grinning like someone who'd just cashed out at Caesar's, raised his own glass in acknowledgement. The woman's face, tucked behind that wave of dark hair, seemed to gleam at him, as if she was powered by some other-worldly illumination at the core of her body. He knew he was drunk, but he also knew that he could feel no pain — and feel no rejection — when he was drunk. Shoot at enough rabbits, you'll eventually hit one.

Shoving himself off his stool, he staggered to the restroom, fired a laser-beam of electric-yellow urine into the commode, then studied his glazed and sallow reflection in the mirror. He then hocked an oyster-sized gobbet of phlegm into the sink before stepping back out into the barroom.

The woman, much to his chagrin, had vanished.

"That ladies' room is a curse," he complained to Steve as he settled his tab. Damp, crinkly bills appeared on the bar top. "Someday, NASA's gonna find a bunch of Jersey broads circling the Milky Way like satellites. Mark my words."

"Marked," Steve agreed, not bothering to give Jimmy back his change.

It was a weeknight and the parking lot was only mildly populated. The surrounding businesses — an auto-body shop and a bank — were all dark. Directly overhead, the moon was a fat pearl wreathed in smoky black clouds.

A figure was approaching him at a rapid pace from the far end of the parking lot. Had he not had so much to drink, he might have noticed the person right away, might have even avoided the whole ordeal entirely, but that was not the case. As it was, he was all-consumed by the Herculean task of fishing his car keys from the pocket of his coveralls. An impossibility, it seemed that the keys had somehow enlarged and were no longer able to be extracted through the too-small opening of his pocket.

It wasn't until the person was less than three feet away that Jimmy de Campo looked up. Bleary-eyed and confused, the figure appeared as nothing more than a shadow that had detached itself from the night and come to life.

"Who the — "

His words were silenced as the figure struck him across his left kneecap with something long, solid and unforgiving. A strobe of blinding light flashed before his eyes. The pain that followed was like nothing he had ever felt before — a hammer-strike to the core of his marrow. He collapsed to the pavement just as the figure — dressed all in black and with a balaclava over their head, like a cat burglar in an old movie — swung the unforgiving staff again, this time connecting with his right shin.

Jimmy heard the bone break. It was a sound that echoed out over the otherwise silent parking lot like a firework, and it was a sound he would hear night after night while doped to the gills on pain meds in the weeks to follow.

The figure stood directly above him, the fat, round moon silhouetted behind the figure's masked face. Like a halo. Indeed, he was briefly accosted by the certainty that this figure *was* some sort of celestial or spiritual being, albeit one here for revenge for every misdeed he'd ever managed to perpetrate throughout the course of his drunk and miserable life.

He was struck several more times, his consciousness wavering as his legs were pulverized. At one point, when he rolled over on his back and ceased holding up his hands in useless defense, it felt as if his legs had been reduced to bits of broken glass and gravel in his jumpsuit. The back of his head resting on the cold, damp pavement of the parking lot, he watched as the figure raised the instrument once more. Even in his fading consciousness, he saw that it was a crowbar. He saw, too, that his attacker was not a man but a woman: he could see it in the stance of the masked figure, but also in the ringlet of black hair that had shaken loose from the balaclava and curled down his attacker's shoulder.

The woman raised the crowbar above her head, its silhouette bisecting the face of the moon. He knew in that instant that she was going to smash his skull to rubble. And in truth, he welcomed it. The pain in his legs was so great that, strangely, it had rendered him mostly numb. With some detachment, he wondered if this mad woman had busted something vital in his spine, severing the nerves.

But then she lowered the crowbar. It was a chilly night, and he could see plumes of vapor issuing from the facemask of his attacker. The woman's chest rose and fell, rose and fell, the undeniable accentuation of breasts beneath the ribbed black sweater, rose and fell, the steaming of her hot breath in the cold night, rose and fell, rose and fell…

And then she was gone.

4

It was other-Aaron whom I had to temporarily employ in order for me to listen to James de Campo's story. A stand-in for sanity's sake. I had detached from myself, had fitfully withdrawn into the vast and anonymous caverns of my mind where reality was like a fuzzy and unfocused movie projected on a rippling screen. And even within these protective confines, I couldn't fully escape it. I *saw* you there, doing these things. I heard the scrape of the crowbar as it connected with the asphalt, saw the explosive sparks it elicited each time its curved head scoured across the ground. A miner's pickaxe sparking off stone.

James de Campo continued his story in the calm, dilatory tones of someone under mild sedation. Perhaps this was a tale he'd told many times before, maybe even in one of his AA meetings. There was the drunk couple who stumbled upon his shattered and quaking body sometime later that night, half conscious and hallucinating in the parking lot of the Cougar's Den. The wail of an ambulance and the blessed black shroud that fell over him the moment he was jostled off the ground by paramedics. A prolonged hospital stay, and the jangly, aching discord in his lower extremities that he still felt, all these years later, every single day. The pain in that hospital bed had been so great and terrible that it had felt otherworldly. The only thing greater was his need for a drink. But after just a few days in the hospital, and as he slipped in and out of consciousness, he received a visitor who seemed to rob him of his addiction all in one fell swoop. Like a snap of fingers.

"A vision," he said, and it was only here, in this moment, that a fire gleamed behind those sly fox's eyes. "I knew she wasn't real, but she had come back. The vengeful angel. Only this time all in white, burning like a forest fire, and instead of a face she wore the moon."

As he said this, my own gaze shifted toward the paint-by-numbers Jesus on the wall above the TV. Those feral wolf's eyes raged like twin suns.

"Had a stroke while I was laid up in the hospital, too. It made me useless on one side as well as my legs. Never felt so helpless. Went through a year of rehab, on the stroke and on the legs. Christ, the legs. My body ached so bad I wanted to die. But I sobered up, because there wasn't any way I could do both. And anyway, every time I felt the urge to drink, I'd just sit there and close my eyes for a spell. And every time I closed my eyes, I kept seeing her shining moon-face right there above me, staring down, that crowbar poised to whack my head apart like some Halloween pumpkin."

With some difficulty, he bent over and hooked a set of fingers underneath the left-leg cuff of his sweatpants. Grunting, he hoisted the pant leg to mid-shin. That was far enough: I saw the lumpy, alien terrain of his lower leg, the Frankenstein stitching and tender bolt holes that, all these years later, still looked disconcertingly fresh. Apparently satisfied by the look on my face, he let the pant leg drop back down then eased himself back in his chair.

"By the time I'd completed a year of rehabilitation, I was stone sober, and my mind had cleared. It was like a storm blowing through a town, leaving bits of debris everywhere, but also clearing the skies at the same time. And it was in that clarity — the calm after the storm, I guess you'd call it — that I realized who that woman had been. God almighty, but it took me a year to put a name to that face."

"You're wrong," I told him. "It wasn't her."

Those sly fox's eyes widened in mock surprise. "Oh, no? Because you knew her so well? Listen, bud, I'm sure I've pissed off enough women in my lifetime that any number of 'em might want to bash my face in, Lynn Thompson included, but I only know one gal who'd actually try to do it."

I let this sink in. My immediate reaction was to not believe him — it just couldn't be true. It wasn't *you*, Allison. Moreover, in 2013, we were already together, living in the apartment in Eastport. I wanted so badly to think it was bullshit, and that this man was a drunk and an abuser and possibly even a murderer… but I couldn't. I couldn't believe these things because in my heart I knew they weren't true.

My mind slid back to that time you returned from what you'd said was a media bazaar in New Jersey, only to return shaken up, discordant, and with blisters along your palms like you'd been swinging a —

(crowbar)

— baseball bat. The only truth in all of this, Allison, was that you had been a stranger to me. An absolute stranger — this other-Allison operating under a cloak of deceit throughout the duration of our marriage. It took your death and the insight of strangers to get me to realize this.

"To be clear," James de Campo went on, his voice a touch weaker now. "I didn't get sober because your wife came to me like some kind of angel. I didn't see what she did to me that night as some divine intervention that I gotta change my ways. I'm not that far gone, pal."

"Then why'd you get sober?"

"So I could fucking kill her." And he grinned, revealing teeth like peanuts behind his silver goatee. "She came for me once, tried to open up my belly, got my arm instead. Came for me again, years later, and made it so I'm a cripple. Not just that, though. It was the way she hesitated near the end." That horrible grin stretched across his sallow face. "That crowbar ready to bash my skull. One whack and it's lights out, boys, and for good. But she didn't do it. She bashed my legs to shit in the heat of the moment but she lost her nerve to finish the job in the end. That's what I remember most from that night, other than the pain. The way she stood there, catching herself in that last moment. Stopping like that. Thinking it through, maybe."

"Enough," I said.

"And so I thought, shit, what if she finds the nerve some day? What if five, ten, fifteen years from now I'm stumbling out of another shithole like the Cougar's Den, and there she is, dressed all in black except for a big shiny moon where her face should be. That crowbar resting on her shoulder like she's Cal fucking Ripken up at the plate.

Who knows? Maybe this time she won't hesitate. Maybe this time she'll finish the job. So what do I do? Well, fuck, buddy — I get *straight*. I get *sober*. And I bust my ass through a year of rehab so that I'm *strong* again, or at least as strong as I'm gonna get. And then I waited for her to come around again. I was ready, and I was waiting. But I was getting anxious, too. Riled up, I guess. I called up her momma — 'Where's your girl, Lynn?' — but she said she ain't seen that old Allie-Cat since she was a teenager."

The sting of your nickname on his lips forced my heart into my throat. I opened my mouth to challenge him but nothing came out.

"Whether she lied or not, who knows?" de Campo went on. "Allison never had much regard for her momma, neither."

"You're lying. Her mother's dead." It was my voice, sure, but issuing from some distant plateau.

De Campo laughed. "Dead? That's news to me."

"Allison said — " But the words hooked in my throat.

"Don't you have no clue who you been playing with, buddy?"

Jesus Christ, Allison.

"So what *then*?" de Campo continued, his voice cracking in the process. "I'll tell you what *then*, pal. I waited for her to show herself. All these years, I sat and I waited for her to show herself. I swore it would happen. I swore it. But now here you are telling me that ain't gonna happen. Is that what I'm to understand? That the little Allie-Cat bought the fucking farm and here I am busted to shit for it?"

There was nothing I could say to that. In the cage, the cockatiels began to squawk.

"Was a good run," de Campo said. He reached into the stretched-out collar of his sweatshirt and yanked the sobriety medallion from his neck. The chain snapped soundlessly. He set the medallion trailing its broken chain on the table beside the television remote. "I think you better show yourself out, good buddy," de Campo said as he shifted, wincing, in his recliner. "I'd get up, but, well…" His words concluded in a gruff chortle that segued into a coughing fit.

I rose from the couch and went to the front door as de Campo clicked the TV back on. He cranked up the volume, the televangelist's voice crackling through the speakers. In the cage, the birds became frenzied, nipping at the bars with their knobby gray beaks. Feathers spiraled about the room.

"I bet I'll see her moon-face again tonight," de Campo called back at me. He did not look in my direction, only stared at the television. "It's been years since I last saw it, but I'll bet she makes an encore performance tonight."

I tugged on the doorknob but the door didn't budge. A momentary pang of irrational terror caused me to think that I'd never get the door open and I'd die here in this house, while the plastic-faced man on TV howled about damnation and the birds in the bell-shaped cage chittered and squawked and squirted greenish globs of shit onto their flooring of newspaper. But then I realized the deadbolt had been turned, so I cranked it, yanked the door open, and hurried out into the rain just as a peal of thunder, loud as Armageddon, clashed across the sky.

"We're doomed, brothers and sisters!" I heard the televangelist chide a second before I slammed the door shut.

I took off down the porch and slid through a puddle at the end of the concrete walkway. I fell on my ass, my teeth rattling in my skull. Scrambling around the car toward the driver's side, I dug my keys out of my pocket just as a second clang of thunder cracked the sky in half. I jumped in the car, cranked the ignition, and your sappy music erupted from the speakers. Pausing to catch my breath, I glanced back up at James de Campo's house and saw a face in one of the windows at the far end of the house. Brenda. As I stared at her, she retreated back into the gloom, a section of curtain replacing her scowling visage.

Don't you have no clue who you been playing with, buddy?

That I should believe James de Campo over you, Allison, was troubling. I felt foolish, tricked. I struggled not to believe him, but the night in the bathroom with those blisters on your palms kept rerunning through my mind as a rebuttal to any argument I tried to brook. What had you said to me that night? *I've spent a lot of time in darkness, Aaron, so much so that I've churned it up and stirred it to the surface and made it this real, tangible thing. It lives alongside me. It moves when I move.* Had I mistakenly thought you had been speaking of your sister when, in fact, you had been confessing to what you had done in Jersey? What you had done with a crowbar?

I steered the Sube away from the curb, my entire body suddenly cold and wet and shivering.

5

I drove around for a while before stopping at a family-style Italian restaurant to force some food down my gullet. Yet I could only choke down half a breadstick and a rather soggy meatball before throwing in the towel. My stomach wasn't up to the challenge. It seemed my investigative priorities had changed over the past hour, Allison. No longer was I hunting your sister's murderer and the murderer of all those other teenage girls — the monster I had come to think of as the Woodvine Killer; now I was hunting *you*, or so it felt like, desperate to unlock whatever secrets remained hidden in your underground chamber. A mother, for one thing. Still alive.

— *Perhaps*, suggested other-Aaron, who was now seated opposite me at the two-person table in the restaurant, *searching for the killer and searching for the real Allison are the same thing.*

I drank my entire glass of water in several thirsty gulps. Irked by his constant pragmatism, I didn't want to hear from other-Aaron at the moment.

I managed to force down the other half of my breadstick before paying the bill and slinking back out into the rainy night. In the car, I dialed the cell number Peter Sloane had given me. I expected to get his voicemail, so I was surprised when he answered after the first ring.

"Aaron," he said. "Did you go? What happened?"

"It's not de Campo," I told him. "He's a piece of work, all right, but his legs are beat to shit. He couldn't kill a squirrel."

Sloane made a contemplative humming sound on the other end of the line.

"Allison's mother is still alive," I said. "At least, she was a few years ago, according to de Campo."

"All right," Sloane said, not comprehending.

"Allison told me her mother had died before we met. When she was still living in Woodvine."

"Well, I can confirm that Lynn Thompson was still alive when I left Woodvine in 2006. As for what's happened to her since, I can't really — "

"She's alive," I said, cutting him off. "I know she is. Allison had been lying to me. Just like she lied about what happened to her sister, she lied about her mother." I shook my head, the early twinges of a migraine sparking to life behind my eye sockets. "I just don't know why."

"Some people just want to forget," Sloane said. "They want to start over fresh."

"Peter, what the hell's going on?"

"You mean rhetorically, or are you actually expecting an answer from me?"

"I don't know what I'm expecting. I don't know what to do." I paused. "That's not true. I know what I'm going to do."

"What's that?"

"Go to Woodvine. Find Allison's mother."

"Is that a good idea?"

"I don't think I have a choice. I feel like I'm falling apart."

"What about this killer? You putting it on the backburner or giving up completely?"

"Shit, I don't know. I don't know what I'm doing anymore. I started out looking for one thing and now I'm looking for something else. Except it doesn't feel like looking. It feels like… I don't know. Something else."

Strangely, I thought of Bobbi Negri's mother saying, *We haunt ourselves.* It caused a chill to ripple through my body.

"Aaron," Sloane said. "I was able to make a phone call for you today. Norfolk Police Department. Margot Idelson, the girl murdered in 2006?"

That chill turned into an icy hand that clenched my heart. "Yes?"

"You were right. Her wrists had been secured behind her back by some kind of wire. They were still on her when her body was found, strangled to death. Police kept it out of the papers."

"Jesus Christ…"

"I'm waiting on calls back from some of the other departments, but I think we both know what they'll tell us."

"Right."

"Allison was right," he said.

I shut my eyes. Rain pummeled the roof of the Sube.

"Maybe you're right, too," Sloane said. "Maybe there's an answer waiting for you in Woodvine. Be safe, Aaron."

He ended the call.

I pulled out of the parking lot and, in the rain and beneath the cover of darkness, headed west toward Pennsylvania.

PART FOUR

THE
MISSING
CIRCLE

CHAPTER FIFTEEN

1

Places have secrets, too.

During the entirety of our relationship, and as best as I can recall, you spoke of your hometown only once. It was during a drive to Lancaster for a weekend in Dutch Country for our one-year anniversary. You had reservations about going, but *I* had reservations at a five-star bed and breakfast which I'd sprung on you as a surprise. I knew you'd grown up in Pennsylvania, but you never spoke about it. You had alluded to the darkness you'd left behind in your hometown, a darkness born from the tragedy of your long-gone family: the accidental death of your father, the drowning of your sister, and the subsequent demise of your mother, who'd wasted the rest of her life in the bottle, angst-ridden from the losses your family had suffered. When you turned eighteen, you had run away and never looked back. There was nothing for you there anymore. Your past had come up during our courtship, of course, but you had made it clear it was a past you desired to remain in the past. I had respected this and never pushed you for information, never tried to draw things out of you. But then on that drive through Pennsylvania, something — some small but crucial wheel — began to turn inside your mind.

Out of nowhere, you said, "Do you know what they call the area between Philadelphia and Pittsburgh?"

"What's that?"

"Pennsyltucky."

I chuckled. "How far are we from where you grew up?" Despite your feelings about your hometown, it felt natural to ask this question in that moment. In fact, it had come out of me before I realized what I was saying. But when you didn't respond, I decided to let it go. I turned up the music and kept my eyes on the road, pretending I hadn't said anything.

You turned and stared out the passenger window. We were coasting along a strip of asphalt that clung to the side of a large hill. To the right of the road, the landscape fell away to long stretches of sun-dappled valleys and the periodic clusters of small towns. At some point, you clicked off the music.

"Woodvine, Pennsylvania," you said. "It was a refinery town. The sky was perpetually dark from the smoke of the gas fires, and when the refinery eventually closed down, the air still tasted like soot. All the men had black fingernails and the women had purple pouches under their eyes. It was the missing circle of Dante's hell. It pulled you in, you know? As a little kid, I'd wake up screaming, convinced that our house was on fire, but it was just the smell of the refinery — a smell that seeped into our walls and our bodies. Made all our food taste horrible, although I didn't realize this until after I left town and experienced places that *weren't* chemically poisoned.

"My dad drove a truck. He thought he'd escaped the pull of the refinery. Joke's on him, though — he was killed in a wreck out in the Midwest while driving a big rig. I was just a kid. I only remember him as a shape — large, sullen, broad-shouldered, with big, rough hands. Always smelling of booze. My mother took a job at the refinery after the accident. She had those purple bags beneath her eyes, too. She worked there until she fell and got hurt. The company paid out, and then the whole refinery closed a few years after that. My mom, she ultimately drank herself to death. This was because of what happened to my sister, not my dad. Not losing her job at the refinery."

"Your sister who drowned," I said. You had mentioned it on one or two occasions, but it had always come up as if being drawn from you, like siphoning a poison from your veins. "What was her name again?"

"Carol. She drowned in the Elk Head River, which ran through town. Its waters were gray with runoff from the refinery, the banks always scummy with this strange yellow foam. There were always dead fish along the riverbank, too, and in the summer their corpses buzzed with flies and you could smell them rotting."

It was no wonder you never talked of home and of your family. There was nothing but tragedy in your past.

"Sometimes it would rain for weeks nonstop," you went on, still gazing out the window and at the countryside. "Water would flood through the town, and when it receded, it left behind black ash and mud on everything. There were no birds — the refinery kept them away, the stink of it unappealing. Birds are smarter than people in that way. We stayed and the birds left. Even after the refinery shut down, the birds stayed away. In the winter, it snowed gray clumps, like bits of dirty pillow stuffing blown in from a fire. The *snow* in Woodvine even smelled bad. Dogs screamed all day and night. Cats started walking on their hind legs. Children began speaking backwards for no particular reason. Once, a group of mean little boys from my elementary school pulled a mermaid from the Elk Head River and beat her to death with sticks. And there are places in town where you can exist along two timelines at once. Like, you could be standing on a street corner but also somewhere else in the world at that exact same moment. Sometimes you can see or hear yourself talking through one of those rips in the fabric of the universe."

You turned and looked at me, your face drawn. "There's a man made up of poison gas who lives in an abandoned castle. He'll get inside your skull and drive you mad."

I stared at you, unsure what to say, what to think.

But then you smiled. Laughed. You'd been putting me on.

"Jesus Christ, Allison. I'm not sure where the truth stopped and the bullshit started," I admitted.

"Exactly," you said. "That's exactly what it was like living in Woodvine."

2

I drove about two hundred miles under cover of darkness, stopping once for gas and for a cup of coffee to keep me awake. I did not give much consideration to the dull throb of apprehension that had begun to settle down upon my shoulders like a blanket of chainmail. Another hundred miles through the night, and its presence was now undeniable. The GPS on my phone started going wonky, recalculating my route over and over again. No sooner would I turn off the highway and onto a secondary road, the GPS would reconfigure my route and have me going off in the opposite direction. I must have wasted thirty minutes backtracking. Frustrated and lonely, I kept turning on the CD player just to have those sappy old songs trickle into the car. This made me maudlin, so the music did not stay on very long. Instead, I tried to harness a radio signal from the air but was rewarded with nothing but static. It seemed my cell phone was having trouble connecting to the network, too, which could have accounted for the way the GPS was behaving. Or misbehaving.

Then, on a particularly desolate stretch of road, a deer flashed through the shimmer of the Sube's high beams. Its proximity caused a cry to lurch up out of my throat as it bounded off into the woods beyond the shoulder of the road. I jerked the wheel and the Sube's headlights cut sharply to the left, washing over the blacktop. I spun the wheel in the opposite direction, overcorrecting, and those headlights swung back across the road. Trees rushed up and filled the windshield. I stamped on the brake and the car fishtailed. There was the *rud-rud-rud-rud* of the rumble strip followed by what sounded like the blast from a cannon. The Sube juddered to a standstill, the acrid reek of burnt rubber filling my nose.

My heart racing and my hands squeezing the steering wheel, I sat there catching my breath. I waited for the world to swim back into focus. Once I'd gathered my wits about me, I eased my foot off the brake. The car galloped over the rumble strip and thumped back onto the road. It shuddered and wobbled like an old apple cart. I'd blown a goddamn tire.

"Shit."

I shifted into Park then turned off the ignition. Silence dropped down on me like a shroud. In both directions the road stretched into pure darkness. Trees crowded the shoulders on either side, black and massive and overbearing. The moon was nonexistent; the only light out there was the milky sheen issuing from the Sube's headlamps.

I climbed out of the car and into a night that was frigid and windy. The air felt thin and smelled discreetly of smoke. When the wind blew, it shook the trees with a low, moan-like susurration. I went around to the passenger side and, using the flashlight on my cell phone, saw that the front tire was hanging loosely from the rim. It could have been worse; the blowout could have sent me careening into the trees.

I went to the rear of the Sube and popped the trunk. Beneath the floor mat was a donut and a jack. Also, a crowbar.

Christ, Allison.

The trees whispered and rattled their leaves all around me.

Something caused the hairs to stand up on the nape of my neck, and it wasn't the wind. I reached down and grabbed the crowbar.

— *What is this?* other-Aaron spoke up.

Perhaps it was the culmination of all I'd been through over the past several weeks — or perhaps it was more specifically related to the story Denise Lenchantin had told me, about blowing a tire on that desolate mountain road in the middle of the night — but I was suddenly overcome with the certainty that I was not alone out here. The deer bounding across the road had caused me to jerk the wheel and lose temporary control of the vehicle, sure, but how plausible was it that someone had also sabotaged my tire at some point in the evening? It could have happened easily enough during one of my stops for gas or coffee. Someone could have pulled up alongside me, jammed a screwdriver or a nail into the wall of the tire to weaken its integrity.

The crowbar in my hands, I turned around and surveyed the dark, empty roadway. A gauzy mist was creeping out from between the trees and swirling along the blacktop in both directions.

"Hello?" I shouted, the echo of my voice bowling down the mountain road. "Is someone out there?"

— *There's no one out there*, said other-Aaron. *You are alone.*

Was it so impossible to think that in all my running around, I had inadvertently tipped off the killer? That this whole thing would end right here because he'd been following me these last few hundred miles? That he'd used the same trap on me that he'd used on Denise Lenchantin last fall? I thought of your gun, Allison, still tucked away inside the chest in our closet. Fat lot of good it would do me there if someone were to stroll out from between these trees…

— *Just change the tire and get the hell back on the road.*

I did just that: I tossed the crowbar back in the trunk, took out the donut and the jack, and went to work. The donut was firm and filled with air, but I wouldn't be able to move along too quickly on it. When

I'd finished, I held up my cell and examined the GPS route on the glowing map — a route that continually recalculated and repositioned itself even as I stood there holding the phone steady. A few times, it mapped a course where no road existed, a bold blue line straggling off into the trees. And then that route vanished, too.

I was mopping grease from my hands with a wad of fast-food napkins I'd found in the glove compartment when a pair of headlights appeared on the horizon. I paid the vehicle little attention until it slowed to a stop in the road beside the Sube. I looked up just as a third light — bright as a lighthouse tower — winked on and pinned me there like a felon on the side of the road. I brought one arm up to shield the glare from my eyes.

"Is there a problem?" said a man's voice from within the car.

"Blew a tire," I said. My heartbeat had picked up again, so potent I could feel it pulsing at the base of my throat.

"Need assistance?"

"I'm okay, thanks. I had a spare."

The vehicle idled there, expelling plumes of exhaust that trailed down the center of the roadway before it was carried off by the wind.

"I *am* a bit lost, though," I said. "I'm trying to get to Woodvine."

"Fifty miles east on this road," said the man.

I approached his vehicle, sidestepping out of the glare of his spotlight. The man's face took form behind the spotlight, a pale, square apparition with a military buzz cut. Despite the undercover car, he was in uniform. Pennsylvania State Trooper.

"Fifty miles *east*?" I said. I pointed for clarification in the direction I had come. "That way?"

"That's east."

Somehow, I'd driven right past the town. How had that happened?

"You been drinking tonight?" said the officer.

"No, sir."

"Make sure to clear any debris from the road before you leave."

"Yes, sir."

The cop's window scrolled up and he pulled away — slowly at first, as if struggling with whether or not he should leave me here on the side of the road. I watched as his car picked up speed until his taillights, those beady red eyes, were eaten up by the night.

Something in my head, some gear or cog, rolled over and clicked into place with an audible latching sound. His hot breath against my ear, other-Aaron whispered that he knew what I was thinking.

3

I stayed that night at the Red Robin Motor Lodge, where I stripped out of my clothes and took a long, hot shower. Thirty minutes later, I crawled into bed where I turned through every page of your high-school yearbook, looking for someone in particular. A face I had seen before. A name. Exhausted from driving, I could feel my eyelids grow heavier with each page that I turned. Twice, I nodded off, only to jerk my head up and slam it against the rickety headboard, convinced in my half-sleep that the character for whom I searched had sprung up from these pages and had fled from the motel room while my eyes were shut.

I had gone through the yearbook several times before, of course. I had a recollection of a particular page — a particular photo — and now I was desperate to confirm the notion that was pinballing around inside my skull. A notion that had occurred to me as I'd watched the Pennsylvania State Trooper drive away down that lonely stretch of road earlier that night. And just when I thought the page did not exist — that I had somehow conjured it up in my mind — I saw it. Right there. Page fifty-eight.

I sat up in bed for a very long time. When I finally switched off the little lamp beside the bed and eased myself down onto the stiff, overly starched pillowcase, I remained staring at the ceiling and at the zebra stripes of moonlight filtering in through the blinds. Wondering if I hadn't been so wrong back in the car, when I had frightened myself by humoring the possibility that the Woodvine Killer had somehow gotten wind of my involvement in all this, and that he was tracking me right at this very moment. That he knew where I was headed and was close by, maybe even in this very same motel, maybe in the room next to mine. That I might have already confronted him about your theories without realizing his true identity. Maybe the burst tire hadn't been an accident after all. The same thing had happened to Denise Lenchantin, hadn't it? My mind kept returning to that, and this time, other-Aaron did little to dissuade me from it.

It was the clicking sound that had echoed in my head after the Pennsylvania trooper in the unmarked police car had driven away that returned to me now — a sound very much like the snapping of fingers. It was the sound of *realization*, echoing throughout the curved and lightless chamber of my skull. It was, too, the words other-Aaron had whispered in my ear.

— *Denise Lenchantin said it was someone pretending to be a cop. Yet who's to say the man was pretending?*

It was Peter Sloane's picture on page fifty-eight of the yearbook.

4

I dreamed of you ghosting toward me across the surface of a river, your body shrouded in an early morning mist, your flesh pale and bare except for a bright red sweatshirt that really wasn't red at all, just a faded pink, but saturated with the blood from a gushing head wound, so red now that it was black, SAINT FRANCIS YOUTH LEAGUE printed on it in scrawling script, and your arms reached out for me and your neck was a corkscrewed purple stalk impressed upon by furious fingers, and your eyes were hollow pits, and when I awoke, I did so screaming and clawing at the air, as if I could rip through the fabric of this life and crawl screaming into the next.

5

Around ten o'clock the following morning, as I sat devouring a breakfast of Dunkin' Donuts in a shopping center where, at the Midas across the street, I was having a new tire put on the Sube, my cell phone rang. I thought that maybe it was Sloane, and so I hesitated, but it was Trayci again. I'd forgotten she'd tried to get in touch with me yesterday afternoon. I decided to answer it so she wouldn't think something terrible had happened to me.

"Where the hell have you been? I've been trying to reach you for days."

"Hey, Tray, nice to hear from you, too."

"Don't be a dick. What've you been up to? Owen said he stopped by the house last night but you weren't home."

"Whose house?"

"Yours. Whose do you think?"

"What was Owen doing in Maryland?"

"He had two nights in Baltimore for a conference, thought he'd be a good brother-in-law and take you out to dinner. Your loss, I guess."

"Shoot. Well, that was nice of him. Tell him I said thanks."

"Where *are* you?"

"Uh, I'm doing some traveling," I said.

"Traveling."

"I thought it would be good to get out of the house for a while."

"Exactly *where*?"

"Pennsylvania," I said before I could come up with a suitable lie. "Visiting some old college buddies."

"Let me get you a plane ticket, Aaron. Come out and see the kids."

"I can get my own plane ticket, Tray."

"Then do it."

"I've got work. Once I'm done translating this book I'll come out. I promise."

"You said you finished the book last month."

I closed my eyes, rubbed a set of fingers along my brow. A headache was stirring to life behind my eyes. A part of me wanted to confide in my sister just what I was doing, but I also did not want to worry her. "Just working on some rewrites," I lied.

"So you can do some traveling with old college buddies but you can't visit your sister and her family."

"You're not really angry, are you?"

She sighed. "No, Aaron, I'm not angry. I've just been worried about you. You need to answer your phone when I call. And maybe I'm just... I don't know. Overreacting? I hope so." A pause. "I've been having a recurring dream that something bad is going to happen to you."

"Tray," I said. "Nothing bad is going to happen to me. You're being silly." Yet my voice shook as I said this.

"Aaron, I've been waking up in the middle of the night like you're in my room, standing over my bed. Watching me. Like a ghost."

It made me think of Rita Renfrow, and what she'd said as we climbed the staircase to the second floor of her house and to her daughter's bedroom: *I keep dreaming that there's someone in the house. A man.*

"Really, though," Trayci said. "How're you holding up? Be honest with me."

"I've been able to keep my mind busy," I said, which was the truth. Visiting dark places, tracking a murderer, but busy nonetheless. No lie there.

"Have you given any thought to seeing a therapist? I think it's a really good idea."

"I don't know, Tray. I don't want to wallow in that stuff."

"It could help. You're not one of those closed-minded macho idiots, Aaron. You know it could do you some good."

"I'm just not in that place yet. But when I am — *if* I am — then I promise you I'll look into it. I'll talk to someone."

"And you'll come out here, spend some time, right?"

"I will. It'll be nice to see the kids. It's been a while."

"Just do me one favor, huh? Answer your goddamn cell phone when I call, will you?"

"You got it. My bad."

"Okay." She sighed. She was three years older than me, and I was suddenly picturing her sliding me around the tiled kitchen floor of our childhood home in a laundry basket, me shrieking with laughter, Trayci's bright, buoyant, wild face filling up the canvas of my world. "I love you, little brother."

"I love you, Tray."

I ended the call, surprised to feel a smile on my face despite the headache that was drilling for oil in my skull. For the first time since your death, Allison, I actually considered going out to Minnesota and spending time with Trayci and her family — of actually moving forward with my life instead of moving backward and creeping through your bleak, hopeless hunting ground, and now, today, with my sights set on your hometown and a mother you told me had died years ago, I was attempting to dig up your past to separate the truth from your lies. I should close the book on all of this, forget it, move on with my life. Your secrets had been your secrets for a reason, and I should let them be. And as for the Woodvine Killer... well, that had been your obsession, not mine.

Except that now it *was*. It was mine, too.

Spiritual transference.

CHAPTER SIXTEEN

1

Dense black storm clouds had gathered above Woodvine, Pennsylvania, as if the town were brooding over some wrong-doing or perhaps plotting something sinister. For a time now, as I drove down the crumbling ribbon of asphalt that led into town, fluffy black filaments snowed lazily from the sky and collected along the Sube's windshield. It wasn't until a procession of smokestacks appeared on the horizon that I realized it was ash. *In the winter, it snowed gray clumps, like bits of dirty pillow stuffing blown in from a fire*, you had once told me. I understood you now.

The refinery stood against a storm-darkened sky, a construct of steel girders, concrete walls, cylindrical smokestacks that, back when the facility was still operational, had belched thick, noxious smog into the stratosphere. I imagined that, back in the day, one might not discern between the gray, low-slung clouds and the seepage from those massive smokestacks; it all would have commingled into a churn of poison gas that hung above the landscape like the sword of Damocles. I stared at the refinery as I drove by. Something about it bothered me, and I was glad to leave it behind in the Sube's rearview mirror.

Woodvine came into view soon after. Tumbledown white houses, a collection of them, lined the streets. A whitewashed church of indecipherable denomination stood powdered in gray soot. Downtown was a grid of single-story cement buildings and gas stations, of laundromats and bowling alleys, a bank and a coffee shop, a pawn shop with wire mesh drawn down over its plate-glass windows. A boarded-up movie theater at the far end of an empty, bombed-out parking lot. And drinking establishments — I counted seven of them as I wound up and down the narrow downtown streets. They outnumbered the churches.

At the crest of a hill stood Elk Head High School, a medieval brick saltbox that would have looked perfectly at home with bars on its windows, concertina wire on the fence and a sniper's tower in the rear. It was a weekday and school was in session, cars shimmering in the parking lot, a few teenagers smoking cigarettes on the curb out front. There was a brick sign on the lawn with the school's name embossed on it, the faded green elk's head emblem right beside the name.

I parked across the street and stayed there for a while. Something wanted me to. On the passenger seat was your yearbook. I opened it to page fifty-eight — to the black-and-white photo of a younger Peter Sloane standing before a classroom full of students. The caption beneath the photograph read: *"Detective Peter Sloane speaks with students about police work on Career Day."*

Back at Sloane's bar, when I'd explained that the killer was in your yearbook, Sloane had been quick to brush that theory aside. When I kept insisting, Sloane had fingered James de Campo, pointing out the man's photo in the yearbook. Had that been a deflection? A way to steer suspicion away from himself? Or was I overthinking this whole thing?

With my cell phone, I snapped a photo of the black-and-white image of Sloane. I texted that photo, along with the link to the newspaper article about the grand opening of Pistol Pete's, which featured a more recent photo of Sloane, to Denise Lenchantin's cell phone. She hadn't gotten a good look at the man who'd approached her on that deserted mountain road that night, but perhaps something in Sloane's posture or face might jog something in her memory. It was worth a shot, anyway.

I dialed her number to explain what I'd just sent, but the call went straight to voicemail. I left a message, asking her to look at the photos and see if the man in them sparked anything for her, then told her to call me back as soon as she was able.

Peter Sloane knew where I was. That last phone call to him, I'd told him where I was headed. *Maybe there's an answer waiting for you in Woodvine*, he'd told me. Only the answer had been right here in the yearbook all along, hadn't it?

Hadn't it?

I cracked my window and had a cigarette. I had two. I thought the ash had blown from the tip and set the back seat of the Sube to smoldering — I even looked back there, ready to pour the remnants of my cold coffee over the scorched upholstery — but then I realized I wasn't smelling burning upholstery at all. It was the air outside. It was dense and smoky and acrid. I watched as bits of gray ash collected on the windshield, a spot here and a clump there. The two kids smoking cigarettes on the curb had departed, and I could see two distinct patches of bare white curbstone where they'd been sitting. I glanced up the sloping lawn toward the school and saw them ambling slowly toward the parking lot, the backsides of their jeans dusted in gray. The refinery had shut down when you were a child, Allison, yet the pollution it had caused — the environmental trauma — had lingered. How many decades needed to go by before the remnants from that refinery were finally washed clean from the town?

A police car glided up the street in front of the school, the Woodvine Police Department shield on its door. Its rack lights looked like they were blanketed in mold.

Suddenly itchy, I moved on.

There was a park with a decrepit-looking bandstand in the center of a dead-grass field. A man walked his dog through a scrim of gray grass. A woman wearing a headscarf and clunky orthopedic shoes stood on the corner with an armload of groceries; she watched me drive, a look of dim impatience on her bronzed and wrinkled face.

I had located the address of your childhood home in an online directory, and had populated that address onto a satellite map. It showed a solitary house set back from a long stretch of road on the western side of town, surrounded by trees, and with the serpentine shimmer of the Elk Head River running nearby. I knew I was close when I crossed over the river by way of a picturesque stone bridge. A makeshift wooden cross staked into the earth on the shoulder of the road prompted me to pull the car over and get out.

Tugging my jacket closed, I approached the wooden cross that stood at an angle among the weeds on the shoulder of the road. The first thing I noticed was the doll's arms nailed to the cross. I thought of the armless doll in your hope chest back home. The cross itself was weather-worn, but I could still make out the faded print of your sister's name along the vertical stave, bracketed by those two rubber, bodiless appendages. The writing was faded but legible. I looked down the embankment beyond the cross at the languid brown water of the Elk Head below. Its surface was furry with soot, and there were yellowish clumps of foam gathered along the muddy banks, just as you'd said.

Something urged me down there. Before I could rationalize what I was doing, I was descending the embankment toward the river, using exposed tree roots and low-hung branches as hand- and footholds. It took some time and effort to get down, and by the time I set my mud-caked shoes on the solid, hard-packed soil of the riverbank, I was winded.

The Elk Head River was nowhere near as wide or imposing as

the Delaware or the Potomac; this was just barely more than a creek, maybe three and a half feet deep at its center, and about forty feet across, if that. In one direction it wound through a forest of white pines, red maples, black walnuts, and the shaggy, drooping boughs of yellow-tinged weeping willows. I found it remarkable that anything could thrive amid such pollution. In the other direction — to my immediate left — the river tunneled beneath the stone bridge until it reached hazy daylight on the other side. I peered beneath the bridge through a curtain of dangling ivy. In that instant, I was overcome by the certainty that it was here, right here in this exact spot, where your sister's body had been found.

I stood there and listened to water trickling from a drainage pipe tucked into the stone wall of the bridge. I heard another sound, too — a sound so much like someone sobbing that it caused a chill to ripple through me.

Swiping aside the tendrils of ivy that hung down from the overpass, I passed beneath the bridge while digging my cell phone from my coat pocket. I switched on the flashlight app, and held it out before me like a priest wielding a crucifix at someone possessed. The flashlight's beam was too meager to penetrate the gloom beneath the bridge, except for a pencil-thin laser beam that stretched only about a foot in front of me.

I looked at the drainpipe. It was maybe ten inches in diameter, bisected by a single wrought-iron bar. A trickle of gray water spilled from it and pattered to the swampy earth below. The mortar around the pipe was mostly chipped away, the concrete blocks that comprised the abutment porous and crumbling. As I approached it, a smell like diesel exhaust exhaled from the mouth of the pipe.

I could still hear it — a sound, disembodied, thin as tissue paper, carried on a breath of air, something that sounded impossibly like someone sobbing from some great distance issuing from the drainpipe, causing my entire body to grow cold and the hairs on the back of my neck to rise up like quills.

I directed the meager beam of my cell phone's flashlight directly into the mouth of the pipe. The darkness in there swallowed it up. Still, the sound of someone sobbing was unmistakable.

"Who's there?" I said while simultaneously backing away from the pipe, my heart slamming painfully against my ribcage. "Is someone there?"

No sooner were those words out of my mouth than I was no longer standing here under the bridge, but back home in Harbor Village, gazing into our bathroom sink as a beam of light blinked up at me from the drain. Where I'd heard a man's voice come through the pipes, speaking the very words I had just now spoken: *Who's there? Is someone there?*

And on the heels of this, your own enigmatic description of your hometown, that one day as we drove through Pennsylvania, coming back to me, no longer a joke at my expense or a metaphor for how you'd grown up in this place, but sheer, inarguable fact; your words, your words: *And there are places in town where you can exist along two timelines at once. Like, you could be standing on a street corner but also somewhere else in the world at that exact same moment. Sometimes you can see or hear yourself talking through one of those rips in the fabric of the universe.*

I stood for a long time beneath that bridge, my body trembling, my mind grasping to cling to the solidity of the world. I stared at the gray water spilling from the mouth of the pipe, hearing nothing but the quiet babble of its progression now. No sobbing from that pipe. No other-Aaron at the other end of it.

No.

After a time, I turned and headed back up the embankment. By the time I stepped back out into daylight, and despite the chill in the air, I was sweating profusely.

2

Cane Road struck me as the type of remote strip of asphalt where outcasts and pariahs were unceremoniously dispatched and forced into obscurity. Desolate, absent of life — a forgotten memory on the outskirts of a forgotten town. Poplars scraped the gunmetal sky, their shaggy conical bodies powdered in marrow-hued grime. Mailboxes jutted at crooked angles from both sides of the road, their hulls peppered with buckshot, their misshapen aluminum doors gaping mouth-like in shock. There was a sizeable deer carcass in the middle of the roadway, its white-tufted belly split down the middle, its guts a glistening, viscous decoupage smeared along the ash-powdered blacktop. It hummed with flies. As I cut a wide berth around the carcass, I saw that the deer's head had been lobbed off. Cleanly. Someone had made off with a roadkill trophy.

Your childhood home was buried among gnarled, leafless oaks wrapped in fog at the end of a long gravel driveway. Two posts had been hammered into the earth on each side of the driveway, a chain with a NO TRESPASSING sign hanging from it running between them. I parked on the side of the road and got out of the car. Birds warbled in the nearby trees and the air felt electric with an oncoming storm. I stepped over the chain and ducked beneath low-hanging tree branches and vine-like tendrils that unspooled from the trees and whispered along my shoulders and the top of my head. Overhead, storm clouds had gathered, an archipelago of stark black shapes rimmed in dizzying gold. As I advanced up the driveway, the trees appeared to part, first allowing glimpses then a full view of the structure that lay hidden back there among the trees.

Your childhood home was gone. In its place stood a crumbling, skeletal structure, fire-scarred and insubstantial. The roof was no more; only a handful of charred beams remained, arching above an empty, decimated, two-story chasm. The front porch had been split in half, as if a fireball had come tumbling out the front door and rolled down the steps, trailing black smoke and reducing everything in its path to cinders. I looked up and saw a stone chimney looming against the overcast sky, stately as the Tower of Babel.

I approached the ruin, having to step around fallen beams, fire-blackened two-by-fours and sections of wall. The detritus lay in thick underbrush, and I could see vines curling around a downspout and along the remaining walls on the western side of the house, which suggested that this fire had not been recent.

The remaining porch steps looked about as reliable as a booby-trap, so I went around the side of the structure — it was so far gone I couldn't think of it as a "house" — where yellow insulation poked through the scorched rents in the wall, flapping in the breeze. I heard a melodic tinkling sound and glanced up. Remarkably, a wind chime still hung from one of the eaves, a collection of pitted brass cylinders strung together with catgut.

The windows along this side of the structure were gone. I peered into one of the gaping, charred portholes and saw the devastation that was the interior of the house. Nothing remained; the fire had devoured everything straight down to the foundation. Small green plants sprouted from the ashy soil and there were great profusions of multicolored flowers running along the interior perimeter. The air, I suddenly realized, was electric with bees.

My mind spun. I had come all the way out here, retracing your childhood footsteps in order to peel back the final layer of who you were, Allison, only to find a dead end. As much as I hated to admit it to myself, it felt like you had somehow orchestrated this whole thing in order to prevent me from knowing you, fully and completely. Stalemate.

Something moved inside the house, some subtle transfer of energy I felt rather than glimpsed through the cracks in the building's facade. Was it you, haunting the remains of your childhood home? There was a door here, the concrete steps leading to it a crumbling, loose pile of rubble. I climbed atop the pile and peered through the crack between the door and the frame. I could see nothing inside the house except the faintest shimmer of daylight spilling between the exposed rafters. I backed away and the door shook loosely in its frame. Pressing on it, I felt just how accommodating it was. There was no doorknob, but in the place where the knob had been was a hole cut into the wood. I slipped my fingers into the hole and felt the door give easily enough. I opened it, bent forward, and stepped across the threshold.

There was a noise, and a sharp, sudden pain.

The world went black.

3

I watched as a thing with blazing red eyes and steam seeping from its pores spoke in quiet, dulcet tones to a teenage girl with golden hair. They stood together on a stone bridge in the middle of the night, the moon a fat pearl floating in the sky and its reflection rippling on the surface of the river below. The girl spoke to the thing, laughed along with it. She could not see that the thing's head was filled with gas and that its eyes were boiling in their sockets. She could not see that the inner workings of the thing had been corrupted and that a poison shuttled inside it, corroding the bits and pieces that had once made it human. She talked and she laughed and the thing talked and laughed along with her. Clouds of steam billowed from its mouth as it laughed, but the girl did not see it.

Not at first. And when she *did* finally see it, it was too late. The thing was upon her, scorching hot and whistling like a teakettle, eyes that had become bright red headlamps and teeth like finger bones. For a moment, it changed and became a thing in a hooded sweatshirt holding a handgun, pointing it not at some teenage girl, but at you as you stood in a suburban boutique, before it changed back into the monster. The last thing the girl knew was the burning, acrid stench of gas fires, and the heat that radiated from the thing's hands, which had fashioned themselves into claws, monstrous once more, and were now squeezing, squeezing, squeezing the life from her body...

4

I opened my eyes to a sky intersected by charred black beams. I was on my back, my mind muddled with confusion. As I struggled to sit up, a lightning bolt of pain fired through the center of my skull, causing me to wince. I touched a tender spot in my scalp, just above my hairline, and my fingers came away slippery with blood. As I sat there staring at my fingers, I felt more blood trickling down my face and stinging my left eye.

Beside me on the ground was a brick, a bit of blood and hair stuck to it. Not without pain, I craned my head around and saw that I was in the burned-out remnants of a house. A dim recollection returned to me — of pushing through a fire-scarred wooden door and the world going black. I looked at the doorway through which I had come, and saw that there was a collection of loose bricks above the frame. I had unwittingly jarred one loose as I had come through the door, and it had walloped me on the head, robbing me of my consciousness before I'd even hit the ground.

With some difficulty, I climbed to my feet then braced myself against the wall of your childhood home — what remained of it — and hastily swiped the blood from my face. The wound in my scalp felt like it was on fire. I remained leaning against the wall, catching my bearings, until a laugh shook itself loose from my throat.

My head throbbing, I baby-stepped my way back down the gravel driveway toward the road. As I stepped over the chain at the mouth of the drive, I saw a woman walking toward me from across the street. She looked to be about my age, maybe younger, and was dressed in a maroon flannel shirt and jeans so faded they looked white. Her chestnut-colored hair was pulled back in a ponytail.

"Hello," she said, smiling. "Interested in the property?"

"What happened to the house back there?"

"There was a bad fire there years ago."

"Was anyone killed?"

She slowed her gait as she crossed the street toward me. Her smile faltered. "No, sir. No one was killed. I'm Tara Whitney. I live across the street." She gestured at an ugly mustard-colored rancher caged behind a knee-high wire fence. The yard was crowded with lawn ornaments and countless dream-catchers of various sizes and colors hung from the eaves.

"What happened to the woman who lived here?" I asked. "Lynn Thompson?"

"Well, I'm not…" she began, then immediately went silent. She was staring at me as if in shock.

"What?" I said.

"You're bleeding."

"Christ." I touched the tender spot on my scalp again then wiped my fingers on my pants, which were filthy anyway.

"What happened?"

"It's embarrassing."

She took a step closer to me to examine my wound. Winced at the sight of it.

"Does it look bad?"

"Might need stitches," she said.

"Wonderful."

She looked me in the eye again before retreating a couple of steps back. "I'm sorry, who are you?"

"My name's Aaron Decker. I married Lynn Thompson's daughter."

"Her daughter?"

"Allison," I said. "Allison Thompson."

Tara Whitney's face brightened. "Allie-Cat! Oh my God!" She laughed, covering her mouth. "I haven't seen her in years! Is she with you?"

It felt like there was a hornet struggling to free itself from my throat. I coughed into one fist and said, "Allison passed away last December."

Still smiling and shaking her head, Tara Whitney said, "What's that?"

"She died."

The smile drained from her face and her arms came up, folding themselves over her chest. One hand went to her mouth, and I heard a *tink* as her modest gold wedding band struck her front tooth.

Thunder bowled across the dark sky. A drop of rain fell on my cheek.

"I'm so sorry," she said from behind her hand. "My God. Allison Thompson." She shook her head, her gaze hanging on me with great weight.

Then the downpour came, crashing to earth and soaking us in a matter of seconds. Tara cried out and I pulled my coat up over my head.

"Come," she said, holding out a hand for me.

"What?"

"Come with me."

I took her hand and she pulled me across the street toward her house.

5

"I used to be best friends with those girls," Tara Whitney said as she applied ointment to the gash in my head. I was seated at the kitchen table, a towel, which she had given me to dry my hair, draped around my neck. I listened to the rain hammer the roof and sluice down the windows that looked out onto a weedy garden crowded with plaster cherubs and large plastic sunflowers. The ointment stung, causing me to draw air through my teeth each time the cotton swab came in contact with the wound. "I grew up in this house. This was my parents' house. My dad's in Florida now, my mom's passed away. Eric and me, we've made it our own, this house. Eric's my husband."

"When was the last time you saw Allison?"

"Not since she left Woodvine. We were teenagers. I'm two years older than she is." She peeled open an adhesive bandage and brushed back my damp hair. With her tongue crooked in one corner of her mouth, Tara held the bandage against the cut.

"Ouch," I said, and kicked one leg out from the chair.

"Don't be a sissy." She placed her hands on both sides of my face and stared intently at my eyes. "Doesn't look like you've got a concussion, though I'm no doctor." She released my face, then took a few steps back to study her handiwork. "Anyway, that should be okay. Looks like you won't need stitches after all. Maybe."

"Thank you."

"Don't mention it." She went around the other side of the kitchen counter and took two mugs down from a cupboard. "Had she been sick?" she asked, and when I didn't reply, she said, "It's okay. I don't want to pry. I'm sorry."

Lightning briefly illuminated the windows.

"Some guy started shooting people at a strip mall just before Christmas. Witnesses said Allison tried to stop him."

Tara leaned against the refrigerator. She covered her mouth again. Her eyes were as large as searchlights, staring right at me.

"I'm sorry," I said. "It's not a very nice story. I don't think I can keep telling it."

"I just don't believe it."

I smiled weakly at her from across the gloomy kitchen. There was a pain in my chest now, severe as a knife wound.

"I bet those witnesses were right. That *was* Allison. She would've tried to stop the shooter."

"What caused the fire to the house across the street?" I asked. I was desperate to change the subject, but I was also curious. Upon seeing it, my mind began considering the worst about you, Allison. Sorry to say, but things had changed recently, and I wasn't sure who the real you had been anymore.

"Well, I don't really know. It happened several years ago. I remember watching it, the fire, over the treetops. It was the middle of the night and the whole sky was lit up. They had trucks come in from three different towns to put it out. The house was destroyed but they were worried about a forest fire getting out of control. It was the middle of summer; we were in a drought. The woods turn to kindling around here in the summer."

"Was Allison still living there when it burned?"

"No, she'd left Woodvine a few years before. She left when she was eighteen."

"Was Lynn Thompson home when it happened?"

"She was, yeah. I remember her sitting in the open back of an ambulance with a blanket around her shoulders. She was lucky to get out alive."

"Is she *still* alive?" I asked.

"Lynn lives in Beaumont now, the next town over. I keep in touch with her because I'm the real estate agent on her property."

"Allison told me her mother was dead."

"Oh," said Tara. The coffee machine burped, and she seemed grateful for the interruption. She filled two mugs. "Milk?"

"Black is fine."

She came over and set both mugs down on the table. Outside, the storm continued to rage.

"It'll pass soon enough," Tara said, casting an eye out the window as she joined me at the table. "Storms come quick and furious out here, but they don't last. They're like little explosions."

"You don't seem too shocked that Allison had told me her mother was dead."

She made a face that suggested it was none of her business, then hid behind her coffee mug.

"I guess they had a real bad relationship," I said, watching the rain against the windowpanes. "Allison and her mother."

"Lynn had never been an easy person to get along with. She's mellowed out some over the years, but she was never really a mother to those girls. And, I mean, things happened." She clutched her mug in two hands, brought it to her lips, but did not drink it. A curtain of steam rose in front of her face. "I guess you know about Allison's sister Carol? What happened to her?"

"I know she was murdered. I know that, for a time, Lynn's boyfriend, a guy named James de Campo, was considered a suspect by the police."

"That guy was a terror," Tara said. "I don't know if he killed Carol or not — my husband thinks he did it — but he was a real piece of work. That's how Allison and I became close, when that guy moved into their house. Before that, I'd been friends mostly with Carol — she was my age — but after Jimmy moved in across the street, Allison spent a lot of time out of the house. She stayed over here some nights. I thought of her kind of like my little sister back then."

"What about Carol? Did she stay here a lot, too?"

Tara set her coffee back down on the table. "Carol had changed by then. When she died, we hadn't been as close as we were when we were kids. That happens sometimes, but with her, it was kind of sad."

"Why's that?"

"Because she was a victim. I mean, I didn't realize it at the time, but that's what she was."

"A victim of her mother's boyfriend? Of abuse?"

"A victim of her mother," Tara said. "But, I mean, a victim of circumstances in general, I guess. You don't grow up in a house like that and become Snow White, you know what I mean?"

"Lynn was abusive?"

"Lynn was just an all-round train wreck. Drugs, alcohol, you name it. And every guy she ever brought home was ten times worse than she was. Those girls didn't stand a chance." She looked me up and down. "Except maybe Allison did. I mean, she *did*. She got away from here. And for the record, you don't look anything like the type of guy I would've expected Allie-Cat to wind up with. What are you, a lawyer or something?"

I laughed, though my body felt depleted of all humor.

"Anyway, she was a tomboy," Tara went on, half-smiling in recollection as she stared out the windows at the rain. "Her fingers were always dirty, her hair always uncombed. There was nothing very *girly* about Allison Thompson."

"You wouldn't have recognized her in a million years," I said, taking my cell phone from my pocket. I opened up the photo album and handed her the phone. "Go on. Scroll through them."

"Good Lord," she said, holding the phone just a few inches from her face. "Is that really her? You're right — I never would have recognized her. She looks like a goddamn runway model. That black *hair*. Where are the bouncy yellow curls?"

"Beats me. Her hair was dark when we met."

"No, she was a blonde, just like her sister. Beautiful long golden hair. After Carol died, though, she cut it. Short, like a boy's, and choppy. I think she did it with a pair of scissors in the bathroom."

"Is that right," I said, my mind returning to what James de Campo had said about you showing up on his doorstep looking like someone who'd been eating out of trashcans. I'd already seen you this way in your yearbook photo, of course, yet I still couldn't reconcile that tiny black-and-white image with the woman I had married.

"She marched to her own drummer, all right," Tara said.

I drank my coffee while Tara scrolled through the photos on my phone. Outside, the rain began to taper off.

After a time, she handed me back the phone, then stood up from her chair. "Hold on a sec," she said, then vanished down the hallway. When she returned a few minutes later, she was carrying an old shoebox. A few strands of hair had come loose from her ponytail and floated like gossamer in front of her face. There was a tattoo of a star behind her right ear.

Tara dragged her chair next to mine then set the shoebox on the table. She opened the lid and I saw that it was filled with photographs. They were scattered about in there, in no particular order or arrangement, just loose and existing and touching each other like memories do.

"Hold on, let me find it," Tara said, rifling through the photos in the box. "I know it's in here. I think it's — here! Here it is."

She handed me a photograph of a thin-framed girl of about ten or eleven, hair like plaited sunshine, a half-smile on the girl's face that might have been a smirk. It was you, Allison. There was complexity behind your eyes even then. Your head was tilted as if to examine your own shadow that stretched out on the pavement at your feet but your stare clung to the camera.

Something hitched inside my chest. I tossed the photo back into the shoebox and then took a sip of coffee, forcing my gaze away from the picture and back out at the dwindling storm. Fat pearls of water dropped from the eaves and ran in squirmy rivulets down the windowpanes.

Tara was perceptive enough to register my despair. She set the lid back on the shoebox and pushed it away from us. She had the good sense not to apologize.

"I want to talk to Lynn," I said. "I need to tell her about what happened to Allison. Could you give me her address?"

Tara exhaled audibly. "I'm not sure that's such a good idea."

I looked at her. "What do you mean?"

Tara shook her head. "Like I said, she's never been an easy person to get along with."

"I think she needs to know that her daughter is dead."

"For Lynn, Allison has been dead for years. Dead to her, anyway. I'm not sure it would mean anything for you to tell her what happened. I'm not sure she'd care."

"That can't be true," I said. "She's still her mother. I feel like she should know what happened." There was something else, too, that I needed to know — something about the house, and the fire that had reduced it to rubble — but I didn't say this aloud.

Tara checked her wristwatch. On the counter, the coffee machine made a hissing noise.

"Let me change my shirt," she said, getting up from her chair. "I'll drive you."

6

It was a twenty-minute drive through verdant farmland that glistened in the aftermath of the storm. Beaumont was gleaming metal grain silos and billiard halls and gas stations that looked as extravagant as miniature amusement parks. I had balked at the idea of Tara driving me out here, but she had insisted. "If I'm wrong and you *do* have a concussion, I wouldn't be able to live with myself if you drove off into a ditch," she'd said as she pulled on a bright pink rain slicker from her hall closet and grabbed her purse. I'd relented.

We did not talk about you, your mother, or your sister on the drive to Beaumont. Instead, Tara asked questions about me — where did I live, what did I do for a living, did we have any children? She made a valiant effort to be engaging — and I'll admit that I liked her; she was very sweet — but I felt like there was a tornado gathering momentum inside my chest.

During the drive, I kept checking my cell phone to see if I'd missed a call from Denise Lenchantin, or maybe a response to my text messages. But no, I'd missed nothing. She hadn't gotten back to me... and this fact caused a new breed of worry to rise up in me. I had told Peter Sloane that I had spoken with Denise, so he knew she was out there talking about the encounter to whoever would listen. Maybe she couldn't identify the guy's face, but she certainly could describe the car. And what had Sloane said to me when I'd told him the type of car the killer had been driving? *An old sedan with a spotlight on the door? Hell, I still drive one. It's not as uncommon as you'd think. It's not like you have a license plate number.*

Jesus Christ, how could I have been so blind? Had I inadvertently put Denise Lenchantin directly in Sloane's crosshairs? Was it possible that the reason she hadn't gotten back to me was because Sloane had taken a drive out to West Virginia and done something to her? A terrible certainty, bleak as cancer, settled over me.

"Did you know a man named Peter Sloane, who used to live in Woodvine?" I asked Tara as she drove. "He was a police detective back when Carol was murdered."

— *Po-leeeece-man*, other-Aaron corrected inside my head.

"Sloane?" she said, twisting her mouth from side to side in thought. "Nope. Doesn't ring a bell. Why?"

"Just a guy I know," I said, and turned to gaze out the window.

By the time we pulled up outside a squat cement building with a sign over the door that read, in cursive pink neon, THE GAS FIRE GRILLE, my hands were trembling in my lap and I'd exuded a tacky film of sweat that made me feel like something that lived under a rock in a swamp.

I'll admit that there was another thought niggling its way into my brain, something that had been gathering momentum ever since I came upon the burned-out remnants of your childhood home. All that I had learned about you on this journey, Allison — the misery and grief of your childhood, the calculating resolve you shouldered into adulthood, the violent revenge you were able to enact upon James de Campo in the parking lot of that bar — suggested you were a woman capable of anything. Anything at all. Even now, my wrists burned with the phantom sensation of those plastic bands you'd looped around them during our lovemaking, something that had seemed odd and out of character but not terrifying at the time. But everything had a new meaning now. A new you, Allison. Just how bottomless was the well inside your soul? Had your childhood home burned to the ground due to some freak accident, or had you crept back to

Woodvine at some point in the past, under the cloak of darkness, hell-bent on punishing your mother for being such a lousy parent? A mother who let monsters like James de Campo slip through the bulwark of your innocence? A mother who was helpless to prevent the death of your sister? I can almost imagine the firelight reflecting in your eyes as you watched it all burn to the ground…

We got out of the car and went to the door of the Gas Fire Grille. Tara suggested she speak to Lynn first, and that I should wait by the bar. I agreed, although my nerves wanted nothing more than to get this over and done with.

The interior of the place was like every other dumpy chain restaurant, with kitschy bric-a-brac on the walls. I went to the bar and ordered an ice water while Tara went off to break the ice with Lynn. I watched her approach a thin, muscular woman dressed in black spandex pants, running shoes, and a sleeveless black shirt. She wore a stained green-and-white apron slung rakishly across her pointy hips. As they spoke, the woman looked past Tara and directly at me from across the room. The distance between us was too great to make out any details, except for the pale white face bracketed in curling strands of straw-colored hair.

Forcing myself to look away, I sipped my ice water and watched a man in a Mountain Dew windbreaker negotiate a dolly loaded with cases of canned soda through a doorway behind the bar. The door kept swinging closed before he could get the wheels of the dolly over the jamb. He cursed, scratched his balding gray head, then proceeded to twist the dolly around backward so he could prop the door open with his buttocks as he pulled it.

When I looked up again, I saw your mother moving toward me beneath a ceiling garishly lit with green-tinted light bulbs. She was wiping her hands on a towel which she tucked into the front pocket of her apron as she approached.

A pang of sadness radiated through me at the sight of her face. Scrape away the hard edges and the perpetual frown lines, the years and the heartache, the complexion ravaged by drug abuse, and this woman could have been you, Allison. In fact, this woman was so wholly, undoubtedly your mother, it was as if nature had conspired to replicate your family's lineage with perfect acumen to fulfill some sacred and unknowable pact.

"Tara tells me we're related," she said, her voice hardened from years of smoking. She leaned an elbow on the edge of the bar, cocked a hipbone toward the ceiling. The flesh of her right arm was shiny and pink, stretched taut from skin grafts. There was a prominent ridge where the good flesh met the bad, like a demarcation line between two feuding countries. "She also says you've got some bad news about my daughter."

My mouth went dry. I mustered enough courage to say, "My name is Aaron Decker. Allison and I were — "

"What happened to my daughter?"

That hornet was back in my throat, the feisty bastard. I said, "She passed away last December. I'm sorry to tell you this. I'm so sorry."

A vertical crease appeared between Lynn Thompson's eyebrows. Otherwise, she remained stoic. "How?" she said.

"She was… there was a… someone…"

"Go on," she said, tapping her hand on the bar. "Let's hear it."

I cleared my throat and said, "She was killed. Shot. Someone shot her. There was a shooting at a strip mall near our home. She was killed. She was shot. Allison was shot." The words avalanched out of me.

The crease between your mother's eyebrows deepened, but the expression on her face — one of mild agitation at having been called away from her job clearing empty dishes off tables — did not change.

"Anything else?" she asked.

I just stared at her.

"I got work to do," she said.

"Wait," I said, struggling to find my voice and to line up my thoughts into some semblance of coherence. "Allison told me you were dead."

"I was," she said. "Just like she was dead to me."

"How does that happen? She was your daughter."

She leaned close to me, so close I could smell the cigarettes on her breath. In a low rumble, she said, "Who the fuck do you think you are?"

This stymied me. I could say nothing, only stare into eyes that were so much like yours, except these were rimmed in a seething, fiery anguish.

"I'm sorry," was all I could manage to say. The same thing everyone had been saying to me, Allison, since your death, and now here I was, helpless to say anything wiser to your estranged mother.

"I'm sure she told you all sorts of shit about me," Lynn said. "Let me tell you something, bud. My life wasn't easy. I'm only human. I had problems, you know. I got fucked up on a lot of shit. Men, mostly, but a lot of other shit, too. I ain't proud of it. Hell, my own mother was a waste, how should I know any different? And now you come here to lay this on me. What'd you expect?"

"I just thought you should know what happened."

"Yeah, well, mission accomplished," she said, straightening up. But she didn't walk away; instead, she stood there sizing me up, looking at my clothes, my haircut. Judging me. For a moment, I thought she might hit me up for money or something.

I took a deep breath and said, "Can I ask you about the house?"

Lynn frowned. "What?"

"The fire," I said. "What caused the fire?"

Something like a laugh creaked up out of Lynn Thompson's throat. "You with the insurance company, too? My lucky day."

"Was it Allison who set the fire? Did she come back here?"

"Once Allison left, she ain't never come back. Not once."

"Then how'd the fire start?"

Her eyes narrowed to slits. "This is what you're here asking me?"

"I need to know. I need to know just how far she went."

Lynn plucked a cigarette from behind her ear, held it up. "Passed out on the couch with one of these in my hand," she said. "That good enough for you?"

I felt my body grow loose. An icy hand had been slowly squeezing my heart; it released its grip now and I could breathe again.

"You think that batshit crazy daughter of mine came back here to burn the place down? Take me out in the night?"

I said nothing.

"I'm think I'm all talked out," Lynn said, taking a step back from me while tucking the cigarette back behind her ear. "Thanks for the laughs."

I watched her strut back across the restaurant. By the time she reached her next table of customers, she had a smile planted on her face.

Tara, who had been watching from the far end of the bar, came over to me. "You okay?"

"Sure. Hell. Never better."

"Your hands are shaking."

"They've been doing that for months," I confessed.

7

Back in Tara's car, we sat in the parking lot of the Gas Fire Grille where we passed my last cigarette back and forth like a couple of high-school kids. The rain was holding off for now, but judging from the tumultuous black clouds creeping toward us from the east, it wouldn't be long before we were treated to another deluge.

"I tried to warn you," Tara said, reclining in the driver's seat, her window partially cracked. Across the street were two billboards, one depicting the somber face of Jesus Christ, the other advertising a strip club called Pole Position. "Did you have any other business out here?"

"No."

"So you're heading back tonight?"

"There's a motel out by the highway. I'll probably stay there tonight, head back home tomorrow morning." Of course, what I was thinking was that if I didn't hear back from Denise Lenchantin by this evening, I'd be driving back out to West Virginia tomorrow to see if I could locate her. And if not, then I'd go to the police and tell them what I suspected about Peter Sloane.

— *Po-leeeece-man*, other-Aaron whispered inside my head.

"Where you gonna eat?" Tara asked.

"I can't even think about food right now. My stomach's all jumpy."

"Hell, come over for dinner tonight. Meet Eric. He'll be home by five."

"That's very kind, Tara, but I couldn't impose on you like that. This has already been way too much."

"Hey, now." She turned toward me, jabbed a fist against my shoulder.

"Ouch."

"Listen, man. You came out of nowhere and dropped this bombshell on me about my old childhood friend. Least you could do is stick around and have a home-cooked meal with me and the hubs."

"All right." I smiled at her, my face feeling old and tired and made of sackcloth. "How can I argue with that?"

"Right on, man."

"Just don't punch me again."

Tara laughed.

8

By the time we reached the mustard-colored ranch house on Cane Road, the rain had tapered to a drizzle again, and the windshield wipers were squeaking and leaving black smudges along the glass. I thanked her for the ride and she told me dinner was at five-thirty sharp. I thanked her again, this time for her hospitality.

Back in the Sube, I sat behind the wheel for a time, replaying what your mother had told me. I felt guilty for thinking you capable of something so heinous as burning your house to the ground with your mother inside, but I also felt relief for knowing that I had been wrong. Here I was, a fool, desperate to cling even tighter to this alien thing that drew further and further away from me. Unanchored, unmoored — drifting, drifting.

My vision blurred. I swiped a hand across my eyes and my fingers came away wet.

I headed back toward town, planning to purchase a bottle of nice wine to bring to dinner and maybe grab a shower back at the motel room, when my cell phone trilled. I checked the screen and saw that it was Peter Sloane. I pulled the car onto the shoulder of the road and stared at the phone, unsure if I should answer it or not. Would it be too suspicious if I let it go to voicemail?

I answered it.

"I've got some news," Sloane said. "Confirmation from the medical examiner in the Megan Pollock case. Aaron, she was found with her hands still bound behind her back by a length of wire."

My mouth was dry. I stared out of the Sube's windshield, where the smokestacks of the defunct refinery rose up beyond the trees at the horizon.

"Did you hear me?" Sloane said.

"I did."

"Aaron, where are you now?"

"I'm in Woodvine, Peter," I said, wondering if this was something he already knew. Had he followed me out here? Had he been the one to tamper with my car tire? Or was I making huge leaps in logic?

"I think it's time we reign this in. There's enough here to go on now. Why don't you come back out here and we'll sit down, get all our ducks in a row? I've got people we can take this information to. They can put the rest of the pieces together."

I stared at the outline of the refinery against the darkened sky. "I don't know, Peter. There's still some stones I'd like to turn over first."

"What stones? Aaron, I think we should talk. Come on back out here. I've still got friends on the force who can look at this stuff."

"Not just yet," I said. "Give me one more day."

"What else can you do, Aaron?"

I closed my eyes. My head throbbed. "I just want to make sure I'm not overlooking something," I said.

— *Po-leeeece-man*, said other-Aaron.

And that was when I realized what I was looking at. Those smokestacks rising up over the trees at the horizon. I counted them in my head.

"Aaron? You still there?"

"Listen, Peter, I'll be in touch, but I gotta go now," I said, and disconnected the call.

My satchel containing the murder files sat beside me on the passenger seat. I tore it open and dug through it until I found the loose sheet of legal paper. I held it up against the windshield, so that your sketch of those six rectangular columns stood next to the outline of the refinery smokestacks on the horizon. The pattern of those smokestacks matched the drawing.

"Jesus Christ," I muttered.

I was startled by the ringing of my cell phone again. I checked and saw that it was Peter Sloane calling me back. This time, I rejected the call and let it go to voicemail.

9

There was a paved road that led to the refinery, its sun-bleached blacktop marred by spray-painted graffiti. Slogans warning travelers to turn back were emblazoned on the surface of the road in neon pink, orange and lime green. Stick figures had been sprayed along the blacktop as well, featureless effigies whose bodies looked ill-proportioned and crude. I slowed the car to a crawl when I spotted what looked like a nude person standing on the shoulder of the road; as I drew closer, I saw that it was a department-store mannequin tied to a post like some hideous version of a scarecrow. Several more of these dummies rose up from the shoulders of the road as I progressed toward the refinery. A placard hung from the neck of one of the mannequins, the phrase SURRENDER DOROTHY spray-painted on it.

"What the hell is this place?" I said to myself, leaning over the steering wheel to get a better look at the refinery as it came into full view.

Indeed, it looked like something out of Oz, only an Oz that had been decimated by nuclear war. Those six massive smokestacks rose from a rectangular concrete building, with two rows of milky, wire-meshed windows running from one end to the other. Everything was crowded with scaffolding and steel girders, but I could still see the graffiti that crowded the entranceway of the building. Most prominent — curled like a welcome banner above a set of large metal doors — was the phrase THERE IS MADNESS HERE in stark streaks of red spray paint.

I stopped the car and shut it down. From my vantage, I could see that the metal doors of the refinery were not sealed; a column of darkness separated them, wide enough for a person to slip through. Two more mannequins stood guard out here, one on each side of the entranceway like a pair of doormen. One of the mannequins wore what looked like a conductor's hat.

I got out of the car and crept along the busted slabs of asphalt toward the building. The smell in the air was undeniably different out here. It was as if hidden things still burned. If gas fires had souls, then their ghosts haunted this place.

The smell only increased as I approached the doors. I looked up and surveyed the dual rows of grimy windows, each one set behind a cage of wire. Birds' nests poked through the meshwork.

I took out my cell phone and activated the flashlight app. That meager, pencil-thin beam drilled a hole through the column of darkness between the two doors. Inside my head, other-Aaron stirred like something prodded by a white-hot poker.

— *Why in the world would you go in here?* he spoke up.

"Hush, now," I said, and squeezed myself through the opening in the doors.

10

I found myself standing at one end of a long, narrow corridor. The ceiling was high and there were rectangular windows up near the rafters, but their panes were so filthy that little daylight was able to penetrate. Moreover, the feeble javelin of light generated by my cell phone could hardly illuminate anything more than three feet in front of my face.

The place smelled awful. I tugged my undershirt up over my nose as I advanced down the corridor. Ahead, I could make out the vague suggestion of an open doorway. As I passed beneath a milky panel of light coming through one of the high windows, I noticed something affixed to the wall off to my left. I went to it and saw that it was a child's doll, its cloth body black with mold, its hollow rubber head and limbs the color of ash. It was hung by a harness of thin wire and nailed like a picture frame to the wall. Farther along the corridor I came to a second doll, this one strung upside-down by its legs. As if this sight wasn't disconcerting enough, I noted that both the doll's eyes were missing and that a black sludge had dribbled from its empty sockets.

My eyes had adjusted somewhat to the gloom by the time I reached the open doorway at the end of the corridor. I passed through it and into a large open space, where the dual rows of windows permitted more light into the chamber. I tucked my phone back into my coat as my eyes adjusted further to the murky half-light.

The chamber was filled with dolls.

They surrounded me, hives of them, assembled in heaps and dangling from wires and strings from the rafters. They were propped in corners, in pyramidal wedges of cloth and plastic and rubber. Dusty marble eyes stared at me from every corner of the room.

All of them — lashed together with wire.

The centerpiece of this nightmare was another mannequin — or, rather, an amalgamation of mannequin parts, assembled in such a fashion so that the thing was spiderlike, a confluence of arms and legs branching from a central torso held in place by tight bands of electrical wire. In each molded plastic hand it clutched a doll, like something about to feast. Its head was featureless, twisted funny on the blunt stalk of its neck. The thing wore a shawl of cobwebs, thick as a death shroud.

It stood in the center of the room in all its hideous, multi-limbed glory. The dolls all faced it, as if in worship. Painted in spidery red letters on the floor, spiraling in a never-ending gyre around the godlike mannequin:

GAS HEAD WILL MAKE YOU DEAD

I staggered backward, unable to pull my gaze from the monstrosity. Your voice resonated in my head: *There's a man made up of poison gas who lives in an abandoned castle. He'll get inside your skull and drive you mad.*

My back thumped against a spongy wall of dolls, and I spun around in time to see one of them begin to twist and undulate and come alive. I trained the beam of light on it, my hand shaking. The doll bulged outward from the others, one molded rubber arm shifting in a slow-motion salutation. I watched its head tip backward, straining the stitching at its neck, and could *hear* its movement, somehow even more terrible than actually *watching* it move. It was tied to a support beam that was covered with countless other dolls, except this one was *alive*, was —

Something dark and sleek poked through a tear in the doll's body. My breath caught in my throat. I wanted to pull the flashlight's beam away but I was powerless to move. I stared as the thing squirmed its way free of the doll's body and dropped audibly to the cement floor.

It was a rat roughly the size of a small dog. I watched it sniff the air then scurry along the baseboard toward a deeper part of the room.

I should have felt relief, but the movement of the doll and the appearance of the rat had only served to heighten my senses. There was something else in here with me, an indistinct shifting of reality that conspired to resolve itself as an actual *thing*. It was the chamber itself, its walls closing in on me, those dusty dolls' eyes drawing closer, closer. Something in here… something…

— *There is madness here*, other-Aaron whispered ghostlike in my head.

"Then let's get the fuck out," I responded, and fled from that terrible place.

CHAPTER SEVENTEEN

1

There was a police car parked in the Whitneys' driveway when I arrived at five-thirty. I parked the Sube across the street and was about to get out when my cell phone vibrated. The hairs on the back of my neck periscoped, and I worried it might be Peter Sloane again. But it was Denise Lenchantin's name and number on the display. Relief washed through me.

"Is this him? Is this the guy?" she blurted before I could utter a hello.

"Do you recognize him from those photos?" I asked her.

"No. I told you, it was too dark and I didn't get a good look at him."

"Not even a *sense* of him from those photos? Nothing?"

A pause. "I mean, it *could* be. It could also be a million other guys. I just don't know."

I leaned my head back against the headrest, rubbed at my eyes.

"This article says this guy is a retired cop," she said. "So he wasn't just pretending that night, was he?"

"I don't know," I said into the phone. "I don't know anymore."

"What should I do, Aaron?"

"Just be careful," I told her. "Keep one eye looking over your shoulder at all times."

"Now you're scaring me."

I thought of that terrible monstrosity comprised of mannequin limbs back at the abandoned refinery, the profusion of dolls climbing the walls, and a shiver rippled through my body. Yet Denise Lenchantin was still alive; Peter Sloane hadn't crept up on her in the night and choked the life out of her. Not yet, anyway.

"Aaron?" she said, and I realized I hadn't spoken in a while.

"Listen," I said. "I don't know if this is the guy or not. Just please be careful, okay?"

"Yeah. Okay. You too."

I promised I would be, then disconnected the call. My hands were shaking, and I took several minutes to regain my composure before climbing out of the car.

The rain had stopped for now, but the evening sky was a tumult of aggressive-looking thunderheads swirling in a soupy miasma above the treetops. I climbed the porch steps of the Whitney house, a bottle of Apothic Red in my hands, which I'd purchased from a liquor store in town.

A baby-faced man with a buzz cut answered the door. I held out my hand to shake his, but he snatched up my wrist and tugged me across the threshold. Before I knew what he was doing, he had gathered me in a tight embrace that drove the bottle of wine into my sternum.

When our hug was over, he held me at arm's length. "Hey, man, I'm so sorry. Tara told me about Allison. I can't believe it."

"Thank you," I mustered.

"I'm Eric."

"Aaron."

"Come on in."

I followed him down the hall to the kitchen. Burgers were sizzling in a pan on the stove, and Tara was at the counter slicing tomatoes. She smiled when she looked up and saw me. "I hope you like Spam-burgers," she said.

"She's joking," Eric said.

"Whatever it is, it smells delicious." I set the bottle of wine on the counter. "This was really very nice of you both."

"Hell, we loved Allison, man," Eric said. He went to the fridge, took out two cans of Bud, and handed me one.

"The police car outside," I said. "You're a cop?"

"Five years now," Eric said. He clinked his beer can against my own then took a slug.

"Still can't believe I married a fucking cop," Tara said.

"Kiss it, babe," Eric said.

Tara stuck out her tongue at her husband, then redirected her gaze to the bottle of wine I'd brought.

"Tell me where the glasses are and I'll pour you some," I told her.

"Hell no," Eric interjected. "She made a deal with me. No drinking."

"I'm pregnant," Tara said, as if apologizing for something. She placed a hand against her belly, which was still washboard flat.

"No alcohol, no cigarettes," Eric said, ticking each item off on his fingers.

"No sushi, no lunch meats," Tara added, frowning.

"That was the deal. And she's stuck to it, man. Impressed the hell out of me."

Tara met my gaze. We'd smoked cigarettes that afternoon, after meeting with Lynn Thompson.

— *Secrets abound*, whispered other-Aaron.

"Well, congratulations to you both," I said, and raised my glass in celebration.

2

We ate dinner on a small screened-in porch at the back of the house. It was chilly but the constant movement of wind felt good and made me feel alive.

Tara and Eric talked for a time about growing up in Woodvine. These stories inevitably coincided with stories about you and your sister, but to my surprise, I did not become maudlin or uncomfortable in hearing them; they were nice stories, and while they made me miss you more, they also comforted me in some strange fashion. I guess it was nice to hear that there were good things in your childhood, too.

What was clear was that neither Tara nor Eric had any real love for the town. They recognized it as a dead end, a remote and struggling landscape on the fringe of society.

"Why not move?" I asked them.

"Shit," Eric said. "Where would we go? You need money to pick up and move someplace. Her folks, they had two mortgages on this dump."

"We've really started thinking things through now that we're gonna have this baby," Tara said. "Started saving some money, too. I got my real estate license last fall. Remember I told you I'm the listing agent for Lynn Thompson's place across the street?"

"No one's buying a burned-out fuckin' house, hon," Eric said.

"It's not the house, you dummy, it's the land. Someone buys that, they can build ten houses on it."

"Is that right?" Eric said, nodding appreciably. Throughout the course of dinner he'd gone through a case of beer, and had only recently opened the bottle of wine I had brought; he was on his second glass of that now.

"Anyway," Tara said, "I don't want to raise a kid out here."

"She's been having nightmares," Eric said. He looked at his wife, compassion on his soft, round, alcohol-reddened face. He looked more like a drunken cherub than a police officer.

"Doc says it's normal with pregnancy," Tara amended. "Crazy dreams."

"Monsters coming to steal away the baby," Eric said, clawing at the air between him and his wife.

"Really," I said.

"It's all perfectly normal," said Tara.

"Speaking of nightmares, I went out to that old refinery this afternoon. I went inside the place."

To my surprise, Eric laughed. In a sort of singsong voice, like someone reciting a nursery rhyme, he said, "Gas Head will make you dead."

"Oh, stop it!" Tara said, and slapped him on the shoulder.

"Yeah, Gas Head. What the hell is going on out there?" I asked. "It looked like some weird goddamn shrine or something."

"Well, it sort of is, I guess," Eric said.

"It is *not*," Tara countered.

"Then what would you call it?"

"What *is* it?" I said. "Who put all those dolls out there?"

"Kids," Tara said.

"From town," Eric added.

"Kids from town are going up into that place?" I asked. I couldn't believe it.

"Well, not so much anymore. But back when we were kids, you bet. I went in there a bunch of times myself."

"To smoke weed," Tara whispered around cupped hands. She tipped me a wink.

"I never smoked weed, T."

"Liar." To me, Tara said, "He thinks 'cause he's the law now he can't say he's ever done anything illegal."

"I never smoked any fuckin' weed, T," Eric insisted.

Tara shrugged her shoulders. "Suit yourself, bub." She mimed toking a joint.

"So wait," I said. "Hold on. Why were kids going up to that place? Those dolls look like they're some sort of… I don't know…"

"Sacrifice," Tara said, her eyes going wide.

"Yes," I said. "Exactly."

"It's Gas Head, man," said Eric.

"It's bullshit," Tara countered, yawning. "Eric's just being a dick."

"No, tell me," I insisted. "What is it supposed to be?"

"It's just a stupid urban legend," Eric said. "Every town's got a boogeyman, right?"

"That's how our parents kept us from hanging out on the refinery grounds when we were kids, after the place closed up," Tara said. "Go there and Gas Head will poison your head, ruin your mind, and eat you from the inside out."

"His body made of smoke! His eyes like pools of oil!" Eric crooned.

Tara said, "It's just like how Godzilla was made from radiation or nuclear fallout or whatever? Well, Gas Head comes from the old gas fires of the refinery."

"No, Dumbo," said Eric. "He doesn't *come* from the fires, he *is* the fires. Or what remained of the fires after the place shut down."

"He's the smoke, not the fires, jerk," Tara corrected. "And quit calling me Dumbo."

"Anyway," said Eric, "it sort of had the opposite effect. You tell a kid not to do something, what do they do? They do exactly *that*. Place became a hangout for a while. We used to go and drink beer — "

"And smoke pot," Tara said, wrinkling her nose playfully at her husband.

Eric ignored the comment. "Seriously, though," he said, setting his wineglass on the table and sitting forward in his chair. He appeared to sober up. "Bunch of people got sick because of that place back when our folks worked there. We were just babies, man, so we don't really remember nothing, but we all know the stories."

"Sick how?" I asked.

"In the head," Tara said.

"Brain cancer?"

"Crazy cancer," Eric said. "Bunch of suicides, stuff like that. They shut the plant down for a while, but came back and said there was nothing wrong with it. Unrelated events."

"Which was bullshit," said Tara. "Unrelated, my ass."

"Anyway, it didn't last long. AstroOil, the parent company, they were facing some lawsuits, too, I think. They shut the place down for good a year or so after that."

"How many people killed themselves?" I asked.

"I think around a dozen," Eric said, looking at Tara for confirmation.

"Could be more," Tara said. "Can't really remember."

"Jesus," I said. "That's a high number of people to commit suicide all in the same workplace."

"No, no, man," Eric said, waving a hand at me. "You misunderstood. They weren't *working* at the refinery. These were people here in *town*."

"What?" I said.

"There were others who had to leave town, too," Tara said. "They were all out of sorts, you know? I don't know. Getting paranoid. Needed to clear their heads."

"That's when people first started talking about Gas Head," Eric said. "It started out as the term people used for the poor bastards who killed themselves, like it was some disease or something — 'They got a bad case of gas head,' shit like that. But then later, as things went back to normal — "

"Normal as it gets around here," Tara added.

" — and the refinery closed up for good, people just started talking about it like it was some kind of monster or something. Like, an actual *thing*. Gas Head. He'll make you dead. Watch out, and keep outta that old building. It's all just some local superstition."

"My mom used to say that if I didn't finish my vegetables, Gas Head would seep through my bedroom window at night and poison my head. For years I imagined this creepy white cloud of smoke coming into my bedroom while I slept and blowing up my nostrils, filling my head with smog. Scared the shit out of me."

"But you ate your vegetables," Eric said.

"Anyway, kids started to bring dolls up there like some sort of offering to Gas Head," Tara said. "Like Eric said — a superstition, you know? You offer up a decoy to appease Gas Head, and Gas Head would leave you alone. That sort of thing went on for years, but it really ramped up after Carol was killed. And I'm not just talking about little kids believing in this stuff, either — I brought a doll up there myself and I was in high school at the time. At first they were just tossed at the doorstep of the place. But over time, people started going inside, setting them up in that room."

"And all those mannequins?" Eric said. "Some high-school kids hauled 'em up there, set the whole place up. It became like a goddamn Gas Head shrine."

"But no one goes up there anymore," Tara said. "And Allison, she never went. She didn't believe in it. She hung *her* doll from a cross on the road, near the river where Carol's body was found. As if in defiance of the whole Gas Head thing."

"I saw the cross on the drive in," I said.

"That doll hung there until Allison left town," Tara said. "She took that doll with her."

I opened my mouth to say that I knew this, that I'd found the doll in your hope chest and had it in my possession, but decided against it at the last moment. It just seemed too personal to share.

"Fifteen years later, and Carol's murder is still unsolved." I was looking at Eric as I said this. "Is anyone in the police department actively working this case?"

"With no new evidence, there's nothing more to go on than there was back when it happened," Eric said. "You ask me, it was their mom's boyfriend, what's-his-name."

"James de Campo," I said.

Eric snapped his fingers and pointed at me. "Bingo."

"What makes you so sure it was him?"

"Look, I didn't really know the guy back then, except maybe I'd see him in the halls at school. He was the head janitor at Elk Head. But I've also heard stories about him from her." He jerked a thumb at his wife. "Tara watched the shit play out live from right here across the street. Fucking guy was apparently a drunk who got a little too handsy with Lynn Thompson and her girls. Cops were always at their place."

"That doesn't make him a murderer," Tara said.

"Listen," Eric said. "You do this job long enough, you realize that the simplest, most logical answer is usually the right one. Besides, I've seen the file. He was the only suspect back then. His alibi was shit and he'd gotten into a fight with Carol just before she stormed out of the house. Then he disappeared for a few hours, claiming to get drunk by himself somewhere."

"Did you know the police detective who was working the investigation back then?" I asked him. "A man named Peter Sloane?"

"Only from the file. I was in high school back in 2004 and didn't much hang out with cops."

"Sloane left the department back in 2006, two years after Carol's murder. Would the department have a record of why he left?"

"Depends on the circumstances. You trying to track this guy

Sloane down or something? He wouldn't be able to tell you anything that you can't already find online about the case."

I felt uncomfortable mentioning the yearbook connection you had uncovered, and how Sloane's photo was in it, to these people. Anyway, I wasn't one hundred percent convinced that Sloane was the killer. It was only one photo in a book of hundreds.

"And if it wasn't de Campo," Eric said, "then it was probably one of Carol's boyfriends."

"Was she dating anyone in particular at the time?"

Tara's mouth opened but no words came out. She glanced at her husband then back at me. I couldn't interpret the expression on her face.

"What?" I said.

"She was kind of, like, dating around a lot," Tara said, then looked instantly ashamed. "Like, a *lot*."

"Does anyone in particular stand out? Maybe someone who would have left Woodvine soon after her murder?"

"We were high-school seniors by then. Half of us left once school was out. Most everyone wanted to get out of here."

"You think some boyfriend killed her?" Eric said. He'd set his wine glass on the table and was sitting forward in his chair again. He looked interested.

"Allison thought it might have been someone she'd gone to school with. Someone you all went to school with."

"I'm getting chills," Tara said.

"If it was someone we went to school with," Eric said, "then why do you think he would have left Woodvine soon after the murder? What makes you think the guy didn't hang around? Maybe he's still here."

"Because I think he killed someone in Virginia two years later," I said. "And I think he's been relocating ever since."

They both stared at me — Tara with a look of unmasked fear, Eric like someone who'd been told a joke and was still puzzling out the punchline. Maybe I'd said too much.

"A serial killer," Tara said, leaning far away from me in her chair. She hugged herself as if suddenly cold.

"Looks that way," I said.

Eric laughed. "Shit," he said. "Right." He looked at Tara. "He's joking, babe."

To me, she said, "Are you?"

I considered my options. Ultimately, I said, "Yeah. Just a joke. Sorry. It was distasteful."

"Goddamn," Eric said, grinning. "But can you imagine?"

"You didn't know Carol like I did," Tara said to him. "It isn't funny."

"I didn't say it was *funny*. Come on, T. Chill out."

"I would, maybe, if you'd let me have some wine."

"Tara…"

"A sip won't hurt the baby. Even the doctor said so."

There was only about that much left in Eric's glass. He handed it to Tara, who studied the dark crimson puddle at the bottom of the glass with mixed emotions. She looked up at me from over the rim of the glass, a smile suddenly brightening her face.

"I don't think a sip would hurt either," I agreed. "Although I'm no doctor."

"See that?" Eric said. "You've got permission from a guy who's hunting serial killers." He laughed, then turned to me. "I'm just joking."

I smiled, nodded. I was suddenly very tired. Moreover, I wasn't sure where to go next, Allison. When I discovered Peter Sloane's photo in the yearbook, I thought I'd uncovered some truth. But in actuality, what did it mean? Sloane's photo in the yearbook was not a smoking gun. It was not a confession or DNA evidence. Furthermore, I found it increasingly difficult to reconcile the old guy with a heart condition to be a serial killer traveling up and down the east coast while running what appeared to be a modestly successful bar and grill. I was at a loss, Allison. I had come this far only to fail you.

Tara shot the last of her husband's wine, then smacked her lips and made a show of how delicious it was. I laughed.

"Christ," Eric said, taking back his empty glass. "I can't believe you drank it. You were doing so good."

"What I really want is an ice-cream sundae," Tara said.

"With pickles on top, right?" said Eric.

"Gross." She wrinkled her nose. "But maybe…"

I helped Eric clear the table while Tara lit a propane heater on the porch. The night had grown cold and dark; each time I glanced beyond the screened porch, I felt like I was staring off into space.

"Toddy Jenkins," Eric said to his wife as we shuttled plates and glassware from the porch to the kitchen. "Remember that guy? Talk about a serial killer in training."

"Yuck," Tara said. She stuck her tongue out between her teeth.

"Who's Toddy Jenkins?" I asked.

"Big slob we went to high school with," Eric said. "He got kicked out of Elk Head for hiding in the girls' bathroom. He used to watch chicks take a squirt through a hole he'd drilled in the stall."

"Swell guy," I said.

"He used to wet his pants, too," Tara added. "Remember, Eric?"

"Just once," Eric said, as if this onetime foible was forgivable of a high-school student.

"Ooh," Tara said, clapping her hands. "And Donald Freese!"

Eric laughed. He snatched up our napkins from the table in one beefy, hairless hand, held them above his head, and peered up at them with a lecherous gleam in his eye. "He used to hide under the bleachers and look up girls' skirts."

"Lovely," I said.

"Go on and finish the wine, Aaron," Eric told me.

"Give me a hand," I said, and poured what remained into my glass and his. When he went back into the kitchen, Tara rushed over, took a healthy swallow from both her husband's and my glass, then held up one finger in front of her lips in a *shhh* gesture. "My lips are sealed," I told her, "but your teeth are purple."

"Hey," Eric said, coming back out onto the porch. "Speaking of creeps, do you remember old Glenn what's-his-name? Everyone called him Glenn the Friend?"

"Lord," Tara said, covering her purple teeth with one hand. "He was a creep, all right."

"He was everybody's buddy until he caught you doing something wrong," Eric told me. "Glenn the Friend. What an asshole that guy was."

"Remember, Eric, that time he caught us fooling around in your dad's car?"

"He caught us more than once, T."

"No, he didn't. Just that once."

"You're wrong."

"I'm *not*, Eric. If you got caught fooling around in a car by Glenn the Friend more than once, it was with some other chick."

"This guy," Eric said, ignoring his wife and looking at me. "He was a real piece of work. I'm like seventeen and trying to get some action in the backseat of my old man's Buick, and this numb fuck rolls up like he's state police."

I laughed.

"I mean, the guy was a real grade-A asshole," Eric said, picking up his own wineglass from the table. "In fact, he worked with de Campo on the janitorial staff at the high school. He used to drive this big ugly car with a police light on the door."

I looked up from my wineglass, the blood-colored surface of which had been lulling me into a state of semi-catatonia, and said, "What's that?"

"He'd have the headlights off and drive around behind the school at night, where all the kids were fooling around," Eric continued. "Then he'd turn on the headlights and shine that big spotlight on everyone."

"Childress," Tara said, snapping her fingers. "That was his name. Glenn Childress."

"You said this guy was a janitor at your school?" I asked.

Eric nodded.

"Oh, he was so gross," Tara said. "I was walking home one night from the 7-Eleven and he pulled up right alongside me. Next thing I know he's got that spotlight shining in my face. Scared the shit out of me. He wanted to give me a ride home but I refused. He got, like, mad at me, and drove behind me the whole way until I reached my house. I still remember it like it was yesterday. Gives me the creeps just thinking about it."

"This town is full of crazies," Eric told me. "One of the reasons we'd like to get out."

"Whatever happened to this guy?" I asked. Despite the chill out on the porch, a fine sweat had begun to exude from my pores.

"Glenn the Friend?" Eric shrugged. "Beats me. He's been gone for years."

"Maybe Gas Head got him," Tara said. She went over and wrapped her arms around her husband.

"Maybe he *is* Gas Head," said Eric. He blew in his wife's face and she bit his shoulder.

3

It was a quarter to nine when I got back in my car and headed down Cane Road toward the highway. What fatigue that the wine had brought on over dinner had been replaced by a steady thumping in the center of my brain. When I reached the Elk Head River bridge, I pulled onto the shoulder of the road and turned on the car's interior light. My satchel was in the foot well of the passenger seat; I yanked it onto the seat, opened it, and dug out your high-school yearbook. There was an index at the back of the book where all the names were listed alphabetically. I ran my finger down one column until I located the name CHILDRESS, GLENN.

It was the same page where James de Campo's dark, furtive grimace leered out at me. De Campo, the head custodian. Beside him was a younger fellow, perhaps only in his mid-twenties in the photograph. The caption below this photo identified him as Glenn Childress. Unlike de Campo, he wasn't attempting to affect a smile. He had his lips drawn so tightly they looked like wires. Small eyes spaced a bit too far apart, their stare not precisely at the camera, but at something off in the distance. A prematurely receding hairline that formed an unruly black mullet down to his shoulders. His surname was embroidered on his work shirt.

My blood went cold. Not because I realized I was finally looking at the man who had murdered your sister as well as those other girls, but because I realized that I *knew* him. I had met him before. I had spoken to him and been in his company. I had shaken his hand.

I closed the yearbook, slid it back into my satchel, then pulled back out onto the road. The Sube thumped along the uneven concrete of the bridge. I kept my eyes trained on the shaft of darkness ahead of me, too frightened — and too certain — that I might see ghosts if I averted my gaze over the side of the bridge.

When I hit the highway, I motored past the motel where I had stayed the night before. My exhaustion had been replaced with an urgency that powered my body like an electrical current. I drove the four hours back to Annapolis, stopping only once to purchase a large cup of coffee and to pump gas into the Sube.

It was after one in the morning when I turned into Harbor Village. I eased into our driveway, crept into the house, and climbed our stairs while my body trembled from a combination of caffeine and sleep deprivation. Our closet light was flashing on and off, on and off, on and off.

I emptied myself onto our bed and slept for about a million hours, until daylight came screeching through the bedroom windows. I got up, showered, dressed, and was halfway down the stairs before I turned around and re-entered our bedroom. The closet was dark now; when I flicked the switch, nothing happened. All that flashing throughout the night must have burned out the bulb.

In the semi-dark, I knelt down, opened your hope chest, and shoved a heap of your sweaters to one side. I felt the cold metal of the revolver at the bottom of the chest, along with the box of ammunition. I took the gun and the ammo with me, toeing closed the lid of the chest with my foot. Then I paused, reopened the chest, and removed your armless doll from its plastic body bag. I took that with me, too.

In the car, I stashed the ammo and the gun in a duffel bag, which I had filled with random articles of clothing. Beside me, I propped your mutilated doll in the passenger seat. Then I called Peter Sloane. He answered after the first ring. I told him everything I knew — who the man was, and where he was located. Sloane listened, and when I was done talking, a long silence fell between us as we both digested everything I had said.

"Okay, listen to me, Aaron," Sloane said. "I know you think you've got this guy, but do you remember what I said back at my place? That you might just be following Allison's logic and not necessarily a trail of evidence leading you to the killer? Do you remember?"

"Peter, this has to be the guy."

"Hear me out. There is no evidence that links this man to any of the murders."

"The car with the spotlight on it," I said. "His face in my wife's yearbook. And that story the Whitneys told me back in Woodvine. It all adds up, Peter. He's the guy."

"Aaron, *listen* to me. Your wife heard a story about a guy who reminded her of someone she knew from her hometown. *That's* the guy you've tracked down. But that doesn't mean he's the killer. He's just who your *wife* thought was the killer. Do you see the difference?"

"I understand what you're saying, Peter. But my gut is telling me something different. Allison was right about this. I can feel it."

"Then let's take everything you have to the police. I can find a sympathetic ear."

"I've tried that before, Peter. Besides, you just said it yourself — there's no actual evidence connecting this guy to any of the murders. What good will going to the police do?"

"They can research it, track his movements. In other words, conduct an actual investigation. Things you can't do."

"And if they come up empty? If they're unable to tie this guy to the murders because they can't find any evidence? Then what, Peter? The guy just walks? He just gets away with it? And not only that, but then we've tipped him off."

"It's the only thing left to do," Sloane said.

"It's not the only thing," I told him.

Sloane exhaled audibly on the other end of the line. "Aaron, what are you talking about?"

"I'm going to go there and see if *I* can find evidence."

"Like what?" Sloane said. "What sort of evidence do you think you'll find out there?"

"The car," I said.

"Even if you found that car, Aaron, it wouldn't be *proof* of anything. It's just confirming what we already know. We *know* this guy Childress owned a car like that. It doesn't tie him to the murders."

"We know he owned it fifteen years ago. But if I can show he *still* owns it, that'd be more than a coincidence, right? That'd be something."

A heartbeat of silence on the other end of the line. "If he still owned the car, that might be something. Maybe not probable cause for a warrant, but something. We'd still have to get the police involved."

"So let me get down there and see what I can find. Let's make this case as strong as we can. I have to do this, Peter. I have to be sure."

"You just watch yourself, Aaron. Be careful."

"I'll be in touch," I said, and disconnected the line.

I started up the Sube, and your music spilled out of the speakers. This time, instead of shutting it off, I cranked the volume. No simple eighties tune this time: the Sonics serenaded me with "Strychnine" as I careened out of Harbor Village, down past the plaza where you had been murdered, and hit the highway at nearly ninety miles an hour.

CHAPTER EIGHTEEN

1

The Valentine Motel shone like a lighted train car against the backdrop of a darkening sky. Its neon VACANCY sign sizzled in the oncoming darkness above the trees, pink lights mirrored on the surface of puddles that seemed to be placed at strategic intervals across the parking lot. Dusk had settled over the landscape as I'd driven up the side of the mountain, ribbons of red, orange, yellow, and violet stacked on the western horizon and radiating through the forest; with the sunlight quickly draining from the sky, I could feel the evening's frigid embrace in the marrow of my bones.

I steered the Sube into the motel's parking lot, tires crunching over chunks of gravel. The lot was empty, with no other vehicles in sight. Beneath the motel sign, the plate-glass windows of the motel's office discharged a dull, milk-colored light that simmered in the early evening. The windows were slightly concave, giving the whole office the appearance of a large fishbowl. From my car, I could make out the wood-paneled walls on the interior, the fishing trophies and photos behind the front desk. I could see no one inside the place.

All twelve of the motel rooms that spanned the length of the parking lot were dark. Their windows looked like portals to other dimensions.

I parked in the lot, turned off the car, let the engine cool. *Tick,*

tick, tick. Switched off the headlights and watched your palm print dissipate from the windshield. *Tick, tick, tick.*

Other-Aaron was looking at me from the passenger seat, your mutilated doll in his lap.

"What?" I said.

— *Good question*, he responded. *What, exactly.*

I took a deep breath then got out of the car. Cold mountain air stung my face. I crossed the parking lot toward the motel's lobby, the joints of my bones strapped together by an intricate if unreliable system of loose wires, pipe cleaners, and stretched-out rubber bands. Other-Aaron kept pace with me, but gone was his sage advice and his air of prim confidence; I'd dumped him quite unceremoniously into the deep end of illogic, where he was struggling to keep afloat.

— *What exactly do you think you're going to accomplish here?* he asked. *Just like Peter Sloane said, even if you find the car, what does that really mean? Sloane is right — you've followed Allison's train of thought and that led you to this man. You did not follow a logical pattern of clues tying him to any of the murders.*

I willed other-Aaron out of my head. Now was not the time to start second-guessing things.

The lobby's interior was warm and scented with lavender and pine. There was no one behind the desk, no one in the darkened little alcove beyond where two cane-backed chairs stood before a dark TV screen. There were fresh vacuum tracks on the rose-colored carpet. I scanned the wall of photographs behind the desk, the fishing trophies and prized catches, a first aid kit bolted to the wall, and the little velvet board on the desk with its rows of colorful flies affixed to it — all the things I'd noticed before, when I had been here under wholly different pretenses. Back when I'd been a different man, you might say, Allison. Back when you'd been a different woman, too, I suppose. In my eyes, anyway.

There was a buzzer on the counter, what looked like a doorbell bolted to a block of wood. I pressed it, heard the buzzing behind some distant wall, and immediately thought of the revolver buried in my duffel bag which I'd left back in the car.

— *See? You're not prepared for this. What good will that gun do you in the car?*

It was not Glenn Childress who emerged out of the gloom beyond the two cane-backed chairs and the dark television set. It was his wife. An angular, wire-thin woman with mousey brown hair and clothes that looked ill-fitting and hand-sewn. She possessed the beseeching, quizzical stare of a barn owl, only there was nothing predatory about it. She'd been the one to check you in when you came down here last fall, Allison. The woman who'd spoken to me about you when I'd first come down here, too. Yet if she recognized me now, she made no show of it.

I asked for a room. When she learned I had not booked a reservation, her pale face went grim. "Currently under a two-week restocking moratorium from the DNR," she said, poking at the keys of her computer. "Hope you're not here to fish."

"That's unfortunate."

"There's rafting trips." She nodded at a rack of brochures that stood against the wall beside the plate-glass windows. "Guides at the mouth of the river leave at seven sharp. Fifty dollars will get you the day trip plus lunch. Nothing fancy, mind you. Peanut butter and jelly sandwiches."

"I don't mind peanut butter and jelly."

"They go soggy on the river."

The creak of a floorboard drew my attention back to the unlit alcove toward the rear of the place. I waited to see if Glenn Childress would appear in the darkened doorway.

"Credit card and ID," Childress's wife said.

I dug my Visa card and driver's license from my wallet, handed it to her. She fed the card into a machine and I returned my gaze to the alcove. But then something stirred the hairs on the nape of my neck to attention. I glanced over my right shoulder and spied other-Aaron's wan countenance reflected in the night-dark window at my back.

— *This is a mistake*, he said. *You should go to the police.*

The credit card machine beeped. Childress's wife handed me back my card and driver's license, and I tucked them back in my wallet. When I looked up, I saw that she was studying the wound in my scalp. I had removed the bandage and had shaken my hair down over it as best I could, but the area around the knot had begun to bruise, making it look as though I had a smudge of dirt across my forehead.

She handed me a brass key affixed to a plastic fob with the motel's name on it. "Room Four," she said. It was the same room we'd both stayed in on our previous visits.

I thanked her, told her to have a nice evening, and shoved myself back out into the encroaching darkness.

2

This suffocating little box of a room. Wallpaper with its green and brown fish, a twin bed packaged in a burnt umber bedspread, the ghosts of cigarettes haunting the threadbare, oatmeal-colored carpet. All of this beneath a large Texas-shaped water stain on the ceiling.

There was a circular card table on the far side of the room, the two mismatched wooden chairs gathered around it like seedy conspirators. The bathroom door stood partway open, a vertical shaft of black space not unlike the opening of a defunct mineshaft —

or the old AstroOil refinery back in Woodvine — beyond the door. The red Cyclopean eye of a smoke detector stared down at me from the ceiling.

It was all stage dressing. I switched on the futile little lamp beside the bed, the bathroom light, the solitary bulb over the dingy shower stall that blazed with an unholy reddish glow. I was looking for cracks in the foundation of the world, the zipper on the back of the rubber monster suit. I peered beneath the bed and opened all the dresser drawers. A section of wallpaper had curled away from the wall; I pinched it between my thumb and forefinger and administered a series of quick tugs until I could see the gummy, colorless drywall beneath. Had I expected to find some hidden missive under there? If I cut the carpet down the middle and splayed both halves in an autopsy fashion, would I locate a secret hatch to another world, a world where the realness of these past several months might be diluted by an alternate state of being? *You and I exist outside this plane, where space and time are wound into a ball and not in a straight line*, you'd once said to me. I cannot recall the reason for you saying it, cannot recall what we had been doing at the time; yet your words were clear as a handbell in the center of my head. *We will always be together because we have always been together. We are acting out all our moments simultaneously right now. Ghosts are time travelers not bound by the here and now.*

I pulled the drapes closed, propped your creepy armless doll on the nightstand, then opened my duffel bag while I sat on the edge of the bed. Wrapped in a pair of my boxer shorts was the revolver. Unreality washed over me as I picked it up, set it on one thigh. Looked at it. There was a child's playground seesaw in the center of my brain, other-Aaron at one end of it, me at the other. We did not go up and down, up and down. We remained perfectly balanced, the two of us, while a strong wind gradually gathered momentum and advanced toward a full-blown tornado all around us.

I released the cylinder and loaded each chamber with a round. It was frighteningly easy. A child could do it, as they say. I thought of you as I loaded the weapon, and of the man who had taken your life. Had Robert Vols, your murderer, fired his father's pistol on numerous occasions before he decided to finally fire it at you? Had he gone on family hunting trips when he was younger, shot skeet, used a pellet gun to pop cans at the local dump? Or had that asshole woken up that morning with that single-minded, burning purpose scorching a hole in the fabric of his diseased gray matter, itchy with it, unsettled and sweaty and twitchily disturbed, thinking for the first time, *It's right up there, that gun, right in their bedroom, that thing that could end lives, that thing that will make the sweating and the twitching go away*?

Once six rounds were in the cylinder, I locked it back in place. The gun was heavier with bullets in it. Like someone handling plutonium, I rewrapped the gun in my boxer shorts then tucked it carefully back into my duffel bag. I buried the remaining ammo underneath.

From my satchel, I removed the file of the murders, opened it, and proceeded to place all your documents on the small circular table that was wedged between the bed and the wall on the far side of the room. Each girl's face smiled up at me as I placed her photo down on that rickety clapboard table. Margot Idelson, murdered in 2006. She would have been nearing thirty years old now, had she lived. Shelby Davenport, murdered in 2008, in nearby Bishop, North Carolina. It wasn't Davenport's murder you had been down here investigating back in October; by then, you had already spoken with Denise Lenchantin, had already learned the identity of the killer from hearing her story. You had come here to end it. That was why you'd bought the gun. You had come here to kill Glenn Childress. Only problem was, he hadn't been here when you arrived. His wife had checked you in. You'd stayed two days hoping he would show, and you gave some bullshit story about car trouble so you wouldn't arouse suspicion. But Childress never showed. And after two days you had to leave. You had to get back home to me, so I would not become suspicious, either.

After Shelby Davenport's murder, there was a period of roughly two years where nothing happened, at least as far as your records were concerned. But then in 2011, Lauren Chastain was unfortunate enough to run into Childress in New Jersey, only to have her body discovered on the swampy, cattail-rimmed bank of the Delaware River a couple weeks later. Another brief respite for Childress until Megan Pollock was found in a black and blue jumble of limbs in 2013 in Whitehall, Delaware. Jump ahead to 2016, and there was Gabrielle Colson-Howe, dead and purpled and bloated beneath the Harry Nice Bridge in Newburg, Maryland, strangled with such ferocity that her head had been twisted backward on her neck. Two years later, Holly Renfrow had crossed paths with Childress, only to fall into the Potomac River with her wrists bound behind her back and drowned.

I heard the seesaw creak inside my head. Other-Aaron's side ticked incrementally closer to the ground. He was positing a question.

"I feel it, too," I told him, leveling the seesaw out again. "They're spread out all over the place. How did he find these girls?"

It was the question that kept returning to me, kept nagging at me. Had Childress simply traveled the byways of the east coast, up and down and state to state, searching for teenage girls whose appearance so closely resembled your sister Carol's? Had it been that random? Or had he lurked behind the anonymity of the Internet, scouring social media sites for girls who fit the desired description?

— *Social media would explain how he knew Holly's name*, said other-

Aaron. *But then to locate her house? Had Holly been careless enough to post her address online somewhere?*

The seesaw went *crrrriiiiiick*.

3

B ehind the motel and partially obscured by trees stood a double-wide trailer where, presumably, Glenn Childress and his wife lived. There was a clothesline that ran from the rear of the motel to a pulley attached to one corner of the trailer, a few plain white bath towels hanging from it. Now, in the stone-gray light of evening, the towels looked like ghostly, flapping apparitions.

I stood smoking a cigarette in the clearing between the motel and the trailer. Ivy crawled up the walls of the trailer, crept along the roof, spooled around the stovepipe that jutted up from the shingles. All the windows were dark.

It wasn't the trailer that interested me, but the large automobile parked alongside it, hidden beneath a brown canvas car cover.

I took one last pull on my smoke before tossing it to the ground and crushing it out beneath the heel of my shoe. I closed the distance between the motel and the trailer at a quick clip, realizing that there was still enough daylight along the western horizon to frame me in stark relief for anyone who might happen to look out one of the trailer's windows. If someone was in there watching me right now, I wouldn't know it.

As I got closer, I bent in a crouch and made my way over to the car. A few feet from it, the texture of the ground changed beneath my feet. I heard things crunch and break, which caused me to freeze in midstride. I looked down and saw that the ground was covered in broken bottles and shards of terracotta pottery. There was a mound of junk piled up against the side of the trailer, broken lawn chairs and an old bookcase and less identifiable items all thrown together in a schizophrenic heap. I maneuvered around the junk as quietly as possible, stopping to catch my breath and give the muscles in my calves a break only when I reached the car.

Sweat stung my left eye. I reached down and lifted the hem of the car cover, pulled it up over the grille, the hood, the windshield.

It was an old Thunderbird, its rusted frame an iridescent whitish blue beneath the moonlight. Its two front tires were flat.

It was Peter Sloane's voice that returned to me now: *There is no evidence that links this man to any of the murders.*

Had you led me astray, Allison? Had I followed your irrational obsession instead of following the clues? Was all this one big charade?

I remained there, crouching beside the car, my mind awhirl with a million different outcomes and consequences, unanswerable questions and illogical leads. After a time, I pulled the cover back down over the car. Bits of broken glass crunched beneath my shoes.

Beyond the trailer, the woods rose in a black swell. I discerned a path — large enough for a vehicle to pass through — vanishing into the trees. There was a wooden sign posted at the path's entrance:

CAMPGROUND CLOSED FOR THE SEASON
NO TRESPASSING

I crossed over to the path, my head down, my hands stuffed in the pockets of my peacoat. I hoped that if anyone were to see me, I'd look like the perfect example of an ignorant fool out for an evening stroll and nothing more.

The path cut through the woods for a time until it emptied onto a vast clearing. Kayaks were stacked on a wooden trestle and there was a collection of small cedar cabins tucked among the trees, each one dark and vacant in their off-season retirement. I caught a whiff of ancient campfire smoke, yet instead of it being a comforting smell, I thought of Tara Whitney's childhood fear of the terrible thing called Gas Head: *For years I imagined this creepy white cloud of smoke coming into my bedroom while I slept and blowing up my nostrils, filling my head with smog.*

I heard running water, so I followed the slope of the land until I arrived at the cusp of a shallow brook, its surface cloudy with mist. Along the opposite bank, the trees formed an impenetrable shroud, shielding this part of the land from the road farther down the side of the mountain. The sensation was one of complete isolation, despite knowing that the motel and the road beside which it resided was probably less than half a mile down the mountainside.

I peered through the trees to my right and saw that a gravel passage wound farther into the woods. I followed it until a thing began to take shape among the trees — a large, barn-shaped garage with a set of double-doors at the front. A sign above the doors said DANGER — ELECTRICAL EQUIPMENT INSIDE, and a sign bolted to one of the doors said DO NOT ENTER. A hefty chain was lashed through the handles of the doors and held in place by a padlock, as ancient and rusty as something salvaged by divers from a sunken ship. There was a single window on the west-facing side of the building, its grime-caked windowpane glowing with the reflection of a distant sunset. I carved an arc in the grime with the heel of my hand and peered inside. The interior was crowded with items, hulking shapes indistinguishable in the gloom. I noted, however, another vehicle beneath what looked like a sheet of blue tarpaulin. Staring at it, I felt the back of my throat constrict. I was suddenly, unwaveringly certain it was an old sedan under there.

"Hey there," said a man.

I jerked away from the window as if zapped by a current of electricity.

Glenn Childress stood maybe twenty feet from me, a sturdy fellow with a dark mullet and a great expanse of pale forehead. He wore a denim jacket and jeans so faded they were practically white. He held a large flashlight in one hand — one of those heavy-duty Maglite jobs — but there was still enough daylight in the sky so that he hadn't needed to turn it on.

He chuckled good-naturedly at having startled me. "Didn't mean to spook you," he said. "Although, truth be told, you gave me a bit of a start myself. Wasn't expecting to find anyone out here."

"I was just out for a walk," I said.

"Well, I can certainly understand the allure of the woods out here," Childress said, smiling amiably enough. Across his chest was what I at first mistook to be a Sam Browne belt, but when he turned his body to inhale a great lungful of air, I could see the barrel of a rifle poking up over one shoulder. "Not an ounce of pollution out here. Pure as the driven snow, as they say. Only problem is, camp's closed for the season. We don't open back up 'til summer." He jerked a thumb over his shoulder. "Big ol' sign out by the road behind the motel."

"I must have missed it."

He waved a hand at me, still smiling. "Ah, no harm. I assume you're the fella checked into Room Four earlier this evening?"

"That's right."

"Well, we should probably head back there. It'll be dark soon, and this ain't the best place to be wandering around once the sun goes down."

Without waiting for a response, Childress turned and began trudging back through the trees. Already the night was creeping through the underbrush, and stars were beginning to poke holes in the firmament. I followed him through the woods, my gaze locking onto the rifle strapped to his back. I was aware now that the temperature had dropped considerably and that an owl was singing a dirge in a nearby tree. I cast a glance back over my shoulder at the garage with the DANGER sign over the doors; it was already being swallowed up by the encroaching night.

Childress slowed his gait so that we could walk in tandem. He was watching me now, studying my face. The muscles of his jaw appeared to tighten.

"Say, fella, do I know you?"

"I was here about a month ago, asking about my wife."

"That's right," Childress said, snapping his fingers; the sound echoed through the trees. "I remember now. Something about she died, is that right?"

"She did, yes."

"Well, that's just…" He shook his head, his lips tightening. "It's just terrible, really." A cloud of vapor wafted from his lips. "What brings you back this way?"

"Turns out my wife had come here to see an old college friend," I said. "I didn't realize it at the time. Anyway, I thought I'd come out and tell her about my wife's death. I didn't want to do it over the phone, but I guess I should've called first. She isn't home. So here I am."

"Well, that's mighty nice of you," Childress said. "Who's the friend? Maybe I know her."

"Julie Sumter." It was the first name that popped into my mind.

Childress made a sour face. "Don't sound familiar. She here in Chester?"

"Bishop," I said. It was the nearest town to Chester, down in the foothills of the mountain — the town where Shelby Davenport had been killed back in 2008.

"Well," Childress said. "Can't say I know everyone down there in Bishop. I hope she takes it well. And I hope you find some peace, too, fella."

"Thank you." I stepped over a spindly deadfall. "You've owned this place long?"

"Few years."

"What'd you do before this?"

Childress froze. I stopped short beside him, suddenly perspiring despite the cold evening air.

"Hear that?" he said. He held up one finger, his bloodshot eyes scanning the treetops. I noticed patches along his square jaw where he'd missed some spots shaving. "You hear the son of a bitch?"

I listened but could hear nothing.

"Hold this," he said, and handed me the flashlight. The thing was as heavy as a medieval mace.

It was then that I *did* hear something — a machinegun rat-a-tat somewhere in the upper branches of a tree.

Childress swung the rifle in front of him, jammed the stock against his right shoulder, and pointed the barrel into a cluster of treetops. Just before he pulled the trigger, I heard the sound again — *tat-tat-tat-tat-tat*. He fired, and the sound of the gunshot whip-cracked through my skull. Overhead, a bird spirited off into the darkness.

"Goddamn woodpecker," Childress groused, lowering the rifle. A halo of gun smoke drifted about his head. "Keeps drilling holes in the cabins. I'll get him yet."

4

We parted ways at the road: Childress raised a hand in a farewell salute as he headed in the direction of the double-wide trailer while I continued down the hillside toward the motel. Thunder growled in the distance.

Despite the cold, my clothes had grown damp with perspiration. I entered my room and turned the feeble bolt in the door. It didn't seem sufficient; someone could kick that door down on the first try.

I looked around the room, saw the chairs by the table. I dragged one over to the door and tried to prop the back of the chair up under the doorknob, like they do in the movies, but the height was off. I looked around the room for something else. But there was nothing. I wondered if I should even stay here tonight. I wondered if I should find someplace else, someplace safer.

— *He saw you peering in the window of that garage*, other-Aaron spoke up. *You told him Allison's friend lived over in Bishop, where Shelby Davenport was killed. You made him suspicious.*

I went back outside and walked to the end of the parking lot, where two large dumpsters sat among dense foliage. I kept glancing behind me, expecting to find a smoke-black figure advancing toward me in the darkness — Glenn Childress, with his skull smoldering and his eyes blazing red. *Gas Head will make you dead.*

There was a picnic table here, an old charcoal grill on wheels, a few metal trash barrels. Lifejackets hung from pegs on the outside of a large wooden shed, the double doors partway open. I peered into the shed and saw shelves burdened with painting supplies, tools, industrial cleaners, and bleach. There was a flashlight in a toolbox on the floor, a sturdy Maglite like the one Childress had been carrying. I picked it up, pressed the button, and a beam of white light cut through the darkness. I shut the flashlight off and tucked it under one arm.

Leaning against the rear wall of the shed were some heavy wooden oars. I took one and carried it back to my room, where I propped the paddle-end beneath the doorknob like a barricade.

5

I spent that evening in Room Four with the lights off and the drapes pulled, except for a vertical ribbon of window through which I could observe the motel's parking lot. I dragged one of the chairs from the table and propped it in front of the window. I sat there peering out as a light rain began to fall, your loaded handgun on one thigh. I didn't feel safe taking my eyes from the outside world for too long. It was as if Childress, not fooled by the lies I'd told him back at the campsite, might come for me in the night.

My exhaustion and fear was counterbalanced by a heart-thumping urgency to *do something*. When I shut my eyes, it was the faces of dead girls that ghosted toward me through the fog. Each time I edged toward sleep, I'd jerk awake, certain that someone — some formidable presence — was here in the room with me, standing right over my bed. I had conversations with people who were not there. You were one of them, Allison. Peter Sloane was another. Glenn Childress was yet *another*, and in my partial dream state, he sat in the other chair at the table staring at me while I talked to him from my perch before the window, my arms and legs powerless to move, as if I'd been administered some potent sedative. Childress was entirely cloaked in shadow except for his eyes, which shone like two silver coins set above a fire. The longer I stared at this visage, the closer those coins drew toward one another, until they joined to form a single iridescent sphere of light. Yet when Childress leaned forward to address me, his body creaking like something made of wooden planks and rusted bolts, I saw that it was actually other-Aaron.

— *There's a man made up of poison gas who lives in an abandoned castle. He'll get inside your skull and drive you mad.*

A pale wraith resolved itself within the black rectangle of the bathroom doorway, its body comprised of white smoke, its eyes two black pits swirling like tornados in the center of its skull-like face. It moved with the fluidity of something weightless, and when it finally dissolved, it left a smell like burning rubber in its wake.

I spilled out of the chair, mostly in some aquatic state unfit for traversing on land, and staggered for a moment in the unconscious dark. My head ached and I didn't remember why until I reached up and felt the swollen knot protruding from my forehead. A part of me wondered if everything that had happened since that loose brick had clobbered me on the skull back in Woodvine had been a hallucination brought on by trauma. I was fumbling around aimlessly in the dark of my motel room when the bathroom light came on.

There you were, perched on the toilet lid, pale legs drawn up to your chest, your body nude and nearly translucent in the meager glow of the light. You looked up at me, and I was terrified to find your eyes were dark pits, and there was a moldy rot working around your hairline. You looked like something someone had dug up from deep in the earth.

Your mouth unhinged and inky black drool pattered onto the ceramic tiles. Steam began to seep from your mouth, your ears, your nostrils. Your eyes, those black gems, began to boil and liquefy in their sockets. *It lives alongside me*, you said as steam billowed out of your mouth. *It moves when I move. It's in the bedroom right now, waiting for me to come back…*

I cried out, and fell from the chair onto the floor. That was when I realized I had been dreaming. I lay there breathing in great whooping gasps, staring at the darkened ceiling, while my heart tried to punch a hole in my chest.

I fumbled my cell phone off the nightstand and saw that it was a quarter to five. Sitting up, I saw that the rain had stopped; the world beyond the window drapes was as black and lifeless as some remote planet. I slipped the phone in my pocket, then set the gun on the nightstand. I tugged on my coat, pulled a knit cap down over my head, grabbed the Maglite, and then crept back out into the night.

6

What had felt like no more than a ten-minute walk earlier that evening now seemed twice as long beneath the freezing cover of darkness. I slipped past the double-wide trailer with its pitch-black windows and its curl of smoke unspooling from the stovepipe, and headed straight down the path that wound out toward the campground. The rain had ushered back the mist; it clung to the trees and simmered before me like something I could reach out and manipulate with my hands. I didn't dare turn on the flashlight until I was halfway down the path and well out of sight of the double-wide. And even then, I winced as that stark bolt of light burst from the head of the torch. The fog was so great, the light reflected off it, creating a glowing white wall of smoke directly in front of me. I switched the light back off and continued on.

The fog seemed to dissipate once I reached the clearing. I could make out the angular shapes of the cabins around the perimeter of it, as well as the rack of kayaks closer toward the river. I moved quickly across the clearing and found the path that led to the garage that was buried deeper in the woods.

The garage rose up out of the dark, its corrugated metal roof radiating with the crisp, azure light of the moon. I jogged to the single window on the west-facing side of the building, the bulky flashlight in the pocket of my coat whapping against my ribs. I took out the flashlight, pressed it against the dirty windowpane, and clicked on the light. I had hoped at least a meager trickle of light might penetrate both the gunk on the window and the cavernous darkness inside the garage, but it didn't; I could see less than I could earlier that evening.

I wedged the flashlight back in my coat and tried to raise the window. The sill was wet from the rain, the wood spongy, and I couldn't get it to budge.

— *That's either the car in there or it's not*, said other-Aaron.

"Screw it," I said, taking out the flashlight again. I yanked the knit cap from my head, wrapped it around the head of the flashlight, then used it to break the window. The strike was muted, the broken shards tinkling to the floor inside.

I reached in, thumbed the latch, and jockeyed the window up. As I withdrew my hand, a jagged tooth of glass bit into the flesh along my arm, drawing blood. Wincing, I glanced at the wound, saw it wasn't terribly bad, then climbed in through the window.

At some point it had started to drizzle again, though in my haste I hadn't noticed until I was standing in the garage; the rain hammering on the metal roof sounded like mallet strikes on a steel drum.

I cast the flashlight's beam along the section of blue tarpaulin. It was held in place by elastic cords affixed to the chassis of whatever vehicle was beneath it. I began undoing the cords, the tarp crinkling like something alive, the cone of light issuing from the flashlight jouncing along the walls as I worked.

I grabbed a section of the tarp and pulled it back…

…to reveal a John Deere tractor with a plow attachment on the front.

Something very much like a laugh threatened to claw its way up my throat. I took a couple steps back, just letting the flashlight beam linger on the vehicle. Rain hammered the roof with increased urgency.

"Son of a bitch," I muttered.

I redirected the flashlight to take in the rest of the garage — the tools hanging from pegboards on the wall, the clutter on a series of standing aluminum shelves, the mound of used tires, farming equipment, and all-weather gear. One shelf in particular was stocked with automotive gear — a few car batteries, jumper cables, a dented chrome fender, countless headlights gaping like blind eyes. A detachable spotlight — the exact type a police sedan would have mounted on the driver's door — sat right there on the shelf. The flashlight's beam reflected from its concave glass dome, so that it looked as if the spotlight had come on.

I took a few cautious steps toward it, as if the thing were emitting waves of radiation and I didn't want to get too close. My breath shuddered from my lungs, clouding the air in front of my face with vapor.

Something tickled the right side of my face. I shone the light on its black, slender, partially curled body, and my initial impression was that it was some variety of impossibly thin snake. But as my gaze rose higher, I recognized it for what it was…

Spools of electrical wire hung from a bracket in the ceiling.

7

A steady sheet of rain was falling as I crossed out of the woods and headed back down toward the motel, the neon pink glow of the marquee and the lighted lobby windows guiding me like a beacon. In the rain, the trek back from the garage and across the campground had been more treacherous than earlier, and I had slipped and fallen several times on the slick mud. By the time I reached the parking lot of The Valentine Motel, I was soaked straight through to my underwear and striated with mud.

I had tried to reach Peter Sloane on my cell phone, but there was no cell service on the mountain; the call would not go through. I tried one last time, standing beneath the motel's marquee, the warm phone to my ear. Nothing — no service.

I peered through the fishbowl windows of the motel's dimly lit lobby. It was empty, with a sign on the counter that said PLEASE RING BELL FOR SERVICE. The sign sat next to the old rotary phone.

I crept inside, warm air blasting me in the face, and went to the counter. I half expected the phone not to work, but when I pressed the receiver to my ear, I heard the dial tone. I called Peter Sloane's cell number. It rang twice before Sloane answered.

"Who's this?"

"Peter, it's Aaron."

"What number is this?"

"I'm on the motel landline. There's no cell service out here." I noticed two globules of blood on the countertop; it took me a few seconds to realize it was blood from my arm wound, dripping from my sleeve. "Peter, I didn't find the car, but I found the spotlight and I found several spools of electrical wire. He's keeping them in a garage in the woods."

"Have you had any interaction with him?"

"Earlier today, yeah. He was out — "

"Get out of there."

I thought I'd misunderstood him. "What?"

"Get out of there, Aaron. You've convinced me. Let's go to the police."

"But we still can't connect him to any of the murders." I reached across the countertop for the first aid kit bolted to the wall, but then froze. One of the framed photographs on the wall had snared my attention.

"Aaron," Sloane said. "Do you hear me?"

"Holy shit, Peter," I breathed into the phone. "Holy *shit*..."

"Aar — "

The lights blew out and the phone went dead. Outside, lightning streaked across the sky, followed by a roar of thunder.

The dead receiver still to my ear, I dug the Maglite from my coat pocket, clicked it on, and projected its beam onto the collage of photos hanging on the wall behind the counter. Photos of men and women holding large, sleek, metallic-looking fish. Photos of people in orange life vests cruising down a river. Among them all, one photograph in particular stood out. Maybe I had even seen it on my first trip to this place, when I'd first come down here looking for answers to what I thought was a different sort of question. A framed photograph that, under any other circumstances, would have been wholly and completely innocuous...

It was a photograph of young girls, perhaps twenty in all, standing before one of the cabins at the very campsite beyond this motel, each one wearing a shirt that said SAINT FRANCIS YOUTH LEAGUE in bold red letters. Holly Renfrow was the third girl on the left.

They'd all gone to the camp. That was how he'd found them.

— *Get out of here.* It was other-Aaron, echoing Peter Sloane's sentiment.

8

It took me three tries to jab the key into my motel-room door, the rain pelting my back and plastering the hair to my head. Inside, I swiped the wall for the light switch, momentarily forgetting that the power had been knocked out. I went to the window and yanked open the drapes, flooding the room with moonlight.

The dead girls' files were still scattered about the table. I gathered them up into a hasty pile, but midway through this process I happened to look up and see that your armless doll was no longer perched on the nightstand. It was now tucked up against the headboard, its remaining eye aglow with moonlight. The oar that I had used to barricade the door lay slantwise across the bed.

I looked at the nightstand and noticed that the revolver was no longer there, either.

Someone — or something — shifted in the darkness behind me. I turned and saw a figure standing in the bathroom doorway. The figure advanced into the harsh neon light of the room and took form.

It was Glenn Childress, and he had your revolver pointed at my chest.

9

Childress's face was void of expression. Beads of perspiration glistened on his high forehead, each one reflecting the moonlight coming through the motel-room window. His colorless eyes hung on me from beneath the prominent ridge of his brow.

"I know who you are," he said, his voice low. "I looked you up. It wasn't hard."

I said nothing.

"I looked your wife up, too. Plenty of news articles about her. Pictures and everything. I'll admit, with her dyed black hair, it took me a moment to recognize her. But then it hit me. She looked so much like her sister."

Your yearbook was among the files on the table, opened to your sister's memorial page. Childress placed a hand on your sister's photo. He kept the gun trained on me.

"You think you've got it all figured out," he said, "but you don't. You see me, you see some monster. You see something ugly and detestable that needs to be stopped. But you don't see what *I* see."

Somehow I found my voice. Said, "What do you see?"

Childress caressed your sister's yearbook picture. "Corruption," he said. "Pollution. A pollution of the soul. Girls who start out innocent and with their whole lives ahead of them, yet somewhere along the way, they become poisoned. They rot."

He glanced down at the yearbook. Half his body was silvered in moonlight, the other half awash in shadow.

"I watched it happen to her. She was the first. I could do nothing but mourn what was happening to her until someone spoke up and told me what needed to be done."

"Who spoke up?"

Childress returned his heavy gaze to me. He tapped his temple with one blunt index finger. "Glenn the Friend," he said. "It's what the kids at the high school in Woodvine used to call me. But they didn't know it was the man in my head they were actually talking about."

He took a step in my direction, and I backed up until I was against the wall.

"We've all got two people inside us. A voice, a whisper. An alternate consciousness. Most people, they don't listen to that voice. I was no different at first. When I first started hearing it, I didn't know what it was trying to tell me. But then I *listened*… and it showed me the darkness that existed in others. In *her*."

He slammed the yearbook closed.

"I saved her," Childress said. "That's the thing you don't understand. I didn't *hurt* these girls, I *saved* them. They were doing terrible things to their bodies, their minds. They were going rotten. What did I do? I squeezed every ounce of poison from their bodies and left behind something pure and wholesome and clean again, just like the day they were born. You can see it happen; it's a real thing. When I *heal* them" — he brought one hand up in a fist — "you can see the innocence flood back into their eyes. And when I'm done, I let the water baptize what's left."

"You murdered them."

"I stopped them from getting worse."

"You tracked them down. You pretended to be a cop so they'd go with you."

"They came to *me*!" he shouted, teeth clenched. "Carol Thompson came to *me*. She was presented as the first, and I cleared that poison right out of her. And so I had my calling. I followed the voice, and the voice led me here. And they are brought to *me*."

"That's not true," I told him. "That's just the excuse you give yourself to keep doing what you do. The girl in West Virginia."

I nodded toward Holly Renfrow's file, atop the stack on the table. Childress didn't take his eyes from me.

"She fell into the river before you could strangle her. You didn't get to do it yourself, so you approached a woman whose car had a flat tire on the side of the road. That woman wasn't brought to you, as you say; she was a convenient target and you were riled up and ready to kill someone."

Lightning flashed at the window. I shied away from its glare but Glenn Childress remained motionless.

"There's something else I know," Childress said. "You haven't gone to the police with what you know. If you had, I'd be answering questions in a jail cell right now. But you, like your stupid fucking wife, decided to go this route alone. And now here you are."

"That's not true," I said.

I heard him cock back the hammer of the gun.

"It doesn't matter," he said in a low voice. And then again: "*It. Doesn't. Matter.*"

A dim red light began to emanate from the bathroom. It turned Glenn Childress into a hulking, featureless silhouette. The glow intensified until it cast a radiant red glow on everything in the room.

Childress watched his shadow stretch along the wall. He turned and glanced over his shoulder at the light spilling from the bathroom doorway.

I grabbed the oar that was lying slantways across the bed and swung it at Childress's head, just as he was turning back around to face me. I felt the heavy wooden oar strike the side of his skull. The force wrenched a strangled cry from him. He went down, knocking over the table on his way to the carpet. The gun went off, a report that sounded like cannon fire in the room. On the floor, Childress raised his head, and I could see a startling perforation along the left side of his head, from temple to jaw. The blood — black in the eerie red light spilling from the bathroom — spurted from the wound and filled his left eye socket.

Childress crawled behind the overturned table toward the corner of the room. I mistakenly thought he was retreating from me until I saw that he was groping for the revolver that had flown from his hand in the fall and now lay against the baseboard.

I struck him a second time between the shoulder blades with the oar, then dropped the thing and scrambled over to the gun. I scooped it up in both hands and spun around to face him. My heart was slamming in my chest.

Childress looked up at me. He managed to prop himself in the corner. The gash along the left side of his face pumped blood onto his denim jacket.

He was wheezing, his chest hitching. He drew one leg up then leaned his head back against the wall, gasping for air. I stood there with the gun trained on him, both hands wrapped around the hilt.

Glenn Childress raised one hand.

"All right," he groaned. "All right."

I watched as he touched the gash at the side of his face. His palm came away black and shiny with blood. He stared at it, and something like a laugh erupted from between his blood-streaked lips.

Another flash of lightning, and I saw Childress's shadow projected on the wall — multi-limbed and monstrous, just like the mannequin I'd found in the abandoned refinery back in Woodvine. Or so it seemed.

I leveled the gun at his head, and pulled the trigger.

10

Ears ringing, I lowered my arm. The gun dropped to the carpet. I could smell the gun smoke, cloying and acrid in my nose. Another smell, too — like burning oil. I watched as the smoke rose from the wound in Childress's skull, swirling as if alive. The smoke collected at the ceiling, a formidable mass that appeared to shift and move and churn with a certain disquieting measure of sentience. I dug the flashlight from my coat pocket and switched it on. The cloud of smoke undulated in the beam of light, slowly rotating like the eye of a storm. A tendril of smoke detached itself from the cloud and snaked dreamily along the ceiling and in my approximate direction; I tracked its progress with the flashlight. Like a cobweb, the smoky tendril levered itself down from the ceiling until it broke apart and vanished altogether. I redirected the beam to the clot of smoke directly above Childress's ruined skull. A jumble of serpents, it roiled and eddied and churned. I stood there with the flashlight trained on it for an unknowable amount of time, until it had all but dissipated into the air.

Something crackled in the bathroom. I leaned across the threshold and saw that the red light was coming from the heat lamp above the shower stall. As I stared at it, I watched its intensity diminish until it faded to a glowing pink ember at the center of a bulb recessed in the ceiling.

Before I could fathom how that light should work when all the rest of the motel's power had been knocked out by the storm, the lights in the room blinked on.

11

I stepped out into the rain, feeling about as substantial as a man constructed from paper. An inkling of daylight poked through the distant trees while the moon, still partially shrouded in mist, hung directly overhead. The frigid air bit into my sweat-slickened flesh, and the rain felt good on my face. There was a marching band clambering around inside my skull.

I had every intention of heading to the lobby to call the police, but I was frozen when a pair of headlights swung into the parking lot. It was a silver sedan with a spotlight on the driver's door. I raised my hands above my head, too rattled to stop and wonder who could have called the police, as the car came to a stop directly in front of me. The driver's door opened and a man in a leather jacket over a western-style shirt climbed out.

It was Peter Sloane.

"Jesus Christ," he said, rushing over to me. He put a hand on my shoulder and I lowered my hands. I didn't realize how much I was shaking until Sloane's hand steadied me. "What the hell happened, Aaron? Are you hurt?"

"Childress," I said. I was vaguely aware that I was floating in a daze, unable to anchor myself to reality. "He's in Room Four. He's dead."

Sloane squeezed my shoulder. He put his face close to mine. "What happened, Aaron? Tell me what happened."

I told him what had transpired in the room, including Childress's confession. When I got to the end, I told him how Childress had raised his hands and said *all right, all right*, but that I had shot and killed him anyway.

Sloane glanced over his shoulder at Room Four. The door was still ajar, the light from the room spilling out into the wet parking lot.

"It was self-defense, Aaron," Sloane said.

I shook my head.

Sloane grabbed me on either side of my head and forced me to look him in the eyes. "Listen to me — it was self-defense. Do you understand? Do you?"

I nodded my head.

"Say it. Say you understand."

"I understand," I said. "It was self-defense."

Sloane released his hold on me. The rain glittered like jewels on his leather jacket.

"There's a campground up the hill," I told him. "All of Childress's victims had gone there. That's how he found them."

Sloane was nodding his head, but he had stopped looking at me. Instead, something over my shoulder had attracted his attention. I turned and followed his gaze.

Dressed in a pale yellow robe that was soaking up the rain, Glenn Childress's wife moved with the dreamlike lassitude of a sleepwalker toward Room Four. She stopped as she reached the open doorway and simply stared into the room.

"That's his wife," I said. "I think I need to sit down."

I dropped to the pavement while Childress's wife did likewise before the threshold of Room Four. She glowed like something divine. Sloane rushed over to her, crouched beside her. If she made a sound, I couldn't hear it over the storm.

CHAPTER NINETEEN

1

There is a word in Japanese, *yugen*, that has no English equivalent. In Japanese, it is the awareness that the universe transmits a profound and mysterious beauty that can only be understood by the man or woman engaged in the comparable beauty of human suffering. You had plumbed the darkest depths of this world and left a part of the curtain pulled away so that I, too, might peek behind it. This bleak, rusty machine we call life. This unexpected beauty.

2

There was police involvement soon after the events that transpired at The Valentine Motel — of course there was.

I spoke at length with two investigators from the joint Chester-Bishop Police Department, a female detective named Goodall who possessed the soulful, dulcet voice of a rhythm and blues singer, and her heavyset male counterpart, Detective Hart, who had the nervous habit of reducing his coffee cup to a pile of Styrofoam snowflakes. Sloane pulled some strings, and in less than five hours an attorney friend of his arrived from Asheville. This attorney, Juno Patel, arrived having already contacted three of the six families of the deceased, and was able to confirm that the girls had indeed attended Glenn Childress's camp at some point in the year prior to their deaths.

The four of us sat together in a room with no windows, your notes, newspaper clippings, yearbook, and photos of the murdered girls on a stainless-steel table between us. There was a spray of blood across the cover of your yearbook, Allison, a rust-brown beading that arched above the green foil-stamped head of the elk. Bagged as evidence was the revolver, which they showed to me only once so that I could acknowledge that it was in fact the same handgun I'd taken with me across state lines and used to kill Glenn Childress.

In that windowless room, I walked Goodall and Hart through everything as best I could, frequently backtracking to fill in the gaps I had inadvertently overlooked the first time telling it, or to add clarifying statements to things I had previously said. When it came down to telling them about the final few moments in that motel room, I went with the story that Peter Sloane had advised: I told them that there had been a struggle during which I had managed to get the gun away from Childress; while holding him at gunpoint, he had come at me. My killing of Glenn Childress had been in self-defense. Juno Patel conveyed his endorsement with periodic nods of his head throughout my telling of the story.

Hart had a problem with me. Mostly, he had a problem with me transporting an unlicensed firearm across state lines, which I then used to kill a man. Patel was not ruffled by this; he began questioning why Detective Hart would want to play the sympathy card for a man who was clearly a serial killer — a serial killer who'd been living undetected among them in this otherwise peaceful mountain town, no less.

"Serial killer," Hart scoffed. Despite Patel having connected three of the six victims to Childress's campground, it was clear that Detective Hart found the concept wholly preposterous.

Juno Patel just grinned. Shark-like.

By the end of that day, Patel confirmed that the remaining three girls had also attended the camp. The connection was irrefutable. Detective Goodall said that my approach to this whole thing was reckless, and that I could be charged for a variety of crimes. In the end, however, she said that the district attorney had declined to press any charges against me. Detective Goodall wished me well. Detective Hart said nothing — he just stewed at his desk, picking apart his Styrofoam coffee cup with his blunt, brown fingers.

3

Obsessions are hard monkeys to shake. For the days and weeks following the events of that early morning at The Valentine Motel, I continued the process of peeling back layers and exposing things to the light. So did various police departments and journalists. Many things became clearer soon after. Many other things took more time to wriggle free and reveal themselves in the daylight. Much of what I learned came from Bobbi Negri; her ability to dig up the truth was rivaled only by your own ability, Allison. The more she traveled backward into Glenn Childress's eerie past, the more certain she became that this story — all of it — should be a book.

"And not just about Childress," she said to me one afternoon over the phone. "About you and Allison, too. A woman tracking a murderer for over a decade, and the husband who picks up where she left off."

I told her I wasn't interested in writing a book about it. In truth, I was trying to let it all go. I'd spent enough time in the dark.

"Why don't you do it?" I suggested. "You know it all just as well as I do. More so, if you include whatever creepy skeletons you're still digging up in Childress's past."

"But it's your story. Yours and Allison's."

"We don't want it anymore."

Bobbi ultimately ran with it. She promised that if the book sold, she'd split the advance with me. It sounded like blood money, so I told her I didn't want any profits. I told her that Bill Duvaney had started a charity through the newspaper, named after your column, Allison's A-List, whose mission was to help girls who'd been abused, neglected, or otherwise needed assistance. I suggested she could send my share of any book royalties directly to the charity.

"You're a conscientious fellow," Bobbi said, chuckling on the line. "Do you want to hear what I found out so far?"

I almost said no, but in the end told her to lay it out for me just this once.

What Bobbi Negri learned:

A few years before Glenn Childress had murdered anyone, he had been working as a custodial engineer at the AstroOil gas refinery in Woodvine, Pennsylvania, when he started getting headaches. They were bad, so bad that sometimes he couldn't get out of bed in the morning. After a while, he went to see a neurologist in Philadelphia. The neurologist found nothing wrong with him.

It was around this time that a number of other Woodvine residents became inexplicably ill. Some of them committed suicide. Some others picked up and left town, claiming that the air in Woodvine was poisoned. Everyone pointed fingers at the gas refinery. AstroOil shut the place down pending the results of numerous air-quality, safety, and equipment tests. The test results came back unremarkable, but that did not quell the concerns of the people living within the shadow of the refinery. Politics and public pressure ultimately resulted in the refinery closing its doors for good. This resolution was not met with unanimous approval; the refinery had employed over half the town's population, and now the residents of Woodvine, Pennsylvania, were faced with staggering unemployment in the wake of those refinery doors having been closed.

Glenn Childress ultimately took a custodial job at Elk Head High School, under the supervision of James de Campo. While purely supposition on Bobbi's part, this was probably how Childress first became aware of Carol Thompson. Carol had attended the school, but would have also interacted on occasion with de Campo, who had been engaged to Lynn Thompson at the time.

While working at the high school, Childress had also applied to the Woodvine Police Department, but was rejected for a variety of reasons, to include failing the psychological portion of the examination. It was around this time that Childress purchased a shit-brown 1996 Oldsmobile Cutlass Ciera. He mounted a spotlight to the door and began patrolling the parks, schoolyards, and back alleyways of Woodvine during the night.

Glenn Childress murdered Carol Thompson in the summer of 2004. Records showed that Childress had also begun suffering from his headaches again — or perhaps they'd never left him — and that he had gone to see another specialist in Philadelphia. The findings were no different this time than they had been the first.

Not long after the murder of Carol Thompson, Glenn Childress thought it best to leave the town of Woodvine, Pennsylvania, for good. He traveled east in his Oldsmobile sedan, got jobs on cleaning crews at various restaurants, municipal buildings, civic centers. In all this time, he garnered not even a single parking ticket. At least outwardly, Glenn Childress appeared to be a model citizen.

He eventually journeyed south to Chester, North Carolina, where he found work assisting an elderly couple with the upkeep of their motel and campsite. It was a quiet, remote place that suited Glenn Childress just fine. Perhaps the isolation had even helped with his headaches. But it would soon prove to be the perfect hunting ground for whatever monster was hiding behind the mask of Glenn Childress's face.

In the summer of 2006, Childress readied the campsite, then watched as a consortium of teenagers and preteens tumbled off buses from various parts northeast. It was on one of these diesel-grimed Greyhounds that Margot Idelson arrived — or, rather, was served unto him. One can only speculate what may have transpired between Childress and Idelson for the seven days she stayed at the campsite, but my guess is that *nothing* transpired. Not at that point. He would have been too cautious. He had studied her from afar, perhaps only lingering in the periphery of her awareness, something toothy and clawed biding its time from behind a veil of sagebrush. At first, conceivably, he had been transfixed by the physical similarities she shared with Carol Thompson — her slender frame, startling eyes, a mane of blonde, wavy hair. Perhaps, too, he had recognized something in her that had flipped his switch — the *pollution* that he had professed to me that night in the motel room. Whatever it was, he had waited for Margot Idelson to return home to Norfolk, Virginia, before going after her and killing her there. How had he located her in Norfolk? It was confirmed by the FBI, who later got involved in all this, that Childress collected the girls' names and home addresses from letters they'd write home while staying at the camp.

The following year, Childress bought the motel and campsite from the elderly couple, who'd been yearning to retire. Childress stayed quiet that year, busying himself with this new venture; if he'd targeted anyone else during this timeframe, no one has ever found any evidence of it to date.

In 2008, after getting arrested for underage drinking, Shelby Davenport was sentenced to community service. She spent two weeks traveling from nearby Bishop to Chester, where she and some other youths assisted Childress in preparing the campsite for that summer's impending campers. Whatever Childress saw in Shelby Davenport, it was enough to risk the proximity; he murdered her that same year in Bishop, no more than thirty miles from the motel. No suspect was ever considered in the girl's murder.

In 2011, Childress met a mousy, skittish woman named Sheila Longbaugh who worked at a laundromat in downtown Bishop. Sheila had known the Davenport family — they lived across the street from each other — so one might surmise that this was what sparked Childress's initial interest in the woman. Perhaps he'd grown nervous at having murdered someone so close to the motel and was hunting for information that only the Davenport family and their close friends and neighbors might know. Whatever the case, their courtship lasted two months, after which they were married at the local courthouse in Bishop. Sheila quit the laundromat, moved out of the rundown duplex she shared with her mother and stepfather, and went to work alongside her newfound husband at The Valentine Motel. For Sheila, owning a motel and campground was a business venture the likes of which she'd never dreamed. Maybe she was even happy for a while.

They tried getting pregnant right away, but after three miscarriages, Sheila was told by her doctor that it just wasn't in the cards for her. This sunk her into a deep depression, which lasted for several months. Whatever impact this might have had on her husband's state of mind is open for speculation. During this time, Childress managed to travel all the way to Vineland, New Jersey, to murder Lauren Chastain, a girl who'd spent a week at the campsite earlier that summer.

The following year was another quiet one, or so it seemed. Childress had much of the motel remodeled. The construction on the place went on longer than anticipated, and he had to cut the camping season short that year. But then the following year, in 2013, a teenage girl named Megan Pollock caught his eye as she stepped off a bus in the parking lot of The Valentine Motel, a backpack slung over her shoulder and a sleeping bag rolled up under one arm. Childress waited months before driving to Whitehall, Delaware, where he strangled the girl and left her body in a twisted heap in the woods off a highway, on the bank of a muddy brook. The autopsy report determined she'd been strangled with such brute force that her neck had been broken in three places. In my mind, this had been the result of Childress having to make up for his previous year of dormancy, only to come out of the gate with a rage and fervor uncontrolled and nearly superhuman. But that's just a guess.

There was Gabrielle Colson-Howe from Newburg, Maryland, in 2016 — a three-year gap since the Pollock girl's murder. Bobbi Negri had a theory that Childress had not been dormant during those three years at all, but that we simply did not know who his other victims had been. Bobbi suggested that it wasn't possible for you to have identified *all* of Childress's victims, Allison, and that your dossier had not been complete. And do you know what? She was right... although I'm getting ahead of myself.

Lastly, of course, there was Holly Renfrow from Furnace, West Virginia, murdered in the fall of 2018. I followed the news out of Furnace more closely than any of the other towns, until I came across a brief article accompanied by Hercel Lovering's photo. Chief Lovering cited a "clerical error" for mistakenly finding Das Hillyard guilty of Holly Renfrow's murder. After some disagreement with the local magistrate, Lovering resigned from his post as police chief. I thought it might give me some paltry satisfaction to learn this, but it did not. It just made me feel cold inside.

The nightmares I suffered soon after the events at the motel were of a fierce and merciless breed. Even in my waking hours, an image persisted — Glenn Childress's dark form drifting across the Elk Head River bridge, his labored exhalations smoking in the chilly autumn night. Gray ash snowed down from the sky but never seemed to collect on this dark and curiously immaterial figure… as though he wasn't fully of this world. I saw his car idling on random street corners at night, the sedan's headlights dwarfed by the ocular glare of that single door-mounted spotlight.

You think you've got it all figured out, he'd said to me in that motel room, *but you don't. You see me, you see some monster. You see something ugly and detestable that needs to be stopped. But you don't see what* I *see.*

A part of Glenn Childress had survived that night and had pursued me back to our townhome in Harbor Village. This was dreadful enough, but it was made unbearable by the notion that his monstrous presence had eclipsed yours. Since my return, the closet light had stopped coming on by itself. The Alexa speaker no longer spontaneously played your shitty music. I could no longer discern your handprint on the windshield of the Sube. *We will always be together because we have always been together*, you'd once told me. *We are acting out all our moments simultaneously right now. Ghosts are time travelers not bound by the here and now.*

To escape the emptiness of our home, I visited my sister Trayci. She was happy to have me, and I was happy to spend time with her and my nephews (Owen was away on business travel). We went fishing, bowling, had a pizza and movie night, but I soon began to feel unsettled.

"Allison's not with me anymore," I confessed to Trayci one evening as we sat in her living room polishing off a bottle of wine. "After she died, it still felt like a part of her was with me. In the house, even. But not anymore."

"She'll always be with you, Aaron. You know that."

I was searching for you, tortured by your absence. Torturing *myself*. And it was the insight of Bobbi Negri's mother that kept returning to me whenever I considered this: *We haunt ourselves.*

Yes, Allison. We haunt ourselves.

It felt like a great weight was slowly crushing my chest.

4

Bobbi Negri had been right — there were more victims. Your tally of seven (including your sister) was ultimately augmented to eleven. The police learned of this after discovering Childress's Cutlass Ciera in a storage facility in Bishop. Snared in the carpet fibers of the vehicle were strands of hair from some of the victims you had identified, as well as hair from others you had never keyed in on. In the trunk of the vehicle were leather driving gloves, spools of electrical wire, and fake police credentials.

Sloane told me all of this one afternoon as we ate lunch at a restaurant in Washington, D.C. He and Dottie had traveled to the city for vacation, so I agreed to meet him for an hour while Dottie visited a museum. Obsessions being what they were, Sloane had had a tough time letting it go, too. He kept in touch with detectives from the various police departments working through their individual cases, and also with detectives Goodall and Hart, who were closing the loop in Chester.

"You know," Sloane said, "Goodall, she mentioned something in passing last time we spoke."

"Yeah? What's that?"

"That the forensics concerning what happened in that motel room don't exactly comport with your version of the story."

I paused with my Michelob halfway to my lips. "Meaning what?"

"Meaning that the angle in which Childress was shot, coupled with the blood spatter on walls, suggests he was low to the floor when you killed him. Not standing up and coming at you."

"Oh." I set my bottle on the table.

"It's nothing anyone is interested in pursuing, so I wouldn't sweat it," Sloane said. "I just thought you should know."

"And if someone does come asking about it?"

"I don't think they will," said Sloane, "but if they do, you stick to your story. It was self-defense."

"And if that doesn't satisfy their forensics?"

"Hey, it was a traumatic event. Who can be expected to remember every tiny detail?"

"Right."

"The motel's closed down, you know."

"Yeah, I saw that."

"Apparently it's become something of a tourist attraction. People are tearing it apart and making off with souvenirs."

"What happened to Childress's wife?"

"She was questioned extensively by police then ultimately let go."

"They thought she might have known something?"

"I guess it's hard to fathom your spouse doing something so dark for so long and you not knowing about it."

"I can fathom it," I said.

One corner of Sloane's mouth tugged upward in the approximation of a smile.

"She went there to kill him, you know," I told him. "Allison. It's why she had the gun. It's why she erased the hard drive on her laptop. My guess is her next step would have been to destroy all the files in her trunk. No connection to the crime."

"But Childress wasn't there when she showed up for him," Sloane said.

"No. He wasn't."

"So you did it for her. You finished it."

"I keep seeing him, Peter." It came out as a confession. "When I close my eyes. When I dream. When I'm awake, too. I keep hearing that gunshot. The sound of it got trapped in my head."

"You'll forget in time."

"He said that everyone's got two people inside them. He was crazy, but I think he was right about that. Allison was two different people. I learned that along the way. She had a different side to her that was capable of things I would have never thought possible."

"So do you, Aaron," Sloane said.

"There's something I never told you."

Sloane eyed me and he took a swig of his beer. "Go on," he said.

"When Childress died… I mean, after I'd shot him, Peter… I saw smoke come out of his head. Right out of the bullet hole."

One of Sloane's eyebrows arched. "And?"

"It wasn't just a little bit of smoke. It moved like something alive. I watched it go up to the ceiling and move around up there. For a second, it was like it was considering whether or not it should go inside *me*."

"What are you talking about, Aaron?"

"Gas Head."

Sloane set his beer bottle on the table. "It was a story to scare kids, Aaron. Make-believe."

Shamefaced, I looked down at my half-eaten club sandwich.

"You know what?" he said, his tone suddenly upbeat. "I think it's time you and I quit wallowing in all of this. It's over. No more talk about Glenn Childress or Gas Head or murders or anything else. We're done."

"I think that's a great idea," I said.

After lunch, we chatted on the sidewalk for a while until Sloane spotted his wife across the street in the crowd, waving at him.

"Listen," I said. "Thank you for everything, Peter."

"Thank you, too, Aaron."

We embraced, and then I watched him stroll across the street. He joined his wife and they merged with the crowd until they disappeared from my sight.

I would never see Peter Sloane again.

5

On some random afternoon, as I sat in our (formerly) shared home office working on a translation, I received a telephone call from Rita Renfrow. She wanted to thank me for finding the real killer and not giving up. She said she was resting much easier now, although the grief over her daughter's death was still great.

"It's probably something I'll always carry with me," she said.

I thanked her for the call, and then she asked me a question.

Her voice barely above a whisper, she asked if Childress had said anything about her daughter before he died. *I would've liked to hear him say what he'd done to her and that he was sorry*, Rita had said when we'd spoken in her yard, back when she still believed Das Hillyard had murdered her daughter. *He should have at least given me that.*

My answer to her was the second and final lie I would tell concerning this matter, counting the one about self-defense I told detectives Goodall and Hart.

"Yes, Rita. He did. He apologized. Before he died, he said he was so sorry for taking Holly away from you."

Rita was quiet on the phone for a very long time. At one point I thought maybe we'd gotten disconnected, but then I heard a quiet sniffle, and I just remained on the line with her, not saying anything. We stayed like that for a long time. In the end, she whispered, "I'm glad you killed him."

I said nothing.

She offered a final thank-you and a goodbye, and ended the call. I sat there staring at the phone, and for the first time in a long while, I didn't feel completely horrible. It was as if that weight that had been crushing my chest had eased up the slightest bit.

And then there came a knock on our front door.

I went down the stairs and was halfway across the foyer when the person knocked again, more urgently.

I opened the door to find a woman standing there. The first thing I noted was that she was wearing a long black woolen coat, which was an unusual choice for a midsummer day. The second thing I noticed was that the woman standing before me was Sheila Childress. Our eyes met, and as recognition dawned on me, I could see that her eyes were red and glassy, as if she had been recently crying. Unsure what to say or do, I just stood there staring at her.

The crazy thing that returned to me in that moment was a memory from your work party that we had attended back before we were married, the one at Bill and Maureen Duvaney's house. Madam Golganor, the drunk, foul-mouthed psychic, with her crystal ball that was MADE IN CHINA. The warning she had given me, imparted by a woman in a red beret: *Don't. Open. The. Door.*

Sheila Childress produced a small handgun from the pocket of her wool coat. She aimed it straight at my chest and pulled the trigger.

There was nothing at first, except the feeling that I'd been struck in the upper chest by a great force of wind. I fell backward into the foyer and lay there, blinking haplessly at the chandelier above my head. I couldn't breathe, couldn't draw in any air. The pain came next, spreading its burning tendrils throughout my body, each one stemming from the molten supernova where my heart was supposed to be.

Sobbing audibly, Sheila retreated from the doorway. Somehow I managed to raise my head and watch her totter down the steps toward the road. Some of our neighbors were coming over. I looked down further and saw that I was wearing a bright red shirt, only I had been wearing a white t-shirt a moment earlier, and none of it made any sense. My head dropped back down onto the floor. There were three chandeliers up there now, rotating like a —

(Great Cosmic Clock)

— pinwheel. The lights flickered on and off, on and off.

Distantly, I heard another gunshot. People screamed. I couldn't fathom what was happening. I couldn't remember what I was doing lying here on the floor, my body cold in the middle of summer, my shirt red instead of white, my vision breaking down and growing dim, my mind not here, not here. A figure swam in front of my field of vision, recognizable yet unfamiliar all at once. Other-Aaron, his face grim, his voice a gunshot of its own in my head.

— *Be still. Be still. Be —*

6

—*h*ere, suddenly looking down at myself, a reversal of roles, a mind within a mind and a soul within a soul, seeing the life drain from my eyes, ascending and descending all at once, as I watch me die. And there I go, that solid, skin-and-bones version of me — *gone.*

7

I am suddenly standing alone in the dark of our townhome. I sense you here somewhere, Allison, but I cannot find you. I smell your perfume; I hear the wisp of your feet on the carpet. I traverse the hallways, hunting, searching. I do not find you; only a blurry image of myself, this skin-and-bones other-me who also wanders the halls in search of you. I am everywhere at once, everywhere this other-me goes. Because we haunt ourselves.

I am there in the doorway to our office as other-me comes up the stairs and sees me. He comes toward me but I am already retreating into the black. I am everywhere, everywhere.

I am standing in one dark corner of a gloomy parlor while an old woman in a wingback chair stares directly at me and says, *What about your friend, Jeffrey? Who is that?* And the other-me comes close, reaches out, and grazes the cold mist that is me.

Everywhere; everywhere…

I ghost through the house playing your music, Allison — it comes on when I think of it — and I am always playing it, always, and I am turning the pages of your yearbook, and when other-me comes into the house, he sees the image of your sister right there in front of him, and I keep playing your music…

I am in the bathroom of The Valentine Motel, making the red light over the shower burn like a supernova…

I am in our bedroom closet, knowing now where you keep the key to the padlock on your hope chest, and knowing that there is only one way you and I can ever be reunited, Allison, and so I compel the other-me to begin the quest. I dig the key out of your running shoe and place it on the mystic pedestal…

When other-me loses hope, I flash the closet light on and off, on and off, on and off. Because if other-me is going to open that door and die in the end, I need to get him there. It's my only way back to you, Allison. My only way.

We haunt ourselves.

And then I am in our bedroom, Allison, watching you leave. Red beret and houndstooth coat. Saying, *Come with me.* Kissing other-me's forehead before you leave. I rush to the version of myself still in bed, reach down, try to grab him, pull him up — not to stop you, Allison, because nothing can stop what has already happened, but for one final glimpse of you before you depart this world for the next. And other-me must sense my presence, because he rises with a confused sense of urgency, and goes to the window to watch you leave one last time.

8

And then this world fades and the next one begins. I am floating in space. Yet I sense that I am not alone. Somewhere, two voices are counting down from ten. Somehow, I can hear them.

The blinding light from two headlights cuts through the darkness. Blinding, yes — but I can stare at it without it hurting. Do you know who I see back there, beyond the headlights? Behind the windshield? A version of you and me that is at once wholly familiar yet fleetingly alien. People on another plane of existence, and in another time. People I've known and loved and am quickly forgetting.

I turn around and see you there, Allison. Floating in the black with me. You are backlit by a fluttery spangle of white light, cool and not too bright.

You've got a hand extended toward me.

I take it.

In the car, the other version of you tells the other version of me, *Two figures. Holding hands. Just for a moment — there and then gone.*

I squeeze your hand, Allison.

Come with me.

This time, we leave this world together.

AUTHOR'S NOTE

On June 28, 2018, my friend was murdered along with four other people while at work. A monster entered her office building with a shotgun and opened fire. The number of dead was announced but no names were given right away. I spent hours worrying if my friend, Wendi Winters, a reporter for *The Capital*, was okay. And I realized that even if she was, there were still five people dead, and there were friends and family members out there just like me hoping that they were okay, too.

I met Wendi in 2006, when she came to my house to interview me about a book I'd written. Because she was a jack of all trades, she'd brought a camera, too, and took a photo of me standing by a fence. My wife made some snacks and we sat around our living room just talking. She hugged us both when she left.

We kept in touch, and would meet infrequently for coffee, to discuss my writing, and to talk about our community, of which she was so fervently supportive. She invited me to her media bazaars, and we would check in with each other from time to time to see what was going on in our respective worlds. She got to know my family and me, not because it was her job as a reporter, but because she was a steadfast chronicler of our community; the heart of this nascent village; the truth in things. Because she was a good person who enjoyed getting to know people.

Wendi traveled with me during the writing of this novel. She remained in my mind and heart, and I think this book is better for it, because a piece of her has made it into this story. In fact, it was my grief over what happened to my friend that started the story-machine in my head rolling. This book is a product of that grief, but also of our friendship. Because, sometimes, books are therapy.

Rest easy, Wendi.

RONALD MALFI

June 3, 2019

Annapolis, Maryland

ACKNOWLEDGEMENTS

This book originated from a dark place, which means it takes the hard work and talent of a great many people to make it bright and good and palatable for public consumption. Many thanks to my editor, Sophie Robinson, whose keen eye helped elevate this story from what it could be to what it ultimately is, and to Hayley Shepherd for carrying us across the finish line. Thanks to my agents who toil quietly behind the scenes to keep the machine rolling — Cameron McClure, Katie Shea Boutillier, Matt Snow, and the tireless Cassie Graves for all her scheduling prowess. Gratitude to my friends and family who provided insight as I bounced ideas off them or read early drafts of this novel — Kevin Kangas, Tyre Lewis, my wife Debra, and my dad, Ron Malfi, Sr. Lastly, my appreciation for my two daughters, Madison and Hayden, who are always there to lift Dad from the dark depths of his writing into a world of sunshine, goodness, and love.

Ronald Malfi is the award-winning author of several horror novels, mysteries, and thrillers. He is the recipient of two Independent Publisher Book Awards, the Beverly Hills Book Award, the Vincent Preis Horror Award, the Benjamin Franklin Award, and his novel *Floating Staircase* was a finalist for the Bram Stoker Award. He lives with his wife and two daughters in Maryland.

ronmalfi.com
@RonaldMalfi

For more fantastic fiction, author events,
exclusive excerpts, competitions, limited editions and more

VISIT OUR WEBSITE
titanbooks.com

LIKE US ON FACEBOOK
facebook.com/titanbooks

FOLLOW US ON TWITTER AND INSTAGRAM
@TitanBooks

EMAIL US
readerfeedback@titanemail.com